Jefferson's Promise

A Mystery

By Gene Daniels

Jefferson's Promise
Copyright © 2014 Gene Daniels
CreateSpace Independent Publishing Platform

Cover credit: Gibson Design Associates, Inc. Charlottesville, Virginia.

This book is a work of fiction. All characters, events, organizations and institutions are either the product of the author's imagination or are used fictitiously.

ISBN: 10: 1499292813
EAN: 13: 978-1499292817

For Jeanne

"The Thomas Jefferson Foundation and most historians believe that, years after his wife's death, Thomas Jefferson was the father of the six children of Sally Hemings mentioned in Jefferson's records, including Beverly, Harriet, Madison, and Eston Hemings . . .

A committee commissioned by the Thomas Jefferson Heritage Society, after reviewing essentially the same material, reached different conclusions, namely that Sally Hemings was only a minor figure in Thomas Jefferson's life and that it is very unlikely he fathered any of her children."
["Thomas Jefferson and Sally Hemings: A Brief Account" retrieved from:
http://www.monticello.org/site/plantation-and-slavery]

"Never suffer a thought to be harbored in your mind which you would not avow openly. When tempted to do anything in secret ask yourself if you would do it in public. If you would not be sure it is wrong." [Thomas Jefferson to Francis Wayles Eppes, Monticello, May 21, 1816. Edwin M. Betts and James A. Bear, Jr. (Eds.), *The Family Letters of Thomas Jefferson*.]

"In the Jeffersonian family code, one not only kept secrets from outsiders; one kept secrets from oneself." [Joseph J. Ellis, *American Sphinx: The Character of Thomas Jefferson*.]

Prologue

A January wind swirled snow around the streetlights as two homicide detectives arrived at a three-flat on one of the District's unkempt streets. Flashing lights from several squad cars ricocheted against the building and an adjacent concrete overpass, adding their own kind of chill. Onlookers milled around on the sidewalk fronting the building, the majority African Americans, many dressed in coats covering night clothes.

The detectives stepped outside their car, pausing to take in the scene. Two uniformed officers blocked a door to the building. One began walking toward the detectives. The light snow bounced off his leather jacket, melting as it fell onto the sidewalk.

"What have you got?" the senior detective asked the approaching officer.

"Not sure. You'll need to take a look. It's not pretty."

The patrolman turned to escort them toward the building's entrance.

"Call came in at 11:32. Domestic dispute with gunshots heard. When we arrived we opened the entry door and found a woman lying at the foot of the stairs."

"Alive?" The second detective asked, but his attention focused on the crowd of faces watching them.

"Didn't look that way. Blood all over the floor and her clothing. Couldn't find a pulse. I radioed for the paramedics and backup. Then we started up the stairs."

"Why not wait for backup?" the senior detective inquired.

"We called up to announce we were coming, but got no response. Decided we should take a look to see what was going on," the officer responded, avoiding a direct answer to the detective's question.

"The apartment door at the top of the first flight of stairs was wide open. The only occupant was a thirty-something, heavyset, white male. We found him sitting on the living room sofa. There was a handgun on the floor in front of him."

Snow continued to fall as the police officers halted near the entrance to the building.

"The guy was moaning, not crying. Just moaning. From the sofa he started waving and pointing toward the stairs. Really upset. We didn't see any point in starting a conversation. Cuffed him, waited for you guys and the ambulance."

The patrolman looked to see if the detectives had questions.

"If you don't need me I'll get on with helping to find out if anyone witnessed what went down. My partner and another cop are upstairs keeping an eye on the suspect."

"We'll take it from here. Thanks," the senior detective replied.

The junior detective, Hispanic in appearance, slight of build but with an athlete's body, went in first. He immediately saw what the patrolman had described. The woman, a light-skinned African American, lay curled in nearly a fetal position within a pool of blood, her grey dress torn, exposing red underwear. The detective studied the victim's face. He judged she was quite young, maybe not even twenty, and rather attractive despite the abrasions across her nose and cheeks. Those marks, he wondered, fists or stairs? The detective looked again at her blood-soaked body, then at the two paramedics pressed against the wall in the small, poorly lit hallway. He likened the scene to that from low-budget crime drama on a cable movie channel.

"Nothing we could do. She was dead when we got here," one of the medical responders said, interrupting the detective's thoughts. "Looks like she was shot several times. We're waiting for lab people and the photographer."

The senior detective, an African-American male, both older and much larger than his partner, moved from behind into the crowded space. He looked for a few moments at the body, then bent down and pulled the woman's dress over her underwear. The detectives acknowledged the paramedic's comments, took one more look at the dead woman, then at each other, before carefully stepping around the body and starting up the stairway.

A young female officer, gun drawn, met them at the apartment door and ushered them inside. The detectives nodded toward another uniformed cop standing next to a doorway leading to a small kitchen, which revealed a sink overflowing with unwashed dishes. The senior detective instructed the woman officer to put away her gun.

Holstering it, she said, "He won't say anything, not even his name. Kept whimpering for a while, but has quieted down." The two street cops stood aside as the detectives took over.

A well-worn sofa along the far wall faced a large flat-screen TV to the right of the door they had just entered. Beer cans littered a nearby end table. Both detectives looked closely for the first time at the man sitting on the sofa. He was dressed in dirty jeans and a Redskins T-shirt.

Crossing the room, the detective-in-charge pointed to the gun still on the floor, telling his partner to leave it in place. He stationed himself a few feet from the sofa, looking down at its occupant. The cuffs stretched the man's arms behind his back. His head hung down, face hidden from view. The younger detective remained standing in the middle of the small living space.

"I took care of her you know," the man on the sofa mumbled, barely loud enough for the police officers to hear.

"She'd been on the streets and I took her in. She's just a kid. I made her someone other than a whore. She was a nobody. We were happy, I thought. I told her we could have kids. I promised to take care of them. Then tonight, when we were getting ready for bed, she comes at me with a knife."

He looked for the first time at the detectives.

"What was I supposed to do?" he asked, his voice now louder.

More like forty-something, the junior detective observed, not thirties as the officer outside had reported.

"Where's the knife?" the senior detective asked.

"I don't know. She had it earlier. I swear."

Both detectives looked toward the two cops standing across the room.

"Haven't seen it," the female officer said. The second officer shook his head.

The junior detective walked out of the apartment to the landing in the stairwell. The medical team still stood next to the body at the bottom of the stairs.

"You guys find a weapon of any kind? A knife maybe?"

"Nothing we've seen. Do you want us to move the body?"

"No, not yet."

The paramedic's response appeared to signal the man on the sofa not to say anything more. And he didn't, no matter what questions the detectives put to him.

"Let's take him in," the senior detective said to no one in particular. He then looked over at the uniformed officers. "Flip a coin if you like, but I want one of you to seal the room and wait outside the door until the forensic crew gets here. The other can take charge of our football fan."

The detectives followed the police officer and the Redskins T-shirt out of the apartment.

"The crime-scene people can look for the knife," the black detective told his partner as they descended the stairs.

The body had yet to be removed and wouldn't until the forensic team finished. At the foot of the stairs they stepped around a sticky puddle of blood. The suspect noticeably avoided looking at the dead woman on the floor. A police photographer, just on his way in, stood aside as the group exited the building.

The T-shirt was put into a squad car for the ride to the station, where questioning would resume. That night, however, little came out of the shooter's mouth. Only that his name was Thomas Jamison, and that the woman, Sarah, was his wife of two weeks. And that he wanted a lawyer. Jamison was booked, locked in a cell, and charges prepared, a lawyer to be located in the morning.

A clock above the doorway showed 2:10 a.m. when the detectives signed out and headed through the building's rear exit to the parking area. Once outside, the senior detective placed a hand on his partner's shoulder.

"See ya in the morning," he said, and started for his car. After a few steps, he called to his partner who was walking away.

"Mike!"

His partner turned around.

"Yeah?"

"Haven't I been telling you? It's all about cleaning up bloody messes."

The young detective drove the short distance home. Snow fell heavily now, sticking on grassy spots and the tops of some cars. He knew his wife's car would be parked behind their townhome and that it was his task to find a space on the street, hopefully on the same block. Theirs was one of six three-story houses on a block in the northeast quadrant of the city, a short distance from the Capitol. They could afford living in the neighborhood only because his wife's uncle bequeathed her enough money to pay down most of the asking price. If and when they moved, given D.C.'s competitive housing market, they knew they'd get more than their money back.

The detective quietly inserted the key in the front door. His wife, a nurse at a city hospital, wouldn't have gotten home until nearly midnight. By now she'd be asleep in bed. He smiled, thinking how she would open her eyes when he crawled into bed, then put her arm around him before falling back to sleep, like she had done many times before.

But she wasn't in bed. Nor would she ever put her arms around him again. Removing his key from the door, he pushed it open and stepped into the foyer. His wife lay at the foot of the stairs leading to the upper levels, her bathrobe in disarray, exposing her underwear. It was blue. Congealed blood surrounded her mouth and nose, her open eyes vacant. Shutting out the panic that took hold of him, he tried for a pulse and dialed 911 on his cell. He collapsed onto the floor next to her, tears streaming down his face, reaching for her hand.

He wouldn't remember what he said to the operator, nor much of anything else that night. Memories that remained were faint images of people talking and moving about. Someone, probably his partner, helped him climb the stairs and sit down on a recliner in the living room. Everything felt unreal, as in a dream, like he wasn't really there.

According to the medical examiner, his wife suffered massive cerebral hemorrhaging when her head struck the slate floor in the townhouse vestibule. Unconscious and untreated, death occurred within an hour, the report concluded. She had most likely tripped over their basset hound. The first responders found the dog beside the couple, whimpering, a front leg twisted to the side. When expecting her husband late, she always made sure the light remained on in the entryway and the door chain detached so he could get in with his key. She apparently had been descending the stairs for one last check of the door locks. Their lumbering basset, hoping to be taken outside, frequently sidled alongside when they came down the stairs, dangerously under foot.

Chapter 1

Seated at his sister's dining room table, Michael Chance knew something was wrong. He wasn't comfortable in his body, and worse, at times he couldn't be sure it *was* his body. As far as he was concerned, these dinners arranged by his sister were not helping his experiences of being outside himself, looking in.

Mike had been staying with Kelly and her family following the months he was adrift after his wife died falling down their townhouse stairs. "Falls are the second or third leading cause of accidental deaths," a neighbor felt compelled to tell him a few weeks after the world-shifting events of that fateful January night.

During his nine years on the D.C. police force, Mike had quickly moved up the line from street cop to detective, first burglary and then homicide. What motivated him to request the transfer to homicide hadn't been clear. Was it linked to feelings about police work in general? He and Kirsten had resumed talking about starting a family. Maybe that was it--how to mix parental responsibilities with being a cop. Was he trying to convince himself that police work suited him no matter what the future might hold? Whatever the reason for requesting the change, homicide held open the promise of rekindling the enthusiasm he once felt for his career. Maybe even provide a chance to get some seriously bad people off the street.

Mike partnered with Justin Johnson, a tall, 220-pound black man with twelve years of homicide experience. Some years past, a duty sergeant misread, or feigned as much, when announcing Justin's name at roll call, and exclaimed, "Justice! Man, that works here." The name took. No one called him Justin or even J. J. again.

At 5'10" and 170 pounds, Mike figured he lucked out partnering with the big guy. His Hispanic mother had gifted him some color, along with black hair and brown eyes. This once led Mike to tell Justice that they made good partners since both were people of color. Justice looked at him, smiled, and said, "Mike, there's color, and then there's *color*. Maybe you could work a little more on yours!" A smile nearly always lit up Justice's face when he talked to him, or for that matter when he spoke to anyone other than lawbreakers.

Mike went on compassionate leave following his wife's death, but found it difficult to envision a time when he would return to work. Nightmares and recurring memories of Kirsten's body at the foot of the stairs never ceased. His psychiatrist diagnosed severe grief reaction with aspects of PTSD and prescribed anti-depressants. But life continued as sadness piled on top of sadness. He barely managed enough energy to handle the simplest daily chores. A fellow officer said she would keep his basset hound, Coronado, until Mike was ready to have him back. It seemed for the best, given he found it hard to take care of himself, let alone the dog. That the animal's presence continually brought back memories of Kirsten's accident aided his decision.

He continued in therapy for only a month before giving up that anyone could convince him a meaningful future existed without Kirsten. In April, after the umpteenth visit to check on him, his sister told him, "You can stay with us while you get back on your feet." *Insisted* is the better word, since Kelly announced she wouldn't leave his townhouse, despite the ungodly mess he'd let it become, if he didn't promise to come stay with her family.

Kelly and Steve Cummings lived in Charlottesville, in the shadow of the Blue Ridge Mountains to the west, a two-hour drive from D.C., home of the University of

Virginia and Thomas Jefferson's Monticello. They owned one of the ubiquitous brick, colonial-style, box houses seen in many of the city's neighborhoods. Because the lot sloped in back, it allowed the previous owner to add a small in-laws' apartment, with an all-season sunroom above it. Both spaces afforded pleasant views of a wooded area abutting the backyard. An outside entrance from the driveway allowed private entry to the apartment. A stairway inside ascended to the first level of the main house. The Cummingses usually rented the space to a university student, but Kelly informed Mike the place was his for as long as he wanted.

The family had moved to C'ville, as the locals call it, ten years earlier, when Steve garnered a faculty appointment at Virginia's prestigious state university. He had recently finished his Ph.D. in psychology at Georgetown. That same year, Kelly completed her undergraduate degree in accounting.

Kelly and Steve had one child, Tammy, who had just turned twelve. Mike loved being around his niece, although she sometimes reminded him of the unfulfilled dreams he and Kirsten once shared. Tammy exhibited the typical adolescent self-centeredness that kept conversations revolving around her. This suited him perfectly and they got along great. Tammy was out with friends at a pizza party tonight and he lamented her absence. Her chatter might have saved him from needing to make conversation.

Kelly was younger by two years and since they were kids, his biggest cheerleader. Mike remembered in sixth grade how she sat in the front row of the regional spelling bee in which he competed. Every time he spelled a word correctly she grinned and gave him thumbs up. She still ranked as his biggest supporter, no doubt the main reason he didn't lock himself in the townhome and do who knows what following Kirsten's death.

The siblings grew up in Alexandria, Virginia. Their father commuted to the District for work at the travel and tourism office in the U.S. Commerce Department-- until he died suddenly of a heart attack two years ago. Their mother surprised them by quickly moving back to her native New Mexico. She traced her family roots back four-hundred years and the arrival of Spaniards to the outskirts of what is now the artsy city of Santa Fe. She hadn't been well since their father's death, but Mike and Kelly trusted their mother's sisters in New Mexico to watch out for her.

Shortly before Kirsten's fatal accident, their mother broke a hip when she fell while walking on uneven pavement. The injury left her unable to travel for Kirsten's funeral. She called Mike daily in the weeks following, begging him to visit her. He knew that wouldn't work, not then, at least. He wasn't ready to have the conversations his mother would want. His sister regularly called their mother and promised many times that both she and Mike would visit soon.

Kelly served the first course, a cold vegetable soup prepared from locally grown produce, which quickly earned compliments from everyone at the table. Mike struggled to pay attention to the conversation, while at the same time hoping to avoid joining in.

It was now August, seven month's since his wife's death. In the past month or so he sensed his depression slowly lifting, but at the same time he recognized something else wasn't right. He became conscious of the out-of-body experiences a few months ago. At first he tried to shake them off, as if they were a bad dream he could escape by awakening. The episodes, however, took on a life of their own, lasting sometimes for days, even weeks. When they occurred, he wondered whether he was simply an automaton, moving through the world but not in it. He was numb, not feeling, yet aware he was

11

there, still present, but not quite present. Something definitely was wrong, but he didn't know what.

He knew that Kelly and Steve observed the changes in him--the detachment, then agitation, the anxious looks he gave them. After considerable coaxing they got him to talk about his feelings, or, as Mike said, his "unfeelings."

"It will sound silly," he told them. "You'll think I'm nuts."

"No, please," Kelly urged. "We want to understand."

Taking a deep breath, Mike avoided eye contact as he attempted to describe what he was experiencing.

"It's hard to explain, but I frequently feel like I'm outside myself, floating somewhere above. I'm looking down, no longer in control of who I am. Like my mind isn't my own. Sometimes I don't recognize my own words. Even everyday objects can appear strange or unfamiliar. On top of it all, I can't help thinking about death and dying. But it's all very abstract. I don't really feel anything. My emotions are shut down. I'm sorry. I know this doesn't make any sense."

With shoulders slumping, Mike looked earnestly at his sister and brother-in-law.

"I sometimes think I'm going crazy."

Steve was not a clinical psychologist, having chosen an academic path researching human cognition, but he offered to talk to some of his colleagues. "Let me see if any of the clinicians have an explanation for what you're experiencing," he said.

A few days later, Steve said that Margot Rider, a practicing clinician in the psychology department, might have some ideas about the behavior exhibited by the individual Steve described. She would be happy to see him as a client if it seemed appropriate.

His first appointment had been two weeks ago. He found himself thinking about that initial meeting with

Dr. Rider while conversation at the dinner table bounced in various directions around him.

Although a faculty member at the university, Dr. Rider saw clients off grounds in a small office, conveniently located less than a half-mile from the university Rotunda. Maybe ten or fifteen years older than Mike's thirty-six years, she was professional in both dress and demeanor. At the same time, she didn't exhibit the "clinical" attitude Mike felt had characterized the police psychiatrist. He perceived an authentic concern, a warmth even.

Dr. Rider sat quietly while Mike reviewed his life going nowhere. He described the aching sadness since his wife died, then the emotional void he recently experienced, the detachment from life, the unreality of it all, and the terror.

"It's possible," his therapist said, "that your depression and anxiety are simply increasing in intensity. These can wax and wane. It may be the basis of your more recent feelings of losing a sense of self. There are some other possibilities, however.

"You've lost more than your wife. You've lost those things that give us stability--job, partner, friends, even your previous surroundings. All of these losses likely are contributing to what you now experience. You aren't grounded anymore, and that can be frightening."

"I can testify to that!" Mike agreed with a slight smile.

"From what you've told me," Dr. Rider continued, "I think something other than depression is going on. I'll need to learn more about you before I can be sure. Next time we meet I'll want you to take a few simple tests and complete some questionnaires. And don't worry, you aren't losing your mind. Your feelings may even be somewhat reasonable given what you've gone through. But let's take it a step at a time. In the meantime, continue taking your anti-depressants."

During his second therapy session, Mike spent the hour dutifully writing responses to the many items on the materials Dr. Rider provided. She promised to share what she learned from his answers the next time they met. That would happen Wednesday of the coming week. Mike couldn't help thinking about what Dr. Rider would tell him, and if she would be able to help him.

When Kelly gathered up the soup dishes and made preparations in the kitchen for serving the main entrée, conversation at the table slowed. The man sitting across from Mike was one-half of tonight's invited socializers (sympathizers?) for the widowed brother. Mike remembered the couple's last name was McCabe, but he was no longer sure of their first names. A cop named Dennis McCabe once worked with him in burglary.

During drinks before dinner, Mike mainly had stared into his beer while talk went on around him. Not that he missed seeing the occasional I'm-so-sorry glance from their guests, especially the woman. She appeared ready to say something whenever she looked his way. He did recall Kelly saying that the man (Paul?) was a professor, a colleague of Steve's at the university.

From the kitchen Kelly called to her husband, asking for help serving the main course. Left alone with the evening's dinner guests, Mike's anxiety level skyrocketed. The McCabes looked his direction and smiled. Mike realized he needed to say something. He asked Paul, or whomever it was in that chair, what he taught at the university.

Paul--it was his name--replied, "As I said in the other room . . ." Mike realized he definitely had not been paying attention earlier. "I'm a history professor specializing in the American revolutionary period. Not a bad place to be, right, in Charlottesville? Jefferson's Monticello, and the Monroe and Madison houses so close by."

"Of course. I've been to Monticello several times. Twice with Kirsten. We even went once to Montpelier. I've never been to Monroe's place."

Paul's wife, Cynthia, spoke up. "Kelly told us about your wife's accident. We're so sorry. When was it, about six or seven months ago? And you were on the D.C. police force, weren't you?"

"It happened in January."

Not six or seven months, not six or seven years, Mike thought. It happened a lifetime ago. He couldn't help staring. What did she want from him? He really didn't want to be here. He wasn't ready to talk about himself, the extraordinary woman he lost, and his life going nowhere, despite what his sister might think.

"I was a detective, burglary and then homicide," he managed to get out.

Kelly and Steve came back into the dining room carrying dishes. Attention mercifully shifted to his sister's soufflé. Mike decided he really had to talk with his sister about these dinners. He didn't think he could take another one without leaving the table and throwing a dish or two on the way out. He began to lose focus.

Why am I so far away? Where am I? I hear voices. What do they want from me?

Chapter 2

Conversation at the Cummings's dinner table took on a predictable normalcy associated with such gatherings until the history professor paused, looked at his hosts, then uncertainly toward Mike.

"I wonder if you'd like to hear something that recently brought a bit of excitement to my usual dull days in the library?"

Mike hadn't been listening. He learned he could hide his feelings of remoteness. At least he hoped that was true. No one seemed to have noticed that he had been temporarily someplace else. He looked at the faces around the table. Everyone appeared to be studying him, expectantly so, he thought. He assumed a question had been asked, maybe more than once. He tried a brief nod of his head for an answer, hoping it was the right response.

Both Kelly and Steve quickly nodded also. Smiling, they said, "Of course," almost in unison. At the same time they appeared to loosen their grip on their silverware. Mike wondered what he had just agreed to.

"I hope you'll find this interesting," Paul McCabe began.

"Oh, they'll love to hear it," his wife chimed in. "You can't be in Charlottesville and not be interested in Jefferson and Sally!"

"We're certainly interested," Kelly said.

"Definitely," Steve added, looking at his wife and then at his brother-in-law. Mike stared at his plate.

"Well," Paul began again, "if I can just lay a little groundwork so we're all on the same page. Then I can tell you what happened last week.

"As all of you know, Jefferson is said to have had an

affair with his slave, Sally Hemings. The affair, by the way, possibly began in Paris. Both Sally and her older brother, James, were Jefferson's servants when he was a minister to France.

"I have to say, Jefferson didn't help himself by never explicitly denying an affair with Sally. But, for a long time, many historians decided there weren't enough facts to support the accusations. After all, over the years Jefferson became one of the most hallowed of the Founding Fathers."

Mike desperately wanted people to talk about anything except his life going nowhere. "But I thought the DNA findings settled all of this," he said. "A scientific study, if I remember right, maybe ten years ago. It showed Jefferson was the father."

Kelly beamed, as if Mike was back in middle school and just spelled *victuals* correctly at the regional spelling bee.

"No, Mike, the 1998 DNA study didn't settle it, although the noose got drawn tighter. The DNA study shows a link between an individual carrying the Jefferson Y chromosome and one of Sally's sons, Eston, the youngest. But not specifically Thomas Jefferson. If it's okay for now, just trust me on this, and then I can get through this story before people fall asleep into their plates!"

"Oh, they wouldn't do that," piped up Cynthia.

"No, we want to hear this. Keep going," Kelly said. "But while you do, let me clear some plates and find out who wants coffee with dessert. I can hear from the kitchen."

While Kelly collected dishes, Paul continued his narrative.

"Many professional historians believe that at least one, very likely all, of Sally Hemings's children were by Jefferson. There are records of six births. We don't know for sure what actually occurred. Even if we accept that they had a sexual relationship, exactly what went on between Jefferson and Sally is unknown. Was she a lover? Was she forced upon? Was she prostituting herself in trade for something?"

"But if Jefferson forced himself on her, why would she come back from France with him?" Steve asked. "I understood she could have been freed in France and stayed there."

"Yes, she could have stayed in France. In Paris at the time it was illegal to own slaves. We just don't know what happened. For instance, did she literally lay down in response to her master's orders? Relations between female slaves and their white masters weren't all that uncommon.

"Remember, she was maybe only fifteen or sixteen at this time. Her mother and family, owned by Jefferson, lived in Virginia. If you are asking, did she have a choice, a real choice, that is, we don't know. Were they in love? Again, we don't know."

Here the professor paused for his last remarks to sink in. As if on cue, Kelly brought in a dessert of sorbet and homemade cookies and began pouring coffee for those wanting it. When she sat down the lecture resumed.

"By all accounts Sally was a beauty. Very light-skinned. She had a white father and two white grandfathers. In fact, Sally's father, John Wayles, was Jefferson's father-in-law. That made Sally a half-sister to Jefferson's wife, Martha. She died, after ten years of marriage, a couple years before Jefferson went to Paris. Sally came to Paris a few years after that. I have always wondered whether he might have seen something of his wife in Sally that attracted him. As half-sisters they likely had more than a passing resemblance. Steve, maybe that's a question for you psychologists?"

Steve stopped sipping his coffee and replied quickly, "Not my specialty, sorry."

McCabe smiled at his friend's swift parry, then continued. "You can see how important it would be to find out what really happened in Paris between TJ and Sally. And, of course, in the years following. But enough background. Let me get to the interesting part.

"A couple of weeks ago I got a call from a friend who runs a rare books and historic artifacts shop. I've helped him out occasionally by researching items he considered purchasing for resale. He's got a great collection of old broadsides, some even from Jefferson's time and even more from the Civil War period. Elmer--that's his name--wanted to know what something might be worth that would settle once and for all the Hemings-Jefferson question. Well, except for digging up TJ's remains and doing more DNA tests, I'm not sure anything will end the debate on his possible affair with Sally. But, as you can imagine, I was certainly ready to hear him out.

"Elmer said he got a call from a man who claims to be in possession of a letter or some kind of document written by James Hemings. Importantly, the caller said the artifact mentions an agreement between Jefferson and Sally Hemings. As you pointed out, Steve, James and Sally could have stayed behind in France as free persons. So why did they leave? Was some sort of deal worked out?

"If an agreement was reached, it could be the 'treaty' Sally's son, Madison, claimed Jefferson made with his mother in Paris. Madison Hemings said his mother didn't want to return to this country, but that TJ persuaded her by promising special privileges. And that her children would be freed when they turned twenty-one. Madison also said his mother was pregnant by Jefferson when she returned to Virginia. He claimed TJ eventually fathered all her children, which of course included himself.

"If Madison Hemings told the truth, and many people think he did, then Jefferson fathered all of Sally's children. And the number would be seven, not six."

Here the professor paused to eat the sorbet which was melting on his plate. Others also gave their attention to dessert and the table became quiet. Once he finished eating, McCabe began again.

"It's extremely unlikely Jefferson would put something in writing linking himself sexually with his female slave. If they reached some agreement, it must have been a verbal one. And we have to assume James Hemings would have known about a relationship between TJ and his sister. Remember, he was with them in Paris. So perhaps James Hemings made a record of what transpired, maybe to protect his sister and her children should Jefferson renege.

"Many slaves couldn't read or write. For example, historians aren't sure if Sally could. However, we know that James Hemings could read and write very well. If there is something out there written by him, the only thing we know for sure is that it was written before the end of 1801. He committed suicide late that year."

The professor looked around the table to see if he was losing his audience.

"Sorry, I'm getting too detailed here. Professors tend to run off at the mouth."

His wife started to say something, but McCabe stopped her with a wrinkled brow.

"The bottom line is this. Depending on the exact details, some sort of written statement from James Hemings attesting to a treaty or promise, whatever you want to call it, would not only tighten the noose but practically spring the trap door under Jefferson's feet. I can tell you it would shut up a lot of people who see the whole affair as preposterous."

McCabe paused once more. He asked Kelly for more coffee and apologized again for making his story so long. Mike had been fidgeting in his seat while the professor talked. Both his sister and brother-in-law now glanced in his direction. McCabe also looked toward Mike before continuing.

"I'm almost at the end. Please hang in just a little longer. It seems Elmer made an appointment with the caller to bring the document to the store. Then he contacted me. Well, as to what it could be worth? I know some untenured assistant professors who would kill for it. Maybe some full professors, too! Just kidding!"

The comment brought laughter from those at the table, except one. Mike looked on impatiently, wondering where this was going and how much longer it would take to get there.

"Lots of people would relish a look at this," McCabe said. "Besides academics. Consider, for instance, the descendants of the Jeffersons and the Hemingses. I have to wonder if maybe someone from one of these families discovered this document in their attic and decided to cash in."

Mike felt a headache coming on and decided this story had gotten a bit too long and heavy. "So, what happened?" he asked. "Did Elmer see the letter?"

His question came while Kelly was in the process of pouring from the coffee pot. She looked up and almost spilled coffee on Cynthia.

"That's the funny part," McCabe said. "Elmer called a few days later to say the guy never showed up. Tried the number left on his phone, but no one answered. Elmer waited a couple of days, still hearing nothing. He then called me to say he now thought the guy was working some kind of scam. That he backed away after Elmer made it clear his store dealt only in *legal* artifacts."

Mike tried to fathom what purpose Paul McCabe's

story served. Actually a non-story as far as he was concerned. Maybe academics have to get their kicks wherever they can, he thought. He centered his eyes on Kelly, but she looked down at her coffee.

"Well, that's too bad it wasn't something worth pursuing," Mike said, starting to push his chair away from the table, judging now was a good time to ask to be excused. His head hurt to the point he felt sick. He really needed to get away. McCabe's words, however, held him down.

"Just let me finish if I can. I know I've probably bored everyone."

Before Paul could make eye contact, Cynthia blurted, "No you haven't. Please tell everyone what happened next."

Kelly and Steve said words to the same effect. Both looked imploringly at Mike, with expressions that clearly said don't-leave-now. Resigned, Mike realized he had more to endure.

"Okay, bear with me. I'm near the end. Or did I say that already?" Paul chuckled.

"Last week I brought this story to a group I meet with occasionally. They're hard to describe. Mostly amateur historians. Jeffersonphiles. Also politically minded people who are looking for ways to invoke Jefferson in some cause or other. The group calls itself 'The Jefferson Bunch.' They meet every month or so to discuss the Founding Father. Sometimes outside speakers are invited. That's how I got to know the group. Kind of community outreach. But you get a free meal and some wine out of it, and they're genuinely nice people. Good students of history. I actually like doing it.

"I wasn't scheduled to attend this past week, but a colleague of mine was going to tell them about the stairways at Monticello and she asked me to come along. Believe it or not, there are various opinions about why

Jefferson designed the staircases as he did. Steve, you'll appreciate this, there are even psychological ones relating the design to Jefferson's supposedly closed personality."

McCabe looked at Steve, who smiled at the reference to his discipline, but chose not to respond.

"After Elizabeth, my colleague, finished her presentation, we were standing around, conversing over wine. I happened to mention to someone the call I got from the artifacts dealer who told me about a mysterious Hemings letter. The story quickly got buzzed around the room. Everyone wanted me to sit down and go through all the details so people could ask questions.

"We talked for almost an hour--about what the document could be, what insights it might contain, and so on. The group, I should add, is rather mixed regarding their views of a Hemings-Jefferson affair. Fortunately, by then Liz had left for another appointment. My story got a lot more interest than hers!"

Mike figured he just witnessed academic one-upsmanship first hand.

"Well," the professor said, "the group wants to investigate! They asked if I would be willing to talk with Elmer, to see if I can find out anything more. Possibly find a way to identify the owner of the letter. The group just couldn't see not doing something in case the letter was for real. Legally obtained or not. Sorry, Mike."

McCabe looked over at Mike who was focused on a spot somewhere above his sister's head.

Not waiting for a response, the professor moved to a conclusion, but only after looking tentatively toward Kelly and Steve.

Taking a deep breath, McCabe said, "I made it clear that I really didn't have the time to pursue this. Even if I did, I told the group I wasn't the right person to do so. But I said that if I thought of anyone who might help, I'd let them know. When Steve and I were playing squash a couple of days ago, I told him the story, and he told me about you, Mike. That you're a cop on indefinite leave and perhaps looking for something to occupy your time. You know, until, well, when you're ready to go back to the District. I hope that's right?"

Four faces turned toward Mike. He saw Kelly's pleading look, just like he used to get when he was sixteen with a driver's license and she and her friends needed a ride. Now he knew the purpose of tonight's charade. He had been set up, backed cleverly into a corner. He needed to have one long talk with Kelly and Steve. What did they expect from him? They should have known he wasn't ready to play detective again. Not yet. Maybe not ever.

Looking down at his dessert plate, avoiding eye contact with those around him, he pushed his chair back from the table.

More to himself than to the others, he said, "I'm afraid I really can't help you. I have this splitting headache. So, if you'll excuse me."

Not that he was listening, but no words were spoken at the table as Mike exited the room.

Chapter 3

The morning after the dinner party, during which Paul McCabe broached the idea of chasing down the owner of the so-called Hemings document, a conversation Mike rudely had cut off, sparks flew in the Cummings household. An angry and teary-eyed Kelly made it clear to Mike he had let her and Steve down, and not just because he had abruptly left the dinner table with some lame excuse of a headache. They had been working very hard to deal with Mike's grief and then the more recent changes in him. It affected all of them. Tammy was concerned, too, she said, and not just about Mike. She worried about her parents dying. What would happen, Tammy asked, if her mother died? What would she do? What would dad do? Would he be able to keep his job? Would they be able to keep going?

Kelly admitted the dinner had been a setup. They planned it after Steve heard the Hemings story from Paul McCabe. They had wanted to give him something interesting to focus on--a little task until he was ready to tackle bigger ones.

Mike didn't know how to respond to his sister's impassioned speech. He knew Kelly still didn't completely understand the terror he experienced when he found himself simply going through the motions of an existence. He recognized he was a burden on the Cummingses. He also had disappointed his mother by not visiting her in more than a year. And there were the many friends of Kirsten, as well as his colleagues on the force, who had extended their sympathy, all of whom he had never acknowledged.

As Kelly spoke to him, her voice softening, she reached out and placed her hand on his shoulder. He immediately felt he was no longer there. His sister kept talking, but he saw the scene in the kitchen as if from some remote mountain top. He was in a movie, acting a part, following a director's commands and not his own.

Are there reasons why we are here? What happens when we die? Where is she? Is a life alone worth living? How do we know we are alive? Am I alive?

"Mike! Mike, are you listening? I'm sorry to come on so strong, but it's been hard. We all love you, but you owe it to yourself and to Kirsten's memory to get back on track. You have to start being active again. For your own sake."

Mike lifted his eyes to Kelly's face and slowly nodded in agreement.

"I'll do what I can," he said quietly.

* * *

Mike's appointment with his therapist turned out to be at a convenient time for his brother-in-law to drive him. He still didn't feel comfortable behind the wheel. He managed everyday activities well enough, but worried that thoughts of being outside himself might distract him. He was thankful when Steve volunteered to chauffeur him.

Dr. Rider greeted him and came around her desk to sit in a comfortable chair opposite his.

"Let me first tell you what I picked up from your responses to the questionnaires you completed last week," she began. "What you are dealing with fits with the experiences of a client of mine whom I treated a few years ago. What the mental health field recognizes as depersonalization disorder. My client was younger, a college student actually, in her early twenties. She had been sexually abused as a child and suffered from depersonalization off and on for maybe seven or eight years.

"Feeling that you're outside your body looking in, detached from one's self, can be triggered by severe stress or traumatic, even life-threatening, events. It's a defensive reaction, a way the mind can protect itself. Not an unreasonable strategy when you think about it. Basically, if reality is too awful, we move outside it. Like I said, it's called depersonalization disorder, DP or DPD, in the jargon of our business. But it's also more than simply a defense mechanism helping us cope with tragedy. It can become a state in itself. It's as if that defensive reaction takes root and won't let go."

She checked Mike's reaction before proceeding. His eyes focused on her. His mind worked to absorb what she was telling him.

"You're a bit older than many people who experience their first DP episode. The causes of your onset, however, are similar to others with this disorder. And so are your symptoms.

"So let me begin with some basics about DP. First, and I've mentioned this before, you aren't insane or going crazy. Having psychotic episodes or anything like that. For some individuals it comes and goes. For others, it's quite constant, a chronic condition. Frequently it begins with a reaction to drugs. Marijuana, for example. From what you wrote, you haven't been into drugs, correct?"

Mike shook his head. "You may not believe it, but even in this day and age I never did drugs. Was a sports nut in high school, soccer and baseball. You were off the team if you were caught using. When I did a couple of years of college I was interested in law enforcement. I knew messing with drugs would ruin my chances of being a cop."

"Good. It will make your treatment easier," Dr. Rider said, before commenting further. "I'm not sure if I did, but I should have mentioned earlier, that even most of those who suffer from chronic depersonalization can get along passably well. Hold a job, interact socially with others, and so on. They may not look like they have a problem, but they know they do. Trying to explain their problem to someone often doesn't lead anywhere. Perhaps as a consequence they learn to hide it from others. Then there's the anxiety that somehow they'll be found out. You, better than anyone, know these experiences can be extremely stressful."

Mike recognized that Dr. Rider was describing him.

"One of the interesting things about DP episodes is that many so-called normal folks have them. Most of us at one time have felt 'out of it' or 'floating above it all.' 'Detached' from everything. Like in a dream. These experiences typically don't last long and can arise for lots of reasons. Nearly everyone has experienced an occasion when familiar objects lose their familiarity. Words on a page, for example. It's called 'derealization' and can be part of DP."

"It happens to me," Mike said. "I can be looking at something, something I'm familiar with, and it looks strange. It's like I've never seen it before. It's scary."

"I'm sure it is. So let's see if we can get you back in control. I want to say something about your treatment. I'm sure you've been thinking about what we'll be doing here. Maybe how long it will take. Even if a treatment will work."

"Yes, thanks. I'd like to know what's going to happen," Mike said somewhat neutrally, hopefully hiding his growing fear that he couldn't be "cured."

"Let me be up front with you, full disclosure, so to speak. I said I think I can help you and I believe I can. Will we be able to restore your sense of self to what it once was? Get you back to where you were? I believe we can. Some people suffer with depersonalization for years, while you say you've only been experiencing it for a few months. However, I wouldn't be surprised if you've experienced DP episodes longer than you realize, likely going back to the time your wife died. Your grief and depression over her death may have kept you from recognizing what was going on."

Mike thought about his life in the months immediately following Kirsten's accident, but he found little to grab hold of. It was if he hadn't been alive then. He turned his attention back to Dr. Rider, and said, "I'd like to see if you can help. It's better than doing nothing. And if you have some tricks up your sleeve, I want to see them."

Dr. Rider, laughing, said, "No tricks. And I don't do magic. I'm afraid I don't even do anything special. No mud bath, exotic diet, laying on of hands, inkblots to look at, whatever. My approach basically is what the field calls cognitive behavior therapy. Although I may add some things based on what I learned treating my previous client with DP. I'll want to work on your thought processes and then on some behaviors. Not tricks, just tools of the trade.

"So let me tell you what comes next. During these sessions we'll be talking about what you've gone through this past year. I'll also want to know about any previous experiences you might have had with feeling outside yourself. It's possible that some individuals have a tendency to experience depersonalization, even something they're born with. I sometimes wonder if it's a way emergency responders cope. Like pulling people out of a train wreck or from a bomb scene. Fleeting or temporary DP experiences wouldn't be unreasonable in those cases. I guess I should have included being a cop in that list."

Mike heard Justice's voice in his head. *It's all about cleaning up bloody messes.*

He saw himself standing next to Justice and the paramedics, the dead African-American woman in the entryway, bruised and soaked in blood. Like watching a movie. The camera then zoomed in on Kirsten, lying at the foot of the stairs, blood on her face, not moving. Unable to touch him. Talk to him. Love him. What did he feel? He didn't know.

Where is this all going? What happened to my life? Whose life? Who am I really?

"Mike, look at me!"

Through the haze Mike saw his therapist looking down at him.

Dr. Rider sat down, smoothed her pants and opened her notebook again, all the while her eyes on Mike.

"I saw you zone out. I decided to do something to distract you. Jumping up from my chair was the first thing that came to mind. I hope I didn't scare you."

"You definitely got my attention, but I'm still in a bit of a fog."

"That's understandable, but if you're up to it, let's keep going."

"I'm okay. Let's keep at it."

Dr. Rider reached into a canvas bag at her side. She pulled out a small notebook and offered it to him.

Mike took it and flipped through the pages.

"There isn't anything in this."

"No, there isn't. Not yet. I want you to keep a diary. Each day I want you to record your feelings of depersonalization. Write down your thoughts, then try to rate them on a 10-point scale. A 1 would be very little if any sense of losing yourself. Feeling normal, like your old self. A 10 would be the strongest sense of depersonalization. Use a 10 when you think you are completely outside your body, questioning who is in control of your mind or body, when things don't look familiar. Describe your behavior at the time and what you felt, then rate your feelings as best you can. Do you understand what I'm looking for?"

"I think so."

"Good. The goal is to get you thinking about what you're thinking, to find out what's going on in your head. We're going to look at how your feelings of being numb, emotionless, vary from moment to moment, day to day, and over weeks. Most importantly, we're looking for triggers. What is it that brings on a sense of detachment. It's important to write down both what you were doing and what you were thinking at the time."

Dr. Rider's next question caught Mike off guard. "How would you rate your sense of detachment right now?"

"Now? Here?"

"Yes. What are you feeling?"

Mike wasn't sure how he felt, or if he wanted to share his current feelings with his therapist. He stared at the empty notebook in his hands, then said, "Well, I would have given it a 2, maybe a 3, when I first came in. I was feeling pretty good actually. But I found as the session went on, when we talked about what's wrong with me, I began to feel more detached. My mind got fuzzy. Sorry, I can't think of a better word. I can see myself in this chair, but I don't feel like it's me in the chair. That especially happened a few minutes ago when you mentioned people coping with bloody messes."

Did she really say *bloody messes*?

"I'm sorry," he said. "I know you're supposed to be helping. I have to say a 6."

"That's fine. It stands to reason that as we explore your problem you'll feel some stress. We know your reaction over the past months, maybe even when working as a cop, has been to deal with stress by moving outside yourself. There's no need to apologize. I would have been surprised if you hadn't felt stressed when we talk about some of these things that are bothering you. Good work!"

Maybe she gives gold stars, Mike thought somewhat

sarcastically. Nevertheless, he appreciated her enthusiasm for his efforts.

"I'd like to ask you to do something else for me. Well, for you. From what I've learned, you've been pretty inactive these past months. Watching TV, taking walks. Your responses to one of my questionnaires indicate you sleep a lot."

"I guess that's true," admitted Mike, embarrassed by his lack of initiative to do practically anything.

"I would like to see if you can change that. See what you can do to get involved with something. A hobby even. Have you been exercising? You look like you're in pretty good shape."

"I'm not where I'd like to be. These past months have taken a lot out of me. I haven't exercised like I used to."

"Please try to do it. Regular exercise, that is. It's important to demonstrate to yourself that you're in control of your body. There are some great continuing education courses at the university, if that interests you. Something to focus on other than your feelings. Do you think you can find something?"

Mike learned during his previous therapy that it was best to go along with what the therapist requested. "I'll see what I can do," he said, hoping he could.

"Before you go, let me suggest some strategies for dealing with DP episodes. When you find yourself drifting, try distracting yourself. For example, you might concentrate on something in your environment. Think about what it is, what it's for. What color and shape is it. It can be anything. If you're eating, it could be food on the plate. Or look at a picture on the wall and ask yourself what's in it. Maybe pay attention to how people around you are dressed. It really doesn't matter what. Do you think you can do that?"

"I think I can manage that."

"One other trick. Oops! I said I didn't have tricks, but

it is a little trick. When you find yourself slipping, distancing from yourself, start repeating a phrase like, 'I am Mike Chance. I am real. I am here.' What do you think? Can you do that, too? I'm not saying do all these things at the same time. I'm just suggesting another tactic. Would you try that once in a while?"

Mike agreed again, but found out Dr. Rider wanted more.

"Okay, say those words aloud for me."

"Ah, all right. I'm Mike Chance. I am real. I'm here," Mike responded, feeling rather silly.

"Repeat that to yourself when you feel you're slipping."

When he emerged from Dr. Rider's office, the sunny skies that ushered him had turned gray. He paced up and down the sidewalk, waiting for his brother-in-law to pick him up. When a light rain started to fall he moved under a nearby awning. The weather didn't help his mood. Still feeling disoriented following his therapy session, he found the mantra circulating in his head.

It stopped when he irrationally began worrying that passers-by might be listening.

Chapter 4

The Jefferson Bunch had been around Charlottesville since the 1970s. The number of members fluctuated, being in some years as many as ten or twelve. A member is someone who likes to talk about Thomas Jefferson, shows up at a meeting of the group more than once and, if seeking "official" membership, hosts a light dinner and conversation in their home.

The group seeks to mimic Jefferson's famous dinner parties at Monticello, especially those in his retirement years, when he hosted visitors nonstop. True to Jefferson's practice, wine is offered only after the meal is finished. Members are partial to Virginia wines, which Jefferson, contrary to myth, rarely tasted. Certainly not from any grapes planted at Monticello. His wines, at quite some expense, arrived from Europe. The host picks the topic for an evening's discussion, usually in the form of a quote, historical anecdote, book synopsis, or recent news item. Lately there had been much discussion about Jefferson's views of "big government."

Jonathan Turner had accepted the role of host for the group's upcoming meeting. He began his career teaching history at a local high school. After earning a master's degree, he secured a teaching position at a nearby community college. Jon had been with the group for nearly ten years, making him one of the oldest current members. In his early seventies and a confirmed bachelor, he had hosted more than two dozen dinners over the years. It helped that he liked to cook.

The host assumed responsibility for coming up with a topic for consideration, doing some background reading, moderating the discussion, and sometimes playing devil's advocate. At tonight's meeting, however, the group would be treading over old ground and Jon didn't look forward to it. The Bunch had talked about the purported Hemings affair numerous times. From these previous discussions Jon knew the members fell into three factions: the he did, the he didn't, and the we don't know and perhaps never will.

Two weeks ago the Bunch heard from Professor Paul McCabe about a two-hundred-year-old letter that could shed more light on Jefferson's relations with his female slave. Excitement among these Jefferson students grew when they considered the implications. The group decided they wanted to know more, maybe even try to locate the owner of the letter. Members asked Professor McCabe to head-up an investigation, but he declined. He did say, however, that he'd give some thought as to who might be able to help them.

The previous weekend McCabe e-mailed that he had met Mike Chance, a Washington police detective currently on leave, and that he had tried without success to enlist him in the hunt for the owner of the letter. A few days later the professor e-mailed again. Having thought it over some more, he now believed the whole business wasn't worth pursuing. If there was something out there, he communicated to Jon, it would come to light eventually. Jon forwarded the professor's messages to the Bunch's members.

Not all the members wanted to give up. Peter Trent desired the group to find someone else to investigate, a private eye if necessary. Peter had the money to finance such an effort, given his prosperous restaurant on the historic pedestrian mall, but he acknowledged he didn't want to pay all the bills. He suggested the group meet to vote on whether they should sponsor an investigation. No one objected to this democratic process. The only condition voiced by several members was that at least two-thirds of the regular attendees be present.

Jon knew that Peter Trent fell in the "he did" camp.

Peter believed the evidence strong enough to implicate Jefferson in fathering, if not all Sally's children, at least most of them. In Peter's view, the DNA study linking a Jefferson male to one of Sally's children, the evidence revealing Jefferson's presence at Monticello nine months before each of six deliveries, and the first-person reports by Monticello visitors who mentioned children with Jefferson's features, made the case against Jefferson practically airtight.

Another long-time member, Charles Wingate, adamantly defended the "he didn't" position. Charles owned a local publishing company and lived in nearby Keswick. A staunch defender of Jefferson's reputation, he argued, *ad nauseam* in Jon's opinion, that Thomas Jefferson, Founding Father of the country and devoted husband to Martha and loving father to his surviving children, would never take a slave mistress. Charles emphasized that whatever evidence existed that "he did" was circumstantial and not convincing. A man as principled as Jefferson just wouldn't do it. Charles repeatedly reminded everyone that Jefferson's granddaughter once said it best: *It is a moral impossibility.* Simple as that. End of argument.

Whenever Charles perched atop his soapbox reciting platitudes about Jefferson's spotless character, Peter Trent would roll his eyes and start slinging dirt. He liked to remind Charles of the Founding Father's history of misadventures with the opposite sex.

"You forget, Charles, that Jefferson once made advances toward Betsey Walker, his best friend's wife! And what about all that time he spent in Paris with the married woman, Maria Cosway? He definitely had an active sex drive."

Charles eyed Peter as a father might look at an ignorant child.

"Peter, Jefferson acknowledged his moral lapse

regarding Walker. He was obviously regretful and unlikely to do anything like that ever again. Nothing serious happened in the Cosway relationship. We all have moments of weakness."

"Who's to say he didn't have more than a few moments!" Peter interjected. "You're living in fantasy land. You really have no clue as to what the Founding Fathers were really like. Jefferson wasn't the only one of this supposedly sainted group to chase skirts, and married ones at that. Why do you think these guys were any different from the string of politicians over the years caught in compromising positions?"

Jon figured that Peter was looking for one more piece of good evidence for Jefferson's paternity, one that would make Charles shut up.

The upcoming discussion and vote concerned Jon for yet another reason. The composition of the group changed in the past year with the addition of two new regulars. Jeremiah Maxwell was an African-American minister who recently started a church on the southeast side of Charlottesville, practically in the shadow of Monticello. Andrea Hudson was the other new member. She worked as a political consultant out of her home in Charlottesville, but frequently traveled to meet with out-of-town clients.

For the most part, Jeremiah proved to be a genial contributor. He typically wore clothes that always appeared too large for his wiry 6 feet, 160 pounds. Jeremiah always got people's attention because he spoke in a disconcerting, stentorian voice which seemed to belong to someone twice his size. He seemed to genuinely enjoy the group's get-togethers, but from the beginning, Jeremiah made clear his views on Jefferson.

"I want to be honest with you folks. I've come to learn as much as I can about Mr. Jefferson." Jeremiah paused in that first meeting and looked once more around the room, clearly prepared to say more. Seeing that everyone was listening, he continued, "But, and here I hope I don't find disagreement, we must begin with the fact that Jefferson was as big a racist as ever existed. He may have written 'All men are created equal,' but he didn't mean it. That's a fact. He bought and sold black people. Gave them as presents. He had us whipped. He talked about my people in the vilest manner. He said apes liked to mate with our women. That we were an inferior race and should be sent back to Africa. We weren't fit to live next to whites."

All of this came out too bluntly for Charles Wingate. The publisher stirred uneasily in his seat, before nearly exploding, "Reverend Maxwell, we all know that Jefferson said some things that look bad when taken out of the context of the times. Yes, he owned slaves, but so did many of the Founding Fathers. Holding slaves was legal. This meant there was an issue of property rights. And people realized that the economy of the South, if not the whole country, would collapse if slaves were set free all at once. Slavery wasn't of Jefferson's choosing. The Founding Fathers were shackled with slavery. Shackled! Those were George Washington's words. But even so, Jefferson spoke of the evil of slavery. He . . ."

"Mr. Wingate! I'm not talking about the circumstances, the excuses, the context, or about blatantly immoral laws. I'm referring to the absolute facts. And the facts are that he worked people, my people, from dawn to dark. People who had no choice in the matter. People who had no freedom except to please the white master. He considered us, at best, little children requiring his protection. And I can tell you it wasn't Jefferson who was shackled!"

Jon had felt obliged to jump in at this point. "Reverend, I think we all know where you're coming from. No one here disagrees with those facts."

Jon saw his comment didn't quite satisfy Charles, who, red-faced and breathing hard, fortunately chose not to respond. Jeremiah, however, wanted the last word.

"I fear you all will never be able to understand where I'm coming from. What's important for you to understand is that I have feelings. Yes, deep feelings about how my people suffered. There are some things that touch me in ways that cannot touch you. Never will. I don't want to be anything but honest with you. This is definitely a man we need to talk about, even learn from. But if I'm going to participate, I believe we must have our discussions rooted in honesty."

Jeremiah steadfastly defended the validity of African-American oral history. If Sally's son, Madison, told a newspaper reporter his mother was Jefferson's concubine, that he and his siblings were all fathered by Jefferson, it undoubtedly was true. Jeremiah accepted Madison's statement that Sally gave birth soon after she returned from France.

"Just because no record of a delivery has been found doesn't make Madison Hemings a liar," he argued. "These weren't just distorted or fabricated memories. Few African-American slaves could read or write. Oral story-telling was their tradition. So why shouldn't we accept Madison's story?"

In a subsequent meeting, Jeremiah pointed out that Jefferson was far from a true Christian. Truth be told, Jeremiah had said, he thought of Jefferson as a borderline, maybe actual, atheist. Although Jeremiah accepted the title of reverend, he admitted he hadn't graduated from seminary or earned any divinity degrees. He liked to say he heard God's voice telling him to spread the gospel. One couldn't ask for better credentials, he explained.

An acquaintance of Jon's had attended the minister's church for a while. He told Jon that Jeremiah had a gift--

the most eloquent and downright passionate sermons rolled off his tongue. All the more captivating, his friend said, because he spoke in a surprisingly deep, booming voice.

Many people came to the new church, Jon was told, because of the reverend's preaching and a dynamic gospel-singing choir. Others no doubt came out of a genuine fear for their souls, since Jeremiah preached that the hell fires of eternal damnation would consume those who did not recognize Jesus Christ as their savior. When Jeremiah learned Jefferson denied Christ's miracles and resurrection, the virgin birth, and much of what Jeremiah held true, he knew he had a perfect example of someone gone astray. Having laid out Jefferson's beliefs, or more correctly his non-beliefs, Jon's friend related how the preacher would shout a litany of queries from the pulpit:

"What do you think happened to Mr. Jefferson's soul?

"What makes us great in God's eyes?

"Is it great deeds? Beautiful words? Is it money to build a great house? To buy expensive wines?

"What must we do to follow the Lord? Who do *you* say Jesus is? What do *you* believe?"

At these moments Jeremiah would turn from the pulpit and point in the general direction of Monticello, his hand shaking. "The man who wrote 'all men are created equal' kept our people in chains." His voice thundered through the church. "Those were real chains. But what about the chains of unemployment, of sickness, of poverty? How should *we* look after others? As Jesus did, or as people like Mr. Jefferson did?"

Jefferson was more than Jeremiah's foil. It was clear the Reverend Jeremiah Maxwell considered the author of the Declaration of Independence to be the devil incarnate.

The minister's participation in the Jefferson Bunch introduced a degree of tension in the group. This was particularly the case if anyone mentioned race, which often couldn't be avoided. Charles once claimed that Jefferson wouldn't stoop to having sex with a black slave. Jeremiah's expression soured, and he raised his hand to stop Charles from continuing. What else did many white slave owners do, the minister suggested, but have sex with black women they held in bondage. Jefferson's father-in-law provided a good example, Jeremiah pointed out.

Charles insisted he meant "servant," someone obviously beneath the Founding Father's station in life. Since Jefferson and other respectable white Virginians typically called their black slaves *servants*, everyone in the group knew what Charles really meant. Discussion went downhill after that.

No, Jon did not look forward to the approaching meeting.

Chapter 5

By late Friday afternoon, Jon had finished preparing dinner for the evening's meeting of the Jefferson Bunch. This included spending time deciding on the two bottles of wine he'd serve from his modest collection. Jon felt obligated to play host again. He had taken charge of channeling all the e-mails setting up tonight's vote, and thus saw himself partly responsible for the group meeting on such short notice. Besides, it gave him a chance to try out a new vegetarian chili recipe.

Jon counted seven regulars this year. In addition to himself, Charles, Jeremiah, and Peter, the list included the other relative newcomer, Andrea Hudson. Attractive and always impeccably dressed in professional attire, she had ties to a Washington-based consulting firm. Andrea admitted to the group that she was here to learn as much as she could about Jefferson.

She said she wanted to make sure her clients could name at least some of the Founding Fathers. And if asked to identify a favorite among this revered group of white men, she wanted it to be Jefferson. George Washington might work. No one had a bad thing to say about him, but he provided too few recognizable quotes. Besides, she recognized that many people view the first president as aloof, on a pedestal, almost regal, if that isn't sacrilegious to say. She knew it shouldn't be one of the Federalists, Adams or Hamilton, for instance. Their push for stronger executive powers wasn't where the tide pulled these days. They were also too unknown to most people.

Jefferson had to be the one, she told the group. Everyone knew he drafted the Declaration of Independence. Fewer knew James Madison was the force behind the U.S. Constitution. Plus, the fourth president just didn't stick out in people's minds. But everyone knew about Jefferson, America's favorite Founding Father. In fact, probably the world's favorite Founding Father. His words often reverberated when dictators were being overthrown.

She was aware Jefferson brought some baggage-- especially the failure to free his slaves. Nevertheless, there were the many quotes from the great man denigrating the institution of slavery that could be employed in his defense. She agreed with Charles Wingate, if we throw out Jefferson, who's next? Few weren't culpable. Even Lincoln, the Great Emancipator, wasn't in favor of social and political equality between blacks and whites, such as letting blacks vote or marry whites.

She also recognized that she needed to tread carefully around the whole church and state separation thing. As Jeremiah liked to point out, Jefferson was anything but orthodox Christian. Andrea knew many of her clients and more importantly, their constituents, didn't want to hear this. She happily discovered Jefferson was full of contradictions and thus ripe for editing. "I am a Christian," he once began. Then clarified what he meant in somewhat unorthodox fashion. Well, those four words would suit just fine, she said.

Craig Gibson and Mark Abernathy rounded out the recent members' list. Craig taught political science at a Charlottesville high school, having taken over from Mark following his retirement. Jon hesitated to guess how these two would vote, although based on past discussions he saw them being in the we-will-never-know camp. Jon knew Jeremiah didn't have difficulty believing Jefferson had sex with his slave and perhaps he'd want proof. On the other hand, maybe the minister wouldn't feel there was any need to show what he already took for granted. Andrea was on a mission to gather whatever information about Jefferson would be helpful to her clients. Peter clearly desired to investigate further the possible document. Jon also knew where Charles stood. Although he didn't like siding with the publisher, preferring a middle ground, Jon believed that with his own no vote, the motion to mount an investigation might possibly be defeated. He didn't want any part of it.

Six of the regulars attended the meeting. Mark carried Craig's regrets, saying a family matter needed attention. Given Craig had three teenage children, that could mean anything. Jon realized the vote might now be closer than he thought.

A long-standing tradition called for the evening's topic not to be discussed until the group sat down with wine following dinner. Despite a more than usual tension in the room, tonight's dinner conversation stayed away from Sally Hemings and Jefferson. Talk centered around local issues in C'ville, particularly the impact of the weak economy on local shops and restaurants. To a certain degree the city found itself cushioned against the most severe economic downturns. The presence of a university with more than twenty thousand students, two large hospital complexes, and several major federal agencies, including a national government information center the locals simply call the spook center, helped keep the economy moving. Many pensioned retirees resided in Charlottesville as well.

By mutual agreement, the host limited each member's after-dinner wine to no more than two glasses. Jefferson reportedly never drank more than that, and these typically were watered down. In this way they honored tradition, but also protected those who were driving, as well as the pocketbook of the host. The rule also helped maintain a degree of decorum that Jon knew for a fact sometimes had been lost before imposing limits on alcohol.

With everyone settled in his spacious living room, Jon assumed the role of moderator.

"As you all know, we're to vote tonight on whether we support Peter's idea to go ahead with an investigation--to see what can be found out about the mystery caller and possible James Hemings letter. It isn't clear if this is some kind of fraud, that no such letter exists. And even if there is a letter, can we, or rather someone we hire, find it. Speaking of the question of hiring someone, this brings up the question of money. We haven't yet talked about how much as a group we are willing to put up. How much does a private investigator cost?"

"Aren't we ahead of ourselves, Jon?" Charles asked. "Let's find out if this is something the group wants to do before we get into details. I certainly don't want to do it. It isn't really any of our business. Launching an investigation, that is. We're a discussion group, for crying out loud. Not a bunch of provocateurs with nothing else to do."

"Hold on a minute, Charles," Peter declared. "We are, or at least have claimed to be, students of Jefferson. As serious students maybe we should be thinking of this as research. What is a student but an investigator of knowledge?"

"I know talking about money is getting ahead of things," Andrea jumped in, "but I think I should tell everyone that I know someone who is willing to put up some money to help find out if this letter exists."

"You mean you talked this over with people outside the group?" queried Jeremiah. "I thought we promised Professor McCabe not to go too far with this. You know, so we don't alert the media."

"Give me more credit. I talked with this person in

very general terms. No specifics. I made it clear our conversation should be kept in confidence. I knew of his interest in historic artifacts from the Jefferson period. I simply mentioned that we, the group that is, might be on the trail of something big related to Sally Hemings. He asked me not to reveal his name, but to keep him posted. If we get to the point where we can be more specific then he might be interested in helping out with the cost of an investigation."

"Just like that?" Jon asked. "No strings?"

"There are some conditions. But let's wait until the vote to hear them. I just thought it important for people to know that money may not be an issue. At least not as much as we might think."

Jon looked around at members of the group. He realized this may not go in the direction he wished. Money would be a problem for some, himself included. Andrea's comments appeared to take that off the table. Resigned to whatever the evening might bring, he said, "Okay, let's get down to voting."

"Just wait a minute," interrupted Charles. "I've thought long and hard about this. It's all a lot of nonsense. Who are we to be digging up dirt on Jefferson. He deserves more, and I think . . ."

Peter Trent cut him off. "Damn it, Charles, we aren't digging up dirt. It's already out there. It's fact finding. Nothing else. If Jefferson screwed Sally based on some kind of offer he made her then everyone should know about it. God almighty, he's a dead old white man. Many historians believe Jefferson promised Sally something, maybe her kids' eventual freedom. Why shouldn't we find out for sure if we can. And if Andrea knows someone who will help pay the bills, then it's even better. With business the way it is these days I certainly don't want to be shelling out a lot of cash. Thanks to Andrea, apparently we don't have to. Jon, let's vote."

Jon looked around. Before Charles could respond, he said, "Right. Let's just get this over with, then we can see where we go next. I, for one, don't want to get involved with this adventure."

"Is that your vote?" Jeremiah asked. "I thought we would be doing this anonymously. You know, by secret ballot."

"So did I," Mark added.

"Perhaps we should have considered that," Jon said, taking a conciliatory tone. "But I think it's pretty clear to everyone where we all stand. Let's keep it transparent. I'm voting 'no,' as I just said."

"Well, you can put me down for a 'no,'" Charles stated. "The whole idea is ridiculous."

"Okay," Jon said. "We have two no votes. I guess we know where you stand, Peter."

"Damn right. We could make our mark on history if we found this letter."

Jon looked at Andrea Hudson.

"I assume, Andrea, with that benefactor in your pocket you are going to vote yes?"

"I am," she said emphatically. "And not just because I know someone who will help out. I had already decided that Sally should have a full hearing. Anything we could find out would be important both to the debate and to her legacy.

"She gets painted as Jefferson's slave concubine and not much else. Then there are those who want the two of them to be in love. As if that makes everything okay. Just forget he owned her. Think of them as some happy honeymoon couple! What does a fifteen or sixteen-year-old know about love!"

The male members of the Bunch looked her way. Andrea missed many of their previous discussions of Sally and Jefferson. Consequently, the group hadn't heard much from her on this topic. Tonight they learned that Andrea came prepared to make her views known.

"Consider her legacy if Jefferson wasn't the father of her children," she continued in front of her silent audience.

"Some people suggest that Jefferson's brother, Randolph, slept with her. Or maybe even Randolph's sons. You all know other names come up as well. Some say she may have had multiple partners. To me, that makes her out to be someone other than what she might have been--a strong woman in a tough situation. Maybe she stood up to Jefferson. Someone thought her capable enough when she was only fourteen to escort his eight-year-old daughter across the Atlantic. She managed to get around in a foreign country. All this while waiting on both Jefferson and his daughters."

This was the most animated the group had seen Andrea. Several of the members moved uneasily in their seats.

"We know she could have stayed in France as a free woman. But imagine how scary that must have looked to her. Her mother and siblings, except for James, were in Virginia. How would she have managed on her own? We don't know what her brother planned, but we know he came back, too. You have to think she'd be lost, alone in France without her brother. So did she really have a choice?

"What did she consider her best option? I for one would like to know if she worked out a deal to help herself and her family. She certainly wouldn't be the first woman who prostituted herself to make a better life for her children. Where's the shame in that? That would give her a heroine's role as far as I'm concerned."

None of her listeners could decide on the right response. Mark seemed absorbed with looking at his shoes. Charles's jaw had dropped, his mouth open. Peter smiled. He saw her speech as a pitch for a yes vote from any undecideds. Jeremiah's countenance didn't reveal much. Jon took a deep breath and broke the silence.

"Okay. Mark, I'm guessing you're down for a no vote, right?"

"Well, I was going to vote no," Mark said somewhat indecisively. "And I know Craig wanted to vote no also. But when I talked this over with my wife, she said some of the same things Andrea just said. Why do you men, she said, emphasizing 'men,' not want to know what really happened to this girl? Everyone talks about the great man Jefferson, she said. No one seems to consider Sally's point of view. Joyce really surprised me. I didn't know she was into all of this. Anyway, Jon, I guess I think both she and Andrea have a point. So I have to vote 'yes.' But I'm sure you can count Craig's vote as 'no.'"

"Wait a minute!" Peter shouted. "This is a vote of members present. Right, Jon? We didn't agree to take proxies."

"I have to agree with Peter," Jon replied. "To be fair it should be a vote of those present. We clearly have a quorum with the six of us here. Any votes in the past have been by majority so I assume that's what we're doing tonight. So far we have three yes votes and two no votes."

At this point the members turned toward the preacher.

"Reverend, what do you say?" Peter asked, clearly expecting a yes vote and producing the result he wanted.

All eyes were on the minister, not unlike when he stood in the pulpit on Sunday mornings. Jeremiah paused to bask in the spotlight. He then smiled at his audience and spoke slowly in his deep voice.

"I have considered this question for a few days now. I have prayed over my decision and I think I heard from God."

Seated to the minister's right, Peter rolled his eyes.

"I want you all to know this group means a lot to me. As a black man in the South, I mean. Twenty-first century or not, it's still the South. But surrounded by all you kind, white folks," he continued with the same smile, "I have appreciated the opportunity to talk candidly, honestly, about things that are important to me. Religion. Race. Injustice. So . . ."

"Your vote!" Peter exclaimed, no longer able to sit through Jeremiah's homily.

"I'm getting there," Jeremiah shot back. "I just want to preface my vote with a kind of thank-you to the group. I don't want anyone misinterpreting my vote in any way other than it comes from my heart."

Jon had no idea where this was going. Looking around the room it was clear Jeremiah had lost others as well. Only Peter seemed to glimpse some hope for his side.

"I have to vote 'no,'" Jeremiah announced.

"You can't!" Peter said, once more raising his voice, at the same time rising from his chair.

"You heard Andrea. It won't cost us much. We can make a difference. I thought you were smarter than this!"

An awkward silence filled the room. Jeremiah glared at Peter. Before the minister could reply, Jon responded, hoping to put a lid on things.

"Peter! Calm down. We had a vote. We are tied. The motion didn't carry. From what Mark says, if Craig were here the investigation would definitely have been voted down. I think the result tonight says we aren't going into the private-eye business."

Peter remained standing while addressing the group. "Well, it doesn't mean I can't get involved, even if you people have no backbone. How can you call yourselves students if you won't do a little work outside of class! Yes, let's just all get back to talking about Jefferson's dinner dishes! It's safe and goes nowhere. Andrea, what do you think?"

"I need to consider this some more," she answered. "The person I mentioned probably wouldn't really care who led an investigation. Only that there was one. But if the Jefferson Bunch decided against getting involved, he may decide the whole thing is a wild-goose chase. We'll have to see. Personally, I would like to explore this further."

"Mark," Peter said, looking straight at him. "What do you think. Your wife seemed to agree with Andrea and . . ."

"I'm sorry, Peter." Mark shook his head. "I agree this letter would be an amazing find. Despite what my wife thinks, given our split, and Craig's view, which I think we should consider even if he isn't here, I believe we should drop the whole thing. It would likely be a waste of time. It isn't clear this letter is for real. If it is for real, it will probably turn up."

"Well," an emotional Peter declared," I don't have to wait and see. Good night everyone."

He turned abruptly, grabbed his jacket from a chair in the hallway, and marched out the front door.

When the remaining members got to their feet ready to follow, Jon noticed that no one had touched their wine, a Cabernet Franc he obtained from a local winery. Watching Charles put on his coat, Jon could tell the decision pleased him. Mark also appeared satisfied with the vote. He got the outcome he apparently wanted, but could tell his wife he stood up for Sally. Andrea would report to her client and see where that went. And Jeremiah? Jon couldn't decide what motivated the preacher's vote. Peter's brusque interruption had quashed any more discussion.

As he ushered the last person out the door, Jon realized he felt good about the meeting. Except for the uncomfortable moment between Peter and the reverend, he believed everything turned out for the best. Peter Trent could do what he wanted without involving the group in a questionable endeavor. Jon wanted to think more about Andrea's comments concerning Sally's legacy. For now, however, he had the task of pouring wine back into bottles. Then there were dishes to do.

Chapter 6

Virginia's state capital lies seventy miles southeast of Charlottesville, located at the falls of the James River where Piedmont cascades into Tidewater. The city of Richmond boasts a major university, world-class museums, and numerous desirable features of a modern city. Yet the past casts a heavy shadow on the city. It was the capital of the Confederacy during what many Southerners called the War of Northern Aggression, as well as home to the largest slave market north of New Orleans for nearly forty years before the war. After the war and into the 20th century the city was a major center of massive resistance to integration efforts. Richmond constantly seeks to re-define itself.

A drive down Monument Avenue reveals the city's efforts toward reconciliation with history. The tree-lined boulevard, with a massive statue at each of six traffic circles, stretches east and west from Franklin Street on Richmond's west side. The first and largest monument erected, a memorial to Robert E. Lee sculpted in France, was unveiled in 1890, before tens of thousands of onlookers. Over the next thirty years, other paragons of Southern resistance, J.E.B. Stuart, Stonewall Jackson, and Jefferson Davis ascended to lofty pedestals. A statue honoring Matthew Fontaine Maury, who helped acquire ships and construct naval defenses for the Confederacy, was positioned in 1929.

In 1995 city officials broke ground for a sixth monument, honoring the Richmond-born tennis player, Arthur Ashe, the first African American to win the Wimbledon men's singles title and a prominent civil rights supporter. City leaders intended Ashe's statute to help heal racial tensions, but in the attempt they ignited deep-seated passions. Some Richmonders believed a monument commemorating a tennis player, a black one at that, defiled the memory of the Confederate warriors so proudly recognized on the avenue. Others did not want an African-American champion to be viewed alongside those who supported the institution of slavery. Still others simply prayed the city would learn to live comfortably in the present while acknowledging its past.

George W. Arthur was born and raised in Richmond, deeply immersed in the legacy of the Confederacy. Members of the Arthur family fought for the South in the Civil War and many of their descendants worked to make sure that the Confederate boys and men, and the Cause they fought for, were not forgotten. George's parents were among them.

In the 1960s, George's mother and father found a hero in Alabama's Governor George Wallace. When their first male child was born in early spring of 1963, they christened him with the Alabama governor's name. Later that same year, they watched on television when their son's namesake stood up to Federal Marshals at the University of Alabama in order to prevent blacks from enrolling. The Arthurs supported Wallace in his presidential runs, showing up at rallies with their own little George Wallace, whom they introduced to everyone they met. At one rally the governor went into the crowd to greet personally his supporters. He stopped to pat their George on the head. Of course, the Arthurs quickly told the governor they named their son after him. The candidate smiled and said, "Thank you, folks. You have made me proud." George's parents told that story frequently.

Young George lost track of the number of times his father took him on a tour of the Confederate Museum or to visit Hollywood Cemetery. The cemetery overlooks the falls of the James River. Gently rolling hills, streams and ponds, with stands of various hardwood trees, including holly, made a pastoral-like setting.

Two American presidents and the Confederate States President, Jefferson Davis, are buried at Hollywood. So, too, are thousands of Confederate soldiers and officers, including the Southern dead disinterred from the Gettysburg battle site following the war. Confederate soldiers had been buried where they fell, on hillsides or in farmers' fields, or simply thrown into trenches, usually with little in the way of identification. Re-interment at Hollywood began in spring of 1872 and continued throughout the summer. Men who fought under Longstreet, Pickett, Hood, Early and other Confederate officers, and who died in places with names like Seminary Ridge and Little Round Top, came home.

As a youngster, George Arthur's father would lead him past the cemetery markers, seeking out names he recognized, frequently stopping to tell a story of the man and his death. He always paused respectfully at the hilltop grave of General J.E.B. Stuart. Now there was a soldier, his father would begin. He'd tell George about "Jeb" Stuart's many exploits in the Battles of Bull Run, Antietam, Williamsburg, and Fredericksburg. How Stuart took over from Stonewall Jackson when that great general was wounded by friendly fire at Chancellorsville. Tears ran down his father's face when he told George how Stuart fell, in May of 1864, mortally wounded at the Battle of Yellow Tavern, only a few miles from Richmond.

The only time George remembered his father criticize General Lee or President Davis occurred when he told George how, in the fateful last months, the two leaders considered freeing Negroes if they would join the fight against the Northern armies.

"Why the hell did they think we were fighting! I just don't understand," his father exclaimed, shaking his head. "We fought to keep the niggers in their place. 'Segregation now, segregation tomorrow, segregation forever.' Those were Governor Wallace's words," he told young George.

"Lee and Davis started discussing emancipation just so we could win," his father complained. "What kind of victory would that have been? John Wilkes Booth said it right," his father went on, "this country was for the white man, not the black man. Booth had guts."

George did not need to ask what his father meant.

At the end of each tour through the cemetery, his father, voice now low, would describe what happened in early April of 1865 when Confederate soldiers and many of the townspeople fled Richmond and a large part of the city burned to the ground.

"The fight was almost over then. At least for some. But not for the Arthurs," his father stated as his eyes swept the sea of Confederate graves.

At the dinner table on April 15th of each year, the day Lincoln died, after saying grace George's father offered a toast: "To Booth. The man who brought down the tyrant Lincoln." George learned that others in the South celebrated privately the first assassination of a sitting U.S. president, the man whom they believed crushed the South's way of life. When George grew older, in his own house he, too, toasted the Old South on that day. The date was easy to remember since it was the same day the feds took his tax money to support God knows what liberal causes and to impose unnecessary regulations that kept him from succeeding in business.

Approaching fifty, George Wallace Arthur stood six-feet tall, with a lanky build tanned by regular exposure to the sun during weekly golf rounds. Chiseled facial features suited the lean body he always dressed neatly and expensively. Many women considered him attractive and George liked that kind of thinking. A successful

Richmond business man, he moved in the best social circles and owned a large house on Monument Avenue.

Although he gladly carried the governor's name, George exercised caution when introducing himself. Most people knew him simply as George Arthur. The forty employees of his carpet company called him Mr. Arthur. He was especially circumspect around the Northerners who continue to invade the South seeking employment or a warmer climate for retirement. George recognized they would never understand the South and its traditions--what it had been through. Since they could be potential buyers of carpet, his business cards simply identified him as George W. Arthur, Owner, Southern Fine Carpets.

George also knew people who were more than happy to refer to him as George Wallace Arthur. He met with them once or twice a month--to play cards, talk politics, drink beer, and wonder out loud how this country ended up with a nigger in the White House, fags getting married, and millions of illegals taking jobs from decent white folks born in the great U.S. of A. These meetings also had a political agenda. Many of those attending were Ku Klux Klan members, George being one. Although membership in the Klan was secret, some members openly acknowledged their participation. Those who preferred secrecy had ways of identifying themselves to each other. George, mainly for business reasons, belonged to the second group.

An uncle once told George "the Klavern did its share" when those civil rights workers came south. In the last couple of decades, however, his uncle said, the Southern Klan had attempted to clean up its image. It sought to make waves on the political front by supporting conservative candidates for local and state offices. At one time the Klan talked of running a previous Grand Wizard for United States President. Occasionally its supporters sponsored music festivals when they judged the singers' lyrics could help young people know what is right for their country. We're not a hate group, his uncle asserted.

Klan members met in various homes around the area, but most frequently in the home of Billy Lee Jackson. When he divorced his second wife, Billy ended up with a house on Richmond's south side, a big hole in his savings account, and monthly alimony payments taken straight from his paycheck. The split-level ranch sported a large finished basement and wet bar, behind which Billy proudly hung the Confederate flag. A Klan member for more than thirty years, he was now the chief recruiter in the Richmond area. Billy regularly opened his home to friends and acquaintances with similar political views. Especially since the 2008 presidential election, recruiting from this pool of avowed patriots was a piece of cake.

Bob Smith was a frequent guest at Billy's. He grew up in Richmond and graduated from a local high school. His mother raised him and his older sister, Trina, until she died of lung cancer when he was a senior in high school. His father had abandoned the family when Bob was six years old. Whether colored by wishful fantasies, Bob's memories of his father were good ones, although he grew up with misguided feelings of guilt that his father's leave-taking was somehow his fault--he must not have loved his father enough, must have done something very bad, or maybe didn't do enough to help his father take care of his mother and sister. To this day Bob harbored the thought that maybe one day he'd meet his father and tell him how sorry he was for whatever he had done wrong. Now twenty-four years of age, like so many of his friends he hadn't yet "found himself."

Bob had no love of learning, which his high school grades attested to, so that after graduating he hadn't even considered college. Instead, he looked for unskilled employment in or around Richmond. The growth of sprawling shopping areas to the west of Richmond provided the kind of retail jobs he qualified for and, fortunately, generally liked. He lived with his sister, which he had done since their mother died, and commuted from her house in the city to the burbs.

Friendly, somewhat outgoing, and basically honest, Bob made a good salesperson, ambitious enough to be on the outlook for a supervisory position. But no opportunities emerged at the stores where he worked, or, if one did, he got passed over for someone with more experience.

Bob began looking for jobs outside the area. Searching online one day he discovered an ad for an assistant manager at a store on the historic pedestrian mall in Charlottesville. The store specialized in historic artifacts from Virginia's past. Bob knew next to nothing about historic artifacts, nor, for that matter, about Virginia's history. He mostly slept through history courses in school. Bob assumed his ignorance in that area would probably disqualify him, but he did know retail and here was an opportunity to become an "assistant manager." With low expectations, he applied. To his surprise he got an interview with the store's owner and was hired. The job required a move to Charlottesville, which he soon found a fun place to be. The city had good bars and a decent music scene with several venues on the pedestrian mall.

Bob soon learned, however, that while his boss, Elmer Houston, was easy to work for, the job consisted of more assisting than managing. Elmer frequently made trips out of town to hunt down artifacts auctioned at estate sales, sold at relics shows in the region, or offered by private collectors. Elmer also conducted much of the store's business online. This meant someone needed to watch the store while Elmer traveled or worked in his office at the rear of the building. "Assisting" also meant cleaning and running errands, frequently to the post office, since they sold many items over the Internet. At first, many of the customers knew more than Bob about the artifacts, but he soon learned enough of the business to handle the counter traffic. Elmer dealt with anyone bringing an item into the store for possible sale.

A couple of times each month, Bob drove to Richmond to visit Trina and hang out with friends from his old neighborhood. When some of these drinking buddies told him about Billy Lee Jackson's parties, he started attending. He fit right in--so much so that Billy took him aside one night and asked what he knew about the Klan.

"Not much, except they wear white hoods and knock the heads of niggers," Bob responded.

Billy stopped him short.

"All that is part of the past. The Klan today," Billy said, "has important political goals. We need to operate differently now. Well," Billy added with a smirk, "mostly different."

Bob met George Wallace Arthur during one of his visits to Billy's. Arthur, Billy told Bob, was the man who gets things done around here. During their conversation George asked Bob where he lived, what he did for a living. When Bob told him that he worked in Charlottesville at an historic artifacts store, George said he most likely visited the store at one time.

"I'm a collector. Maybe I'll show you my collection someday. Stick around here. We can use people like you."

Bob soon found out what George Arthur meant. At the next party, Billy invited Bob to join the Klan. Feeling flattered, he quickly agreed. After being voted on, Bob took the oath during a formal induction ceremony in Billy's basement. George Wallace Arthur sought out Bob during the socializing following Bob's first formal Klan meeting.

"We don't have many contacts in Charlottesville. You could help out there," George suggested. "You found us. Now find some same-thinking people in your town. Get to know them. Take notes. Try to identify people you think might help us achieve our goals. Remember, as I'm sure Billy told you, we want to affect the political process. So if you come across anything we might be able to use, let us know."

Bob's expression informed George the new recruit wasn't catching on.

"Look, some of these damn liberal office holders are as likely as anyone to have their hands on something crooked. Or they might be playing around with someone's wife. Dig around. Let us know what you find. We can make sure they never get elected again.

"I've also got a special interest in your Monticello guy, Thomas Jefferson. He kept slaves and said a lot of things that make sense. He didn't want niggers living next to whites. Send them back to Africa, he said. In my opinion, as good an idea now as it was then. From what I heard he was screwing one. That's a master's privilege. Keep them in their place, my dad always said. We're still the masters. That's what we fought for. Can't get an army together these days, at least the shooting kind, but there are ways. We just need to get some people in the right place who can make it easier on everybody."

Bob felt good to be singled out. Even if he hadn't given much thought to politics before, he decided this was a cause worth his support. Listening to conversations at Billy's taught him these people wanted the best for the white folks in this country, his country. Everyone agreed that something had to be done before their country was taken over by commie judges and queer politicians. Now they wanted him to help. Maybe he didn't help his father, but he knew he could help Mr. Arthur and his Klan brothers.

"Don't talk about the Klan," George Arthur warned. "Hold off on that. People don't really know what we're about. They still see us as night riders in hoods. On the other hand, if you think someone might be able to contribute, invite them over here for one of Billy's parties. We'll take a look at 'em."

Bob felt sure he could do this. But recruiting potential Klan members wasn't as easy as he first thought. Sure, some of the guys he went drinking with in Charlottesville were, as Mr. Arthur said, "same thinking." However, Bob found it took time to move them off the topic of their last lay or drug buy. They listened when Bob talked politics but only because he bought them more beers than usual. He saw they didn't understand how bad things had become in this country. He needed to teach them but it would take time, and that frustrated him. Bob didn't want to disappoint Mr. Arthur. He wanted to contribute something, show everyone that he could do his share.

An opportunity to make a different kind of contribution fell into Bob's lap. On a Friday afternoon the last week of July, his boss told him about a man who telephoned the day before. Elmer said the man had something important to sell--a letter written by James Hemings, Sally Hemings's brother. It concerned the talked-about affair between Jefferson and his slave mistress. Bob wasn't well-versed on the details of the Jefferson-Hemings relationship, although people frequently mentioned it around town when discussing Jefferson.

Elmer described to Bob the conversation he had earlier in the day with Professor McCabe at the university, whom he had called to gain an opinion on how much the letter might be worth. Although many people accepted the affair as fact, Elmer said the professor claimed, given the present evidence, no one could be one-hundred percent certain there actually had been an affair. If real, the prof said, the Hemings letter would be worth a great deal, especially if the document provided evidence supporting the Founding Father's paternity of Sally's children.

Elmer also mentioned how the caller's voice reminded him of someone who had recently been in the store. Both of them remembered a short, white-haired man with a funny little grey beard who asked about Jefferson-period artifacts. Elmer felt sure it was the same person who called about the Hemings letter. "The voice was his. I know it."

Elmer had set up an appointment with the individual for Monday and invited Bob to be present. They could take a look at the letter, determine how much this individual wants for it, and try to make a purchase.

Bob knew this letter would interest George Arthur. Hadn't Mr. Arthur told him he was a serious artifact collector and also very much interested in Jefferson? He was sure Mr. Arthur would like to own a document proving Jefferson had sex with his black slave. Bob and his boss both looked forward with considerable interest to the appointment, albeit for different reasons.

The mystery caller never showed on Monday. When several days passed without any word, Elmer decided it had to be some kind of scam. He believed the caller must have gotten nervous and backed out. Elmer called the professor to tell him that.

Bob was deflated. He had fervently hoped he would be in on the find and had even thought about calling Mr. Arthur in Richmond when he first heard about the document. Now he was glad he hadn't. Elmer suggested they not talk to anyone about the whole business since they didn't want people running into the store asking questions. After all, his boss said, we don't know anything more than we did before this guy called. It probably was someone trying to pull a fast one, which wasn't all that unusual in their business.

Bob, however, couldn't let it go. He badly wanted to believe this letter existed. What if Elmer was wrong? What if the letter did exist and it wasn't a scam? If there was any chance this caller had the artifact then maybe he could track him down and get hold of the letter. Elmer wouldn't even have to know.

Bob told his usual drinking pals about the episode at the store, but they weren't all that interested.

"Of course he screwed her," one exclaimed. "Everyone knows that. What's a piece of paper going to show! Let's talk about who we've got going, not who some dead president got into bed with."

Bob searched for others who might listen. He began to make the rounds of the bars on the downtown mall. He told the story of the mysterious letter regarding Jefferson and his slave to anyone who expressed interest. It was a long shot, he realized, but maybe someone else knew the man who had come into the store. Bob and Elmer both saw him, so he had a good physical description.

It wasn't hard to find people willing to talk about slaves and sex in the South. His story grew with additions based on his conversations with people--a mix of facts, rumors, and innuendoes, with a bit of twisting of what actually happened in Elmer's store. More and more, Bob viewed the existence of the document as fact.

In his most recent version, Bob told people he had talked to the man with the funny beard for half an hour when he first came into the store.

"You know," he would say, "we discussed Jefferson and Monticello. He asked me what I knew about Jefferson and Sally Hemings. I told him about the secret room at Monticello where he kept Sally, how Sally got the best clothes and food among all the slaves. Never had to work outside the house. Not a day in the fields. You could tell this guy was interested. He leaves, but then he phones me a couple of days later. Says he has a letter written by James Hemings. Well, you could have knocked me over with a feather! I made an appointment to see him but he never showed up. If we could just find out who this guy is and get hold of that letter."

Telling his story made Bob feel important. People talked with him as if he was an expert on Jefferson. As weeks went by, however, he had yet to learn anything new and soon began to lose contact with his usual drinking buddies. They passed up Bob's offer of a beer to drink with someone else, or even drink alone, in order to avoid listening to him rattle on about sex and slavery. Time also wore on Bob. He worried the whole Hemings business would go nowhere. He also had no luck finding more same-thinking folks, the kind he could invite over to Billy's in Richmond. He couldn't see himself keeping this up much longer. Buying all these beers was breaking his budget. Nothing seemed to be going his way.

After a few weeks, Bob mentioned the Hemings story only occasionally. He chiefly targeted out-of-town visitors whom he happened to meet at one of the local bars. He discovered many appreciated learning the inside dope on Jefferson and Sally and, more often than not, in return, they bought him a drink. He knew these out-of-towners wouldn't know anything about a local man with a funny beard and a Hemings letter. Nevertheless, he had grown fond of telling his story. It provided the opportunity to show off his Jefferson knowledge and to drink another beer.

One of his favorite watering holes, not far from his apartment, was a bistro at the Corner, an historic stretch of bars and restaurants near the university. Bob sometimes stopped in after work for a drink and occasional meal. He caught the free trolley from near the store on the mall or walked the mile or so when the weather was nice, which it frequently was in this Mid-Atlantic town.

Bob enjoyed sitting across the street from the prestigious state university in the midst of university types. It gave him the feeling of belonging to the college crowd he was never part of. He sometimes listened in on conversations, although usually he had no idea what the individuals were talking about. None of these people were the right audience for his Hemings story and he hadn't ever considered trying it out on anyone there.

One evening Bob climbed the stairs to the second-floor restaurant and bar with the intention of grabbing a bite to eat before heading home. The place was more crowded than usual and rather than wait for a table he grabbed a stool at the bar. As was his habit, Bob began a conversation with the person seated next to him--the usual small talk about weather and the university sports scene. His bar mate mentioned he was coming off duty from his security job at the university. First time he'd been in this bar since he didn't usually stop for a drink after work. Tonight, however, he planned to meet another guard who wasn't yet off duty. They planned to join some women at a different bar on the Corner.

The man looked around the restaurant, then said, "I'm not sure this is the type of place I'm comfortable in. Folks seem too serious in here."

Bob couldn't hold back. This man wasn't part of the student and faculty bunch. Why not give it another try, he thought. Bob brought the conversation around to Thomas Jefferson and the mystery caller at the store where he worked. Seeing some interest in what he was saying, Bob offered to buy the man a beer. The guard accepted and listened attentively to Bob's story, even asked a couple of questions about the caller. Bob added some of his many improvisations, which lately included claiming the caller had been in the store just last week. In reality, more than a month had passed since he and Elmer learned about the possible Hemings letter.

Looking up from his beer the guard said, "I think I know who the guy is."

"Really? How do you know?"

"Well, I can't be sure, but I used to work security at Monticello before I got the university job. There was this older guy, about to retire soon if I remember right. Grey or white hair, like you said. On the short side. He definitely had a funny little goatee. I remembered him when you mentioned the little beard. He was good to have around since he liked night shifts, which I hate. He'd trade with me when I was scheduled nights. I only have to do night duty at the university maybe one week out of ten."

Bob couldn't ask quickly enough, "What was his name? Do you know how I could get hold of him?"

"I'm not sure of his first name. Maybe Sam or Sammy. Last name is Crawford. I remember I had to write his last name in the duty roster when he switched shifts with me. I'd write 'S. Crawford.' It shouldn't be hard to track him down. I know he lives in town. Check the phone book."

"I'd like to buy you another beer," Bob said, thinking he now had a definite lead on something that would impress his friend in Richmond. His investment in alcohol over the past few weeks had finally yielded dividends.

Chapter 7

Just after 7 a.m. on a Tuesday morning Professor Paul McCabe settled into the chair behind his desk at his university office--feet up, a pile of student papers on his lap, and a cup of coffee in his non-writing hand. He never liked grading papers, but found it easier in the early morning when the grounds were quiet. His colleagues, as well as the department chair and the university deans who were his bosses, generally never sought him out this early. Students never showed up or telephoned at this hour, although he could count on e-mail messages waiting in his mailbox. These usually arrived sometime in the middle of the night, about the time he figured his students finally looked at their assignments.

Enjoying the solitude, and having just begun to made progress on the task of grading, the phone ringing jarred him such that he nearly spilled coffee on a student's paper. Swinging his legs down, he rested the coffee cup on his desk, flipped his pen onto the desk, and reached for the phone.

"McCabe here," he announced as he used his free hand to catch student papers sliding off his lap.

"Professor McCabe, it's Elmer Houston. Have you seen today's paper?"

McCabe assumed Elmer meant the local paper and not the *Post* or the *Times*.

"It's him."

"What in the world are you talking about, Elmer?"

"The man who was shot and killed. It's the guy who was in the store. Remember the guy who said he might have a Hemings letter for sale. His name's Stanley Crawford. It's in the paper. The police are treating it as a homicide."

"Wait a minute, Elmer. First of all, I haven't seen the local paper, so I don't know about anyone being shot and killed. Second, you never told me you met this guy. You said he called you, if I remember right, and then he didn't show up."

"Well, he did call, but that was a day or so after he came into the shop. He wanted to know if we sold artifacts from the Jefferson period. I told him we did, showed him a couple of broadsides, some letters from politicians back then, and a slave cuff. He didn't say much. Spent a few minutes looking in our glass cases and then left. I figured we didn't have what he wanted. Maybe our prices were too high. But when I got the phone call a couple of days later with this guy's story of the Hemings letter, I recognized his voice. He didn't mention he'd been in the shop, but I was sure it was him. His picture is on the front page of today's paper. I recognized him immediately. He's got a rather distinctive profile and a little grey beard around his chin."

"Why didn't you tell me he had been in the store?"

"It didn't seem important, I guess. Especially since he never followed up with the letter. The police are saying it was a robbery gone wrong. You have to think maybe he did have something valuable and someone wanted it."

"Elmer, you don't even know if he had a letter. It just may be a coincidence."

"What do you think, professor? Should I call the police and tell them what I know?'

"You probably should. Even though it may not be relevant. It's been a while, hasn't it? It must be six weeks since we talked."

"That's right. The guy made an appointment for Monday, August 1st. I still have it on my calendar. Never did learn his name. Not until today. I guess it has been a while," Elmer said, obviously disappointed he didn't have more recent information about the murder victim.

The conversation with Elmer did what Paul McCabe's unfinished coffee would have done. He was now wide awake, but little in the mood for grading papers. Despite what he had said to Elmer about a coincidence, he found himself thinking that maybe the mysterious letter and the apparent murder could be linked. He felt he owed it to the Bunch to bring them up to date and turned to his computer to compose an e-mail to Jonathan Turner.

* * *

The same morning Paul McCabe and the rest of C'ville learned about Stanley Crawford's death, Mike Chance arrived in the Cummings kitchen before others in the house. He started coffee brewing and went to retrieve the local newspaper from the box at the street, the only news source Kelly and Steve didn't get online. He sat down to read the paper's coverage of the previous night's events. Only his interest wasn't in the murder so much as the report of the accident involving his niece, Tammy.

The previous night Mike had retired to his apartment after a pleasant dinner with his sister and brother-in-law, his niece being out for the evening. Tammy had been allowed to go with some friends to a movie on the downtown mall since teacher-parent conferences were scheduled the following day and students had the day off. Family togetherness helped lift the fog that he couldn't completely rid himself of. He planned to tell Dr. Rider that the evening was a 2 on her depersonalization scale and jotted some thoughts in his notebook before turning out his light.

Mike knew sleep provided escape, but this night he attributed his tiredness to his recent attempts at renewing an exercise routine. The recurrent thoughts of death and existence, which sometimes kept him awake, were absent. Perhaps he was learning to live with the loss, the hole in his life, the unreality of it all. He decided this was another thing to talk to Dr. Rider about.

Pounding on the door to his apartment interrupted his transition into sleep. He heard Kelly yelling for him to get up, screaming something about Tammy. Guided by the light from beneath the door he reached the door in his boxer shorts and flung it open.

"What is it? What's wrong?"

"It's Tammy," Kelly said, her voice quaking. "I just got a call from the police. They took her to the emergency room at the university hospital. They said she was hit by a car in Court Square. Steve's teaching late tonight and then meeting at one of the pubs with some of his students. He doesn't have his phone on so I had to leave a message. You have to come with me!" she finished breathlessly.

"I'm coming. Let me get some pants on."

As upset as Kelly was, Mike let her drive. He felt unsettled with thoughts of his niece, worried he might experience a full-blown panic attack--something that hadn't occurred since the weeks directly after his wife's death. What should he be feeling? He felt numb. How badly was Tammy hurt? Neither of them asked that question aloud. Kelly concentrated on her driving while Mike stared out the window.

They pulled into the driveway leading to the hospital emergency entrance, slightly bumping a curb, tires screeching as Kelly braked in a temporary parking spot. The siblings hurried from the car into the lighted reception area. Kelly ran past a security guard to the information desk and inquired about the young girl hurt in an accident on Court Square. After learning who they were, the receptionist directed them toward one of the treatment rooms down the hall. Kelly raced ahead of Mike toward a room with large glass doors, with thick drapes blocking view of the interior. Sliding back the glass door, she pushed aside the drapes and stepped into the room.

Her daughter was sitting upright on the bed, a nurse checking her pulse.

The alarm on Kelly's face let Tammy know she needed to quiet her mother's fear. "Mom! It's okay. Just bruised ribs and maybe a broken ankle. They don't know yet until they get the X-rays done. It hurts a lot, but I'm okay. Really."

Tammy then peered behind her mother and saw who else was present. "Uncle Mike! You came, too. I'm so sorry for making you come out."

Mike didn't know how to interpret Tammy's statement, but focused on learning the extent of his niece's injuries. He was too familiar with hospitals, having frequently stopped at the hospital where Kirsten worked for lunch or just a cup of coffee during her break time. He and Justice had been to hospitals more than once to interview injured victims of a crime. The familiar setting helped him concentrate, but at that same time he found himself fighting to keep his anxiety down.

The nurse turned from her patient to address Kelly. "Your daughter is doing fine. A bit banged up, but she's been a real trooper. The doctor examined her and will be back in a few minutes. One of her friends was injured more than she is."

"It's Brandon, Mom," Tammy said quickly. "He's the only one besides me who was hurt."

Kelly stood next to the bed, smoothing Tammy's hair while she fought back tears of relief. "We were so worried. How much does it hurt?" Looking toward the nurse, she asked, "Can you give her something for the pain?"

"Since all her vitals look good the doctor wanted to wait on giving her any medication until they find out if she needs surgery on her ankle."

Kelly looked again at her daughter who clearly wanted to tell what happened.

"It all happened so quickly, Mom. We were walking through the square when a car came flying around the corner. I don't think it even slowed much. The tires did that noise thing. We all jumped back and I think I screamed. Someone did. There were four of us and Brandon had his bicycle with him. His parents let him ride downtown. Unlike some parents I know."

"Tammy, just help us understand what happened," her uncle said, showing his police side. "This isn't the time to take a swipe at your mom."

He could see she wasn't hurt badly and he, too, wanted to cry in relief. The tears didn't come. He looked at Tammy, but couldn't feel as he knew he should. The emotionless movie he starred in continued.

"Sorry," Tammy said, more to her mother than to her uncle.

"Were you on the sidewalk or in the street when this happened?" Mike asked.

"We were crossing the street. I think what happened, at least what I heard the police say, is that the car hit Brandon's bicycle. He was walking next to it. The bike hit Brandon and then me. So we really didn't get hit by the car, but a bike! Now I see why you don't want me to ride a bike to town," Tammy said with a twinkle in her eye. "It could get hit by a car!"

Kelly smiled, tears coming down her cheeks. She saw that Tammy was going to be fine.

The nurse interrupted, "I have to check on the boy who was hurt. Your daughter said there were four of them. The other two kids apparently weren't touched and I was told their parents picked them up at the scene. The EMTs brought Tammy and the boy by ambulance. His parents are with him now.

"The techs were here to take an X-ray of Tammy's

ankle. Stay as long as you like. The doctor may want her here overnight, no matter what. Although judging by her behavior, he may let her go. She's a tough one," the nurse added as she exited.

"You sure are," Mike said, looking at his niece, seeing that pain or no pain, Tammy enjoyed the limelight. Definitely almost back to normal, he decided.

Just then Tammy's father burst into the room with an anxious look, which was soon erased by the smiles on his wife's face.

"I got your message after class. I was at the Corner having a beer with my students when I finally remembered to turn my phone on. I came as fast as I could."

Mike realized he should leave them alone and offered to move the car into the parking garage. He held out his hand to Kelly for the keys. She immediately turned them over without either of them considering that Mike hadn't driven a car in months.

The doctor could see no reason, given the negative X-ray and Tammy's good spirits, that she couldn't go home with the help of crutches and some pain pills to take when needed. The doctor predicted she would want one when the effects of the pill he just gave her wore off.

Kelly and Steve talked with Brandon's parents before leaving the hospital. Their son had a crushed knee cap and some bad bruises from the tumble he took, and would probably need surgery. Like all parents in these situations, they were just glad it hadn't been worse.

On their way home, Kelly told her brother that Brandon's father kept asking whether the police caught the guy who hit the kids. Mike suggested that if they hadn't, the police would likely want to interview the kids to find out what they saw, maybe get a description of the car. Apparently, from what Brandon's parents told Kelly, neither of the uninjured kids could tell the police much of anything. Someone screamed and they saw the car approaching just in time to jump away. They'd been talking to each other when the car came down on them. Without hearing the scream, they might not have gotten out of the way.

Kelly visibly shuddered when she said this.

It was past midnight when everyone got home. Tammy's father held open the front door while Kelly helped her daughter through. Before escorting Tammy up the stairs to bed, Kelly went into the kitchen to fix her hot chocolate and for whomever else wanted some. While she did that, as late as it was, Kelly phoned the parents of the two kids who weren't injured. She wanted to let them know that Tammy was bruised but otherwise all right. Both sets of parents had already heard from Brandon's parents and appreciated her calling as well. They told Kelly that after what happened, it wasn't as if they could just go to bed. One mother admitted it was irrational but she had been sneaking into her daughter's room every fifteen minutes to make sure she was okay.

None of the adults in the Cummings household slept well that night. Kelly and Steve stumbled into the kitchen shortly after Mike. The three sat in the kitchen drinking coffee and talking over the previous night's events. Steve reluctantly left to attend a meeting at the university but said he'd check-in a little later.

Mike was right, a female police officer called the Cummings house soon after Steve left. She inquired how Tammy was doing and asked if she could speak with her sometime that day, hopefully later that morning. Kelly felt Tammy would be ready for the interview in an hour or so and told the officer to come at ten o'clock. The phone rang again before Kelly had put it down. It was Brandon's mother.

After a brief conversation, Kelly told Mike that Brandon was scheduled for knee surgery that afternoon.

"The doctors said he likely wouldn't be playing contact sports or anything that required twisting of the knees. His mother said he may walk with a slight limp, but more surgery in the future might repair it completely. She was just happy he's alive."

"That goes for us, too," Mike replied. "And Tammy could have been hurt much worse."

"I know," Kelly said, "but I have to think she'll get over it. We'll all get through it because we know they're going to be okay. But I'm afraid Brandon's father doesn't think it will be okay. He called the police department first thing this morning to find out if they caught the person who ran into the kids. The police still haven't arrested anyone and he's angry as can be. Apparently, all he can think about is that Brandon won't be playing football! Whatever!"

When ten o'clock approached, Kelly went to check on her daughter who hadn't stirred yet. She hesitated to wake her and instead returned to the kitchen. Tammy was still asleep when the doorbell rang. Kelly looked at the clock and sighed. It was a few minutes after ten and she decided the officer would just have to wait until she got Tammy ready.

Kelly headed for the front door while Mike continued to pore over the newspaper article detailing the killing of Stanley Crawford. The murder was big news in the usually quiet town of Charlottesville. The collision in Court Square involving the kids appeared in a very short article on another page. It apparently got stuck in this edition just before deadline. Mike found it interesting that the two events occurred about the same time and was thinking about the coincidence when Kelly returned to the kitchen.

"The police officer wants to talk to you."

"What? You're her parent. Why me?"

"Maybe they know you're one of them," Kelly offered

with a smile, at the same time swallowing a giggle, which led her to look away from her brother.

"Okay, but I'll bring the officer to talk to you after I see what she wants."

"Please do that," said Kelly with a bigger smile, "but she's a he."

Mike eyed his sister quizzically. He put down the newspaper and headed down the hallway. Kelly had closed the door without inviting the officer in, somewhat impolitely he thought. Shaking his head in puzzlement, Mike opened the door, and sure enough a police officer stood waiting on the front steps. And not, as his sister said, a female one.

"Justice!" Mike exclaimed. "What in the world are you doing here? Man, you're a surprise. Come in!"

Chapter 8

Jonathan Turner forwarded Paul McCabe's e-mail to members of the Jefferson Bunch, alerting them to the identity of the man with the Hemings document, and to the fact that he had been murdered. He soon received two phone calls in response, first from Peter Trent and then Andrea Hudson. Peter wanted to know what else Jon knew about the killing of Stanley Crawford, but Jon told him he couldn't add anything more than what was in the newspaper.

The article reported that Crawford, a retiree, lived with his wife on the east side of Charlottesville. Some additional details followed, apparently obtained from Crawford's wife, Beatrice, by a reporter who was among the first of the news media on the scene.

Beatrice Crawford said she was watching TV when she heard a loud car noise in front of their house. She looked out the window but all she could see were tail lights from a car racing down the street. This happened around 9 p.m., when her favorite television show had just ended. She told the reporter she had been curious about who it might have been and went to ask her husband if he, too, heard the noise. Beatrice considered it too late for any nice person to be making all that racket. Stanley had an office at the rear of the house and always shut the door when he was in there, she said, and even when he wasn't there, she added. She knew not to barge in on him. He didn't like that, she told the reporter. Always knock before you come in, her husband warned her. She did knock, but after getting no response she called out to her husband. Hearing nothing, she opened the door slowly and cautiously looked in.

"I wasn't sure what was going on," she reported. "It

made me nervous. I knew he'd yell at me if I surprised him."

From the doorway she saw her husband lying on the floor next to his desk, the door to the outside entrance ajar. She knew right away he was dead, she explained. He had to be. He wasn't moving and there was blood all over his shirt and pants. She called 911.

The only additional details in the newspaper article had to do with the obvious grief of Crawford's wife and that police on the scene had begun interviewing neighbors. The reporter's account ended by stating the couple had been married forty-two years, with no living children.

Peter Trent asked if Jon knew who this Crawford person was, but Jon repeated that he knew nothing more than was in the paper. Peter then went on at length about how the group obviously made a mistake by not looking for the owner of the Hemings document, even insinuating that the Bunch might have prevented this killing had they been more willing to get off their duffs. Jon took offense but patiently told Peter the group had no idea what they were dealing with. For that matter, it wasn't clear the killing was related to anything except maybe a thief looking for money. Mostly to get Peter off the phone, Jon suggested he talk to Paul McCabe about his recent conversation with the artifacts dealer, Elmer Houston. Peter huffed, saying he might just do that. He also told Jon he had a contact, someone he knew in the mayor's office, whom he believed would know more about the killing.

"Then why bother me with all these questions!" Jon mumbled to himself as he hung up.

Jon's second caller, Andrea Hudson, demanded less of Jon, realizing, unlike Trent, that Jon was just the messenger. Secretly, the news pleased her. Not the killing of course, but the recent series of events seemed to increase the likelihood that there was something to the professor's story about the Hemings letter.

She had not apprized her acquaintance, the one who had offered to help bankroll an investigation, of the Jefferson Bunch's refusal to get involved. She wanted time to think over the best way to keep this individual interested. Her main hope, one she expressed to Jon, was that the Bunch would meet to re-evaluate the situation. Should this happen, after what McCabe learned from the artifacts dealer, and given the previous night's murder, she was sure her client, as she called him, would remain ready to help.

Andrea requested Jon poll the Bunch about scheduling a meeting next week.

* * *

Other than Stanley Crawford's wife, the Reverend Jeremiah Maxwell may have been the person most upset over Crawford's death. He knew the victim personally, a relationship that began several months ago when Stanley began attending Sunday services at Jeremiah's church. More critically, Jeremiah had met with the victim the day before, apparently not long before Stanley Crawford was murdered.

Jeremiah rented a storefront in a strip mall where he held services, temporarily, he prayed. He was waiting until the day he raised enough money to build his own church. The minister took only a small salary out of the Sunday collection. He prayed that his salary, too, would change as more money came through the door. A small apartment attached at the rear of the building served as both church office and living quarters.

Stanley had been one of the few white people in Jeremiah's congregation. Yet he showed no awkwardness when standing in line after the service, waiting his turn to talk with the preacher. When he shook the minister's hand, Stanley typically said how he admired the preacher and how the reverend's message was "right on."

"I was really moved, Preacher. My bones shook. My heart was beating like crazy. I was seeing the light," he commented enthusiastically more than once, if not exactly in those words then something similar. Jeremiah didn't know what to say in response.

Stanley had been raised Catholic, but too many abuses from priests as a teenager sent him running from that faith. Not the kind of abuse that makes headlines. Stanley saw himself humiliated in the confessional by the priests' lectures and the laying on of guilt. These experiences usually followed any confession having to do with sex. Worse than the guilt were the feelings of shame induced by the priest's carefully constructed condemnations. Stanley didn't believe a male teenager existed who didn't experiment with sex.

The experience of receiving communion after a "good confession" from a priest who the day before had listened to Stanley describe stroking himself was just too much. Maybe the priest didn't know it was him. But maybe he did. What right did they have to make him feel dirty, Stanley asked himself. Years later, he learned that many had no right at all. He allowed the Catholic religion to reclaim him once, but that was only to get married. Beatrice said the wedding would take place in a Catholic church or not at all. Shortly after saying "I do," Stanley never went back. When Catholic anger replaces Catholic guilt, it doesn't easily go away.

From Jeremiah Maxwell's standpoint, white folks who show up in a practically all-black congregation were a mixed blessing. Okay, maybe they liked his sermons, or the music. He knew African-American ministers who reported white people showing up just for the music, as if they were on a concert tour. Other white attendees seemed driven more by curiosity. They sought to discover what African Americans did during a worship service, like cultural anthropologists. On the other hand, no doubt some were sincere and honestly "searching."

But Jeremiah knew other white folks, and he put Stanley in this category, attended a predominantly African-American church in order to demonstrate they were *one* with the black community. Their attendance confirmed to the world that they held no prejudices against blacks whatsoever. In this way people like Stanley could prove to others, as well as to themselves, that they were color blind. Better yet, they could follow the same religious path as blacks.

After dropping out of Catholicism, like many lapsed members of the Pope's legions, Stanley did nothing even remotely religious for a long while. Until one day he acknowledged to himself that he was getting up in years. Uncomfortable as the thought was, he knew dying wasn't too far off. This led him to worry there just may be a final accounting after all. But now he wanted something simple--no smoke and bells this time. And no guilt. He just wanted to know what he needed to do in order to earn his place at the right hand of the Creator. Thus, a mixture of good intentions, if scrambling for a place at the heavenly table qualifies, and deeply repressed racial prejudice, brought Stanley to Jeremiah's church.

Stanley had been coming to services for several weeks when he intentionally lingered at the end of the line of those waiting to greet the minister. Arriving at the front, he offered Jeremiah his usual obsequious comments on the service. Then, after looking to see if anyone might still be in earshot, Stanley asked if he could see the preacher privately about a personal matter. It wasn't an uncommon request from church members and Jeremiah always found some advantage in it.

One-on-one conversations offered a chance to explain how God blessed everyone, no matter how bad their problems seemed. He explained that no matter how poor they were in material goods, they became spiritually rich by attending services and supporting the church through their donations. Moreover, with little funds of his own, the minister appreciated an opportunity for a free meal. Thus, in response to Stanley's request, Jeremiah suggested they meet for breakfast the following morning at a small restaurant in the nearby Belmont area.

Stanley was already seated at a table when the preacher arrived. After going through his standard litany of praises for the minister and after making it clear he would, of course, pick up the check, Stanley revealed his so-called personal matter.

"Reverend, I've got something I know will interest you. It's a letter about Jefferson. And Sally Hemings. You know, his slave. The one he had sex with."

"I'm not sure I'm following you," replied the preacher.

"I mean an old letter. Hundreds of years old. It's the kind of thing Oprah will want to talk about. All those professor types at the university will eat it up."

"But what has that to do with me?"

"I'm sure it's important. Worth a lot of money. And I want to share some of the money from the sale. To help you get your church off on a good footing. This church has been a spiritual home for me. Yes it has."

And what better way, Stanley added, to demonstrate his dedication than to help build a physical home as well.

Jeremiah wasn't one to look too far into a man's soul. If Stanley wanted to make some sort of offering in order to deal with unacknowledged feelings of racial prejudice, then so be it. God works in mysterious and apparently sometimes pathological ways.

Jeremiah realized he shouldn't appear too eager for money. While thanking him for his generous offer, he suggested Stanley do some research to discover the worth of the document. At this initial meeting Stanley didn't reveal how the document came into his possession and Jeremiah hadn't thought to ask.

The truth of the matter was that Jeremiah had only the vaguest knowledge of what evidence existed for and against a slave's affair with her owner, who also happened to be a Founding Father. Newly arrived from the north, he had been too busy setting up his church to pay much attention to the gossip concerning Jefferson and Sally Hemings. While Stanley looked into the document's worth, the Reverend Maxwell decided he would do some research of his own. That is where the Jefferson Bunch came in.

Jeremiah originally learned about the group from a conversation overheard at a local book store. The group's members often bought Jefferson-related books from the owner. Over the years she had recommended the group to various customers, making available the name of someone in the group to contact. In this case, it was Jonathan Turner who invited Jeremiah to attend their next session. The minister met with the Jefferson Bunch for the first time about eight weeks ago, keeping secret what he knew about a Hemings letter.

Jeremiah hoped the Bunch would provide him information concerning Hemings and Jefferson, as well as add to his knowledge of Jefferson's religious bent. In fact, as part of the front he presented to the group, Jeremiah decided he should show more interest in religion at their meetings than in the sex life of Thomas Jefferson. Preachers needed to be good actors and Jeremiah played his role well.

He had been quite pleased with his decision to join the group. No matter how all this turned out, the discussions already had contributed to his knowledge of Jefferson in several ways. Even better, they served a delicious meal at each meeting.

Of course he had voted no on the question of investigating the Hemings document. Jeremiah didn't want anyone finding a trail to his door and moving into position to snatch the document Stanley promised him. Well, at least who had promised money from its sale.

Since their first meeting, Jeremiah had talked briefly with Stanley on many occasions. After a service Stanley would come up to the preacher and say something like, "I'm still working on it" or "We'll know soon." Then he would smile and wink while clutching Jeremiah's hand with such force it hurt.

Stanley hadn't been sure how to proceed with selling the letter. He dropped by several stores that specialized in selling historic artifacts, going east to Richmond and as far north as Fredericksburg. He casually asked about the prices of old letters and documents, but he couldn't work up the nerve to show anyone the Hemings document, or even admit he possessed it. He considered attending meetings in the area where collectors bought and sold historic relics and artifacts, but the problem remained the same--in order to sell the letter he would need to explain how he got it. Stanley knew that wasn't a good idea.

Stanley bought magazines on collecting historic artifacts at Barnes & Noble and also searched the Internet. He didn't own a computer but relied on ones at the public library. A reference librarian at the main branch showed him how to identify various websites advertising artifacts for sale. Stanley began to form some definite ideas regarding the worth of the Hemings document. He decided that if someone would pay seventy thousand dollars for a diary written by a Confederate prisoner of war, then the Hemings letter could be expected to bring in even more.

All this took time and Stanley could see the

reverend's growing impatience.

The preacher wasn't just losing patience. He had begun to think there wasn't anything to Stanley's story. If Stanley really had an important letter, why was he taking so long to sell it? Jeremiah decided he needed to learn more about the document.

Following this past Sunday's service, Stanley greeted the minister and made his usual comment about making progress on selling the letter. Jeremiah held Stanley's hand, smiled, and asked him if he could see the letter. The request clearly caught Stanley off guard. He hesitated and then stammered something about having news soon. Jeremiah didn't say anything in response but tightened his hold on Stanley's hand and looked disappointed.

Stanley relented, managed a thin smile, saying, "Well, I guess that's all right. Sure."

He suggested Jeremiah come to his house the next day. Use the door in back that goes to my office, he told the preacher. They agreed on eight o'clock in the evening.

Jeremiah became quite excited about seeing the Hemings letter. He assumed Stanley wouldn't have invited him to his house if the letter didn't exist. Maybe he could help Stanley come up with ways to sell it. Although he believed his congregant meant well in wanting to help his church, Jeremiah sensed Stanley wasn't all that good a problem solver.

The minister anticipated their meeting with the same optimism that had carried him south with only a few coins in his pocket to start a church in Charlottesville. He wasn't sure who might be a buyer for the artifact, but if need be he'd ask for advice from members of the Jefferson Bunch. It would be embarrassing given that he'd been hiding what he knew about the letter. However, Jeremiah knew first hand that God's work sometimes required suffering the thorns of ridicule.

Monday evening, a little after eight, Stanley answered the door in a jubilant mood.

"Preacher Maxwell! I'm glad you came! I have great news. I found a buyer. He called last night. I was going to call you but decided to surprise you." Stanley stepped back to allow the minister to enter. "I'm sorry. Please come in. Do come in. Come in. Please. Sit over there," he said, pointing to a chair next to his desk.

Stanley continued to talk excitedly as he ushered Jeremiah to the chair. He then took a seat behind the desk, facing his minister.

"Like I said, I got a call last night. This person heard I had a valuable document related to Thomas Jefferson. He's a collector. Or maybe an agent for one. Anyway, he's coming tonight to see the letter. I'm thinking I'll tell him I want fifty thousand! What do you think?"

Before Jeremiah could say anything, Stanley continued talking. "We could probably get more but I don't think we should be greedy. What do you say?"

Jeremiah always considered greed a difficult concept. It's the basis of capitalism, isn't it? It makes the country run. Unless people keep wanting more, the whole system comes to a halt. He even knew some ministers who preached that making money was a good thing. Was it greed to want money to construct a house of God? And a salary to live on so he could continue to preach Jesus's message?

Lost in this philosophical rumination, some moments passed before he noticed Stanley was waiting for a response. "You probably know best," Jeremiah finally said, trying to calculate percentages in his head. Would Stanley give him ninety percent, he wondered. That would be how much money? He'd have to do the math later. Stanley rambled on.

"Like I told you, he's coming tonight. In just a little

while. I thought about telling you not to come since he may be here anytime. But I promised that you could see the letter. It turns out it's good you're here now. The letter may be gone soon.

"Here it is," said Stanley, pulling a clear plastic sleeve from the center desk drawer. "You can see it for yourself."

Jeremiah reached for the document but Stanley practically yelled at him. "Don't touch it! You don't want to bend it or anything. It may fall to pieces. It's very delicate. More than two hundred years old. See the date?"

Stanley gently held up the plastic covering for Jeremiah to view the letter. "See, it's dated 1801."

The plastic didn't look all that clean, and from two feet away Jeremiah could hardly see anything through the covering. Or was it the letter that wasn't clean? He could just make out a few lines of script.

"It talks about Jefferson and Sally," Stanley said, pointing at the writing. "I won't show this guy the letter until I'm sure his intentions are for real and he has the money." Stanley's voice then assumed a rather serious tenor. "You can't be too careful. I've got backup if needed."

Jeremiah wasn't sure what Stanley meant by backup and started to ask when Stanley looked at a clock on the office wall. He abruptly put the letter down on his desk.

"You better go now, Preacher," he said. "He might get here early."

Jeremiah slowly stood up and moved toward the door. Stanley followed close behind, speaking in a hushed voice, still clearly agitated about the upcoming meeting with the buyer.

"He should be here anytime now. Don't worry. I'm not going to let it go for small change. I think fifty thousand is a fair price. I'll call you when I've got the money. That could be tomorrow. He probably won't be carrying a lot of cash. I'm not sure I should take a check. No, I want cash."

Jeremiah let himself be shooed out the door with Stanley still talking. He wished he could consult the Jefferson Bunch about the letter and its price. Maybe it was worth one-hundred thousand! Now it was too late. Still, ninety percent of fifty grand would be a good start on his church, he thought. Possibly cover the price of land. More money would come in once land was purchased and the walls started to go up.

As he opened the door to his car he realized he never asked Stanley where he got the letter. Too late for that as well.

Like most everyone else in town, Jeremiah woke up Tuesday morning to see large-print headlines in the local newspaper above the story of Crawford's murder. The killing undoubtedly troubled him more than most readers. He saw Stanley last night! He took the newspaper with him to his one comfortable chair and sat down to learn the details. He read the article several times but couldn't answer his most basic question: How could this have happened? And the more important question: Where would he get the money for his church?

After putting down the newspaper he sat quietly for some time. Myriad thoughts raced through his mind. Someone must have killed Stanley to get the letter and the mostly likely person was whomever Stanley expected last night. Did this person get the letter?

Stanley had clearly been worried someone might steal it. He had said he wasn't going to show it to anyone until he was sure the buyer was for real and had the necessary money. Maybe this person didn't give Stanley a choice. Maybe he threatened him, demanded the letter and Stanley wouldn't give it to him. Maybe that's why he shot Stanley. But did he get the letter?

Crawford's death truly upset him, although he didn't want to examine too closely the reasons for his discomfort. Feeling distressed, he wasn't sure what to do. Should he go to the police? If he did, would they suspect him? What would his church members think if they learned he was mixed up in a murder? He might never get his church building. Jeremiah believed the Hemings letter now rightly belonged to him. It was worth fifty thousand dollars, possibly more, and Stanley had promised that money for his church. But who had it? Jeremiah finally concluded he should let the police look into it first and see where that went.

Later that morning he received an e-mail from Jonathan Turner suggesting a meeting the following week to discuss the Crawford killing and its possible link to the Hemings document.

Chapter 9

It wasn't clear which sibling was happier to see Justice. Kelly and Justice had bonded while the two of them supported Mike in the months after his wife died. They traded visits to Mike's townhome, grocery shopping, and even meal preparation. Justice could make one heck of a meatloaf that fed Mike for several days. Kelly often thought of Justice in the months since Mike had come to live with them. She had considered calling him for advice on how to help her brother, but worried Mike wouldn't appreciate her acting behind his back. So she put it off.

Justice called off and on, but Mike generally wouldn't talk for long. He'd thank him for calling, then say he just needed more time before coming back to the department. Kelly wasn't sure Justice believed him. She knew *she* didn't. Mike's depersonalization episodes were interrupting the progress he had been making. Although the time with Dr. Rider appeared to be helping, Kelly hoped the visit by Justice might be another boost to get her brother back on track.

Mike brought Justice into the Cummings's kitchen where they filled him in on the previous night's events. Justice immediately suggested to Kelly his timing wasn't good.

"No, no," Kelly replied. "Tammy's going to be fine. A Charlottesville police officer is coming to interview her, but you won't be in the way."

"Yes, please stay," Mike said. "We want to hear how you've been doing."

Another phone call supported their pleas for Justice to stay. The C'ville police officer telephoned to say she was running late and wouldn't be there for another half hour.

Kelly relaxed a bit now that she had more time before the officer's arrival and went to check on Tammy. In a few minutes she returned to the kitchen.

"Tammy's awake and wants something to eat. She asked for strawberry pancakes. It's her favorite and I think she's pulling a sympathy move on me. And it's working. But I'll have to use frozen strawberries with this last-minute request. How about you guys?"

The two men declined an offer of pancakes, but sat around the kitchen table drinking coffee, catching up. Justice passed on news of the department, although didn't say anything about Mike returning to work. Mike talked vaguely about his mood swings and admitted he was seeing a local shrink. Kelly soon left, carrying a tray with Tammy's breakfast.

"I really want to thank you for coming to see me," Mike said. "It's been too long since we got together. But you really didn't need to make the trip on my behalf. Although I know Kelly is glad you're here, too."

The big man looked at him, and through one of his trademark smiles, said, "Well, don't consider yourself all that important. Actually, I'm in town to help one of my cousins with our aunt's funeral. Did I ever tell you about Auntie Blossom Hunter?"

Mike's expression revealed he hadn't.

"She was really good to me growing up. Both me and my mom, her sister. Whenever she got up to the District she'd bring us presents. Auntie died three days ago. My cousin asked me to come down and help with the funeral arrangements. I took some personal days off to make the trip. The funeral is Saturday. You see, Mike, you aren't the main reason for my coming here. But why not mix some pleasure with some sadness."

He paused, looking away from Mike, reflecting on some memory from the past. Mike took the opportunity to express his sorrow.

Justice reached for his coffee cup, taking a sip before continuing. "I can't be too sad. Not when someone lives a healthy, loving life until ninety-four. She loved everybody. Her parents knew what they were doing when they called her Blossom. She probably would even have liked you, Michael Miguel," Justice added with a smile.

And Mike grinned, too, as only his family and few close friends knew his middle name. His mother's maiden name was Hernandez. She told him that her ancestors, now his, marched with the first conquistadors when the Spaniards scouted the southwest in the 1500s. How they had later traveled with Oñate during the *entrada* of Spanish settlers into New Mexico in 1598.

"Your ancestors got here before the Border Patrol got going," she joked.

Mike's mother and father met at a tourism convention in Albuquerque sponsored by the U.S. Department of Commerce where his dad was employed. His mother worked for the New Mexico Office of Tourism. Mike's dad had come from Washington to address the Albuquerque meeting. Over the next year they exchanged letters and phone calls, as well as cross-country visits. This led to marriage and his mother's decision to relocate to Alexandria. When their son was born, his mother wanted his given name to be Miguel, her father's name. Her Anglo husband wasn't excited with the choice. They settled on Miguel as a middle name and Michael a first name, which revealed both their sense of humor and notion of compromise.

When Mike's sister came along, his father wanted to name her Kelly. This time their mother went along with the Anglo given name. She insisted, however, on Catalina for a middle name, after one of her sisters. Kelly shared with Mike the brown eyes and dark hair, along with the light brown skin, from their Hispanic mother. Slightly shorter than Mike, Kelly had always been too pretty for words, their father used to say.

While Mike and Justice continued their banter, the doorbell at the Cummings house rang for the second time that morning. Kelly had just returned to the kitchen and went once more to answer the door. She returned with Sergeant Alice Dixon trailing behind her, a notebook in the police woman's hand. Sergeant Dixon looked to be about Mike's age, blond, physically fit, appearing trim in her police uniform. The officer took a look at who was present and immediately rolled her eyes toward the ceiling.

When Justice saw her he yelled, "Dixie! I heard you were in these parts."

"Justice! Don't tell me you left the District!" she said.

Then Sergeant Dixon quickly remembered where she was and why. She turned to Kelly. "I'm sorry Mrs. Cummings. Justice and I worked together in Washington for a couple of years before I took this job."

"That's all right. Justice is Mike's partner. Or was," Kelly added somewhat awkwardly.

Sergeant Dixon appeared confused. She looked at Mike, whom clearly she had assumed was Tammy's father. Kelly recognized the officer's confusion and jumped in.

"This is my brother. He's staying with us. Justice happened to be in the area and stopped in."

That seemed to help, but Sergeant Dixon clearly hadn't sorted everything out when Mike stood up. "Hi. I'm Mike Chance. I was in the D.C. department until earlier this year. I needed some leave time and my sister is putting up with me for a while."

"Nice to meet you. And Justice, we need to get together while you're here. Mike, you too, if you want. For now, however, I'd better get on with my job."

Turning toward Kelly, she asked if her daughter

would be ready to answer some questions about last night's accident. Kelly replied that Tammy was finishing her breakfast upstairs but should be ready for questions.

"In fact, I think she's looking forward to it! Let me show you to her room. We didn't think she should be moving around too much. She's a lot more sore this morning. Also a little more subdued now that she's had a chance to think about what did happen and what could have."

Mike and Justice were still catching up when Dixie returned. Kelly stayed upstairs to be with Tammy and to see if there were any additional requests, or other favors Kelly might grant as thanks to the gods for delivering her daughter safely home.

"She thinks it was a light-colored car," Dixie said, "but that's about all the description she can give. Just so happens this matches what we've come up with."

"You have a lead on who did it?" Justice asked, putting down his coffee cup.

"You heard about the killing, right? Last night, about the same time as Tammy's accident. We're pretty sure the two events are related."

"I was thinking there might be a connection when I read the two reports in the paper," Mike offered. Justice nodded approvingly at his partner.

"A driver approaching Court Square saw a car knock down the kids. He pulled over and called 911. That was at 9:04. The 911 call from Crawford's wife came in a couple minutes later. When we talked with her later, she said she heard a car speeding from the front of the house around nine o'clock. The noise led her to look for her husband to see if he knew what was going on. The Crawfords don't live much more than a mile from the accident scene.

"We also got lucky when talking with one of the Crawford neighbors," Officer Dixon continued. "A man who lives across the street said he looked out his front window when he heard a car noise. He saw a full-sized, light-colored car speeding away. The car looked to be maybe 10 to 15 years old. Definitely not too recent.

"That's the same description we got from the man who called us about the accident in the square. Then we really got lucky. The speeder who injured the kids kept going down High Street and went right through a red light. Scared the hell out of a woman who was about to cross the street with her dog. The car slowed down like it was going to stop, but then sped up at the last minute. When the woman got home she called the desk wanting us to chase the guy right away. Of course that was about fifteen or twenty minutes after all hell had broken loose. Anyway, at that point we hadn't connected the events. The woman with the dog gave the same description of the car. And she also got two letters of the license plate. She thinks it was a Virginia plate."

"Did you get a match on the partial?" asked Justice.

"The woman wasn't sure if the letters she saw were the beginning ones or maybe the second and third. She remembered these two letters because they were the initials of her granddaughter. We're looking at possible plates in Charlottesville and Albemarle County. Even just looking for light-colored cars more than six years old, there are over one-hundred in the area. Of course, we're assuming the car is actually from this area and that we understand what 'light-colored' means. Or that we have the right age of the vehicle. Obviously, we have some work to do. The Albemarle County Police are helping out."

Officer Dixon glanced at a clock on the Cummings's kitchen wall. "I'd better be going. Mike, good meeting you. And Justice, let's get together. Like I said, Mike, you too."

Mike stood up and showed her to the door. When he

came back, Justice had gotten up to leave.

"Things seem to be jumping around here. But I've got to go help my cousin sort out some of Auntie's things. The lawyer is bringing over her will today. If my cousin inherits the house, as he should, he says he's going to sell it. He owns a house in Lynchburg and doesn't want to move. My aunt's house is in one of those neighborhoods where the young white folks want to live. He shouldn't have any trouble selling it. I'll be in touch. Say goodbye to Kelly for me and thank her for the coffee."

After seeing Justice out, Mike returned to the table to consider the new information Alice Dixon had provided. He realized the fog he was used to navigating in wasn't all that bad this morning. In fact, it seemed to have lifted soon after Justice arrived. A 2 or 3 so far today on the Rider scale, as he liked to think of it.

He made a mental note to talk with Dr. Rider about these feelings at tomorrow's therapy session. In the meantime, he was grateful for small miracles. Although Sergeant Dixon had been good about including him in her invitation to Justice, Mike knew he was an outsider. He began to wish he wasn't. Maybe that was a good sign.

Nevertheless, definitely a 2 day.

Chapter 10

Tammy felt better on Wednesday, the second morning following the accident--not so stiff and only a little pain in her ankle. Nevertheless, Kelly kept her home from school given she would need crutches to get around for at least another day. A day at home wouldn't hurt. Besides, she deserved some TLC, according to her mother.

Kelly had appointments in town and asked Mike to keep an eye on his niece until she got back, and perhaps help Tammy get some breakfast when she was awake. Mike's sister did bookkeeping and tax work for a couple of small businesses in town, as well as for several nonprofits. When her daughter graduated from high school, Kelly planned to do the course work and training necessary to earn a CPA certification. For now, part-time accounting, which became full-time in tax season, met the family's needs.

The previous evening Tammy texted and talked on her phone nonstop, sharing her story with friends, as well as catching up with people and events in her social network. Since her friends were in class today and unable, in theory, to use their phones, Kelly told Mike that Tammy should have time to rest and maybe even read ahead in her school subjects. She specifically instructed him to make sure his niece stayed off the swollen ankle. Mike said he'd be happy to watch over his niece. He called Dr. Rider to cancel today's appointment.

Kelly hadn't been gone more than two minutes when Tammy hopped into the kitchen. Mike wasn't sure this was what Kelly meant by his niece staying off her foot. He decided it best not to reprove her and greeted Tammy with a smile. "How's the hopping wounded?"

He helped her to a chair despite Tammy's modest protest, before getting her cereal and some juice, then pouring another cup of coffee for himself. He relished private time with his niece. Their conversation typically centered around school, occasionally about a boy or two she was "just friends" with. That morning they talked about her plans for the coming weekend, when she expected to be let loose again.

They hadn't talked about her accident, nor that the police thought the hit-and-run might be related to the killing of the man on the east side. So it surprised him when she asked, "You're going to get him, aren't you, Uncle Mike?"

"Who are you talking about?" Mike responded, but already with an inkling of whom she meant.

"The guy who hit Brandon and me, of course! You're a cop and you chase bad guys, right?"

"Tammy, first, I am, or was, a policeman in Washington. Not here. Just because you're a cop in one place doesn't mean you're allowed to chase bad guys in another place. Charlottesville has its own police force. I'm sure they're working on finding who hit you. You met Sergeant Dixon. Besides, I haven't been a policeman since, well, you know, since your Aunt Kirsten died. I'm out of practice."

That perfectly rational explanation didn't come close to satisfying his pre-teen niece. "But I told my friends you were going to help catch the guy who did it."

"You what? Tammy, you shouldn't be saying things like that. As I said, even if I wanted to, I wouldn't be permitted. That's the law."

"But that's only if you were being a real policeman, right?"

"What does that mean?"

"I mean, if you were to get this guy on your own, you know, without actually being a cop, then that would be okay, wouldn't it?"

"Tammy, you have to trust the local police know what they're doing. And doing it much better than I could. I don't live here and don't know the people or the area."

"It seems to me that you could at least help. And Mom says it would do you good to investigate something."

"When did your mom say that?"

"You know, after that professor and his wife came to dinner. A month or so ago, I guess. I don't remember exactly when. I wasn't there, remember? When I got home Mom and Dad were talking in the kitchen. I heard her say you needed a challenge and investigating something about an important lost letter would be good for you. You were already in bed. I'm not sure what they meant, and when I asked Mom she wouldn't talk about it. She seemed mad at you. Is this lost letter important because it's worth a lot of money? Or because it might reveal somebody's secrets? That would be so cool! Who wrote the letter?"

"We don't know for sure. The letter may not even exist."

"Why don't you find out?"

"Tammy, we're off track here. Your mom and I talked about all of this. We agreed I would get started on some projects. But chasing down bad guys or lost letters is not part of it. And I've been having some other problems recently. You know I've been going to a psychologist to see if she can help."

"Well, whatever. You look okay to me."

At that moment the phone rang. Mike reached over to the counter to pick it up, then handed it to Tammy. He assumed it was for her even though she rarely got calls on the land line.

"Hello. Oh, hi! Just a second."

Handing the phone back to her uncle, she said, "It's for you. It's Brandon's dad."

Tammy pushed herself upright, standing on her good foot.

"I've got some reading to do. One of my friends texted from the girls' restroom about an upcoming test in English class."

Mike held the phone against his chest while he watched her exit on one foot. He tried to recount the events of Monday night. He remembered who Brandon was, but knew for sure he didn't see the injured boy at the hospital. As far as he could recall he hadn't met the father either. Puzzled, he brought the phone slowly to his ear.

"Hello?"

"Detective Chance, this is Dan Sorenson. Brandon's dad. I'm just calling to say thanks for your help. Tammy told Brandon what you're going to do. You know, getting involved with the case. I want to say how much my wife and I appreciate, you know, as a cop, what you're doing for all of us."

"Mr. Sorenson, I'm really not sure what this is all about. I don't know what Tammy said to Brandon. I mean, she may have exaggerated a bit. I'm on leave from the District right now and not in a position to do police work. My wife died not too long ago and . . ."

"I know, I'm sorry. I heard about it from your sister. And I'm sorry if I'm not getting the story straight about your involvement. I'm just going on what Brandon said. But you have to know, as a cop I mean, how the police everywhere are short-handed. I'm sure any help, especially from a professional, would be appreciated."

"Well, Mr. Sorenson, . . ."

"Dan, please. Call me Dan."

"Okay, Dan. As you can probably understand the local police aren't all that excited about outsiders getting involved with their investigations. Cop or not, I'm an outsider here. I think my niece and I have to talk. I'm sorry if she said some things to Brandon that aren't exactly true."

"Well, it isn't my place to say what you should or shouldn't do. But you know, my son will never play football or serious athletics of any kind because this idiot wrecked his knee. We have to live with that and we'll adjust. But any one of these kids, including your niece, could have been killed. I would hope you might find some time to at least lend a hand. It's your job. You're trained for it. You're here and you have the skills. And, you know, if . . . "

"Mr. Sorensen, Dan, I am concerned. Believe me. I tell you what. I have some contacts on the local force." Thanks to Justice, Mike decided Sergeant Dixon was at least one. "I'll find out how the investigation is going and stay on top of it."

Mike hoped that was vague enough so as not to make him accountable, but maybe sufficient to get Brandon's dad to stop pressing him. He needed to talk to Tammy soon, before she promised more people her uncle would solve the case. If she hadn't already.

Brandon's father thanked him profusely for lending his expertise to the investigation and said he'd be in touch. Not exactly what I promised, Mike thought, but it would have to do. As he started to put down the phone, with every intention of having a serious talk with his niece, the phone rang again. His mind still on what he would say to Tammy, and with the phone still in his hand, he answered without thinking.

"Hello."

"Detective Chance?"

"This is Mike Chance."

"Mike, this is Paul McCabe. We met when your sister had my wife and me over for dinner. I was hoping you'd still be in town. I want you to know I completely understand your reluctance to get involved with the Jefferson document. I must admit that after dinner I felt rather ashamed at being part of what could be called an ambush. Really, I shouldn't have been talked into it, but at the time I was excited about pursuing any leads. As it turned out, there really didn't seem to be much to it. So not getting you involved was fine. But I assume you saw the story in the news, about the guy who was shot and killed? Well, that was the man who came into Elmer Houston's shop looking at historic artifacts. He's the one who claimed to have a Hemings document."

McCabe got no response from Mike.

"After the murder and what looks like a robbery, I'm thinking there just may be something to this business after all."

At that point Mike interrupted. "Professor McCabe, I appreciate your calling." That wasn't exactly true. "But I'm sure you're aware the local police department can handle this." Was this the third time in ten minutes he used that line? "If there's a document out there, one that served as a motive for a crime, then the police will be on the lookout for it. As well as whoever killed this man."

"Mike, I'm sure you're right, but it turns out you could help without getting involved with the police investigation. Remember the group of folks who wanted to hire you to look into this?"

Again no reply, but the professor continued.

"The Jefferson Bunch is meeting again next week. I'm afraid they may still want to get involved. That's why I'm calling. If they have in mind taking some action on their own, from my point of view it would be good if someone with a police background came to the meeting. Someone who could help them understand what the local police will be doing. Explain how these investigations work. Quite frankly, help them see that they're in over their heads if they think they can do something the police can't. When I was at your sister's house there hadn't been a murder. This thing is too much for a bunch of amateurs to take on. I was hoping I might get you to attend their meeting. Keep them from making fools of themselves. What do you think?'

"Professor McCabe, I really don't know what I can do."

"Listen, Mike. I can guarantee just your being there will help keep things focused. The Bunch sometimes thinks they own Jefferson. If they learn what the police are doing from a cop's perspective, that may help squash any notions they might still have about charging into something way out of their league. Besides, you must be curious about the Hemings controversy. I gave you only the briefest overview at dinner. These folks know what a document from James Hemings might mean. You could learn more about this whole business with TJ and his slave. You must be interested. What do you say?"

McCabe was wearing Mike down. The professor's argument caused him to think that agreeing to the request could serve several purposes. His sister would be ecstatic if he stopped playing the poor-me widower. His niece would save face, having promised who knows how many of her friends that her uncle the cop would get involved. And Brandon's dad would be appeased. And to top it off, he could tell Dr. Rider about one more activity!

Mike also saw something of the real cop in him re-awakening. McCabe was right, this Hemings business interested him. Maybe some additional background provided by the Jefferson Bunch would help him see exactly what was at stake. Thinking about getting involved, however, also scared him. He still didn't feel like himself. But maybe his sister was right that getting involved with something would help put him back together. Dr. Rider seemed to think so.

"All right. I'll do it, professor. Where do you want me to be?"

After learning when and where the Bunch would meet, and again promising McCabe he would attend, Mike found that the round of coincidences in today's events wasn't over. The doorbell rang immediately after he put the phone down on the kitchen table.

Justice stood at the door. Seeing the big man renewed Mike's sense that his emotional well-being these past twenty-four hours, despite Tammy's accident, had been clearly linked to his partner's appearance in Charlottesville. Was he actually feeling something? Significantly older than Mike, Justice had an army enlistment behind him and many more years on the police force. He had never asked Justice his age, but figured him for mid-to-late-fifties. Justice had drawn him into that special relationship many police officers have with their partners. He never experienced this kind of comradeship with anyone in burglary, perhaps one of the reasons he opted out of that division.

"I just dropped by to see how you and Tammy are doing. We're getting things ready for my auntie's funeral and I still have some things to do. There will be a reception at the house after she's buried. I hope you'll come. But I have some news, too. Something I would like your opinion about."

"Well, sure, if you think I'm up to giving people advice. Come on in. I'm glad you stopped back."

Mike led the way once more to the kitchen.

"Take a seat and I'll get into advice-giving mode. Tammy is upstairs doing school work. At least I hope she is. She's going to be fine."

"I don't need your advice. Just an opinion. You're too young to give advice," Justice said with a smile, and continued before Mike could comment.

"It's just that I had a surprise coming to me. My

Auntie Blossom apparently saved up a lot of money. Much of it came from a lawsuit she and my uncle settled years ago. Some kind of negligence claim against a contractor who left an open hole my uncle fell into. Broke his skull and almost cracked his spine. He didn't work for some time. It's quite a bit of money actually. The two of them invested it wisely and it survived the recent downturn. Her accountant told me he wasn't even sure she knew how much money she had. My aunt and uncle just let him play with it for thirty-odd years. If they needed money for a car or new roof they contacted him. After my uncle died, she lived on his social security. Counted her pennies, that woman did. Fortunately, this accountant is as honest as they come. He took a small percentage for working with their funds and now she probably has ten times what they started with."

"If you want my opinion, I think that's good," Mike joked.

"Look wise guy, you don't understand all of it. Some of it got left to my cousin. He's a cousin from my uncle's side. The thing is, my aunt's lawyer told me yesterday that most of the money comes to me. And the house, too. I always thought if there was any money it would go to my cousin. He's been taking care of her these past few years. And I never expected she would leave me her house. I guess Auntie felt my cousin already had one."

"Seems like all this is even better, isn't it?" Mike quipped. "Want some coffee?"

"Look, no, but thanks. I haven't time for coffee. Let me tell you the rest. Auntie left me a note. We found an envelope addressed to me among her personal papers. She wants me to move into her house here in Charlottesville. The note said the money should be enough for me to start a business here and keep up the family home. She was in love with that house."

"How are you going to do that from Washington? It's

a long commute." Mike paused, thinking about what he just said. Justice said nothing.

"Wait, I see it. You're thinking about doing it. Quitting the police force."

"Yes I am. I've been thinking about it for a while actually. That is, considering doing something else, moving out of the District with all its congestion and the bad stuff we deal with. I'm no young kid anymore, like you."

"Did your aunt make moving here a condition for accepting the money? Maybe you could rent the house. Keep it in the family, so to speak, and retire here later?"

"Partner, you aren't hearing me. I'm thinking this is probably my best chance ever to get away from crack houses, crooked cops, drive-by shootings, the whole mess, and do something new."

"You're serious, aren't you? Well, I have to say that makes two of us. I've been thinking of not going back. Maybe doing something around here. And if you aren't going to be back there to cover for me, maybe I should just stay here, too."

"Wait a minute. This was supposed to be about me. We can talk about you later. What do you think?"

"I think if you stay in town then maybe there is something in this for both of us. All right, sorry, I'm thinking about me, too. Yes, stay. I think you should do it."

He hadn't been aware that Justice was so unhappy being a cop. Everyone on the force complained about the hours, the ugly stuff they dealt with. Justice didn't appear to complain more than the next person, or himself, for that matter.

Just within reach of Mike's consciousness was the thought that this was more about himself. If Justice remained in Charlottesville Mike couldn't help thinking that he could get his life back together. He felt better than he had for some time. Importantly, it felt good to *feel*. Maybe today was a 1 on the Rider scale, he thought.

Chapter 11

Jeremiah feared the funds to build a church for his newly gathered flock were slipping away from the dock, if not already headed down the river. He desperately wanted to discover exactly what happened the night Stanley was killed, and thought the Jefferson Bunch could help.

Jon had e-mailed to say he set up a meeting for a week from Friday night and asked Jeremiah to hold that date open. Since it was an ad hoc meeting, there wouldn't be the usual dinner and wine, Jon informed him, but there should be a lot to talk about. With luck, he said, the police would apprehend the murderer by then. Jon ended by stating that even if the letter existed, it might have nothing to do with Crawford's death.

Jeremiah knew very well a letter existed. The police, however, might not know that. Until they did, he decided it wouldn't hurt to do some exploring on his own. Jeremiah believed the one person most likely to know about the missing letter was Stanley's widow.

He set about planning another visit to the Crawford house, but judged these days immediately following Stanley's death were too soon. Out of sympathy for the new widow he decided he should postpone a visit until after the funeral. But then he asked himself, "why wait?" An offer to help with her husband's funeral provided a good reason for a visit. Who better to help put Stanley in the ground than his pastor? And it was only right, actually his duty as Stanley's minister, to offer counseling to his congregant's grieving wife. It was the least he could do, he concluded.

Jeremiah put on his best suit, the one he preached in, and on the Thursday following Stanley's death, he drove his recently polished Cadillac to meet the spouse of his deceased church member.

He didn't know Stanley's wife. She had never accompanied Stanley to a church service. Jeremiah assumed, however, her husband would have talked about the church he attended. No doubt she would understand if her husband's pastor wanted to assist with the funeral arrangements, and along the way he could find out more about the Hemings letter. He also assumed Stanley told her about their agreement. It was a lot of money to give away. Not something Stanley would do without consulting his spouse. But if for some reason she didn't know Stanley's plans, Jeremiah stood ready to enlighten her. He felt confident he could make the grieving widow appreciate his church's need.

He had been to the house only once, the previous Monday, the same night someone killed Stanley. He had used a rear door to Stanley's office and if his wife was in the house, Jeremiah never saw her.

The minister knew Stanley had retired, but from what he didn't know. The neighborhood of modest homes he drove through suggested he didn't make a lot of money before retirement. Parking the car and putting on his best smile, he went up the front walkway to the small front porch. He had every intention of doing his best to console the widow, and maybe partake of some cookies and coffee while obtaining the information he sought. Jeremiah had already pressed the doorbell when it hit him that he didn't know the widow's name. It must have been in the newspaper account of Stanley's death, but he couldn't remember. Well, if he wasn't yet on a first name basis, that would soon come. He didn't doubt his power to win over the ladies.

Beatrice Crawford opened the inner door cautiously, trusting the screen door was locked. She hadn't yet become accustomed to being alone in the house. Many neighbors and friends visited the past few days, but when they left she felt more lonely and even a little helpless. She and Stanley had not been all that close, at least in the past few decades. Like many married couples of their generation, they had come to certain understandings which had kept them together. Since his retirement her husband usually stayed around the house, often reading or watching TV in his den-office. His presence in the house gave her some comfort, if not actual companionship.

She really didn't know what all he did in his office, although recent events had shed some unfavorable light on her husband's activities. He allowed her to clean the room once a week, but only after he had a chance to "organize things." Stanley insisted the office was his private space and didn't want her intruding. He kept the door shut, often locked from within.

Beatrice immediately took the tall, thin, black man on her doorstep for a salesman. Why else dress like that?

Jeremiah quickly introduced himself, and in a sympathetic, if somewhat loud, voice explained why he was there.

"I'm Jeremiah Maxwell, Mrs. Crawford. I knew your husband. He was a member of my congregation. But you probably know that. As his minister I'm here to offer you my condolences and to help in any way I can. Stanley was a good man."

Jeremiah waited for a response. Thinking he would immediately be let in, he began to open the screen door but found it locked. Beatrice hadn't moved.

Trying to realign her expectations with what the man just told her, she finally said, "Yes, Stanley told me where he was going on Sunday mornings. I'm afraid he never mentioned you by name. Just that he liked the minister at this new church. My husband said it was very different from what he grew up with. Stanley left the true church, you know.

"I go to Saint Anne's Church and Father Thomas came here yesterday to see me. He's helping me plan the funeral service. Father can't say a funeral Mass since Stanley didn't belong any longer to the church. But Father said he would be happy to say a few words at the interment. I found it very comforting. The funeral will not be in the church, of course. As I said, Stanley no longer accepted God's one true path."

Listening to the widow's soliloquy, Jeremiah came to the realization that he needed to take a different tack. The widow obviously didn't need help with the funeral.

"I don't want to bother you, ma'am. I just felt it my Christian duty to see if I could lend a hand in any way."

Beatrice didn't say a word, staring incredulously at him, trying to think how this strange black man at her door could possibly help her.

Interrupting the growing silence, Jeremiah said, "I'm glad your priest is helping, but I have to admit there's another reason why I came. Stanley told me he might give some money to my church. We're just getting started and we need all the help we can get. In fact, I can say in all honesty that Stanley promised me some of the proceeds from a sale he was about to make. I'm sure he told you about that. If I could just have a few minutes, I can explain."

Beatrice again revised her view of the man on her porch, now convinced he was selling something. Clearly, he wanted money.

Still not making a move to open the screen door, Beatrice replied, "Stanley never said anything about giving away money. But then he never talked much about our finances. He paid all the bills. I'm going to have to go through the bank statements and see if I can figure them out. I'm sorry I can't help you." She moved to close the inside door.

The preacher leaned forward, putting his hand on the

door frame in what he hoped was a non-threatening manner.

"Wait. Please. If I can just have a few minutes of your time. I'm sure these are difficult days, Mrs. Crawford, but if I could just tell you what Stanley told me you'll understand better. It may have something to do with why there was a robber in your house. Maybe why Stanley was killed."

Jeremiah's last remark grabbed Beatrice's attention. When the police asked her about valuables she and her husband kept in their house, she didn't know what to tell them. They never kept any cash to speak of, or none that Stanley ever talked about. Her jewelry was so old and cheap she was sure no one would want it. They didn't have a computer and neither of their two TVs had been taken. If her husband had anything else of value in his office, she wouldn't know about it.

Against her better judgment she agreed to let Jeremiah come in. She decided it might be good to learn more about whatever business this person had with her husband. She unlocked the screen door. Beatrice said that if it was all right she would keep the front door open since she was expecting a neighbor. Can't be too careful, she thought. It wasn't exactly a lie since neighbors had been visiting frequently.

Jeremiah entered a small foyer dominated by a large cross on the wall portraying Christ the Savior dripping blood from a crown of thorns and from a hole in his side. Beatrice made the sign of the cross as she passed the bloody crucifix. Jeremiah tried to look the other way. He entered a living room crowded with furniture, the kind you saw at many secondhand stores. Jeremiah judged these pieces had once been new in this house. In the corner, resting on a small table draped in white linen, stood a statue surrounded by votive candles, some of them burning.

Beatrice saw Jeremiah looking in the direction of the table.

"I have been praying for Stanley to Our Blessed Mother. She'll help him. I know he wasn't one of us anymore, but the Virgin Mary has an 'in' with God."

Jeremiah didn't really understand the holy networking she referred to. He assumed, however, that since Stanley had left the Catholic church he wasn't able to partake of any heavenly favors coming from that direction.

This was becoming more difficult than he envisioned. It was obvious he should tread carefully when talking about his own church. After being invited to sit in a large stuffed chair, his thoughts promptly moved to what exactly he should say to the widow. Having given up on the idea that he would be served something to eat, Jeremiah got right to the point.

"Mrs. Crawford, again let me say how sorry I am for your loss. I talked with Stanley on several occasions. Not just on Sundays. I got to know him pretty well."

Jeremiah wasn't sure how well he really knew Stanley, but he felt his widow should believe that the relationship between her husband and his pastor had been a good one.

"Did Stanley ever mention some kind of old document? A letter perhaps. Something historic even? That he wanted to sell?"

Jeremiah didn't want to come right out and admit he saw the Hemings letter. It could be that Stanley's wife didn't know about it and informing her of that fact might produce some problems. For one, she'd no doubt claim it belonged to her now that Stanley was dead. In addition, once word got out that he knew of the letter's existence, the police would want to talk to him. All in good time, he thought.

Beatrice paused before answering, trying to grasp

114

what the preacher just said.

"I don't know what kind of document you're talking about. I already told the police that nothing seems to be missing. And I don't know what he might want to sell. One time he sold our car without telling me. Simply said it was time to get a new one. It didn't matter to me since I never drive much. That's the way Stanley did things. He sold a lawnmower once that . . ."

Jeremiah interrupted before the list of recycled items grew too long.

"You see, Stanley told me this was something important. A letter from one of Thomas Jefferson's slaves that was worth a lot of money. There are people who collect things like this. Stanley said that if he could sell it then he would be willing to give some of the proceeds from the sale to my church. You have to think maybe somebody else knew about it and came looking for it. Maybe that person killed Stanley."

"Why on earth would he do that?" she asked.

"Maybe Stanley refused to give up the letter and whoever it was got mad and tried to take it by force."

Jeremiah knew he was winging it, but the widow had thrown him a curve with her ignorance of her husband's affairs.

"I mean why would he want to give money to your church? Of course someone might have killed him if he had something valuable. But as I just told you, and like I told the police, I wouldn't have known about everything he kept in his office. Maybe he kept cash around and never told me. I just don't know. But he certainly never said anything about giving money to your church. I'm sorry, reverend, whatever you are, but he wouldn't have told me about that since he knew I wouldn't approve. He let me write a check to St. Anne's once a month. I can't see why we should support you other people as well. I'm sorry. This is all too much for me. If Stanley owned such

115

a document, like you said, maybe his killer took it. I'm sure the police will find it."

Jeremiah saw the widow was getting worked up and decided a quiet retreat was best for now. He didn't know what bothered her most--the idea that Stanley may have stashed away a lot of money without her knowledge, that he had something of value she was in the dark about, or that his church might get some of the Crawford money. Probably the last, he decided.

"I'm sure I've bothered you too much already, Mrs. Crawford. I did just want to come by to tell you how much we'll miss your husband. Maybe I can come again some other time so we can talk more about Stanley. Perhaps I can share with you some of the things he said to me. You know, there are different paths to God."

Jeremiah didn't buy into that idea, nor did he think the widow did, but best to keep things on a positive note, he decided. He soon understood, however, he wouldn't be welcomed back.

While getting up to see him out, Beatrice said, "I appreciate your concern, Mr. Maxwell. Is that what they call you? We call our priests 'Father,' but I guess you know that. You're not a priest are you? No, I guess not. Anyway, I'm sure you try to do well. You know, whatever you do in your church. Maybe I should be happy Stanley found God again, but I think he should have come back to our church. Please don't think me rude, but now that Stanley is dead you really don't have business here anymore."

On his way out the front door, Jeremiah thought it possible the widow was telling the truth and she didn't know about the letter. It was also clear that if Stanley somehow managed to sell it, he wouldn't tell his wife he was giving the proceeds to Jeremiah's church. But Stanley did promise him money from a sale of the letter and Jeremiah felt that promise should be honored. Even if his wife wouldn't agree. He knew for an honest-to-god fact that Stanley wanted to support his church, a place he called his new spiritual home.

Okay, maybe Stanley's motives weren't clear. But why does anyone give away something of value if not to make themselves and others feel better? A 'two-fer,' as he heard someone once say when getting free fries with a burger. If Stanley had planned to buy his way into heaven then the transaction wasn't completed. Who knows where his soul might be! Perhaps his wife didn't know about the Hemings letter, but in thinking over their conversation Jeremiah wasn't sure what she had said. Except that she clearly didn't like his church. He also suspected the widow wasn't telling him everything she knew about her late husband's interests.

On his way to the car Jeremiah realized he never did learn the widow's first name--not that she wanted to be on a first-name basis. He worried his charm might be fading.

Jeremiah drove away with the hope that the Jefferson Bunch would have some idea of how to proceed. He couldn't escape a sinking feeling that the person who killed Stanley now had the valuable document which Stanley meant to sell to help Jeremiah build his church. Eventually he might have to reveal to the Bunch what he knew of Stanley Crawford and the Hemings letter.

But not just yet.

Chapter 12

Bob Smith couldn't believe his luck when he learned from the security guard at the tavern that an "S. Crawford" matched the description of the man claiming to have a Hemings letter. He desperately wanted to impress George Arthur and now it looked like he could. It wasn't long, however, before worries crept in to dampen his high spirits. Maybe it wasn't the right person. And if it was, maybe he didn't have the letter anymore. It had been over a month since the grey-haired man with the goatee came into the store. Bob strived to keep his anxiety at bay.

The phone book listed two Crawfords with first names beginning with "S." The guard thought Crawford's first name might be Sam, but the two S names were Stanley and Susan. This might not be all that hard, thought Bob.

The address in the phone book was in the Woolen Mills area of C'ville, a few blocks east of downtown. The neighborhood once was home to a major manufacturing company producing cotton and wool cloth. During the Civil War the firm made uniforms for the Confederate Army. The same Union soldiers who spared Mr. Jefferson's university burned the factory. It rose from the ashes as the Charlottesville Woolen Mills, once again producing uniform cloth until the 1960s. Small cottages and bungalows, which had once housed mill workers at the now extinct factory, dot this historic area of town.

Bob drove by the house a couple of times while he planned his next step. Seeing the Crawford name on the mailbox by the street told him he had the right place. Now he just needed to confirm this was the right man. He knew he'd easily recognize him and considered simply going to the front door under some false pretext. "Want to donate to the local library?" That was always an option, but he worried Crawford might recognize him and that could be awkward. For the present, he chose to park his car across the street, a few doors down from the house, with the goal of catching a glimpse of Crawford when he came out of the house.

He watched the house for several days. Sitting low in his car, Bob imagined himself a private eye on stakeout. He rarely smoked, but bought a pack of Camels so he could dangle a cigarette from his lips. With an old hat pulled down over his eyes, a cigarette added something to what he considered his disguise.

Leaving the store around 5:00 p.m., he typically pulled up to the Crawford house about fifteen minutes later. He stayed only for an hour or so, fearing his car eventually would attract suspicion and possibly be reported to the police. By the fourth day Bob still hadn't seen anyone venture out of the house. It eventually dawned on him that Crawford probably ate dinner around the time Bob parked outside. He decided to abandon the stakeout and implement his earlier idea and ring the doorbell with some innocuous story. However, just as he started to get out of his car, an elderly woman exited the house and walked across the street to another house. Okay, a woman lived there, probably his wife, he thought. Where was her husband? He now worried that Crawford was on vacation, or no longer living there. Worse, he could be dead.

Agitated, not sure what to do next, Bob finally saw what he had been waiting for. Soon after the woman went into the neighbor's house, he spotted a man back a car out of the Crawford driveway, turn and drive down the street in Bob's direction. Slouched down in the seat, peering out from beneath the hat, Bob managed to get a good look at the driver. He knew right away it was the man who had come into the store. Pounding the steering wheel with delight he inadvertently dropped a lighted cigarette onto his lap, which he furiously slapped at with his hat.

Ecstatic over his success, Bob started his car, found some music on the radio, and headed toward downtown. He pulled into a 7-Eleven parking lot and took out his phone to call Mr. Arthur. He was sure they'd be on a first-name basis when the Richmond business man learned what Bob had accomplished. Then he remembered that he didn't know Arthur's home phone number. Arthur had given him a business card when they first met at Billy's, but it only had his work number. It was after six o'clock. and unlikely Arthur would still be in the office. The news of his find would have to wait until tomorrow.

During his morning break at the store the next day, Bob called Mr. Arthur. He reached a secretary who took his name and after what seemed like a long wait, put him through. Bob quickly discovered Arthur wasn't happy to be reached at his office. "Why did you call me here? What do you want?"

Bob rapidly explained he had discovered something in Charlottesville that he was sure would be of interest. He told Arthur about locating a man who owned a letter written by James Hemings--a letter about Jefferson and Sally. George Arthur listened but only replied that now was not a good time to talk. He took Bob's number and said he'd call him back later this evening.

Bob went straight to his apartment after work, popped open a beer, grabbed some Doritos, turned on the TV, and waited for the phone to ring. He expected Mr. Arthur to thank him for tracking down an important Jeffersonian artifact. But Bob didn't receive thanks. Rather, he got another dressing down for calling the office. Never do that again, he was told in no uncertain terms. If you have to reach me, Arthur said, call Billy first. And as for the artifact, yes, if it was a Hemings letter he would be interested. But when he asked Bob if he had seen the letter, Bob confessed he really didn't know if Crawford still had it.

There was a long pause during which Bob listened to deep breathing before Arthur responded to Bob's admission of total ignorance about the present whereabouts of the letter. When he did reply, at least he wasn't yelling anymore. He actually complimented Bob on finding Crawford. That was a good first step, Arthur said. The next step, he told Bob, was to find out if Crawford still had the letter. He'd also need to ascertain that it was real and not some fake.

Arthur then apparently decided that determining its authenticity probably went beyond Bob's capabilities. He backtracked and told Bob that he should simply find out if Crawford's got the letter. If he did, see how much he wants for it.

"Can you do that?" George Arthur asked, somewhat impatiently.

"I guess so," Bob said, immediately worrying his response might not be positive enough.

"Look, if he has it, tell this Crawford person you know someone who will pay a lot of money for it. Of course, it would have to be authenticated first. You can do that much, can't you?"

"I'm sure I can," Bob replied, with more emphasis this time.

"Good. Call Billy when you get this done. Tell him what you found out. If Crawford has it and wants to deal, then I'll work out a way to make sure it's for real. Don't scare the guy away. I'm interested in this letter. And remember, don't do anything to draw attention to me or anyone here in Richmond. And don't call me at the office! Contact Billy."

Over the next couple of days Bob rehearsed what he would say to Crawford and what questions he might have to answer. His worries now centered on thoughts of possibly botching the whole thing. He finally got up enough nerve to telephone Crawford. Bob told him he represented a buyer of historic artifacts, someone who heard he might have something valuable for sale. This put Crawford on his guard, as Bob suspected it might. Crawford immediately wanted to know the name of the buyer. Bob said he wasn't allowed at this point to give out names. Crawford accepted that, but then wanted to know who said he had something to sell. Bob had been ready for this question as well. He replied he couldn't say, but that it was someone who knew him fairly well.

Then Bob jumped in with, "My buyer is prepared to pay good money if you have what I think you have. He's interested in a letter that talks about Jefferson and Sally Hemings."

After a few moments' silence, Crawford said okay. Bob had made the call late on a Sunday afternoon and Crawford suggested he come to his house the next day. Did Bob know where he lived? No, lied Bob. Crawford gave him directions.

"Come tomorrow evening at nine o'clock. Use the back entrance, the one to my office. That way we don't bother the missus. She likes to watch TV in the evenings."

Bob's mood picked up. Crawford must still have the document. Why else would he have asked him to come to the house? He just needed to make sure, then ask Crawford how much he wanted for it. Mr. Arthur would take care of the rest. If everything worked out, and Bob was now sure it would, this was something he would tell Mr. Arthur personally. He didn't need to go through Billy. He'd make a trip to Richmond after meeting with Crawford.

On Monday night Bob felt confident he was on the verge of accomplishing something important. He hadn't made any headway getting information the Klan could use, or for that matter bringing what Mr. Arthur called same-thinking people to Billy's parties. But setting up a deal for an important Jeffersonian artifact had to earn him some respect from the people in Richmond. The meeting, however, with Stanley Crawford did not go as Bob anticipated. In fact, the meeting never happened. Bob knew Mr. Arthur wouldn't appreciate what did happen.

At nine o'clock Bob parked in front of the house, then walked down the driveway and around to the rear, as Crawford had instructed. A light shone from within an attached room, obviously added on after the house was built. He knocked on the door to the addition, but no one responded. He decided Crawford might be in the main part of the house and began walking to the front of the house. Remembering his warning from Crawford not to disturb his wife, he changed his mind and turned back toward the rear of the house. Hesitating, not sure what to do next, he tried the door. It opened and Bob stepped into Crawford's office.

Stanley Crawford was lying on the floor next to a desk in a pool of blood. Bob took one look at Crawford's body, backed out the door, and ran down the driveway. He quickly got in his car and drove off with tires squealing.

Bob now had a new reason for driving to Richmond. The police would soon be at Crawford's, then the news people. Tomorrow it would be on TV and in the newspapers. He knew Mr. Arthur would hear about it and want to know what part Bob played.

He had to see Mr. Arthur first and convince him he didn't do anything. He needed to tell him that Crawford was dead before he got there. Seeing all that blood spooked him so he ran out. Okay, he shouldn't have sped off making all that noise. But he watched enough cop shows to know that innocent people found at the scene of a crime often get blamed.

From Crawford's house Bob headed back through town. He wanted to stop at his apartment and pick up some things before driving to Richmond. Traveling west on Market Street, the panic that took hold of him at the Crawford residence now escalated. What if Crawford's wife had seen him? Maybe she'd been looking out the window. Maybe neighbors saw him. Maybe someone got the license number. The police might already be waiting for him at home. It didn't help his state of mind that his route through town took him past the Charlottesville police station.

He turned sharply off Market to get to Park Street. Approaching Court Square, he punched in his sister's number on his cell. Driving with one hand on the wheel he held the phone in the other while he waited for his sister to answer. Rounding a corner, too fast, he found he required another hand on the steering wheel. Bob tried to make the turn while holding onto the phone, but it slipped from his hand. When he automatically reached for it, he lost control. The car jumped a curb, swerved back onto the street, and just missed some kids crossing in front of his car. Not exactly missed, he realized.

He saw the group of kids only briefly and knew he hit something, or worse, someone. My God, he thought, what if he hurt one of those kids! No way, though, was he going to stop. Someone would help them. Forgetting the route he had intended to take, Bob turned west onto High Street instead of continuing north from the square. Totally rattled, he managed to locate the phone, now on the floor under his feet. He grabbed it just before reaching an intersection, barely slowing down before racing through a red light.

When he finally reached Trina, he asked her if he could come stay with her in Richmond. Would she wait up for him? He must have sounded upset because she wanted to know if everything was okay. He replied he was tired and needed a break from work. Besides, Bob said, he had the day off tomorrow and he'd like to see her and also maybe get hold of some of his Richmond pals. Fortunately, she was always glad to have him. He sped up a little as he drove toward the 250 bypass, then I-64, and began the hour drive to Richmond.

Driving east, looking frequently in his rear view mirror for the police he worried would soon be chasing him, he worked on what he would say to Mr. Arthur. With a little luck, Crawford's death might not make it into the Richmond news.

He felt a sense of relief after pulling into his sister's drive. Trina happily welcomed him at the door and told him to grab a seat while she got him a beer. When she asked where his clothes were, Bob said they were in the car and he'd get them later. He figured he'd slip out the next day after his sister left for work and buy some things at the thrift store next to the church he used to attend.

Much later, Bob would come to realize that his decision to get away from Charlottesville worked in his favor only for the short run. Based on the partial license plate information obtained from the woman with her dog, and a general description of the hit-and-run car from witnesses, the police had begun tracking down owners of vehicles that matched this limited description. Robert Smith just happened to be near the top of their long list, and a C'ville cop showed up at Bob's vacant apartment on Tuesday afternoon. The officer stuck one of his cards on Bob's door and began knocking on nearby apartment doors.

An older man and woman in an adjacent apartment

said their neighbor kept to himself and sometimes went away for a few days. They were pretty sure he left sometime Sunday or Monday because they had enjoyed a respite from TV noise the last day or so. The elderly gentleman reported that their neighbor's car was an old Buick, tan in color. Another neighbor two doors down told the officer she remembered seeing Smith a couple of times on the downtown mall. She thought maybe he worked in one of the mall's stores.

The officer requested the neighbors contact Charlottesville police when Smith returned. "Just need to ask him some questions."

Bob got permission from his boss to help take care of his sister, who was recuperating from an illness that "has just knocked her out." Over the next few days, he used Trina's computer to follow the news of the Charlottesville killing. The stories repeated the police theory that a robbery had gone wrong. One report stated the police believed the killing to be related to an accident in Court Square where a couple of kids were injured.

Bob began hyperventilating when he read the police had a description of the car leaving the Crawford residence and that it matched a description of the car hitting the kids. He knew he shouldn't be surprised. Not only did he foolishly call attention to his car by speeding away from the house, but he had knocked down those kids. Maybe Crawford's wife saw him leave. The kids probably described his car to the police, although he doubted they would have seen his license plate. The news reports ended with a statement by the Charlottesville police information officer that they had a lead on the person involved and the investigation was ongoing.

Bob knew that to stay on Mr. Arthur's good side, or at least not a bad side, he should be up-front about what occurred. He didn't know if Mr. Arthur had heard about the murder, but figured it wouldn't be long before he did.

He had to convince Arthur that Crawford already was dead when he arrived. How could he be blamed for something that happened before he got there? He couldn't think straight after seeing all that blood! Okay, he got into an accident, but nothing too bad had come of it other than the police might have a description of his car. He would ditch the car. It was on its last legs anyway. What was important, he would tell Mr. Arthur, was that a murdered Stanley Crawford gave clear evidence he had the document. Or he once had. He would offer Mr. Arthur his services to stay on the trail.

On Thursday Bob called Billy and asked for a meeting with Mr. Arthur. He didn't go into details. The whole story could wait until they met. Billy called back and said Mr. Arthur suggested they meet in Hollywood Cemetery the following day. Wait near Jefferson Davis's grave at three o'clock, Billy said. Bob had never visited the cemetery but got directions from his sister after obtaining permission to drive her car.

George Arthur found Bob standing at the gravesite of the President of the Confederacy. He greeted Bob curtly.

"Okay. Tell me what happened."

Bob's stammered as he began his account of Monday night's events. Despite Arthur's menacing glare he managed to tell a coherent story.

"You have to believe me. I didn't kill him," Bob repeated several times.

George Arthur hadn't moved, and continued to glare while listening to Bob's version of his visit to the Crawford residence.

"You know, don't you," Arthur said, "you just opened up a trail to the Klan." Bob immediately sought to reassure him.

"Even if the police find me there's no connection with the Klan. I would never let on that I know you or that I joined the Klan. The police might have a general description of the car, but there are lots of light-colored, older cars. I'll get rid of it. Don't worry."

"But I am worried," George Arthur exclaimed. "I need to think this over. Look, if the Hemings letter exists, there's no telling where it is. If someone killed Crawford before you got there, then it's likely, isn't it, that this person left with whatever Crawford had? When the police catch the guy, they'll probably find the document. Even if this whole thing isn't your screw-up, it's still screwed up."

"What if I talk with the widow?" Bob asked earnestly. "What if the killer didn't get the letter and the widow has it?"

"You got to be kidding. I want you to do as you promised and get rid of the car. Then just lay low for a while. Stay away from Charlottesville and definitely stay away from any Klan members. I'll be in contact when things quiet down. And for God's sake stay out of trouble."

George Arthur left Bob standing dejectedly in the cemetery next to the large monument marking the grave of the Confederate leader. Nevertheless, Bob held on to a faint hope that he could make up for what happened. He needed to redeem himself in the eyes of Mr. Arthur.

First, however, he needed to ditch his car. That required some assistance and Bob knew who could help. Jimmy Cooke was a drinking buddy who had no affiliation with the Klan that Bob knew of. A bit rough on the edges, to say the least, Jimmy's run-ins with the police started back in high school where he and Bob first met.

Bob usually managed to stay clean in whatever delinquent activity he and Jimmy engaged in. Jimmy, however, showed neither the intelligence nor the industriousness to avoid falling into the arms of the police. When arrested, Jimmy usually made matters worse by spewing obscenities at the cops, kicking and screaming as he was thrown into a squad car. It was a miracle he arrived alive at the police station. Upon arrival, his body and his face often were covered with bruises which the police report said resulted from an altercation with an unidentified assailant.

Despite their differences, Bob and Jimmy usually got along well. Bob knew he could trust him not to question why he was abandoning a perfectly good car on a backwoods road some twenty miles west of Richmond. They arranged to meet late Saturday night behind Trina's house.

Jimmy kept Bob's pickup truck in sight as they headed out in the dark. Taking side roads and obeying the speed limits, Bob judged it would be a one-in-a-million chance the cops would stop them. Whatever the probability, after a bad week, to say the least, the odds worked in their favor as neither of them were pulled over on the way out of town.

The two vehicles turned off the highway in a remote spot close to where Jimmy and Bob used to hunt when younger. Bob parked his car in a clearing at the end of a dirt path barely wide enough for a car. He removed the license plates, threw gasoline on the engine, lit a match to it, and got away before the vehicle exploded. Jimmy watched from the seat of his truck, totally impressed, laughing out loud for maybe a minute at the craziness of it all. We should have brought marshmallows, he said, as Bob climbed into the truck. They decided to celebrate the night's accomplishment with a few drinks at a bar in downtown Richmond.

Once Bob started drinking, the memory of Mr. Arthur's anger faded. Still somewhat puffed up over the night's handiwork, and after providing Jimmy a brief lesson on the Jefferson-Hemings business, he told his buddy about the Hemings letter and how he almost had his hands on it. Soon the reason for ditching the car came out. Jimmy got caught up in the story.

"You're shittin me! This Jefferson dude and a black slave? You've got to find it. Everybody will want to hear about it. You'll be famous. It'll go viral."

Both chose to be oblivious to the fact that the police were now involved, and that should they be aware of the document, knowing its whereabouts would be one of their priorities.

"You don't know for sure whoever killed Crawford got the thing," Jimmy said. "Maybe Crawford hid it and wouldn't tell where it was. That could have made the killer mad and he killed him. I would have, if I knew someone was holding out on me. Maybe this Crawford guy gave it to his wife before he got killed. You should find out. Let's go see her. Find out what she knows."

Bob liked the idea. Mr. Arthur didn't even need to know if nothing came from it. After a few more beers the idea seemed even more reasonable. Jimmy wanted to drive to Charlottesville the next day, but Bob knew he shouldn't cross Mr. Arthur. He had to keep out of sight for a while. They would need a cover story when talking to Crawford's wife and over another beer or two, they discussed what might work.

They decided Bob would approach the widow the same way he initially approached Stanley Crawford, that is, before things went bad. He'd tell her he worked for a collector of Jefferson artifacts, that the collector knew her husband possessed an important artifact, and that his client would pay big bucks for it. If she knew anything at all about the document, they figured the possibility of making a lot of money would loosen her tongue.

The two weren't so drunk to recognize that the finishing touches to their plan needed to be completed when they sobered up. Jimmy managed to drive them to Trina's house without hitting anything or being stopped by the police. Bob slid out of the truck and staggered inside. Jimmy never got his truck out of the driveway and fell asleep in the front seat. On her way to work the next morning, Trina recognized Jimmy's truck and peered in a side window. Seeing him curled up in the front seat, she knocked on the window. It wasn't the first time one of Bob's friends didn't make it home after a night boozing, although they frequently managed to locate the wicker sofa on the front porch. Her knock on the window didn't rouse him.

It was close to ten o'clock before Jimmy and Bob sat at the kitchen table downing strong cups of coffee and continuing their plans. The Richmond Sunday newspaper reported Crawford's funeral had been yesterday. It would only be proper, they reasoned, to give his wife time to get over that. In the meantime, they'd wait for the press coverage to die down. When that happened, they'd put their plan into action.

Chapter 13

Stanley Crawford and Blossom Hunter were buried in Charlottesville on Saturday, only hours before a farmer reported a fire in the woods near his property close to Richmond. The deceased had been residents of Charlottesville most of their lives. One white and one black. Although they'd lived in the same town for many years, their paths never crossed until two hearses going in opposite directions passed on the way to their final resting places.

Mike went with Kelly to the visitation for Justice's aunt at the funeral home the night before the burial. It turned out to be one of his most difficult times since his wife's death. When he entered the room with the open casket he immediately experienced flashbacks to Kirsten's accident and funeral. His mind raced with myriad thoughts of death and dying. He felt faint. Perspiration formed on his face. His knees weakened.

Kelly sensed the tension in her brother, moved closer and took hold of his arm. She immediately understood the problem. In hindsight, it had been a mistake for Mike to confront another death so soon, and so real. Kelly saw the distant look in his eyes and turned him slowly toward the door.

"You don't need to be here," she whispered. "Justice will understand."

Mike spent a restless night and was the first person to arrive in the kitchen the next morning. Later, when Kelly arrived, they sat over coffee at the kitchen table and Mike apologized to her for his reaction at the funeral home.

"We both should have known better," Kelly said. "It was a perfectly natural response given what you've been through. We should have foreseen what effect attending the viewing would have."

"I guess you're right. I really don't think I can attend today's graveside service. I'm afraid I'll react the same way. But I do want to go to the reception later this afternoon. I want to apologize to Justice for leaving abruptly last night and for not being at the burial today."

"You know that Justice doesn't need apologies, but I'm sure he'd like to see you."

The house where Blossom Hunter had lived sat back from the street in a neighborhood obviously on the upswing. The houses on each side showed signs of recent renovation. Justice will have to get moving, he thought, in order to keep up with his neighbors.

Loud conversation and much laughter permeated the air as Mike climbed the stairs of the front porch. A black woman whom Mike did not recognize opened the screen door.

"You must be Mike Chance, Justice's partner," she said, motioning him in. "Justice will be glad you could come."

He thanked her and moved into the living room where a relatively small crowd, nearly all African Americans, stood around a table loaded with food.

So much noise on this somber occasion seemed out of place to Mike. He remembered the many hushed, teary-eyed offerings of condolence when people slowly left the gravesite following Kirsten's burial, his mind wrapped in a numbing fog as he acknowledged them. There hadn't been any get-together afterwards. He had returned with Kelly and Steve to the townhouse. They sat for an hour or so, alternately talking about his plans for the coming weeks and being awkwardly silent.

Justice spotted Mike right away and walked over to greet him.

"Miguel! I'm glad you're here. Come with me. There

are some people I want you to meet." Putting his arm around his partner, he guided Mike across the room.

"We can't help but feel good today. When a woman lives that long and does so much for others, how can anyone be unhappy," Justice explained.

* * *

The following Wednesday Mike met with Dr. Rider at his regular time. Because of their missed appointments he hadn't been to a therapy session for three weeks. He remembered to bring the notebook she had given him to write down his feelings of depersonalization. It wasn't an easy assignment. He had written about the trip to the hospital emergency room to see his niece and about his response at the funeral home when seeing the body of Justice's aunt. It was easier to describe how he felt when Justice showed up in town. He hoped he had written enough to satisfy his therapist.

After inquiring about how he was doing and the usual brief small talk, Dr. Rider started right in.

"I see you have your notebook. Great. I hope it's been going okay. I'll want to see what you wrote. However, first I want to talk about your childhood."

Childhood? Mike didn't see what that had to do with losing his wife and a life on hold. Let's talk about last January, he thought to himself.

"I don't need to know a lot," she said. "Just fill me in on what you think are some of the highlights. Maybe even the low lights if you can. As a start, tell me a bit about how you got along with your parents. And your sister."

Mike did, although he occasionally censored what he told her. If his therapist recognized that, she didn't show it, merely nodding once in a while, occasionally asking him to clarify something or taking him down a different path. She asked him to talk about the family's responses to his father's death. Both he and his sister were crushed, of course, but it was his mother, he said, who was most affected. Mike told her how she had been ill off and on since. He admitted not having visited his mother since his wife's death. He provided Dr. Rider with the same set of excuses that came into his head whenever he thought of traveling to see his mother. The psychologist listened carefully, but didn't comment.

Dr. Rider seemed more interested in the summers and holidays he spent in New Mexico.

"You grew up in Alexandria, but you made many trips to New Mexico. That's where your mother's from, right?"

"Right. We'd usually go there during the summers and occasionally during Christmas. She's got a big extended family. My grandparents passed away, but I have aunts and uncles and lots of cousins. Sometimes I think my mother is related to everyone in town. At least the Hispanics."

"What did you do when you were there?"

"Mostly eat New Mexican food! Sopapillas, enchiladas, chicharrones, the works. Nothing like you can get around here. My aunts put out a spread any time we visited. I'd hang around with my cousins. Sometimes I'd hike in the mountains."

"This was in the mountains around Santa Fe? Why do you like hiking? Can you tell me how these hikes made you feel?"

This threw Mike. Why does anyone hike but for some exercise and to enjoy the outdoors?

"Yes, in Santa Fe. I like being outside. The scenery in New Mexico is spectacular. From one of my aunt's houses I could get on a trail leading to the top of some foothills where I had fantastic views of the city and mountains in the distance. It's a wonderful feeling to be up there."

"Did you hike alone or with someone? A cousin or

friend? Your sister, for instance?"

"Generally alone. My sister is two years younger than me and she often did things with the girl cousins. I went hiking with one of my cousins a couple of times, but I guess I mostly went alone. Hiking around the place where you live probably isn't all that interesting for them. I didn't mind being alone."

"You may see where I'm heading. Remember, I mentioned that some people think feelings of depersonalization, being outside yourself, have roots in previous experiences. I'm wondering whether when you went into the desert, so to speak, if you found yourself having feelings like those you now experience?"

"I can't really say," Mike said, not particularly sure of her meaning.

"Go back in your mind's eye, if you can, to one of those hikes. Close your eyes and think about when and where it was, what you were feeling. Can you do that? Then tell me about it."

Mike closed his eyes and worked mentally on revisiting one of his walks in the hills around Santa Fe. It had been so long ago that at first he thought he wouldn't be able to do it. To his surprise he found it relatively easy. He loved those walks, more than he realized when Dr. Rider first mentioned them.

His eyes were still closed when he answered.

"I remember one hike in particular. I was a teenager, maybe seventeen or eighteen. It was nearly sunset. The mountains close to Santa Fe are to the east so when you're up there you get amazing sunset views. The colors are like nothing you ever see around here. On the east coast I mean. And you can see for miles and miles. There is one hill, Atalaya, from the top it seems you can see forever. I hiked there a number of times."

"How did you feel when you experienced those views? Was it anything like you sometimes feel now?

That is, did you feel like you were moving outside yourself?"

"Like I had some mystical experience?" Mike said, his eyes now open, looking at his therapist, not sure what she wanted him to say.

"Not exactly," Dr. Rider said, smiling. "Although I think I did mention that DP has been likened to religious experiences. I'm thinking more of feelings of drifting away, of moving away from your body. Maybe thoughts of the cosmos, of who we are in this universe. I have to say, from what you just described, I probably would be thinking along those lines."

"I guess I may have had those kind of thoughts. What I remember most is simply being at peace, seeing myself on top of the mountain, contemplating the world below. I probably did sometimes wonder about my existence. I mean being alive and what it all means. You know, what's the saying, 'we're just a speck in the dust bowl of space.'"

"I don't know if I heard that saying exactly," she said, smiling again, "but I know what you mean."

"Doesn't everyone have those kind of thoughts?" Mike asked, beginning to worry he just revealed something Dr. Rider would note in his file under "weird thoughts."

"Of course they do. I do. I'm simply trying to see if these are thoughts you've had, whether you can identify them. Maybe tell me how often they occurred."

"Well, I can say it wasn't unusual for me on these hikes to find a rock to sit on and think about things other than myself."

This last comment seemed to give Dr. Rider what she was looking for. She moved to end the session.

"That's all we need for now. Thanks. We won't be analyzing your childhood, but I think I know you better and that will help with what we do here. Our time is up.

In fact, we went over a bit today. You've done great. Please leave your notebook with me. I have a fresh one for you."

Mike had been prepared to tell her about his homicide partner showing up in town, meeting one of the C'ville police officers investigating the murder of Stanley Crawford, and his upcoming appearance with the so-called Jefferson Bunch. She wanted him involved with something and he seemed to have succeeded in doing that. Maybe next time, he thought.

* * *

More than a week had passed since the Crawford killing. Bob Smith twice called Elmer Houston to request more time off. His sister, he told his boss, didn't seem to be responding to the medicines the docs gave her. When Elmer asked what was wrong with her, Bob said "pneumonia," although how he came up with that particular diagnosis is not something he could explain. Elmer seemed to consider it serious and told Bob not to worry. His job would keep. Coming up with a story for his sister, who wondered why Bob didn't go back to Charlottesville and his job, proved to be a bit more difficult. And where was his car, she asked?

Bob didn't want to go back to Charlottesville until he and Jimmy were ready to carry out their plan. He believed it was a chance, maybe a last one, to show Mr. Arthur that he could accomplish something. To give himself more time, he told his sister he sold the car and was in the process of looking for a newer one. The timing worked out, he said to Trina, because his boss laid him off since business had been slow. He could use the time to look for new wheels. He assured his sister the layoff was temporary and that his boss wanted him back the next week. He thanked her repeatedly for feeding him and giving him a room while he was out of work. Trina liked being appreciated and accepted Bob's lies as truth.

On Friday morning, ten days since the Crawford killing, Bob Smith and Jimmy Cooke drove west on I-64 toward Charlottesville, the radio blasting country-western songs. Jimmy was never one for making plans or anticipating consequences. For him life just happened. So Bob had to keep reminding Jimmy to watch his speed. Leave it to Jimmy to have neglected to renew his driver's license or not to take out insurance on his truck, let alone be clocked at 25 mph above the limit. Bob didn't want to tangle with the law, convinced they'd want him for questioning regarding Crawford's murder.

Bob made Jimmy turn down the radio when they neared Charlottesville. He wanted some quiet time to rehearse exactly what he would say to Crawford's widow. By the time they pulled up in front of the house, Bob had his lines prepared. He told Jimmy to stay in the truck while he talked with Mrs. Crawford. Jimmy looked disappointed, but didn't move from behind the wheel.

As Bob opened the truck door, Jimmy reached into a cup holder on the floorboard and retrieved a small envelope. He squeezed its contents into his mouth.

"Jimmy! What's that?"

"Nothin. It's for my stomach."

"You sure you're all right?"

"Yeah. Some kind of digestion problem."

"Okay. But remember, just stay here."

Bob ran his hand over his hair and smoothed his shirt before ringing the doorbell. He noticed that the screen door was unlocked and opened it slightly, ready to be let in. When Beatrice opened the inside door, he choked. He momentarily forgot his prepared speech. Before he could say anything, she quickly challenged his presence on her doorstep.

"Who are you? What do you want?"

He released the screen door, searching for the words he'd rehearsed.

"Mrs. Crawford. First, let me say how sorry I am about your husband."

"Did you know my husband?"

"Well, no, I didn't know him personally."

"Then why are you sorry? Who are you?" she repeated.

This was not going as Bob had hoped.

"I was a business associate of your husband's. We never met, but we were going to do some business together. I talked with him on the phone just before he died. Again, I'm sorry about your . . ."

"Who is that?" Beatrice interrupted, looking over his head.

Bob assumed she meant Jimmy sitting in the truck.

"Oh, he's another business associate," he said, then realized Jimmy was standing next to him.

"He doesn't look like a business man," Beatrice argued.

In his camouflage pants, army issue boots, a T-shirt with a picture of a fishing boat and words beneath it that read, "Kiss My Bass Boat," Bob had to admit she had a point.

"And come to think of it, neither do you," Beatrice said, eyeing Bob more closely. "I don't think we have any business to conduct. Thank you, but I'm busy."

She moved to close the inside door but Jimmy quickly yanked open the screen door and stuck his foot in the way.

"Ma'am, I think you'll want to do business with us when you hear what we have to say. Your husband had something worth a lot of money and we're here to buy it."

Jimmy could always get right to the point. Beatrice still held the door against Jimmy's foot, but he pushed it open, sending her back several steps.

"If we could just come in for a few minutes," Jimmy

said as he strolled inside, leaving Bob with the choice of standing on the front step or following him into the house.

There was another option which occurred to him too late, and that was to pull Jimmy back and for both of them to get into the truck and drive off. It would have been the better alternative.

The widow Crawford, obviously upset, backed into her house while casting a pleading look at the crucifix hanging in the foyer. Bob and Jimmy followed her, with Bob considering how he could regain control of the situation. He was too familiar with instances of being around Jimmy when all of a sudden things got cocked up. But this was different. Jimmy was different.

"Mrs. Crawford," Bob began as he shouldered his way in front of Jimmy, "please don't be alarmed. We have just a few questions then we'll get out of your hair. Like my associate said, we can help you financially. I'm sure you could use some money now that your husband is gone."

"You're talking about that paper, a letter or something, that my husband was supposed to have, aren't you?"

She carefully lowered herself into a large easy chair. Bob motioned for Jimmy to sit next to him on the sofa. Jimmy remained standing.

"Yes, ma'am, we are," Bob said. "And we can offer a substantial amount of money for it."

"A lot of money," Jimmy found it necessary to add.

"I've told the police I don't know whether Stanley had anything like that," she replied, in what was either desperation or simply frustration over the matter.

"My husband didn't always tell me what he was doing. Even if he had something valuable, it doesn't mean he would tell me. I told the police that."

"How do we know you're telling the truth?" Jimmy

jumped in, articulating the thought that was also circulating in Bob's mind.

"Young man, I always tell the truth," Beatrice said through clenched teeth.

She glanced over to the table holding the statue of the Virgin and the votive candles surrounding it. Jimmy saw the direction of her gaze and walked over to the table. Bob watched, not knowing what to expect. He started to say something when Jimmy's next trick took any words out of his mouth. The widow's scream started his heart pounding against his chest.

Jimmy had swept the candles, some of them burning, onto the floor. He then grabbed the statue of the Virgin Mary by the neck.

"Ma'am, we aren't playing around. This god can't help you."

"God?" thought Bob. If Jimmy was doing this for effect he definitely produced one in both onlookers. Beatrice leaned back in her chair, looking as though she would faint. Bob scanned the floor for any burning candles that might set the place on fire. He then looked toward the front door, worried that neighbors might have heard her scream. He'd lost control of the situation once again and tried to regain it.

"Jimmy, put that down. You didn't need to do that. I'm sure Mrs. Crawford is telling the truth."

He had seen enough crime movies to realize that Jimmy had just led him into playing good cop against Jimmy's bad, very bad, cop. Beatrice apparently decided bad cop was for real.

"You should talk to Stanley's minister if you want to know about the letter," she said, clearly frightened.

"Minister?" asked Bob, ignoring Jimmy who was still standing with a strangle hold on the virgin.

"Maxwell. I'm not sure of his first name. Jerry, maybe. He knows about the letter. Stanley told him it was worth a lot of money and promised him money for his church when it was sold. At least that's what Mr. Maxwell told me. He's the one who knows about this thing. I certainly don't. And that's the truth. Maybe Stanley gave him the letter," she offered.

"Where do we find this minister person?" Jimmy asked, once more on point.

"He has a church, a building, a storefront I think he uses for a church. It's on the south side of town, not too far from here. One of those churches for black people. A neighbor told me about it when I explained how Stanley's minister came to the door saying Stanley promised him money. My neighbor saw Stanley going into the church one Sunday. She was afraid to tell me because I go to a different church. It's called Glory Road, Stanley's church, that is. Mine is . . ., oh well, you don't need to know that. The church my husband went to is about two blocks off Avon. The minister lives there, too, I think."

Bob and Jimmy simply stared while Beatrice rambled on. When she paused, Jimmy spoke up.

"Mrs. Crawford," he said, while putting the statue back on the table among the broken votives and spilled wax, "I'm sorry I lost my temper. And we want to thank you for your help. Yes, thank you. But you see I do have a temper. Bob knows that, don't you Bob?"

Bob nodded in clear recognition of that fact. Jimmy looked Beatrice in the eye and it was obvious she, too, recognized it.

"What I'm getting at, Mrs. Crawford," Jimmy said sternly, "is that if you tell anyone we were here, I may get angry again. Do you understand?"

"Yes, yes, I do," Mrs. Crawford said, and slumped back into her chair.

Bob got to his feet, motioning for Jimmy to follow.

"We'll be going now. I'm sorry for the mess we

made."

He reached into his pocket and found a couple of dollars which he put on the coffee table in front of the sofa. "I hope this will cover the damages." Jimmy was all smiles as they headed for the truck. Bob didn't know what to think.

* * *

Beatrice didn't move from her chair for some time. She had been terrified, but now she was angry. Who were they, she thought, to accuse her of lying, and with the Blessed Mother looking on.

She smiled inwardly at the success she had in distracting her unwelcome guests. Beatrice had learned enough since the death of her husband to know what the two men wanted. The police had asked about items of value her husband might have had. They specifically asked if she knew about a letter or document that would be worth something to collectors of historic artifacts. Beatrice told the police she didn't know about any document, nor for that matter whether Stanley had anything worth stealing. When the black minister came to the door with a similar story she began to think maybe Stanley did have some kind of valuable artifact. Today, in her living room, had been two men who thought the same thing.

She hadn't told the police about the minister's visit. He came a couple days before the funeral and her mind had been occupied with the arrangements and, importantly, what to wear. Besides, the police appeared to know already what Stanley might have had.

No, she wouldn't tell anyone about what happened this morning. Except maybe Father Thomas, when the next time in the confessional she confessed her desire to kill these two men. Maybe she'd also mention to Father how she'd told these men about the minister possibly having the document. Since the minister came to her house looking for the document it meant Stanley hadn't given it to him. But it wasn't as if she told these two men the minister definitely had it. How could that be a lie? Father Thomas would understand.

That same afternoon the Charlottesville police issued a state-wide alert for Robert Smith. The bulletin identified him as a person of interest in an accident involving injuries where the driver had left the scene. Robert Smith hadn't been seen since the Monday evening Crawford was killed and continued to be among those the police sought to interview. That in itself might have been sufficient reason to issue a state-wide alert, but information received from the Powhatan County Sheriff's office made the decision easy.

The sheriff's report stated that deputies had investigated a car fire in the woods west of Richmond. Finding no one in the car or at the scene, they placed an order for the car to be taken to a county lot. That occurred a few days later when the vehicle cooled down. It took several more days for someone to record the car's VIN from the engine block and begin the process of locating the car's owner--to determine the circumstances leading to the car fire and to provide a bill for the county's removal.

The Powhatan Sheriff informed the C'ville police that the car, a 1999 Buick Regal, was registered to Robert Smith of Charlottesville. The sheriff requested the local authorities to find out what Mr. Smith knew about the vehicle.

Chapter 14

On the same Friday that Bob Smith and Jimmy Cooke terrorized the widow Crawford, Jonathan Turner again played host to the Jefferson Bunch. He experienced an uneasiness similar to that which arose before their previous meeting. Everyone agreed a discussion of recent events would be worthwhile and Jon asked Professor McCabe to attend in order to help. But he knew there would be another effort by some, Peter Trent for certain, to get the group involved in some way. This time, however, other people were already involved--the police. As far as Jon was concerned, the group needn't do anything but follow the ongoing police investigation. Unfortunately, up to this point, it hadn't revealed much. The murder took place more than a week ago and according to reports in the press, no fresh leads had emerged.

The professor had asked if he could bring Mike Chance, assuming he was still interested, or, as McCabe said, "If I can interest him." Jon couldn't be sure what effect the presence of the detective might have. It was one of the many unknowns hovering over the evening's meeting.

Both Charles Wingate and Mark Abernathy had e-mailed saying they wouldn't make the meeting. Jon wasn't sure why Mark couldn't come, but judged that Charles didn't want to take part in any more discussion of an investigation. Craig Stevens, who didn't make it to the last meeting when the group voted not to pursue the mysterious caller, said he'd be there. Andrea, Peter, and the Reverend Maxwell, also said they'd attend.

* * *

Paul McCabe offered to pick up Mike on the night of

the meeting, but the young detective decided to drive to Jon's house. His car had been sitting more or less idle in the Cummings driveway for many months. Kelly or Steve used it occasionally to keep it running. Tonight was about keeping Mike running. He wanted to test his renewed feelings of competence.

This week's session with Dr. Rider unsettled him. He didn't like talking about his childhood, his and Kelly's reactions to their father's death, or why he hadn't visited his mother. Then there were the hikes in the mountains. He got the feeling that Dr. Rider believed he had been practicing depersonalization all his life! Nevertheless, in the past few days he felt more in control and the fog around him didn't seem as dense. Maybe some of that stuff in his head just needed to be brought up, examined, and put back in proper order, he thought.

Paul McCabe arrived at Jon's house just as Mike pulled up. They walked together up the front walkway while the professor thanked him for coming and apologized once again for being part of the earlier set-up at his sister's house. He expressed the hope that Mike would find the Jefferson group interesting.

After everyone had arrived, the introductions went quickly. When completed, Mike wasn't entirely sure who was who. He matched Jonathan Turner's name and face because Jon met them at the door and they chatted for a minute. He knew who the reverend was but couldn't remember his last name. Jeremiah was a name even someone with DP could remember, he thought to himself. Of course he also was the only black man. Mike remembered the woman's name probably for the same reason, given she, too, was one of a kind here. The others would perhaps become more familiar as the night went on. He hated being unsure of things. Maybe being here wasn't all that good of an idea, he thought. The fog rolled in.

I'm in a chair with a half dozen people looking at me. I'm here. It's me that's here. Michael Miguel Chance. That's me. Why don't I feel like it's me? Dr. Rider said focus on something in the environment. That painting on the wall . . .

With everyone seated in the living room, Jon once more thanked Paul McCabe and Mike Chance for attending. Peter Trent then immediately started the discussion rolling.

"I found out something interesting today. I told you I had some contacts in the mayor's office. Well, someone familiar with the investigation into Crawford's death told me that the forensic unit has yet to release all their findings. It's been over a week. That seems rather a long time to me. I asked my source why that was and he didn't know or wouldn't say. I think we're lucky Detective Chance is here. Do you know what's going on, Mike?"

Everyone looked in his direction. Mike quit staring at the painting on the wall and worked to gain control of himself. Just treat this like a briefing at work, he thought.

"It may or may not be unusual. The length of time it's taking, that is. It could be they're short of staff."

"But wouldn't a murder investigation have priority?" Peter asked.

"I'm not familiar with what goes on here in Charlottesville," Mike replied. "But, you're right. This sort of thing in a town that has few murders would seem to warrant a speedy examination. On the other hand, maybe they needed to send something to the state lab for more analysis. Or, it's possible that a report has been made, but it isn't yet available to the public.

"The police won't want a report made public if the results might interfere with the ongoing investigation. It's possible the police don't want whoever killed Crawford to know what they know. And what they don't know. In my experience it's not uncommon for details to be withheld from the press."

Andrea Hudson had already announced she had a plane to catch early in the morning and tried to speed things along.

"May I suggest that we move on to the main business of this evening."

"I would think anything important having to do with the investigation would be relevant," Peter retorted.

"Yes and no," Andrea answered. "We're here tonight to discuss what our role is, if any, in this whole affair. Maybe we should let the police do their thing and wait for the results of their investigation. If we decide to do that, then I don't know whether we need to talk much about anything, except out of curiosity."

"She's right, Peter," Jeremiah responded. "Perhaps first we need to see what people are thinking. And we owe it to the professor and Detective Chance not to take up too much of their time."

"Okay," Peter reluctantly agreed, "let's talk about what we might do if we were to do something."

Professor McCabe spoke up. "I asked Detective Chance to come tonight to help with just that question. Mike, can we hear your thoughts on this?"

Mike took a deep breath and tried to focus.

"As you know, I'm not on the local police force. But I think you all realize that the police don't like, for lack of a better word, amateurs, interfering with an investigation. There are serious problems with it. I don't just mean the possibility of someone getting hurt when dealing with people armed with guns. Actually, that's not usually what the police worry most about. There's always the possibility that an outsider, someone who isn't aware of what's actually going on, will mess up an investigation and ruin the prosecution's case. Private detectives also fall into this category.

"Consider, for example, if one of you talked with someone who later becomes a key witness. Depending on what you say to this person, or maybe no matter what you say, a lawyer might later claim you gave information to this person that they wouldn't otherwise have had. That could be crucial to a court case. Or if you were to dig up evidence, a lawyer could claim it was tainted since the police didn't have it first. Things like that. I think you can understand what I mean."

Mike paused and looked at the faces in the room. Seeing recognition of what he just said, he continued.

"I certainly would recommend you just let the police do their job. Of course, if any of you know something which might be of value to the police investigation then you should let the authorities know. Withholding pertinent information when a serious crime has been committed can land you in trouble.

"And on that last point let me say something from what I've learned from Professor McCabe. It seems there might very well have been an important historic document in the victim's possession. I'm sure you've already considered that it could be a motive for what happened. But whoever did it would have to know what the document is and why it might be important. Maybe that's where some of you could help the police. What's the nature of this document? What would it look like? I assume it would be written on old paper. How could it survive all these years? Who had it? And importantly, who would want it and why? These are questions the police might want some help with."

Mike turned to Paul McCabe.

"Professor, what makes the Hemings-Jefferson affair so important that someone would want to commit murder just to get hold of a letter about Jefferson and Sally Hemings? I think you said the document or letter could be worth a lot of money. How much are we talking about? How would you sell it if you did have it?"

Mike realized being the center of attention exacted a toll.

Those were my words. I know that. But it didn't sound like me speaking. As if I was on autopilot. I am Mike Chance. I am here. I am real.

"Leave it to a detective to ask about motive," the professor said with a smile. "Your point, of course, is a good one. I'm not sure what the document might be worth. I mean, historians would be interested in what it says, not necessarily the artifact itself. I, for one, would like to know two things. First, is it genuine? Was it really written by Sally's brother? Second, if so, what does James Hemings have to say? Is it relevant to the discourse about Thomas Jefferson?

"I'm sure you know people collect all kinds of documents. Letters and diaries from soldiers in the various wars are bought by history buffs for thousands of dollars. I recently saw a letter signed by a Revolutionary War prisoner selling for ten grand. No doubt there are people ready to pay big bucks for something that put Thomas Jefferson in debt to Sally Hemings. Trading sex for the freedom of Sally's children! It would be a coup among collectors to own such a document."

A few members of the group murmured their agreement.

McCabe continued, "And you've probably heard of art collectors who don't seem to care how they get hold of valuable artwork, just so they can have it displayed in their house. Maybe not even displayed. They just want to own it. I imagine there are collectors of historic artifacts who might behave the same way. It is after all Thomas Jefferson we're talking about. Elmer Houston is the person to talk to about all this. But the bottom line is that it could be worth a killing, so to speak. Sorry, bad choice of words."

McCabe's dark humor brought out a few smiles in the group.

Craig Stevens changed the direction of the conversation by asking Mike about the car accident involving Mike's niece and her friends the night of the murder. The story apparently had made it around the Charlottesville adolescent grapevine, which would have included Craig's children.

Mike found himself talking about what he knew of that night's events. He mentioned his brief discussion with Officer Alice Dixon. Doing so bought him some credibility since he could honestly report that he knew the police were working on a definite lead. He recognized, however, that given the time already gone by, the lead hadn't produced much. At least anything he knew about.

After listening to Mike, Jon looked around the room and moved to bring the meeting to an end. "I think we can agree that it seems best, for now, to wait and see what the police turn up."

Several people made movements to leave, while offering their thanks to Mike and the professor for their input. As the group broke up, Reverend Maxwell made a point of walking out with tonight's guests. The three of them said good-night at the end of the walkway from Jon's house. Jeremiah followed behind the detective in the direction of Mike's car.

To Mike's retreating back, he said, "Detective Chance. May I speak with you a minute?"

Mike looked around and slowed his pace so the preacher could catch up.

"Sure, Reverend."

Coming up to Mike, Jeremiah said, "I'm afraid I haven't been completely open with the group about what I know of this whole business. But what you said about withholding relevant information from the police has me worried. You see, I knew this Crawford person and he told me about a document he had, one related to Thomas Jefferson."

Mike wasn't sure he wanted to learn more, but the cop in him perked up.

"I don't understand. Why didn't you share this with the group? And the police definitely would want to know."

"It's a long story and I'm not particularly proud of it. You see, I have this church. Well, not really a church, a rented space. We're looking to build a permanent building, a real church. Stanley Crawford said he would help. He attended my church even though most of my congregation is black. That happens now and then. Everyone is welcome. One day he asks to meet with me. I'm not sure what's going on, but we meet. Out of the blue he tells me he has an important historic artifact which could be worth a lot of money. He says that when he sells it he will give me money for my church. I know I'm not making myself very clear, but, yes, there is a document out there. I've seen it. I guess the police would want to know that."

"They certainly would," Mike answered. "You don't need to tell me, but you should tell the local police."

"I know, I know. I should have. But now I'm worried I may have waited too long and I'll be in deep doo doo with the police. Would you help me?"

"I'm not sure what I can do. It's very simple. Just go to the police and tell them what you know. They'll no doubt be happy you showed up. I can't believe they would fault you too much. The case is just getting going and they're concentrating on finding the murderer. You may be able to help with a motive."

"I'm sure you're right. But I'm still worried. Would you go with me?"

"Reverend, you don't need me."

"Since you said you know some of the local police I thought maybe you could get an appointment with one of them. Then maybe you could come, too. I don't want them thinking I had anything to do with Crawford's murder. You could vouch for me. Tell them I talked with you after listening to you discuss the case and telling me my duty."

"Look, Reverend, I'm sure you don't have anything to worry about. Just tell them what you told me."

"It isn't that simple," interrupted the preacher. "I was there the night Stanley was killed. Earlier, I mean. That's when I saw the document."

Mike immediately recognized that the minister's worries had some foundation. Being at the murder scene the same night would raise all sorts of questions from the police. He already began to think of a few.

"You see, I began to worry there really wasn't a document. I thought maybe Crawford was just stringing me along. So I insisted I wanted to see it."

"And that's why you went to his house?"

"Yes. He told me to come over last week. On Monday, around eight o'clock in the evening. Well, I did go, and he surprised me by saying he was meeting someone that same night. Someone who was interested in buying the letter. He said I couldn't stay long, but he showed me this letter. He wouldn't let me hold it. Said it was too fragile, almost ready to fall apart. But I did get a good look at it. Sort of yellow dirty paper and faded handwritten lines in what seemed a nice script."

"What did the letter say?" Mike interrupted, growing more interested in the minister's story.

"He read parts of it to me but I don't remember exactly the words. Something about Sal or maybe Sally, and Paris, and a promise Jefferson made. We didn't have time to talk more since Stanley said I needed to get going in case his buyer came early."

The reverend was right, Mike thought. It wasn't that simple. The police would want to talk with him at length about what he knew. And the fact that the preacher was at Crawford's house the night Crawford was killed made things even messier. Mike had hoped to come away from tonight's meeting without any further commitments. That clearly wasn't happening. The events of the last couple weeks appeared to be taking over the direction of his life. Maybe that was good. Get involved with something, both his sister and Dr. Rider had said. The preacher continued before Mike could respond.

"Meet me first thing in the morning at the police station downtown by the mall. Please. We can both go and I'll tell them everything I know. I'd really appreciate it. I'm pretty new to town. And face it, I'm black. Distrust of the police comes naturally. No offense, but they don't always treat us the same as whites."

The reverend successfully placed a burden on Mike that he couldn't simply let drop.

"Okay, I'll help if I can. I'll meet you at 9 a.m. in front of the police station. I'll call Sergeant Dixon tonight and see who she wants you to talk with. It will probably be one of the detectives on the case."

"God bless you. Until tomorrow then," the preacher said before walking away.

Chapter 15

Mike watched the preacher walk back to his car. Mulling over what the minister had revealed held him in place. He still hadn't moved when Jeremiah drove by in his bright beige Cadillac. As he turned toward his own car, his phone rang. Probably Kelly checking up on him, he thought, digging for it in his jacket pocket.

"Hey buddy! You still up?" his partner began. "Dixie's off duty tonight and asked me to have a drink with her. She said to invite you, too, if you want. I told her you may have gone to bed by now since you're on leisure time. But I said I'd check." Justice's smile came through the phone, softening the barb about Mike being on leave.

"No, I'm still up. In fact, I was just about to contact Dixie. I learned something of interest tonight that she'll want to know about. Where are you meeting?"

Mike found the bar on the pedestrian mall just a short step from the C'ville police headquarters. Justice and Dixie had already been served their first round of beers. They welcomed him to their table and Justice went to the bar to order a beer for his partner. Dixie took advantage of Justice's absence to start a conversation.

"I've been telling Justice what we've learned about the Crawford case. Mike, some of this still isn't ready for public consumption."

"No problem. I don't talk with many people around here. Even if I did, I wouldn't talk about an ongoing investigation."

Mike wondered if she had felt it necessary to obtain the same promise from Justice. But then he knew he was an outsider, in more ways than one.

If they only knew what kind of outsider I really am.

I'm outside. I'm outside myself and I can't get back in. Will I ever get back in? Who am I really?

Mike stared intently at Dixie's beer mug while they waited for Justice. After Justice sat down at the table and slid a beer toward his partner, Dixie continued to address Mike.

"I was telling Justice about some interesting facts that have come to light. Things that we need to sort out before releasing too much information. Again, I have to ask you guys . . ." She paused. "Well, I could get in trouble for talking about this."

Justice quickly spoke up. "Dixie, you can trust us. Both of us," he added, nodding in Mike's direction.

"I think it would help me to talk about it. I'm not part of the investigating team, but if I could come up with anything helpful to the case it would be a plus on my record. So let me tell you what I've been told by some team members. I would like to see if you have any insights. The two of you have lots of years of homicide experience."

"That's true for one of us," Mike said, looking toward his partner.

"We have the forensic unit's report, but the chief is sitting on it. There are too many unanswered questions at this stage. We don't want people to start second guessing us."

"I heard the results were delayed," Mike commented.

Dixie looked at him with eyebrows raised. Mike then explained how he knew. He ended with, "I also found out something that's relevant to Crawford's murder. We can talk about it later."

Justice, too, looked at Mike with a puzzled expression. Dixie hesitated before speaking again, clearly processing what Mike had just said.

"An autopsy was done and it looks like the gunshot wasn't fatal. In other words, Crawford didn't die from being shot, not immediately anyway. He bled to death. The bullet hit him in the groin area and severed an artery. There was a bruise on his head which initially suggested he was hit with something. However, the lab guys found skin and some hair on the corner of Crawford's desk. Given the position of the body it looks like he was on his way down when he hit his head."

"You mean after he was shot?" Justice asked, looking up from his beer.

"Yes. We think he was shot, then fell and hit his head on the desk falling down. The report raises one of the unanswered questions. Why did Crawford bleed to death if his wife found him soon after he was shot? She says she found him on the floor soon after she heard the car leave from the front of the house. Was he still alive and she didn't know it? A fire and rescue station is not far from the house. The EMTs got there within five minutes of her call. The medical examiner believes Crawford could have lived for fifteen or twenty minutes after he was shot. The sequence of events isn't adding up right." Dixie paused to sip her beer.

"The detectives went back this afternoon to talk to his wife. They've been looking again at the timing of the two 911 calls--the one from the witness to the accident involving the kids and the one from Crawford's wife. The driver who stopped in Court Square called 911 at 9:04. The call from Mrs. Crawford's came at 9:07. We should have heard from his wife before the car got to the square. The detectives originally assumed she must have been in shock and took longer to call than she realized. When they asked Mrs. Crawford about the timing she simply repeated that she called 911 after finding her husband."

"Perhaps she didn't go into her husband's room as soon as she reported," Justice suggested. "That would have given the driver more time to get away from the house."

"That may have been it," Dixie agreed. "But it's something that needs to be explained. And there's another odd piece to the puzzle.

"We know the bullet came from the gun found on the floor near Crawford's hand. His fingerprints are clearly on the gun, as are some smeared prints from someone else. His wife verified it belonged to her husband. The gun wasn't registered and looked old enough to be something Crawford brought back from his military service in Viet Nam. Mrs. Crawford told us she saw the gun only occasionally, when he cleaned it in the kitchen."

"So you're thinking the intruder didn't come with a gun," Mike wondered aloud.

"That's possible. We don't know, of course, what the intruder might have had. He could have had a gun. The point is, Crawford's own gun killed him. Apparently fired at close range. The team thinks Crawford had his gun out and there was a struggle for it. After being shot he fell and knocked himself out. Left on the floor, he eventually bled to death."

Dixie stopped talking briefly to drink her beer. Justice and Mike did the same while they waited to hear what else she had to tell them.

"Here's the odd piece. The crime scene folks found dirt on the floor, just inside the door. It matches dirt from a flower bed that crosses the backyard. Anyone approaching the house from the rear would have had to go through it. Sure enough, there were footprints in the flower bed. Going both ways! Of course the dirt and prints may have been from someone who visited Crawford earlier. Possibly even a day before. Maybe a neighbor. It's part of the puzzle the detectives are looking into.

"The team doesn't want to discount the possibility the killer walked across the backyard to get to the rear door, then ran back the same way. But Crawford's wife says she heard a car leave from in front of the house. The driveway leads from the front to the rear. Why would anyone walk through the backyard when their car was parked in front? Now people are wondering if maybe there was a second car parked on the side street nearby. From there, you can easily get to Crawford's rear office by crossing the flower bed. One of the detectives thinks there may have been two intruders. They could have worked together, coming up to the house from different directions.

"You ready for more?" Dixie asked, obviously moving to some sort of climax. Mike and Justice smiled at her dramatic emphasis. Both nodded.

"What's even more interesting is that when the lab guys were collecting dirt samples they found something else. One of the techs noticed a break in the boards under the desk. When he pulled up the floor boards he discovered a good-sized compartment. In it was a large metal box. The kind you see used by banks for safe deposit. It was locked and there was no key on Crawford, but they found one under the desk hanging on a nail beneath the top center drawer."

Dixie stopped once more to sip her beer. Both Mike and Justice decided the pause, besides quenching her thirst, aimed for additional dramatic effect.

"The box contained a number of old buttons, nails, some coins, pieces of old plates and cups, an old wine bottle. Among other things. There was a cleaning rag and bottle of gun oil, so Crawford must have kept his gun there as well. Looks like he was collecting historic artifacts, and we think we know where he got them."

"You mean the pottery and stuff?" Mike asked.

"Yes. I'm getting to that. Turns out there were two sets of fingerprints on the box. Crawford's and his wife's. We just got that information yesterday. Her prints weren't initially taken for examination. Not sure why. So the techs didn't have a match. Now we do. Anyway, when first interviewed, she told us she didn't know what her husband had in his room. Said she was only allowed in there once a week to clean. When the detectives showed her the strongbox, she said her husband never told her about it. But her fingerprints on the box clearly show she knew about it.

"Before they learned about the fingerprints the detectives had asked her if her husband collected historic artifacts, maybe stuff from Jefferson's time. You might remember that Elmer Houston, the guy who runs the artifacts store on the mall, told us Crawford had been into the store asking about prices of things. He said Crawford claimed to have a valuable letter or document. Mrs. Crawford admitted her husband did have some artifacts and kept them somewhere in his office. She didn't know where, maybe in one of the desk drawers or in a filing cabinet. These were always locked, she said. Seems like he'd show some of them to her now and then. But she claimed she knew nothing about any document."

"And you know where he got the artifacts?" Justice asked.

"We think so. Crawford worked security at Monticello for a number of years. Retired not that long ago. Beatrice, that's his wife, admitted that over the years her husband would bring home things he claimed he found on the mountain. She knew it was wrong and told him so. He dismissed her criticism by saying there was a lot of old stuff up there, more than those archeologists needed. Beatrice decided to avoid a fight, since they were only little things, like the buttons and coins we found in the box."

"How does the strongbox with her fingerprints fit into this picture?" Justice asked.

"That's part of the puzzle. As I said, the detectives were going out this afternoon to talk with her some more. Both about the strongbox and the timing of events. I was off-duty today and haven't learned yet what they found out. Like I said, I'm not on the investigating team. I have to wait until the information filters down."

"So it looks like he must have taken out his gun from the box and whatever else he had in there before the intruder came. And later put the box back under the floor boards," Mike offered. "Otherwise, how did the box get put back?" He paused, then attempted to answer his own question. "Maybe his wife put the box back when she came into the room and that's how her fingerprints got on it. That would also explain the delay in her call to 911. But why?"

"Obviously we don't know exactly what happened," Dixie said. "We also don't know why the intruder, or maybe intruders, was there. Did Crawford know him? Or her, I guess I should say. Was it an argument, for instance. A robbery gone wrong?

"Right now the investigating team is going with the idea that someone came in, maybe even someone Crawford knew. They struggled, the gun went off and the person fled. It's possible this person took whatever Crawford kept in the box. Maybe it was money. We can't rule out that the intruder knew about the box. But how did the box get back in its hiding place? There were only the two sets of prints. Like you said, Mike, maybe his wife put the box back when she discovered it open on the floor. Again, we don't know yet what Beatrice knew about the box or what she may have done with it the night of the murder. I should find out tomorrow when I hear the results of the detectives' interview. Obviously, Beatrice's fingerprints on the box means she knows more than she's telling."

Mike spoke up, realizing that the preacher's story just became very relevant to the inquiry.

"I think I can help you. I got some info tonight about

who was there and what might have been in the box."

Both Dixie and Justice immediately put down their beers, their eyes on Mike.

"As you said, Elmer Houston claims Crawford told him he possessed a Jeffersonian period artifact, a letter written by one of his slaves. It supposedly talks about Jefferson's affair with Sally Hemings."

"I heard Mr. Houston wasn't really sure the letter existed," Dixie interjected. "At least a real one. It could be Crawford was working some kind of scam. No one in the department is taking the letter idea too seriously. Like I told you, Mrs. Crawford said he collected some odds and ends. Not anything like what Houston told us about."

"Perhaps it should be taken seriously. I have a witness who can testify there really is such a letter," Mike said. "Crawford had it. He showed it to him."

The pair looked at Mike with increased interest. He sipped his beer before reporting on his meeting with the Jefferson Bunch. As best he could, he described the members of the Bunch, then described how the group initially heard about the document and how they wanted to begin an investigation.

"Professor McCabe said the group knew someone who would cover their expenses if they did investigate. Well, at least one of them, a woman I met tonight. Her name is Andrea Hudson. Works for some political consulting firm, McCabe told me. She apparently knows someone who's interested enough in the document to help finance a search for it. The point is, the group was pretty serious about this. That's why Professor McCabe asked me to come to the meeting tonight--to talk them out of the whole investigation thing. I hope I did."

"And you heard about the document at the meeting?" Dixie asked.

"Not exactly. After the meeting one of the group, a

local preacher, one of the regular group members, tells me he knew Crawford. And that he saw the letter. This happened the same night Crawford was killed. And get this, the minister said Crawford expected a buyer for the letter later that night."

"Wow," exclaimed Dixie, who just found a treasure trove of relevant information falling into her lap.

"The minister wants to make a statement. First name Jeremiah. I'm not sure of his last name. I'm supposed to meet him tomorrow morning in front of the police station and help support his story. I told him I'd talk to the police, which I guess I'm doing now. I need to see who wants to take his statement."

Dixie, clearly happy with the information gained from the evening's discussion, said, "I'll talk to Miles Springer. He's the lead detective on the team. I can find out who he wants there when you meet this minister. I'll call you in the morning. Thanks. You've been a great help, Mike."

Her comment didn't make him feel any less an outsider. Nevertheless, Mike appreciated the comment.

The threesome downed what was left of their beers. Dixie thanked them once more for their input. Outside, Mike and Justice waved good-night to Dixie as they walked in the opposite direction toward their cars. Justice said he planned to drive back to the District in the morning now that his aunt's funeral was over and the estate matters settled.

"I don't want to just quit the department," Justice explained. "They're still having personnel problems that began before you came on board. Me leaving right now may not go over too well. But I'm serious about retiring. Well, maybe 'quitting' is the right word, but I want to talk with the captain about the best way to do this."

Once again, Mike felt his overall mood improve when he heard Justice might actually be settling in the area on a permanent basis.

As they parted, Justice added, "I'm looking forward to no more bloody messes. Let people like Dixie take care of them. She's still young, and from what we saw tonight, determined to move up the ranks."

Chapter 16

The whole day had spun out of Bob's control. Jimmy's behavior at the Crawford house freaked him out at first. He yelled at Jimmy as they climbed into the truck, but got no response except giggles. He resigned himself to the fact that no one got hurt. Plus, they were pretty sure the widow didn't have what they were looking for. Between periods of giggles and pounding on the steering wheel, Jimmy pointed out that his threat would keep her from talking. She'll keep the whole thing between herself and that god-woman, Jimmy said.

After leaving the house, the two men stopped at a tavern for lunch and spent a couple of hours drinking beer and playing pool on a table at the rear of the restaurant. Later, Jimmy suggested they buy some chips and a couple six packs, then park by the river where they would wait until dark. At that time they'd make a visit to the minister.

After more drinking, both fell asleep in the truck. It wasn't until sometime after eight o'clock that they drove to the preacher's storefront church. Driving slowly past, they didn't see any lights, nor any sign of a car.

"We'll just wait," Jimmy said, "but first I need more beer."

Since Jimmy was at the wheel, Bob didn't have much say in the matter. They drove back to a carry-out tavern they had passed earlier. Jimmy went in and brought back two six packs of something Bob didn't recognize. Usually they drank from cans, one of the national brands they knew were American-brewed. And because they were cheap. Bob had tried some local draft brews when he made the rounds of C'ville bars seeking information about the mystery caller, but these cost too much for his budget, so he usually opted for a Miller or Bud.

"The bar man suggested we should try this stuff," Jimmy said. "Got some kind of weird name. Look at the dude on the bottle," holding a bottle up for Bob to see. "He told me once you taste a beer with flavor, you won't want to go back to the big-brewery stuff. It comes from a microbrewery. Whatever the hell that means. They don't do cans, but it ain't a foreign beer. Comes from Oregon, he told me." Bob didn't recognize the label and didn't want to know how much it cost. Jimmy was on a roll.

They parked the truck a half block down from where the minister held services. From their vantage point on the opposite side of the street, they had a clear view of the driveway going to the back of the building. Jimmy opened a couple of his newly discovered beers and handed one to Bob. The pair sank down in the seat to wait for the minister. After only a few minutes Jimmy got impatient and insisted on taking a look around.

"Maybe he came in when we were getting beer. His car could be in back. What if he's been there all this time and we're waiting out here for nothin."

Jimmy started to open the truck door.

After today's earlier events, Bob definitely wanted Jimmy to remain in the truck. He quickly put down his beer and told Jimmy to wait, that he'd go and take a look. The beers were catching up to Jimmy and he was still fumbling with the door handle when Bob jumped out and walked toward the storefront.

On a banner above the front door, in large red letters, were the words "Glory Road Church." Beneath that, "Travel Glory Road to Jesus." Bob kept to the shadows as he sneaked slowly around to the rear.

In back, Bob saw what looked like a small apartment with a door to a parking area, but no car. Once again he imagined himself a private detective on the job. He retraced his steps and reported the results of his reconnaissance to Jimmy. The two of them slouched down again in the front seat of the truck and settled into drinking.

Around ten o'clock, a car came down the street and turned into the church driveway, then passed out of sight. The beer had run out and they would have missed the minister's arrival if they had gone back to get more beer and some food, as Jimmy had wanted, an idea Bob had nixed. They had drunk enough, Bob insisted. If he didn't have to pee so bad he would have fallen asleep. Jimmy seemed to have no trouble continuing to drink. Maybe because he had already peed twice on the sidewalk beside the truck. Or perhaps because he had slipped a pill or two into his mouth while Bob wasn't looking.

When the car disappeared around back, Jimmy opened the door and got out.

"No! Damn it," Bob called out, in a voice loud enough to get Jimmy's attention, but hopefully not loud enough for anyone in the nearby houses to hear.

"Look, you stay here. And this time I really mean it."

Bob's words came too late. Jimmy headed for the church building, leaving Bob no choice but to follow.

The Reverend Jeremiah Maxwell opened the rear door following Jimmy's loud pounding.

"Preacher, we're here to be saved!" Jimmy exclaimed. He then pushed the door open, sending Jeremiah backpedaling into the small room that served as his kitchen, bedroom, living area, and church office.

"Who are you?" demanded the irate minister in his deep voice, while working to regain his balance.

Jimmy didn't reply and strolled into the room with an ugly smirk on his face.

"Get out! You've got no business here!" the preacher declared, just as loudly as before.

If Jeremiah hadn't started yelling at them, mainly at

Jimmy, if they hadn't drunk way too many beers, and if Bob hadn't stood frozen on the door step, things might not have gone so badly.

Jimmy didn't like being yelled at--whether by hopelessly irresponsible parents, well-intentioned teachers, or cops doing their duty. Least of all by black people. There are people on the lower rungs of society, as Jimmy saw himself, who look for someone on yet a lower rung. Jimmy long ago decided that included anyone who wasn't white.

The preacher shouted "get out" for the third or fourth time, but Jimmy didn't retreat. Bob remained immobilized. He watched as his buddy pulled a knife from his camouflage pants pocket. Jimmy pressed the button snapping out the blade and walked menacingly toward Jeremiah, waving the knife in front of him.

"Just shut up. You have something we want." Always to the point, that Jimmy.

"I can't imagine what your kind would want from me. Except money. And I don't have any. Take the car if you like. I'll give you the keys. Just get out of here."

Being ordered around was another thing that put Jimmy on edge. Before Bob could react, Jimmy slashed out at the preacher, catching his arm with the sharp blade when Jeremiah raised it to defend himself.

"Oops! Your arm got in my way!" Jimmy said, grinning.

Jeremiah grabbed at his bleeding arm and turned away, moving quickly toward a door at the back of the room. But not quickly enough. Jimmy ran after him and pushed him hard from behind. Jeremiah fell forward onto his stomach, still trying to protect his injured arm. With knife in hand, Jimmy put his knee on the minister's back.

"Perhaps you didn't hear me. I said you have something we want. Now where is it?"

"I don't know what you're talking about," Jeremiah cried out, twisting his neck so he could speak.

"Hold up," Bob shouted, finally moving into action. He walked hesitantly toward the pair on the floor.

"Slow down. Let the preacher talk. Get off him. We don't know he has the letter."

Jimmy didn't get off the preacher. Instead, he rested the tip of the knife on Jeremiah's neck, pushing down hard enough to draw blood.

"My partner's got more patience than I have. Tell us where that letter is. The one that talks about the black whore and the president."

Jeremiah assumed from the first moment the men forced their way into his apartment that he was being robbed. When the one coming across the room mentioned a letter, he immediately came to a different realization, now confirmed by the man kneeling on his back.

"I don't have it. You must know that Stanley Crawford had it. No one knows where it is now."

"Jimmy! Enough!" Bob screamed, not exactly certain what to do.

"You're lying, nigger. Ministers aren't supposed to lie," Jimmy said, ignoring Bob. "You've got exactly ten seconds to tell us where it is."

"Crawford had it," Jeremiah said desperately, his face pressed against the tile floor. "Talk to his widow."

Bob moved toward Jimmy with the goal of pulling him off the minister, but he didn't move fast enough.

"Then I guess you can't help us," Jimmy said with gritted teeth as he pushed the knife into Jeremiah. Bob watched blood spurt from the preacher's neck. He then peed in his pants.

"Shit. Shit. Shit," he yelled. "Look what you've done. You didn't have to do that. What are we going to do now?"

Jimmy got off the preacher, who was moaning, his face on the floor in a pool of blood, his body twitching.

"What we're going to do is get out of here. But not before we search this place. I want to make sure he wasn't lying. Even if he doesn't have the letter, he might have something worth taking."

Bob found enough courage to approach the minister. He knelt down to look at the wound, not really knowing why since he didn't know a thing about first aid. Somehow calling 911 didn't seem a good option. The preacher had stopped making any noise and lay very still. Even in Bob's mixed-up state of mind, he could see that the preacher was beyond help.

"Shit, shit, shit," he repeated again as he stood up, his eyes still on the body in front of him, tears forming.

Jimmy was ripping up the place. Books flew off shelves and the contents of drawers spilled onto the floor. Bob moved away from the minister toward the door.

"I'm getting out of here," he said angrily and raced out the door.

Bob got back into the truck and sat motionless, staring at a streetlight down the block. Jimmy soon opened the driver's side door and slid in beside him.

"He shouldn't have yelled at me," Jimmy offered in way of explanation. "I didn't find anything. Maybe he was telling the truth. Guess we won't find out now," Jimmy concluded with a shrug. He reached for the envelope with the pills.

"My stomach's really bothering me."

Bob didn't say a word on the drive to Richmond. He sat trembling, the odor of his own urine drifting up to him. Jimmy, quiet at first, soon turned on the radio and sang along to country-western songs, even when he didn't recognize the tune. Bob didn't even think to make sure Jimmy stayed within the speed limit.

They pulled into Trina's driveway a little before midnight, the radio still blaring. A light came on in the house as Jimmy stopped the truck, the motor running. Bob sat still, not uttering a sound until Jimmy said something about "mission accomplished." Then Bob started yelling.

"You screwed up everything. You didn't need to kill him."

The pair started arguing back and forth about the day's events. It came out that Jimmy had been laid off his job the day before, which Bob decided must have fueled his anger toward the black minister. Jimmy insisted no one could trace them. They were no worse off than when they started. Even better, Jimmy added, since they knew neither of these people had what they were looking for.

While they were screaming back and forth, a police cruiser pulled in behind the truck. Flashing lights bouncing off the truck's interior grabbed their attention. They stopped yelling, neither of them moved, eyes straight ahead.

After a few moments, Bob turned to look behind them and said his favorite word of the day, "Shit."

Jimmy checked the rear-view mirror and muttered something that sounded to Bob like, "Not me." At that point Jimmy reached under the front seat and pulled out a gun.

Having entered the license number of the truck into their on-board computer, the officers knew the registered owner was James Cooke and there were no outstanding warrants. The officer in the passenger seat notified the dispatcher they were leaving their vehicle. As the cops were about to do that, all hell broke loose.

Bob stared at Jimmy's gun and did the smartest thing he did all day. He opened the truck door and jumped out, rolling on the ground away from the truck.

Jimmy threw the truck into reverse, hit the gas pedal and smashed the truck's bed into the front of the patrol car. He then shifted forward and swung to the left, beginning a U-turn out of the driveway. In the process he crossed a flower garden and accelerated through a neighbor's yard. Dirt and rocks spewed in the air from behind the truck's wheels. From his position on the ground, Bob saw Jimmy stick his gun out of the driver's window.

The two police officers quickly recovered from the jolt and drew their guns while exiting the car. The officer on the driver's side used the car door to partially shield himself, just as Jimmy started firing. The truck careened through hedges, Jimmy's arm bouncing up and down. He pulled the trigger multiple times, aiming in the general direction of the officers. And, given where he laid on the ground next to the driveway, at Bob, who buried his face in the grass with his hands over his head. Since Jimmy wasn't left-handed, and with the truck traveling erratically, what happened next would seem to defy odds. One of Jimmy's bullets found its mark.

Bob heard the officer on the driver's side cry, "I'm hit."

He then heard more gunshots, this time much closer. Bob turned his head to see the officer closest to him firing his gun across the cruiser's roof. Then everything got quiet, soon interrupted by the sound of a loud crash. Jimmy must have run into something, he thought, but he didn't move from the prone position on his sister's lawn.

Jimmy's truck had slammed into a tree across the road. The collision might have knocked Jimmy unconscious or even killed him. That is, if he hadn't already been dead from a bullet to his head.

The officer turned his gun on Bob, who cowered on the ground less than twenty feet away. Quivering in the grass, Bob must have looked harmless enough.

"Don't move," the officer ordered, then radioed their

location, reporting shots fired and an officer down. The cop ran around to the other side of the car to check on his partner, who sat leaning against the squad car, holding his hand over the bleeding wound in his calf. The officer who was unhurt told his partner to hang on, then looked over the hood of the car at Bob, gun pointed in his direction. He yelled again, "Don't move!"

When the officer bent over to help his partner, Bob jumped up and raced toward the back of his sister's house. The officer looked up to see Bob running away and fired several shots in Bob's direction. Bob darted around some bushes and trees, eventually arriving unscathed at the back door of the house.

Trina had been wakened by the truck pulling into the driveway and went into the living room to see who it was. She recognized Jimmy's truck and could see Jimmy and her brother arguing in the front seat. That in itself wasn't unusual. From past experience, Trina knew that most anything could happen when Bob and Jimmy got together. She also knew enough to let their argument run its course.

Watching from the window, she witnessed the police car pull in behind the truck and the subsequent disastrous sequence of events. When the shooting started, she became terrified the bullets would hit her and she ducked beneath the window. When the noise outside ceased the first time, she peeked out. She saw Bob get up from the ground and run to the rear of the house while the police officer fired his gun in Bob's direction. Trina ran to open the back door, screaming as her brother stumbled in.

"What have you done?"

Bob ran past her into the spare bedroom and threw himself on the bed.

Within minutes, additional police cars appeared in front of the house. One jolted to a stop behind the cruiser in the driveway. Others pulled directly onto the lawn. Police officers jumped out, protecting themselves behind car doors, guns pointed either at the house or at Jimmy's truck. It didn't take long for the cops to realize there was no need to point their guns in the direction of the truck. Jimmy wouldn't be contributing anything more to the action.

All attention turned toward the house. Two policemen worked their way cautiously to a position where they could see the back of the house. A senior officer arrived with an ambulance trailing close behind. Several officers helped the wounded cop into the ambulance. Others kept their firearms aimed toward the front of the house, now brightly lit with numerous lights from the police vehicles.

Having been briefed by the wounded officer's partner and handed a bullhorn, the commanding officer spoke loudly the time-worn, melodramatic, but necessary words.

"The house is surrounded. Everyone in the house must come out." Silence. "Come out slowly with your hands raised. Do not make any sudden moves. Come out the front door." Silence. "This is your last . . ."

Trina didn't need to hear anymore. She nudged open the front door and cried out, "Don't shoot."

The officers' guns targeted her as she stepped onto the porch. With hands held high she stumbled down the porch stairs. When she lowered one of her hands to shade her eyes, the commanding officer ordered her to put her hand back up and get down on the ground.

"Crawl toward us," he yelled into the bullhorn.

She quickly dropped to the ground. When Trina approached the closest parked vehicle on her hands and knees, two cops in bulletproof vests bolted out and dragged her to the rear of the circle of cars.

The police commander trotted in her direction, bent

over, keeping low behind the parked cars. In tears, gasping for breath, Trina told him she didn't know what was going on. Her brother was the only one in the house. He ran in and threw himself on the bed. He doesn't have a gun, she said. The senior officer picked up the bullhorn again. For the next fifteen minutes he attempted to coax Bob from the house. He also asked Trina to try. But Bob didn't emerge.

A SWAT team arrived to bring the evening's activities to an end. Members of the unit quickly dispersed to positions near the front and rear entrances. In military fashion they charged into both sides of the house simultaneously, breaking down the doors as they went in. They found Bob just as his sister described, lying on his bed, face down in the pillows, shaking and sobbing.

The police took Bob, not too gently, to headquarters. He was booked and taken to a cell. With multiple shots fired, a wounded officer, as well as a dead local boy, Bob became not just C'ville's, but also Richmond's, person of interest.

The Richmond police didn't talk to Bob until the next morning. It took several hours to close off the crime scene, get written reports from the officer who did the shooting, notify the wounded officer's family, find a wrecker to remove the truck from the tree, and take Jimmy Cooke's body to the morgue. Trina was taken to the police station, interviewed, and then allowed to go home, but warned not to leave town. The police told her someone would be by to talk to her after they interviewed her brother.

There was no way Bob could fall asleep in his cell. He replayed over and over in his mind the series of events leading to jail. The police obviously had followed him and Jimmy from C'ville. Someone must have seen them run from the back of the church, found the minister dead and called the cops. They probably identified the truck somewhere on I-64 when Jimmy drove to Richmond. Jimmy. Shit. He should have known better than to involve him. Jimmy had changed. He wasn't just the simple nut case he had been when they were in high school together.

Bob decided the best thing would be to tell the truth about their visit to the church. It wasn't his knife. He didn't kill anyone. He started to pull Jimmy off the minister, but he got there too late. By now, the police must have found Jimmy's knife and would see the blood on it. They'd know Jimmy did it. They'll believe me, Bob figured. Only a crazy person would go shooting at cops. Jimmy's the crazy one. They'll see that. One of the officers saw him on the ground. Shit, he shot at me. Are they allowed to do that? The cop would tell everyone that he had nothing to do with the shooting at his sister's house.

Bob wasn't sure if the officer who Jimmy shot was still alive. He'd been taken away by ambulance when Bob was in the house and no one said anything to him about the officer's condition. Although he could tell the cops were really mad about the whole thing. The cop could be dead. Another reason to cooperate with the police.

On Saturday morning two police officers came to Bob's cell, handcuffed him, and escorted him to an interview room where two detectives sat at a small table. Neither detective said a word. One nodded toward the only other chair.

Bob had rehearsed his story. Tired as he was, he was determined to make them understand the whole thing had been Jimmy's doing. Scare the minister maybe, but not kill him. The police had to understand that Jimmy did it. And Jimmy shot the cop as he tried to get away. Why else would he do that if he wasn't the one who killed the minister?

The detective-in-charge sat back and played with a

pencil while the other detective turned on a tape recorder. He spoke loudly the date and time, that Detectives Bailey and McDermott were present, along with the prisoner, Robert Smith. The officer read Bob his rights and asked whether he wanted an attorney present. As many cop shows as Bob had watched, he had forgotten this procedure. Plus, it never seemed to come up in the old black-and-white, private-eye movies he liked. Now he wasn't sure what to do. Simply clam up and tell them he wanted a lawyer? But could he afford one? They'd have to give him one. He'd seen that happen on TV lots of times.

While Bob considered his options, the detective next to the tape recorder repeated, "We need you to respond. For the record, do you want an attorney present? Simply say yes or no loud enough for the tape recorder."

Let's wait and see where this leads, Bob thought. He should get credit for helping out. Cops always promised that on TV. He could always stop talking and ask for a lawyer later.

"No," he said in the direction of the tape recorder.

The only detective to speak thus far continued. "I'm Detective Bailey. As you can imagine, you're in a lot of trouble. Your friend Jimmy Cooke tried to kill two of our officers. He wounded one. A bullet smashed his shin bone. It's lucky they both weren't killed. You were there, so we have to think you knew what was coming down. Otherwise, why did you run?"

Bob opened his mouth to explain, but the detective held up his hand for him to be quiet.

"Let's start with your friend who was killed. What can you tell us about Cooke? We know from the officer's report that you didn't do any shooting. We need you to help us understand why Cooke fired at the officers. It seems out of character. It isn't as if Jimmy Cooke's a stranger. We've seen Jimmy before. He's been a troublemaker for some time, but nothing like this. Disturbing the peace. Resisting arrest. Assault. Some pot. That's our Jimmy. On the other hand, we found some bennies in an envelope in the truck. That's something new for Jimmy."

"Bennies?"

"Speed. Lightning. Snap. Uppers. You know what we're talking about."

"Jimmy was taking something for his stomach."

"It isn't for your stomach. They're stimulants. To get high. What planet do you live on!"

Bob looked dumbfounded, and was. The detectives looked incredulously at him.

"We think Jimmy must have done something else, not just the drugs, to make him afraid of the police. Why was Jimmy so scared that he started shooting at the officers?"

Putting down his pencil, Detective McDermott, quiet until now, spoke up.

"There's a list of charges against you being prepared right now. Illegal drugs may be the least of your worries. How long that list gets just may depend on how much you help us."

Fatigue made it difficult for Bob to comprehend exactly what was going on. It seemed as if the police didn't know where he and Jimmy had been. Were they playing with him? Didn't they know about the minister? No one mentioned a murder. However, he clearly heard the detective say something about a list of charges. And he had asked for Bob's help.

"I'm not sure why Jimmy started shooting," Bob ventured, but his mind still on the pills he saw Jimmy take. "I'm glad to help. Jimmy went nuts. We'd been out drinking."

"Where were the two of you before going to your sister's?" McDermott asked.

"In Charlottesville. We picked up some beer and went to a park and sat around drinking."

"Why Charlottesville? Why not just hang around here?"

Bob recognized he might not have answers for all their questions.

"I live in Charlottesville," Bob said. "Jimmy came over to drive me to my sister's. My car's out of commission."

Bob's goal had been to make sure the police saw him as an innocent bystander to Jimmy's attack on the minister, but if the cops didn't know about that, he sure wasn't going to tell them. Maybe the police hadn't really followed them from C'ville. Maybe the situation wasn't as bad as he feared.

The questioning continued and Bob found himself succeeding in withholding information about last evening's earlier events. He kept repeating that he didn't know why Jimmy started shooting, other than Jimmy had been drinking and was a loose cannon anyway. Yes, he saw Jimmy taking something, but Jimmy claimed the pills were for his stomach. Bob swore he never did drugs.

On the other hand, he wasn't sure the detectives believed his story. More than once they showed their frustration at his evasive answers. Finally, Detective McDermott indicated to his partner to turn off the recorder. Before he did, he announced the time and that they were terminating the interview.

When the detectives got up to leave, Bob at last learned why the cops drove in behind them at Trina's house. McDermott looked at him, expressionless.

"You know why the officers were there, don't you?"

Bob looked back with an equally blank face. The detective knew ignorance when he saw it.

"Your friend's back taillight was out. It was a routine traffic stop. A police officer is shot because of a damn tail light! Something's not right and we think you know what it is. The Charlottesville police want to talk to you. No one was looking for Jimmy Cooke, but it seems the C'ville police are looking for you."

Bob couldn't figure out what the detective meant. Had the widow called the police even after they scared her? But how would she know who he was? Maybe she saw the license on the truck and reported it. But then it would be in Jimmy's name, not his. A glimmer of understanding crept into Bob's tired brain.

"The Charlottesville police think you fled the scene of an accident in which some kids got hurt. And from what we've heard, there's more. They think you also may have something to do with the murder of a man named Stanley Crawford. Does that name ring a bell? So we don't believe you're telling us everything we need to know. Someone from Charlottesville is coming later this morning to talk to you."

Shit, thought Bob.

Chapter 17

Saturday morning, a short time before the Richmond police began questioning Bob Smith about the shooting at his sister's house, Kelly Cummings got dressed and headed downstairs to brew coffee and prepare breakfast. Tammy would sleep for another hour or two. Steve soon arrived in the kitchen to grab some coffee on his way outside to clean up a tree limb that had fallen earlier in the week. Kelly had just sat down with a cup of coffee and the local newspaper when her brother came into the kitchen.

"You're up early. I thought I heard you get in pretty late last night," she said.

"Sorry if I woke you. The meeting with that Jefferson group lasted a while and then Justice and I went for a beer downtown."

"I wasn't checking up on you," she added quickly, realizing that she was, and failing to conceal it.

"It's okay. I got more than I bargained for at the meeting. There was someone there, a minister actually, who has some information about the Crawford case. He's African American. Doesn't want to go to the police by himself since he's worried they'll suspect him. Anyway, I'm sure he didn't kill anyone. I told him I'd set up an appointment with the locals and be there when he shows up. We're supposed to meet at the police station at nine this morning. I'm waiting for a call from Dixie, Officer Dixon, who'll tell me whom we're to meet."

"I have to say, Mike, I'm glad you're getting involved. I'm sure everyone will appreciate your help."

"I doubt if I can be much help, but I admit it does feel better to be with cops again. Dixie was with Justice and me last night and brought us up to date on the investigation. It felt good to be included. Especially since I'm an outsider to all of it."

Kelly started to reply when the phone rang.

"No doubt for you," she laughed, reaching over to the counter for the phone and handing it to him. She got up from the table to prepare breakfast.

After Mike finished talking to Dixie, Kelly asked him if he had time for eggs and toast with her and Steve. He declined, quickly finished his cup of coffee, and rose from the table.

"A Detective Springer is going to meet me a little before nine in front of the police station. I'll check back in later."

Mike knew his feelings of depersonalization often were worse in the mornings, but today seemed different, better than usual. The haze, like a coastal morning fog, didn't seem as thick. Nevertheless, still not always sure of himself behind the wheel, he drove carefully toward the historic pedestrian mall.

When he walked out of the parking garage, Mike immediately spotted Dixie standing in front of the police station. She stood a few steps away from a man talking on a cellphone, whom Mike presumed to be Detective Springer. People passed by them on their way to and from the weekly farmer's market held one street over. A September sun and cooler temperatures recently replaced the hot and humid days of the Piedmont summer.

"Hi Mike," she said cheerfully as he approached. "I'm on patrol in a few minutes, but wanted to introduce you to Detective Springer. As I told you, he's in charge of the Crawford case. I think you'll find him in a good mood. There's been a break in the case."

As if on cue, Springer finished his call, slipped his phone onto his belt and turned to meet Mike. The detective extended his hand.

"I'm Miles Springer. The sergeant told me about you. D.C. cop on leave, right?"

Mike nodded as they shook hands.

"And about this minister who has some information about Crawford and a document the victim might have had." Looking at Dixie, "Did you tell him we may have our man on ice in Richmond?"

Mike immediately wondered whether Dixie had withheld information last night.

"I just found out this morning, Mike. I'll let Detective Springer explain. I've got to get moving. Talk to you later."

"Now that I think of it, she was off duty yesterday when we learned a car matching the description of the one we were looking for was found torched near Richmond. The registered owner lives here in town. Someone who was on our list of people to interview about the accident in Court Square. His car meets the description given by witnesses. I understand your niece was one of those hurt. Is she all right?"

"Yes, thanks. She's doing fine. Had some bruises and a banged-up ankle. I assume this is the same person who might be involved in the Crawford murder."

"It is. His name's Robert Smith." The detective said the name quietly as people moved passed them.

"Let's move out of the way while we wait for the minister."

Mike followed the detective, who headed away from the pedestrian traffic. They stopped in an open area next to the police station. Mike looked up and down the street, hoping to catch a glimpse of Jeremiah.

"We don't have all the details yet," Springer continued, "but there was some kind of blowup over in Richmond last night and a police officer was wounded. Smith and a buddy of his apparently tried to get away from officers during a routine traffic stop. Smith's friend was shot by one of the officers. That was the Richmond police chief on the phone when you came up. I'm going to send some detectives this morning to talk with Smith. We think this Smith is the one who killed Stanley Crawford. The timing makes sense and the same kind of car was seen driving away from the Crawford residence. We're sure he hit the kids just a few minutes later. We just may be able to get a handle on exactly what happened."

"Well, that's great."

"Yes, but there's also a new wrinkle."

To Mike's surprise, Detective Springer immediately began to fill him in on recent developments. Mike knew what it was like when pieces of an investigation weren't fitting together as they should. It brought on a tendency to start talking to most anyone about the case--both to hear your own thoughts spoken aloud and to give other people an opportunity to question your thinking.

"I don't know how much Sergeant Dixon has told you, but we've run across a couple of surprises. It turns out Crawford had a strongbox hidden under some floorboards beneath his desk. Something we haven't told the press about. When we first asked Mrs. Crawford about the box, she said she didn't know about anything her husband kept in his office. She said over and over again she wasn't allowed in there except to clean once a week. And usually only when her husband watched. We initially had the impression his wife knew nothing about this box. However, I have to admit that looking back over my notes, I'm not sure she ever flat out denied knowing about the box. Then, and here's the kicker, we discovered her fingerprints on it."

"Is there a reason she lied?" Mike asked.

"There is. Yesterday afternoon my partner and I talked with her some more. We asked her again if her husband kept anything of value, something he might have kept hidden in his office. We brought up again the possibility of a valuable document or maybe money. She repeated that she wouldn't know about anything like that. In fact, she was quite adamant about it. Started to cry. We weren't sure what brought on all the emotion. Maybe because we caught her in a lie. But we also wondered if there was something else going on we didn't know about. It's only been about ten days since her husband died.

"We explained we found her fingerprints on the strongbox. Told her we wanted to know, if she didn't know what he kept in the office, how her fingerprints got on the box. I reminded her that she told us repeatedly she knew nothing of her husband's affairs. After we mentioned the prints, she just sat there for a while. Didn't say a word. As I said, practically in tears."

"Sounds like you had her cornered," Mike commented, looking again for some sign of the minister. Detective Springer didn't appear to notice Mike's behavior.

"We did. To help her with a way out we even suggested she might accidentally have found the box when she was cleaning. Maybe when her husband was out of the house. She didn't know what to say. Some sidetracking followed before she admitted she found the hidden storage compartment when she was cleaning the floor on her hands and knees. She also found the key under the desk. I have a hunch she went looking for the key after she spotted the box. Anyway, once she found the key, she said she knew she shouldn't, but couldn't help it. Looking in it, that is.

"She claimed that was the only time she opened it." Springer paused. He also looked for anyone approaching them before continuing.

"Well, that is until the night her husband was killed. Now get this. When she heard the noise from a car outside, she says she went to her husband's office and found him dead on the floor. This was right after her TV show ended at nine o'clock. All this was reported by the news media. However, what wasn't known, what we didn't know, was what she did next. After entering the room, the first thing she did was locate the box and remove some things she didn't want anybody to see. She wouldn't tell us what these were. Only that it had nothing to do with what happened. She clearly didn't want to tell us what her husband kept there."

Mike watched people walking in their direction. He wondered if nine o'clock had been the agreed-upon time. Detective Springer seemed more interested in completing his account of the widow's interview.

"We went round and round about what was in the box. We assumed she knew her husband kept something valuable in the box and that she wasn't willing to tell us what it was. She insisted over and over again that this wasn't the case, but she still wouldn't tell us what she removed. I actually began to believe her, that it really had nothing to do with the case. She started crying again. Then it hit us. Well, my partner guessed it first. He figured Crawford must have kept porn in there. He asked her if her husband kept girly stuff in the box, like magazines or videos. He actually said 'girly.'"

Springer chuckled. Mike also smiled. Not a word he ever used when talking about porn in the District.

"She didn't know what to say," Springer said, "but you could tell from her look that we guessed right. Eventually she admitted it. Said he kept pictures of sinful women in the box. She claimed it upset her when she first found this stuff. Didn't know what to do. She couldn't just take it since her husband would know she found the box. But she also knew she didn't want the box's contents in the house. Mind you, this was maybe six months ago that she found the box. She couldn't get it off her mind. So, the night he was killed, before she called us, with her husband bleeding on the floor, she took the sex stuff out and put it in the kitchen garbage container. Not satisfied, she took the kitchen garbage and dumped it in the waste can outside. It's in the landfill by now. Can you believe it?"

"People do crazy things," Mike offered, not knowing what else to say, and not wanting to interrupt before he heard the whole story from the detective. His unease grew over the preacher's failure to appear.

"Ever since the day she found the porn, she had been plotting how to get it out of her house. The sad thing is, Mike, the medical people say Crawford likely wasn't dead when she came into his office. His wife may have thought he was dead, but he might have bled to death because she delayed calling for help. So we know why her 911 call didn't come in until 9:07, when she claimed she found him just after nine o'clock. Those five or six minutes might have made a difference. If she had called 911 immediately, maybe he'd still be alive!"

"Some folks have strange priorities," Mike commented, not thinking of what else to say.

Now both men looked up and down the street. Mike checked his watch. It was already 9:20.

"Looks like your guy isn't going to show. We really do need to talk to him. I understand he knew Crawford and can help us know more about this letter everyone is talking about. Something to do with Jefferson and his slave, right? I have to say we haven't taken it too seriously. And his wife, if we can believe her, knows nothing about such a document."

"Yes, it's possible he can help establish a motive for the killing. I would have sworn he really wanted to come," Mike said, still searching the street.

"Maybe some church matters came up," Springer suggested. "I have an idea. Sergeant Dixon just went on patrol. She said she knows where his church is. Let me give her a call and ask her to swing by and see what's up. Come in the station for a cup of coffee while we wait. I'll give the message to the dispatcher."

Mike followed Springer into the station. The detective said he'd be right back and left him standing next to a wall with pictures of police officers who had earned various awards. Mike saw Dixie received one for marksmanship last year.

Something felt wrong. He had thought he wanted to be back on the job. Here he was, back with cops. Okay, not his department, but with fellow police officers. Still, it didn't feel right. Why? Why was he here? No matter what, he would always be an outsider. His anxiety level increased. Everything seemed unreal.

Is this really me, Detective Mike Chance? I don't really belong here. Where do I belong? I'm outside looking in.

When Springer returned from somewhere down the hall, he handed Mike one of the two paper cups he was holding.

"Sorry, I forgot to ask if you wanted anything in it."

"No, nothing. Black's fine. Thanks."

"Let's go in my office. I'm sure Dixon will report back in a few minutes. Charlottesville's a fairly small town. You can get anywhere in ten minutes. Unless it's rush hour, of course. Then we've got big city traffic."

The detective looked carefully at Mike.

"You okay? You seem a little white in the face."

Mike fought through the haze. "Just need some caffeine, thanks."

As they sat down with their coffee the dispatcher stuck his head in the office, started to say something to Springer, saw Mike, then paused before giving his message.

"We just heard from Sergeant Dixon. She's at a

church or building of some sort and something's wrong. You'd better come talk to her."

"I'll be right back," Springer said to Mike, putting down his coffee and hurrying out the door.

Mike didn't have to be a cop to know when things were going south. He looked at his coffee and concentrated on its aroma. It wasn't long before the detective returned.

"Apparently we've got another killing," Springer announced, standing at the office door, his hand gripping the door frame.

"Dixon found what appears to be your minister's body. I'm sending backup, as well as the forensic unit. I have to be on my way, too."

Mike must have looked like he wanted more since Springer said somewhat apologetically, "You'd probably like to go, too. Sorry. You can appreciate the rules. Go on home and I'll give you a call as soon as we find out what happened. And I'm sure I don't need to say it, but, please keep what we talked about to yourself."

Springer said the last few word as he turned to rush down the hall, yelling at someone in an office he passed.

Mike found his way out of the station and walked slowly back to his car. Still an outsider, and he didn't like it one bit.

* * *

The Charlottesville police found themselves stretched thin. The two detectives who had been assigned to interrogate Bob Smith in Richmond were now tied up with the minister's murder. Overseeing the crime scene and interviewing neighbors took most of the morning and early afternoon. Late Saturday afternoon the detectives finally traveled to Richmond to question Smith about the accident in Court Square and Stanley Crawford's murder.

Still hoping to be let off easy if he cooperated, Bob

admitted to the C'ville detectives he went to Crawford's house the night he was killed. He told them about the artifacts store where he worked, how he learned from his boss about the Hemings document, and how he tracked Crawford down. But, he explained to the officers, as he had to George Arthur, Crawford was dead when he got there. Or it certainly looked that way given all the blood on him. Yes, he should have done something other than run, but he panicked. Just ran out to his car and sped off. And, yes, he found out later he may have hit some kids while driving away.

"I tried to call my sister, but I dropped the phone and the car speeded up and swerved when I reached for it. I must have pushed down on the gas pedal. But the kids weren't hurt bad. I read about it in the news. I got scared. I didn't mean to hurt anyone. I'm really sorry. "

The C'ville detectives didn't buy Bob's story about arriving on the scene after Crawford was dead. They briefed the Richmond police on the previous night's killing of the minister and that Crawford and the minister knew each other. Officers from both cities also didn't believe Bob's story that he and Jimmy Cooke did nothing but sit around and drink beer in Jimmy's truck. Everyone agreed Smith and his buddy Jimmy Cooke had to be involved in both murders.

Jimmy Cooke's knife had been sent to the lab for analysis, but it would be Monday before blood samples from the minister arrived for a comparison with any traces on the knife. Fingerprints from the knife and those obtained at the preacher's apartment also were being processed. For now, they left Bob to stew in the Richmond jail, charged not simply with fleeing the scene of an accident, but also resisting arrest and being an accessory to felony assault with intent to kill a police officer. The C'ville police knew it wouldn't be long before murder charges could be brought, but they weren't in a hurry. Bob Smith wasn't going anywhere.

Detective Springer and the homicide team now considered seriously the idea that both Crawford and Maxwell, as well as Bob Smith and Jimmy Cooke, shared an interest in some kind of valuable document. They also had to consider that still others might be interested in a Jefferson-Hemings letter.

Chapter 18

Following his conversation with Detective Springer, which had been interrupted by the news of yet another death, Mike headed back to his sister's house. He drove up Market Street and continued on to McIntire, thoughts about his outsider status riding with him. He didn't fault Springer for not allowing him to visit the crime scene. If their roles had been reversed, Mike knew he would have made the same decision. Cop or no cop, he was an outsider. He wasn't even an active duty cop anymore, if that made a difference, which he knew it didn't. This was the business of C'ville's finest, not his.

Yet he wondered if there wasn't something more he could contribute. Telling Dixie and Miles Springer what the minister knew concerning Crawford and the Hemings letter definitely made a contribution, a pretty significant one at that. But he saw what happened at the police station. They didn't want him around when a new development came along.

On the other hand, he appreciated being invited to the Jefferson Bunch's meeting last night. Although he didn't say much, what he had said seemed important. The professor had been grateful Mike was present, and said so several times on the way out. He recalled that when McCabe requested he attend the meeting, the professor had told him he would learn more about the Hemings-Jefferson story. That didn't happen. The conversation centered chiefly on what the group should do next. When the Bunch decided the answer was "nothing, for now," no one stayed around to talk more about the purported affair or the significance of a Hemings document. Members of the group apparently didn't see anything they could add to their earlier discussions.

After hearing from the detective that the police had the driver in custody who hit Tammy, and who might also be the one who killed Crawford, he had more or less decided the whole business soon would be wrapped up. Springer even suggested as much. However, now that the preacher was dead, he had to think there was more to all of this. Jeremiah said Crawford was expecting someone that night. Assuming it was Smith, did he kill Crawford and then later murder Jeremiah? But why kill the preacher if Crawford had the letter?

Dixie said the detectives were considering whether there might be two people involved. Now Springer said there was someone with Smith when he was apprehended in Richmond. How was this other person involved? Were the killings carried out by two people? Too much didn't add up. Mike hoped Detective Springer would keep his word and update him on recent developments. If not, maybe Dixie would keep him posted. The one thing no one seemed to have a clue about was how the document got into Crawford's possession in the first place.

Mike thought back to what Dixie said last night regarding Crawford's illegal habit of carrying home artifacts from Monticello. Where did he get them? Did he just find them on the ground? That might be possible for buttons, or bits and pieces of old pottery, but old documents don't simply lie around on the ground. They would be stored away somewhere to preserve them. Were they taken from some collection at Monticello? Crawford worked security there. He'd have access to lots of places on Jefferson's mountain. Why hadn't he thought of that earlier? Mike admitted to himself that his mind often still moved at a snail's pace.

He looked up just in time to see the end of the driveway approaching and hit the brakes so hard the tires squealed. Crawford didn't get the letter from a Hemings or Jefferson relative. The ex-security guard stole it from Monticello. The police would probably arrive at the same conclusion sooner or later, but he knew their first priority would be to learn who was doing the killing in town. In the meantime, there didn't seem to be any reason why he couldn't inquire into the document's origins.

Crawford's killer must have been looking for it. If Crawford's killer didn't get the letter, maybe he thought Maxwell had it. Someone must have thought it was still out there. Otherwise, why go after the preacher? But who knew the preacher might have it? Did Jeremiah talk to other people about the letter? Did his killer now have the document? Mike sorted unfruitfully through these ideas while sitting parked in his sister's driveway, until he happened to look toward the house and see Kelly running toward the car.

"I heard the tires screeching. Is anything wrong?"

"No. Sorry. I was just thinking about something. Wasn't paying close attention to driving. I need to be more careful."

Kelly looked concerned, but only said, "Well, come in and have some coffee. I just poured myself a cup. I hope you got some breakfast."

Mike spent the next half hour in small talk with his sister. Later, back in his room, he thought again about the killings and the document. He tried to put things in an order that made sense. Go back to the beginning, he thought.

Crawford tells the store owner on the mall that he possesses a Hemings document. Where did he get it? Did the folks at Monticello have the document and Crawford stole it? Was it part of a collection that Crawford could get to with his security clearance? Someone up there would know if something as important as this went missing, but why wasn't it reported to the police? It was a valuable historic artifact. Did someone at Monticello not want people to know about the letter? Would that mean the folks in charge of Monticello weren't telling the real story about Sally and President Jefferson?

Mike found himself coming back to the question he asked Professor McCabe last night. Who would benefit if such a document existed? Or, perhaps, who would not want the document to become public? Who wanted it so badly they would kill for it?

After some additional, but unprofitable, rumination, Mike decided maybe the professor would be able to help. After all, he was the one who talked him into going to the meeting of the Jefferson Bunch in the first place. Mike figured the professor owed him. He went upstairs to use the family computer in the sunroom. E-mailing would be a better bet than trying to catch McCabe on the phone. Mike hadn't mastered the art of texting and wasn't sure he ever would.

Paul McCabe responded he would be happy to have an opportunity to chat about developments in the Crawford case and how the Hemings document might play a role. The professor suggested they meet at the Starbucks across from the university on Monday at 4 p.m. Mike hadn't mentioned the minister's murder, deciding the local news media would fill in the professor before they met.

Mike walked into the coffee shop a little before four o'clock. He sat down with a cup of coffee at a table where he could see the door. The professor arrived fifteen minutes later.

"Sorry I'm late. Just got out of class. The class before an exam date always seems to get extended. Students hang around wanting to know what's on the exam. I tell them, but in general terms, of course. They would prefer I say precisely what the questions will be. Better yet, what the answers are!"

"I guess things haven't changed much," Mike said. "I only had a couple years of college, but I always got anxious before exams. Tests are a student's curse."

"Well, if it's any consolation, *grading* is a professor's curse. Let me get a cup of coffee, then we can talk. It's all over the news, of course, about the minister's murder. I would like to find out what you know."

The professor returned and suggested they go upstairs to find a more private space. When both were seated at a small table in the second-floor corner, McCabe took a sip of coffee and then shook his head slowly.

"First Crawford and now the Reverend Maxwell. I hope the Jefferson Bunch realizes how lucky they are to be out of this thing. What have you learned? I think you mentioned that you have contacts on the police force."

Now that the news media had spread the story, Mike didn't really know much more about the minister's death than the average citizen. Detective Springer had not called to update him as he promised. An account of the shoot-out with police officers in Virginia's capital had been headline news in newspapers and on TV news shows across the Commonwealth. The Richmond news competed in Charlottesville with media accounts of the minister's murder on the city's south side. Given that it came on the heels of the Crawford killing less than two weeks ago, anyone visiting Charlottesville would think the city was the murder hub of the Piedmont. A Charlottesville police spokesperson identified Robert Smith, currently in custody in Richmond, as a suspect in the killing of Stanley Crawford. He was also possibly linked to the murder of Reverend Jeremiah Maxwell.

Mike did know, however, that the minister saw the Hemings letter and that Jeremiah hadn't showed up for a meeting with the C'ville police the morning his body

Jefferson's Promise

was discovered. Those details didn't appear in the news reports. Also, nothing had been said about a valuable historic document. Either Detective Springer didn't think it relevant or judged best to keep it quiet for now. Mike assumed the latter. A story about Crawford's illegal collection of artifacts and his job as a guard at Monticello surfaced when a reporter wrangled an interview with Crawford's widow. Someone's going to put two and two together soon, Mike thought. After all, if he could figure it out through the fog frequently engulfing him, then anyone could.

"I do know one thing that hasn't come out in the press," Mike began.

"After we met with the Jefferson Bunch the other night, the minister stopped me on the way out. You had already left. My talk about withholding evidence hit home. He knew things the police needed to know."

"Oh?" the professor said, looking over his coffee cup.

"It seems the reverend knew Crawford, but had kept it secret from the group. Not only that, he told me he had seen the document everyone's talking about."

"No kidding. It's for real, then. I have to say, I was having serious doubts about it being genuine."

Mike told McCabe how he agreed to meet the preacher at the police station on Saturday morning, and that he didn't show.

"Well," the professor said, "I'll bet the Jefferson Bunch will want to meet soon to discuss all of this. But what do you think? It looks like there really is a document. But where is it?"

Mike used the professor's comments to begin the line of questioning he had worked out in his head.

"I'm wondering if we could start with some questions I still have about the document."

"Sure, fire away."

"Who would want this thing? You talked Friday night

about why collectors might be interested. And if I remember right, when you were at my sister's house, you mentioned that descendants of the Hemingses or Jeffersons would be interested. Is the document important enough that someone would commit murder to get it? And where would such a document have been before Crawford got his hands on it. Where did it come from?"

"Okay, let me try to answer the first question. I know we talked about its historic significance. Let me expand on that a bit by way of who might be interested. That is, besides historians and the general public, both of whom always like a scandal.

"The topic of Sally and TJ is, shall we say, a delicate, even touchy subject with many people. There are those who don't want Jefferson's name dragged through the mud. They'd rather the whole thing just go away. So, if we assume the letter says Jefferson had an affair, maybe even beginning in Paris, and if you want to protect Jefferson's name, then you would want to keep this information out of the public's sight. Of course, we don't know what this letter says or when it was written, so it's hard to say who would not want to see it come to light. But that seems hardly a reason to kill someone over it. That is, just to get the letter out of circulation.

"On the other hand, there are the descendants of Sally Hemings. Six births are recorded in Jefferson's own memorandum book. You might remember Madison Hemings mentioned a seventh who died shortly after birth. We know four of Sally's children survived to adulthood. Two passed for white and disappeared. But many descendants of Madison and Eston, the two we have knowledge about, believe they are related to Jefferson. Any of these Hemingses would be interested in proof of a relationship."

"Do you think the people at Monticello would want

this document kept out of sight?"

"No. First, the official word from the Jefferson Foundation, the caretakers of Monticello, is that most likely Jefferson fathered most, if not all, of Sally's children. As I told you, however, when I had dinner at your sister's, the evidence is strictly circumstantial. If the letter testified to an affair, then it would corroborate the Foundation's statement. They've put together enough evidence already to believe there was an affair, so it would be icing on the cake for them. These people are excellent custodians of Jefferson and his heritage. Over the years they've opened themselves up to revealing Jefferson as he was. No sugar coating. You can read the scholarly reports, both for and against an affair, on their website. I'm sure they'd be willing to show the letter to everyone, even if it cast doubt on an affair and the Foundation ended up with egg on its face. I guess what I'm saying is that if they knew about the letter, they certainly wouldn't keep it a secret."

"I guess that's a dead end then," Mike said, clearly let down that a promising lead just disappeared.

"Not exactly," McCabe suggested.

"The Jefferson Foundation isn't the only group that has a say regarding what happens on the mountain. There's another group of people in charge of who gets buried in the Jefferson graveyard. They're different from the Foundation people. His grave is only a short distance from the house. People in this association are descendants of Jefferson and they have the official say regarding who can be buried up there."

"I think I can see where this is going," Mike said, becoming upbeat again.

"Yes, I'm sure you can. As it stands right now, the descendants of Sally Hemings, through one of her children said to have been fathered by Jefferson, have been denied burial rights in the Jefferson cemetery. The sticking point is that there are no official records to back up their claim of Jefferson's paternity. There's only the oral history taken from Sally's sons and passed down through the family. That hasn't been enough to convince the cemetery association that these people are related to Jefferson."

"But if James Hemings said his sister had children with Jefferson, then things might change," Mike suggested.

"Possibly. I'm sure there are people descended from Sally Hemings who would relish getting their hands on such a document. Again, if it confirms their beliefs. Now don't get me wrong, I didn't say kill for it. I just meant there's a category of folks, the Hemings descendants in particular, who would be happy to see a letter from James Hemings in support of their claim. I honestly don't know if that would satisfy the known Jefferson descendants. But, again, we don't know what the letter says, so this is all speculation."

"I agree. It's hard to think about who would be interested when we don't know what's in the letter."

"Having said that all this," McCabe continued, "I am sure there are people who might like to see the letter no matter what it says about Sally and TJ. Keep in mind, we don't know who else Crawford might have showed the letter or who learned of its existence. We talked briefly about collectors of historic artifacts on Friday night. There are lots of them. No doubt many would want to own it, no matter which side of the debate it supports. And they'd likely pay a lot to get it. In my opinion, that's the most likely person behind all this--an unscrupulous collector who somehow found out about the letter and desperately wants to possess it."

The professor looked at his watch. "I'm sorry, Mike, I have to go in a few minutes. A committee meeting I'm supposed to chair. I've been missing too many meetings recently."

"One last question, if I may. Do you have any idea where Crawford might have gotten the letter? I have to think it was part of Crawford's artifacts collection. He hit the jackpot, so to speak. But it couldn't have been lying around on the mountain for two centuries."

"No," McCabe said, smiling. "I can't imagine he just picked it up. I once thought that maybe some descendant of Hemings or Jefferson gave it to Crawford. But that doesn't make any sense. Why do that? Certainly not given what we now know about Crawford. He wasn't any expert on historic artifacts. I really can't say how the letter might have surfaced. Another mystery on top of our mystery."

The professor looked again at his watch.

"I'll give it some thought. I'm sorry, but I do have to go."

As the two men walked down the stairs on their way out of the coffee shop, McCabe suggested another way for Mike to find answers to his questions.

"You know, you might get more insight into all of this, better than I can give, by talking to the people at Monticello. Let me contact some folks I know up there. I'll e-mail you what I find out. If I can, I'll try to set up an appointment with someone at the Foundation who might have more information."

Mike thanked the professor and turned down the alley toward the parking lot. Dr. Rider was right. He recognized that getting involved in something helped curb his feelings of depersonalization. Mike wasn't sure, however, that a murder investigation was what his therapist had in mind.

* * *

The day following his meeting with Professor McCabe, the investigation with which Mike was now involved, took another turn. While everyone worked on connecting the dots between the two Charlottesville killings, on Tuesday afternoon Beatrice Crawford stopped by the C'ville police station. Pictures of both Bob Smith and Jimmy Cooke had appeared in the media accounts and Mrs. Crawford had no trouble recognizing both of them. She knew she would never forget those faces. Beatrice soon realized she had nothing to fear by going to the police. One of the men who threatened her was dead, the other in jail. They couldn't hurt her now.

She also had another motive for talking to the authorities. The news accounts said the police suspected the two men killed Reverend Maxwell. Beatrice didn't just suspect, she was sure they did. It had to be them. She sent these men off in the direction of the minister's church. Consequently, she couldn't help thinking that she was partly responsible for his death. If she had called the police immediately after the two men left, the cops might have intercepted them before they killed the reverend. On the other hand, if she had notified the police, even if they were put in jail for a while, eventually they would come back to kill her. Beatrice had no trouble thinking the man the news media identified as Jimmy Cooke would do just that. She would need to talk about all this with Father Thomas in the confessional--explain what happened and how she felt guilty for sending the killers to her husband's minister. She was sure Father wouldn't hold her responsible. But if he did, she also knew he would forgive her.

The police listened with obvious interest to Beatrice Crawford's account of the events taking place at her house the day Reverend Maxwell was killed. She reported how the minister had come to talk to her a few days following her husband's death and asked about the letter or document Stanley was supposed to have. The two men who threatened her were looking for the same thing. She made it clear she only told the evil men about

Stanley's minister because they were going to hurt her. Maybe even kill her.

Other than being aware Stanley had collected things from Monticello, probably illegally, she had no idea what people were talking about. Stanley never showed her any letter. She explained the minister told her that he and Stanley had talked about the document. That's why she told the two men about him. She couldn't possibly have known they would kill him.

That afternoon police charged Bob Smith with the murders of both Stanley Crawford and Jeremiah Maxwell.

Chapter 19

Andrea Hudson met George W. Arthur the previous summer when she attended a political gathering in Richmond. Schmoozing in a room full of party officials, big-time contributors, and office-holder-wannabes was a way to troll for clients. Re-districting following the recent census had created opportunities for new players on the Virginia capital's political stage. Attending the Richmond meeting were many local business executives who desired an opportunity to meet potential candidates for Richmond City Council.

Thirty-nine years old and a veteran of many political campaigns, Andrea knew men found her attractive. Although never married, she had plenty of evidence in that regard. Five-four, slim but hardly anorexic, perfectly coiffed hair, and deep blue eyes, she could boast of being carded at a bar during the past year. Andrea learned to use her attractiveness to advantage, at least when dealing with the male population. When courting potential female clients she made every effort to turn their attention away from her youthful appearance and obvious feminine charms. She accomplished this by coming across as a smart, no-nonsense, business woman, which she was, and which even men recognized after their libido cooled.

A previous client, a first-year state legislator, invited her to the meeting out of gratitude for her work on his campaign. He stood ready to recommend her to Richmond's movers and shakers. The two shared a drink toward the rear of the room while the president of the Richmond Chamber of Commerce gave a brief presentation. Her grateful lawmaker took the opportunity to point out individuals in the room whom she might want to get to know. In a quiet voice behind his drink, he gave Andrea a brief rundown on various individuals attending the reception, including an estimate of their financial worth. At one point, he nodded slightly in the direction of a man across the room standing next to a table holding empty glasses. This was someone she should meet, he said, and provided her some background.

When Andrea moved across the room to greet George W. Arthur, she already knew he wasn't married, ran a local carpet company, was staunchly conservative, and had big pockets, as the saying goes.

"Mr. Arthur. I'm Andrea Hudson." Glancing back across the room at her former client, she said, "Gary might have mentioned that I helped with his campaign last year. I'm here looking for who might be the next council star in Richmond."

George Arthur turned in the direction of her client and nodded when he saw Gary looking at them.

Andrea put out her hand, knowing very well that many Southern gentlemen questioned whether it was proper to shake a woman's hand. Andrea always sought to combat this awkward male silliness, while at the same time making it clear she meant to play as an equal. George Arthur hesitated before taking her hand in a firm grip, an awkward pause originating not from Southern rules of etiquette, however, but from the fact that he was immediately taken by her looks. Andrea recognized it for what it was.

"It's a pleasure to meet you, Ms. Hudson. Yes, Gary told me about you. He appreciated your efforts. I guess we can judge them a success, given he was elected."

"Gary's a natural. I'm sure he would have won without my help." Andrea remembered how hard she worked to make Gary appear to be anything but the country bumpkin he was.

"I appreciate your modesty, but I heard you deserve much of the credit. I'm glad we've met. I happen to know someone who will make another fine candidate. He just needs someone like you in his corner. And, of course, the right kind of backers. I'd like for you to meet him. If you two connect, I'll be glad to help out in any way I can. That's why I'm here."

"Please, call me Andrea, and thanks, I'd like to meet him. I'm told you're a person who is on top of things in town. If I may, I'd like to call you sometime to get your opinion on the political climate, who to contact, what to avoid, and so on. You know the drill."

"It would be my pleasure," said the enthralled carpet salesman. "And call me George. It's only fair both of us be on a first name basis."

On several occasions following her conversation with George Arthur, Andrea met with the man George was promoting for a council seat--young, perhaps a bit too conservative politically even for Andrea, not all that polished, but articulate, good looking, and extroverted. The kind of person Andrea felt she could make into a winner. She signed on and began taking steps to make sure he got on the ballot. Andrea guaranteed George that his man would be popular in the predominantly white district where he sought a council seat. George was delighted and promised to get the word out to people who could help build a political war chest.

From George's point of view, it was a happy combination of circumstances. His man had a savvy political consultant in his corner and when elected would move along a conservative agenda. What made it even better was working with Andrea. He continued to be smitten and went out of his way to come up with reasons for the pair to meet. Andrea had asked for information regarding Richmond's political scene and George could give it. Since this was of benefit both to her and their candidate, Andrea didn't mind making the trip to Richmond from Charlottesville. She frequently coordinated their meetings with travel in and out of the Richmond airport.

On several occasions George suggested they put politics aside and asked Andrea to let him show her around Richmond. They took in the Museum of Fine Arts, the Virginia History Museum, and, since George had a keen interest in the Civil War, the Museum of the Confederacy. One afternoon they toured the Virginia State Capitol, which, George explained, Thomas Jefferson had designed while residing in France. He directed her to the old section of the capitol, no longer used for government business, where the Virginia legislature met in the spring of 1861 to vote on secession.

Upon entering the historic chambers, George moved to the center of the room to stand next to a statue of Robert E. Lee. He announced that it was on exactly this spot that Lee volunteered his services to the Confederacy. Andrea knew she could be mistaken, but she thought George might be on the verge of tears when he spoke.

"Lee was a man of principle who fought for freedom in the South," George commented on their way out. "You know," he continued, "Lee's views on slavery weren't that different from Jefferson's. Both were for sending the Negroes back to Africa. I sometimes wonder if that might have been better for everyone."

"You can't be serious," Andrea said, trying to decode what George meant.

"I mean look at all the problems we would have avoided. You know, the suffering on everyone's part. A war between brothers. Six hundred thousand dead. If the Negroes had been made to leave our country then none of that would have happened. And maybe there wouldn't be so much unemployment today. They really didn't enter this country on their own. They were brought here against their will. I'm sure most would have liked to go back."

Andrea didn't know what to say.

As they strolled the walkways outside the capitol building, Andrea told George about the Jefferson Bunch. He appeared interested and mentioned that one of his hobbies was collecting historic artifacts from Virginia's history.

"I've several artifacts associated with Jefferson," he said. "One is a newspaper advertising the sale of his slaves after he died. Also some pieces of Monticello dinnerware. Things from George Washington as well. One day I'd like to show you my collection."

Saying this, he blushed, realizing what he said sounded like a lascivious invitation to "see my etchings."

Andrea didn't help him when she laughed, and said, "So what else might I get to see?" George continued to blush.

Not very long after that, following an afternoon spent touring the Ginter Gardens, George invited her to his house for dinner. Although Andrea had planned working at home that night on an out-of-town client's behalf, she found she had been enjoying George's company enough to delay her trip back to Charlottesville. She accepted, but jokingly inquired if they would be eating frozen dinners given the lateness of his invitation. George said not to worry, and made a call on his phone. She followed in her own car while George drove to his residence on Monument Avenue. It was the first time she had been to his home and was visibly impressed with its magnificence.

Many of the homes along the historic avenue were refurbished three-story attached dwellings with garages in the rear. George's was one of the few unattached houses, a mansion actually, with a semi-circular driveway in front. The monument dedicated to Robert E. Lee could be viewed from the upper story of George's house. When the Sons of Confederate Veterans marched down the avenue on Lee's birthday, George told Andrea that he always watched from a second-floor window, standing at attention while holding a folded Confederate flag. By this time she was used to George's excesses, as she thought of them, associated with his devotion to the Lost Cause of the South.

Dinner, too, was magnificent, a wonderful Southern meal prepared and served by an African-American couple. Sitting after dinner on the sofa in the lavishly outfitted den, Andrea sipped a locally produced white wine while George drank his third gin and tonic. Her legs curled beneath her, she looked around the room and asked about the paintings on the walls. George didn't look in the direction of the art. He couldn't take his eyes off her. Seeing where his gaze focused, Andrea speculated on where the evening was headed, and whether she cared.

Partly to slow down what seemed to becoming inevitable, Andrea remarked that she hadn't seen his collection of historic artifacts. She asked about his Jefferson pieces. "I've been looking for artifacts in the rooms of your house and I have to say I haven't seen many. I noticed you have the work of some early American painters, but I thought you mentioned historic artifacts."

Her comment unsettled George, and he acted as if he had no idea what she was talking about. Several times following that day in the capitol he had regretted mentioning his collection. He quickly recovered, however.

"I consider the collection rather special. It's concentrated on the period from 1765 to 1865. One hundred years that set the course of this nation, from the

Jefferson's Promise

Stamp Act to the end of the War Between the States. As far as I'm concerned, nothing much happened before 1765, and what happened since 1865 is not something I care to dwell on. I started the collection years ago while my father was alive. In fact, he collected some of it. Just little things at first. Old stamps and coins. When I got ahead financially I was able to expand it. Some of the artifacts are very rare. Besides the Jefferson pieces, I have several books owned by George Washington, with notes and underlining. A pair of Benjamin Franklin's eye glasses. Many historic broadsides from Lincoln's war. I'm sorry, I don't mean to boast. What I was leading up to is that I keep my collection locked up. With so many valuable pieces, my insurance company wants me to make sure the collection is secure. It's downstairs."

"May I see it? Andrea asked.

"Well, okay. Why not. Follow me. Let me refresh our drinks first."

Having topped off their glasses, George led the way down the hallway to the stairs. Andrea observed he wasn't walking too steadily following his third gin and tonic and worried the fourth one he was holding would soon spill.

The lower level had several rooms. Only one, however, had a steel door and an electronically controlled combination lock embedded in it. Andrea looked on while George pressed numbers on the keypad to open the lock. "Fireproof, too," he said.

Switching on the lights, he stood aside to let Andrea through the door. George waved his free hand in a sweeping motion and made a modest bow, barely avoiding slopping his drink on the floor. "Enter, my lady. You are now where I keep my treasures. As the newest treasure in my life, it's fitting you're here. What do you think?"

Andrea didn't know what to think, either about the

corny flirtation or what she saw in front of her. The latter grabbed her attention. Glass cabinets lighted from overhead spots filled the middle of the room. On the walls hung various flags, uniforms, posters, paintings, grainy black-and-white photos, swords, and many old rifles and handguns. She approached the row of cabinets to the left of the entrance, the shelves filled with myriad artifacts: books, medals, buckles, pistols, watches, canteens, epaulettes, spyglasses, and spent shells.

"Wow," was all she managed at first. "This is something, George. There must be hundreds of artifacts here."

"Actually, more than six hundred," he said, his words slurring slightly.

"There are more in the drawers beneath the glass cabinets. Things I haven't had a chance to display, or pieces I rotate in and out of the cabinets when I want a new look. Next time you come, and I trust there will be a next time, I can show you even more."

"Where do I start?" Andrea asked, walking toward a wall of hanging artifacts.

"Things are arranged somewhat chronologically. You're at a good place to begin."

He put his drink down on a small table, and indicated Andrea do the same.

"Let me give you a tour."

George put his right hand gently across her back and directed her to a display, employing his other hand to indicate various objects.

"The pieces on the wall in front of you are from the 18th century. Take a look at the Boston newspaper with the headline reporting the fight at Concord."

They walked slowly around the room. George pointed out artifacts while giving a running commentary of their significance. He stopped at one particular item, a broadside from April, 1865, announcing the search for

Lincoln's killer.

"This is one of my favorite items," he said. "I told you, I think, that I don't collect pieces after 1865. April 1865 was the year and month Lee surrendered. The same month Lincoln was killed by John Wilkes Booth. Only one of those events is something we can celebrate, of course. Lee surrendered on April 9th. Lincoln died on April 15th."

"Of course," Andrea agreed, only later questioning which event George celebrated.

Turning her attention again to one of the walls, Andrea commented, "The oil paintings and photos must be originals. Where did you get them? Those uniforms and rifles look like ones we saw at the Museum of the Confederacy."

"They have theirs and I have mine. In fact, I have some things they probably would like to have gotten to first. Collecting is a rather competitive business."

"Maybe one day you could donate your collection to them."

"Maybe."

While Andrea studied the artifacts, George concentrated on Andrea. His arm still around her waist, at one point he leaned close to her when he spoke of his collection. "You are a treasure," he repeated, while turning her around to face him. He brought his body close and then kissed her.

Based on George's behavior upstairs and then his attention to her downstairs while viewing his collection, Andrea had already surmised something like this might happen. She considered it harmless enough, having previously dealt more than once with this type of situation.

George led her toward the door. Andrea assumed they would continue upstairs. She didn't know how far she wanted this to proceed, but judged there was still time to make some important decisions. Their drinks remained on the table and she pointed to them as they approached the door.

George didn't look where she pointed. Reaching for the light switches next to the door, he exhibited a dexterity Andrea wouldn't have thought possible for someone who had been off-balance after three gin and tonics. He managed to soften the overhead lights with one hand while keeping his other hand against her back, pressing her to him. The hand which accomplished the task of dimming lights now moved across her breasts, then slid down to her thigh. With both hands he pulled her abruptly to the floor. Andrea realized the time for making other decisions had run out.

Chapter 20

On Wednesday, two days after his discussion with Professor McCabe at Starbucks, Mike met with Dr. Rider at his regular time. He brought along the second notebook she gave him. His therapist had wanted him to get involved with something and he seemed to have succeeded. He had quite a list of activities to present her and arrived in a good mood, looking forward to the session.

"What I've done, Mike, is identify in your diary some of the things that cause you to begin slipping into the fog of depersonalization. These are going to be the focus of today's session. It won't be easy, but try to work with me."

Mike took a seat, with an uncomfortable foreboding.

Dr. Rider first taught him some relaxation exercises involving deep breathing, then requested he talk about each of the topics she identified.

"There's no hurry, Mike. We'll take it slowly. If it gets to be too much, just tell me. But I would like you to talk about the things that upset you. Try to relax as much as you can. Breathe deeply and slowly."

He concentrated on complying with her request. His therapist probed gently, requesting he elaborate or clarify, sometimes challenging his thinking, taking notes of things he said.

And so it went for an hour--images of Kirsten, feelings of helplessness, thinking he was crazy, worries about money, fear of disappointing his sister, anxiety over driving a car, concerns about returning to work, difficulties encountered in social situations, questions about the meaning of life, of death. Mike fought off feelings of depersonalization as best he could, focusing on his breathing, reciting his mantra. Nevertheless, he sometimes found himself slipping in and out of a fog. If Dr. Rider noticed, she didn't say anything. When the session drew to a close, she congratulated him on his effort.

"I know this was tough. I put you through the wringer today, but you did great."

Mike could only nod. He continued to breathe deeply, attempting to bring himself down from somewhere above all this.

"We're making progress," she said, watching him closely.

Dr. Rider waited while Mike composed himself and then stood up to see him out. She once again exchanged the notebook he brought in for a new one with blank pages. As he turned to leave, Dr. Rider informed him she would be out of town the next week, but would like to see him in two weeks. She then reminded him to use the strategies she taught him to fight his feelings of being outside himself.

"It will take work, Mike. But, hopefully, you will find yourself feeling more in control. Remember, you *are* in control of your life. Exercise. Get involved in something and keep up the diary."

He had gotten involved! Although he wasn't feeling all that in control when he left Dr. Rider's office. Maybe he never would. Confronting those images of the past year set him back. As the session progressed he knew he had moved up the Rider scale. Today's session ended on a 5, maybe even a 6 or 7, but at least it wasn't a 9 or 10. Maybe that was what Dr. Rider meant by progress. Right now he didn't see it that way. The session had sapped his energy.

Before beginning his drive home, Mike walked to a coffee shop down the block. A latte and some quiet moments to reflect on the session were what he needed.

All the Cummingses were out when he got to his sister's house. He went into the sunroom to check e-mail. A message from Paul McCabe informed him the professor had arranged a meeting with the curator at Monticello for this coming Friday morning. Once again Mike's thoughts turned to the mysterious Hemings letter.

* * *

Monticello, Jefferson's mountaintop home, is several miles to the southeast in a direct line from Charlottesville. The house runs roughly east to west and the city of Charlottesville is visible from the north terrace. It's said that during his retirement years, Jefferson used a telescope to watch construction on the university he designed. Frequently, however, he personally supervised progress, making regular trips on horseback to and from the university. The modern-day visitor to Monticello drives a winding road up the side of Carter Mountain before reaching the gates of this World Heritage Site.

Mike visited Jefferson's mansion the first time on a spring excursion from his middle-school in Alexandria. He remembered the bus trip more than the visit to Monticello. He had been back two more times with Kirsten. They came once before they were married and again later, combining these excursions with visits to Kelly's family. Kirsten couldn't get enough of the place. Inside, she asked the guides numerous questions about Jefferson's inventions, the furniture, the china. Outside, she insisted on walking in the west gardens, as well as along Mulberry Row, the path that once led to slave dwellings and the plantation's few light industries.

On their last visit, Mike learned only a little about the Hemings family and Thomas Jefferson. This came from one of the guides. Discussions with Professor McCabe and the Jefferson Bunch enlarged his meager knowledge bank, but he recognized there was much he still didn't know about "Dusky Sal" and the writer of the Declaration of Independence.

He recovered quickly from the past Wednesday's therapy session and had felt pretty good the past couple days. Maybe the sessions with Dr. Rider were what he needed, he thought--like bad tasting medicine he swallowed for his own good. But Friday morning, when he drove up the mountain toward Monticello, he grew increasingly anxious. He and Kirsten visited almost exactly the same time of year, nearly three years ago. It could have been yesterday. He saw Kirsten in his mind's eye bounding out of the car. The autumn sun glistened in her hair while she led him by the hand across the parking lot.

"Come on," she said. "We don't have much time before the last plantation tour." They hadn't gone into the house that time. Exiting the shuttle on the mountaintop, they walked together, almost running, toward where a line formed for the tour.

Why isn't she here? Why am I alone? Who am I?

He drove slowly, trapped behind a school bus taking children for a tour of Jefferson's home. He tried to concentrate on the kids in the bus and how they would soon be looking around, talking and laughing, punching and hitting each other, running up and down stairs, and perhaps seeing something of Jefferson's house and grounds before getting back on the bus. Thoughts of his own visit as a 7th-grader came back to him. That was a different time. An innocent time. A growing-up time. Before-Kirsten time.

I am Mike Chance. I am real. I am here.

The curator's office was in a building on the road past the Monticello entrance so Mike avoided, for now, confronting the memories of earlier visits to Jefferson's home. Spotting the driveway leading to the curator's office, he slowed and pulled in, right on time for his ten o'clock appointment.

He had expected an office building of some kind, but the only structure on the property was an older looking farmhouse. Leaving his car, he saw a woman standing on a wooden porch watching his arrival. She smiled brightly as he approached.

"You must be Detective Chance. Please come in. I'm Martha Sporlein, the Monticello Curator."

She extended her hand when he got to the top of the stairs.

"Please call me Mike. Thanks for seeing me."

He wasn't sure what to call himself these days. "Detective" didn't seem to fit anymore. He hadn't told Kelly or Justice, but next week he planned to send a formal resignation letter to his homicide chief in the District. Until then, technically, he was still a detective, but on leave from the force. It didn't seem like a good time to explain.

The curator held open the front door and directed him to her office. "It's the second door on the right," she said. Mike went down the hallway and stood aside, letting her enter the room before him.

"Have a seat," she said, moving across the small office and taking some papers and books off the only chair other than that behind her desk. Books and papers, various small objects, including dishes, vases, books, candlestick holders, and what looked like antique instruments of some sort, were displayed on shelves. A stack of paintings leaned against one of the walls.

"Please excuse the mess," she said, sitting down at her desk. She looked around as if viewing her office space for the first time.

"I guess I say that to everyone. All of the Jefferson artifacts pass through here on their way to the big house, the visitors' museum, or into storage. My staff and I do the cataloging, have digital photos made, and then we discuss how the artifacts might be displayed."

"It must be quite a task," Mike said, not sure what else to say, but figuring a compliment was in order.

"We have nearly five-thousand objects associated with Jefferson somewhere up here on the mountain," she said with obvious pride. "I understand from Professor McCabe that you're interested in some of them."

"Well, I'm not sure. I'm sort of on a fishing expedition."

"This is about the murder of Stanley Crawford, right? I'm told some of the archaeology people knew him when he worked up here. I don't think he worked in this area of the property, though. At least not that I'm aware. I guess he could have made his rounds at night when I'd left for the day. It was a serious disappointment when the police said he'd been removing artifacts from the site. Is it really true?"

"Yes. But from what I gather, although I haven't actually seen any of the objects, they're mostly small things. Broken pieces of dishware, nails, buttons, a bottle or two."

"That sounds more like items from an archaeological dig than from the house or storage."

"There is something else. Or at least there may be. I'm not sure what you've heard about the case, but there's the possibility that Crawford possessed a document, maybe a letter, written by James Hemings. One possibility is that it came from somewhere up here."

"Paul McCabe mentioned the letter. And I did see some reference to it in one of the papers. But honestly, when I read that, I thought it must be something Crawford made up. I think that was even suggested in one of the newspaper accounts. That is, that no one knows for sure if the document exists. Or if it does, whether it's a fake of some kind."

"There is a letter," Mike said, pleased the curator was on top of the Crawford story. "But whether it's genuine or not, what it says exactly, or who might have it now, are all open questions. I spoke with someone who saw it."

Let's not talk about another body, he thought.

"Really? And you think the letter might have come from here? Something else that Crawford stole?"

"Like I said, no one seems to know. But where else could it have come from? It seems a reasonable assumption, given that he was stealing other things when he worked here. Is this something Crawford could find here?"

"I don't see how that would be possible. It's my job, as I told you, to catalog everything coming to us. We have things sent to us from around the world. Some artifacts we go out and look for, particularly if we have some clue where they might be found. Like an antique piece of furniture someone is selling and advertises it as Jeffersonian. We even look on eBay. If we can determine it's something Jefferson once owned then we'll try to buy it. Maybe get it on loan. Or better yet, see if we can get it donated! Of course, not everything people advertise as belonging to Jefferson was ever in his possession.

"What I'm trying to say, is that if there were such a letter, I would have seen it. It would be an exceptional find, to say the least. We occasionally get letters from descendants of Jefferson's correspondents. Someone is cleaning out an attic and finds a letter from Thomas Jefferson that was stashed away and forgotten. If we're lucky, they'll contact us. Then we start negotiations. I can tell you a letter written by James Hemings never crossed this desk while I've been here. And that's been the last five years. I'm positive none of the previous curators saw one either. It would have been big news."

"Then I guess the answer isn't up here," Mike said.

"Crawford had to get the letter from someone. But who would give him such an important letter?"

"I'm sorry I can't be of help," Ms. Sporlein said. "To tell you the truth, after talking with Professor McCabe, I was hoping you might be able to locate such a document. It would be a major addition to our collection and possibly provide more light on the Hemings matter."

"I guess I've wasted your time. Sorry. Some people claim that eliminating possibilities is progress, so maybe this is progress."

"Don't apologize. We're happy to talk to people. It wasn't a waste of time to learn more about the Crawford case. And if you say someone saw a Hemings letter, then I'm even more intrigued. I hope you'll keep us posted on what you find."

Getting up to see him out, Ms. Sporlein added something he hadn't anticipated.

"While you're here I thought you might want to talk with Abigail Parker, one of the archaeologists. Like I said, they may have known him. Perhaps you can find out where Crawford got the various objects he's stolen. Hundreds of people visited Monticello in Jefferson's time and, of course, hundreds of slaves with their families lived here. Over the years many things were dropped or discarded in a refuse pile. As you might expect, the archaeologists love digging around.

"I made a tentative appointment for 10:45 and it's almost that. You don't need to see her if you don't want to, but perhaps talking to one of the professional archaeologists can eliminate some more possibilities. And then you'd be making more progress," she said, smiling.

Mike smiled too, but at the same time felt frustrated. This hadn't been the kind of progress he desired.

"Dr. Parker is on the staff of our Archaeology Department. She's been away for a while but knows about all the excavations up here. If you want to talk with her, I'll call and say you're on your way."

"Thanks. I might as well. It just might help."

Ms. Sporlein gave Mike detailed instructions on how to find the archaeology offices. The drive back toward the Monticello entrance once again brought back memories of his previous visits with Kirsten. Mike shook his head as if to shake the images from his mind. He wondered how long it would take to get back in touch with his real self. How long before he would see the world as he once knew it.

I am Mike Chance. I am real. I am here.

The staff archeologist stood at the front door when he drove up to the laboratory, a barn-like structure located about a hundred yards down the mountain from the mansion and the visitor shuttle stop. He got out of his car and headed toward the building. As he approached the archaeologist, Mike smiled inwardly. He hadn't given much thought to what a professional archaeologist might look like. On the drive over it had crossed his mind that he might be meeting a female counterpart of Indiana Jones--tall, tanned, good looking, and outfitted in khaki clothes under a floppy jungle hat.

Dr. Abigail Parker stood about five-six, with a complexion suggesting she worked more in an indoor archaeology lab than outdoors in the hot Virginia sun. Attractive, outfitted in jeans and yellow shirt, she had pulled her blond hair in a ponytail through the back of a Chicago Cubs baseball cap.

"Hi! Detective Chance, I presume. I'm Abby Parker. Martha said you'd like a tour of the grounds and some information about what we archaeologists do on the mountain."

"Thanks. Please call me Mike. I appreciate you taking the time. I just have a few questions."

"No problem. Let's go up toward the house and I'll

show you some of the excavations. We can talk while we're walking."

Dr. Parker described in general terms the goals of the Monticello archaeologists as they climbed the hill toward the house.

"The whole mountain is an archaeology site. Monticello was originally a five-thousand acre plantation. The Foundation now owns about two-thousand acres, including both Jefferson's home site and some outlying farms. We've been doing research up here for several decades. Excavating buildings, gardens, and roads, doing our best to identify what Monticello was like when Jefferson lived here. More than twenty thousand test pits have been made. Most of them around the sides of the mountain."

"Test pits?"

"STPs in our professional lingo. Shovel test pits. Basically, samples of what lies a few feet beneath the ground. If an STP reveals artifacts, or maybe evidence of a structure or a road, then a larger dig is made. Even if nothing is found, we still analyze the soil to help us know what the land might have been used for. With data obtained from STP analyses we can map the plantation, showing where planting took place, the roads used to get around, and where people had residences."

"Sounds like a massive operation." Mike said, hopefully sounding as impressed as he was.

"One requirement for an archaeologist is patience," Dr. Parker said, laughing. "But you probably don't want to hear all this. Martha told me you're investigating the Crawford murder."

Mike realized that the C'ville police might not appreciate his "investigating." He winced as he remembered what he told the Jefferson Bunch about outsiders meddling in a police investigation.

He walked next to the archaeologist as they made

their way up a path to the house.

"I'm really just following up one of the loose ends. I assume you heard that Crawford had a collection of artifacts he took from up here."

"Yes, we've have been talking about it ever since we saw the news reports. I didn't know Stanley Crawford. I've been away for two years, working on a dig at Jamestown. I just returned a couple of months ago. I'm told Crawford retired before I came back, and I don't remember him from the previous time I was here."

"Oh, I thought Ms. Sporlein said you knew him."

"No, I didn't, but two of my colleagues did. Daniel Loomis and Kevin Nesbitt. I only know this because when we heard about the killing and the connection with Monticello, we started asking each other if anyone knew him. Those two said they did."

"When we're done talking do you think I might be able to speak with them?"

"I'm afraid they aren't here anymore. Dan left last week to take a job in Montana. Kevin is still in Charlottesville, but he stopped working at Monticello this past spring. He's finishing his dissertation at the university. I should add that while Dan told me before he left that he knew Stanley Crawford, I only know that Kevin did because one of the other archaeologists said he talked with Kevin recently and they talked about the murder. Kevin admitted he sometimes chatted with Crawford. That's all I know. But if you're interested I can give you Kevin's contact information."

"Thanks. I guess I am interested, but I wonder if I could ask you a few questions."

"Of course."

"My first question is pretty simple, I think. Where do you think Crawford got these artifacts?"

Mike and Dr. Parker had reached the top of the hill. She led him through a gravel parking lot and onto a path along the south side of the house.

"Believe it or not, Monticello visitors sometimes find artifacts lying on the ground. Just last week a young girl found a horseshoe beside a path she and her family had been on. But that's pretty unusual. From what I heard, Crawford had more than a few artifacts. Certainly more than he could possibly discover just by kicking up the dirt."

"I haven't seen all that he had, but, yes, he collected more than a few pieces. Button, nails, bottles, pieces of dinnerware. Things like that."

"Then there are really only a few possibilities. They could have come from an excavation site, the laboratory, or possibly from the storage area. Keep in mind that hundreds of thousands of artifacts have been dug up over the years. Some are on display, but most are stored away."

Dr. Parker stopped.

"Perhaps you know we're on Mulberry Row."

"Yes. I remember it from my earlier visits."

Kirsten had stood next to one of the historical signs, beckoning him to come and read what it said. He couldn't remember which sign or what it said.

Mike looked away from the road to the distant horizon, concentrating on the clouds moving across the sky.

Dr. Parker followed the direction of Mike's gaze. "Beautiful view, isn't it!"

"Yes, it is," Mike said, collecting himself and turning his attention back to the archaeologist.

"Jefferson designed various buildings along this road, including slave quarters and buildings for some of the light industries. A blacksmith shop and nailery, for instance."

"I remember that much from a tour I took a couple years ago. But regarding the slave quarters, I don't remember who lived there."

"The slave quarters up here were multi-family dwellings early on. Something like barracks. They housed the domestic slaves, since their duties required them to be close to the main house. Field hands lived down the mountain closer to their work. The excavation of Mulberry Row took place in the 1980s, long before I got here. Later dwellings housed one or two individuals and maybe their relations.

"Many of the Hemings family lived along this road, at least for a while. Elizabeth Hemings, the family matriarch, lived here and then moved down the hill to a house of her own. Her now famous daughter, Sally, lived here as well. Later, she moved to a room in the south wing of the dependencies under the house."

"What about James Hemings?"

"I was waiting for you to ask about him. He's the one who is supposed to have written a letter about his sister and Jefferson."

"Stanley Crawford had a letter in his possession. I came up here to see if anyone has any idea where he could have gotten it. Ms. Sporlein said she's sure nothing like that ever passed through her office. I'm interested in where Crawford got the artifacts he collected, but even more so, where he got the Hemings letter."

"Well, to answer your earlier question. James Hemings most likely lived here with his mother on Mulberry Row, at least when he was a child. James served a number of roles for Jefferson. When a youth, he acted mainly as a personal servant. He went with Jefferson to Paris when he was about nineteen. Sally came later as maid to Jefferson's daughters.

"When James came back, he attended Jefferson in New York and Philadelphia. He had many duties. Cook. Riding valet. Household manager, and so on. No doubt quite indispensable to Jefferson. James returned to

Monticello around 1793, I believe. I have to admit, I had to look up some of this history before you came."

"I appreciate it. I'm still learning about the Hemingses."

He could see that Dr. Parker enjoyed her teaching role. She smiled at him as she continued.

"Well, James made use of his cooking skills, he was trained in France, and trained his brother as well. Jefferson freed James Hemings a few years later. James then traveled and worked various cooking jobs. It's possible he even went back to Paris.

"He turned up again at Monticello in the summer of 1801. Cooked meals for the Jeffersons, then left the hill in the fall. Soon after that Jefferson learned he had committed suicide. Maybe this is more than you wanted to know!" she said with a slight smile.

"No, not at all. Thanks. I must admit to being more and more interested in all that went on up here. I need to do some reading."

"I should add," Dr. Parker continued, "we assume James stayed with his mother or other members of his family when he came back that summer of 1801. Remember, his mother Elizabeth Hemings moved from Mulberry Row into her own house. The house was excavated in the 1990s, before my time."

"So the artifacts Crawford collected came from one of those excavations?"

"It's possible. These sites produced literally thousands of artifacts, and we've started some new excavations this past year. If Crawford worked at Monticello when any of these were in progress, he might have explored a site and uncovered some artifacts. Of course, he would have to do that when no one was looking. I assume at night. But he would have had a key to the buildings. He could have taken artifacts being processed in the archaeology lab. Probably before they were cataloged. Or maybe from the storage shelves."

"Either way," Mike suggested, "it doesn't seem as if it would be too difficult for someone working security at night to find some artifacts and take them home. It's not like he had boxes and boxes of them. I imagine if thousands are dug up, one would hardly miss a couple dozen. Especially if they were taken one or two at a time over many years."

"You're probably right. My understanding is that none of the items were particularly valuable."

"That's right. Except, of course, the Hemings letter."

The pair walked slowly down Mulberry Row, occasionally moving aside to let a group of tourists pass by them.

"You've got me on that one. We deal in artifacts that can survive hundreds of years buried in the ground. The most interesting thing I've seen excavated from Mulberry Road is some fruit from Jefferson's time. Nothing you'd want to eat now, but still preserved in liquid. It had been in a bottle that somehow got buried, maybe because a wall collapsed on it. We still have it stored in a cool place."

Abby Parker paused and stopped walking.

"But a letter? A piece of paper? Hardly something that would survive since James Hemings's time. I have to think someone is working a scam. I'm guessing the letter is fake."

"I told Ms. Sporlein that eliminating possibilities is making progress. So far today I've been making lots of progress! But somehow it isn't very satisfying."

"I'm sorry I can't be of more help," she said, appearing genuinely concerned.

"You have helped, and I appreciate your time. What bothers me is that I know someone who saw the letter, who said it looked very real."

"It's a mystery to me. What it could be. But then we

have our own mysteries up here. I mentioned that we started excavating some new sites in the past year. Interestingly, one of them is sort of a mystery site."

"Mystery?"

"We found evidence of a building along Mulberry Row near the garden gate. It's a mystery because it doesn't show up anywhere in Jefferson's drawings. No one knows yet what kind of building or what purpose it served. We're still finding artifacts there. Maybe Crawford got some of his artifacts from that site. If you want to make progress by excluding even more possibilities," she said, smiling, "you might want to learn more about that excavation.

"I should have mentioned," Dr. Parker added, "if you were to bring Crawford's artifacts here to let us see them, we might be able to tell you where they came from. Maybe even when they were taken."

"I'm sure the police will do that eventually. How can I find out more about this mystery building and the artifacts at that site?"

"That's where Kevin Nesbitt should be able to help. I was away when they started digging there. We have records of the dig, of course, but until he left, Kevin was the crew chief. He's ABD at the university."

"ABD?"

"Sorry, 'All But Dissertation.' He's writing up results of fieldwork he conducted here. Your best bet would be to talk with him, since he's summarizing what was found. And like I said, he apparently knew Stanley Crawford. It may not gain you anything more, but I'll give you his contact information when we get back to the lab. I'm sure he'd be glad to talk to you about the dig."

"Why not?" Progress is progress, Mike thought.

Chapter 21

The Jefferson Bunch did not meet the week following the brutal murder of one of their members. No one wanted to sit around and speculate about what had happened to the minister. They knew nothing other than what had been in the papers and on TV, and Mike Chance's comments at the previous week's meeting had pretty much dampened any interest in carrying out an investigation. With two murders now associated with the Hemings document, there was even more reason to just sit back and see what developed. Members agreed by e-mail to meet next week.

More than a week passed before Mike heard from his partner. On the Sunday following his trip to Monticello, Justice called from Washington. He had some things to do in the District the next morning and wouldn't get to C'ville until late Monday evening, he said. Would Mike meet him Tuesday morning? Mike agreed and Justice suggested they meet at 9 a.m. at a coffee shop on the pedestrian mall.

Mike inquired about the homicide division and Justice's plans for the future. When he got off the phone he realized Justice hadn't been very forthcoming. Work was fine. The captain had him doing some small jobs, mainly cleaning up paperwork associated with old cases. He hadn't finalized plans for the future.

On Tuesday, when Mike walked west on the mall, he spotted Justice standing outside the coffee shop. His partner came forward and immediately explained they didn't have time for coffee.

"My apologies, but there are some people I want you to meet. They're waiting on us. It's just down the mall."

Justice didn't say anything more about where they

were going or who they were meeting. He made small talk and described the work being done on his newly acquired house in C'ville. They approached a large hotel, which turned out to be their destination. They walked to the hotel elevator while Mike tried to get Justice to explain.

"Come on partner. What's this about?"

"Hold on just another minute. All will be revealed," Justice said with a smile, punching in a floor number.

Mike found his anxiety increasing. Dr. Rider had warned him that DP-related feelings would come and go depending on the situation, and on any stress he experienced. This mysterious trip was stressing him. Being around Justice usually arrested his anxiety, but the uncertainty about what was happening caused him to zone out.

Where am I? I'm on the elevator ceiling looking down. This place feels unreal.

"Hey, partner. Look at me!"

Mike slowly came out of a fog. He saw Justice holding open the elevator door.

"We're here. You got into one of those places your mind goes now and then. This isn't good. I told people you were moving beyond that."

"I'm not sure what you mean," Mike said, trying to locate the voice and comprehend the words he thought he heard.

"What people?"

"I saw you were someplace else in the elevator. You going to be okay? Otherwise this isn't going to work."

"What work?" Mike asked, regaining some equilibrium. "What people? Where are we going?"

"Just follow me," Justice said, starting to walk down the hotel hallway. "I'm beginning to worry this may not have been a good idea."

Mike followed, still working to get his bearings. Why

hadn't Justice filled him in?

I am Michael Chance. I am real. I am here.

Justice knocked on a hotel door. Detective Springer opened the door, said something by way of welcome, then nodded and motioned for them to step inside. He thanked Justice for bringing Mike, who was surprised since he hadn't been aware the detective knew Justice. Two men, both strangers to Mike, and a woman whom he recognized, sat around a table.

"I want you to meet some people," Springer said. "You both know Officer Dixon."

Mike looked over at Dixie and managed a brief smile. Justice gave her thumbs up. The two strangers stood and extended their hands across the table to Mike while Justice took a seat.

"Mike, this is Agent Simpson and Agent Norton. They're both with the FBI," Springer said in introduction. "They've already met Justice."

The agents nodded a curt greeting without going on a first name basis. Mike had worked with the FBI only once before, a shooting in the District involving drugs and money laundering. The FBI supposedly had been keeping an eye on a guy when he turned up dead. Mike remembered they weren't all that friendly and clearly didn't appreciate having to rely on the D.C. police to help clean up their mess.

Mike sat down and glared at his partner.

Detective Springer knew when it was politically correct to yield the floor. "I don't know what your partner told you, Mike, but perhaps it would be good to let these agents tell you why we're all here."

He told me nada, thought Mike, now seriously irritated with Justice.

Agent Norton spoke first.

"Mike, we understand you've had some dealings with a group here in town. The one that meets regularly to talk about Thomas Jefferson."

His opening statement confused Mike and it wasn't due to a DP-induced fog.

"I'm not sure what you mean by dealings. I've been to one of their meetings. They call themselves the Jefferson Bunch. It's nothing more than a discussion group. Like a book club, except they don't necessarily discuss books. They talk about Jefferson, American history, Monticello, that kind of stuff. You can't seriously think these folks have done something to warrant an FBI investigation."

"One of their members, an African-American minister, was recently murdered, wasn't he," said the second agent, looking directly at Mike. "And wasn't it because the minister knew something about a valuable artifact, some kind of letter concerning Jefferson and his female slave?"

"I can't believe anyone in that group had anything to do with the murder," Mike said. "I don't know them that well, but they seem pretty harmless to me. And the only thing they knew about the letter is that it might exist. The minister kept it secret. He told me Stanley Crawford had it. That Crawford showed it to him the night he was killed. I relayed this information to Officer Dixon."

Mike looked at Dixie for backup, who nodded in the direction of the agents.

The ball went to Agent Norton.

"What do you know about Andrea Hudson?"

"Hudson? The woman? I believe she's some sort of political consultant. Travels a lot I'm told. Comes to the meetings when she's in town. I only met her briefly at the group's last meeting."

Mike was more confused than ever.

"Didn't she offer to help bankroll a search for this letter or document?"

"From what I heard, she has some client who's possibly interested in the Jefferson document. When the group first learned about this document they wanted to find it on their own. I was told this Hudson woman said she knew someone who might pay for the investigation. I was invited to a meeting to help them see this wasn't something they should be involved with. After we met they backed off from any idea of investigating. That's about all I know. Sergeant Dixon and Detective Springer know all this."

Mike, still perplexed, looked again at Dixie. Agent Simpson took over.

"Mike, let's back up a bit. I can see your partner hasn't said much about why we asked you here."

Mike turned and gave Justice a look meant to convey his displeasure. Justice only shrugged as the agent continued.

"We're interested in the Hudson woman. Do you know who her client is?"

"I have no idea," Mike said. "I'm not sure anyone knows."

"We know," Agent Norton said with a smirk. "He's someone we're also interested in."

As if a tag team, Agent Simpson took a turn.

"Her client, as she calls him, is a man named George Wallace Arthur. He runs a carpet business in Richmond."

If any of this was supposed to help explain why Justice brought him here, it didn't.

"This man Arthur," continued Simpson, "is a member of the Klan."

"Klan, as in Ku Klux Klan?" Mike asked, becoming more alert.

"The one and only," Simpson said. "The Klan isn't all that active these days, but they're around, and we like to keep an eye on them. We've got someone close to the Richmond group who reports on their activity."

"You mean from inside the Klan?"

"Not exactly. But close. Many of the Klan members hang out in a house in Richmond owned by a man named Billy Lee Jackson. He's a long-time Klan member. They drink, play cards, talk tough about the way the country is going in their twisted view. Not just Klan people, but other right-wing nuts as well. Our informer shows up at these drinking parties. He hasn't been invited to be a Klan member, but he overhears a lot. That's especially the case when the group gets to drinking, which is often.

"He tells us when anything big is going down. In the meantime, we're looking for anything criminal. Last year, an individual we wanted for a bank robbery showed up at one of their drinking parties. We'd been after him for a couple of years. Seems this guy bragged about being on our wanted list. Our informer let us know. We trailed him and made an arrest when he was in a different state so word wouldn't get back to the group in Richmond."

Mike still had no idea where all this was going.

"And you think this Hudson person is tied up with the Klan?"

Agent Norton jumped in.

"We're not sure what she knows about the Klan. But she is tied up with George Arthur. She's been seeing him on a regular basis for the past several months. We're sure he's the person offering to bankroll a search for the Hemings letter. He's an avid collector and doesn't seem to mind if what he collects is legally obtained or not.

"His name shows up now and then as possibly connected to some historic artifacts lifted from museums and private collections. We've traced some of these goods back to Richmond and we're sure Arthur's the one getting them. We think he's been receiving stolen goods for years. Nothing definite that we can use, however."

"How did you find out about Hudson's offer? I mean Arthur's offer?" Mike asked.

"That we owe to Sergeant Dixon," Agent Simpson answered, looking at Dixie.

"Officer, maybe you could tell Detective Chance what you told us."

"Mike, remember when we met on the mall after your meeting with the group? You mentioned a woman, Andrea Hudson, who knew someone willing to pay for an investigation. I didn't think much about it until Detective Springer asked me the other day if I heard anything about this group and about a woman who attended the meetings. He said some FBI agents had been asking questions."

"We knew Hudson had been going to these meetings," Agent Norton stated, without clarifying how they knew.

"I told Detective Springer what you told Justice and me. He passed it on to the agents here," Dixie said.

Justice decided it was time to get involved.

"Detective Springer got hold of me, Mike. He wanted to know about you."

"To see if I was crazy?" Mike inquired, not too happy with being the center of things. Crazy with DP episodes, Mike asked himself, or just crazy as in crazy?

"No, it's just they didn't know anything about you. And Dixie had just met you. Detective Springer wanted someone to vouch for you and Dixie told him to contact me."

"Once we gave them more information on you," Springer said, "Agents Norton and Simpson had an idea how you might be able to help."

"We want to learn more about George Arthur," Agent Simpson explained. "This Hudson woman may be able to help, although we don't want to approach her directly. We're not sure where she stands in this, but we'd like to find out."

"What we need to know, Mike," declared the other

member of the duo, "is if George Arthur has a collection of stolen artifacts and where it is. Right now, we don't have enough evidence to get a warrant to search his place. Assuming there is a collection, we need someone to tell us exactly where it is and what's in it."

"If we have a reliable witness who confirms that he collects stolen artifacts, then we can get a warrant to raid the place," Simpson said.

"And you want to find out if Hudson has seen Arthur's collection," Mike said, beginning to catch on.

"That's it," Justice said, clearly pleased Mike was on track.

Agent Norton nodded his head.

"Our informer tells us he overheard Arthur mention his collection of artifacts. Our man isn't sure where he keeps it, but he heard Arthur boast about it. It's only hearsay. We need something more."

"Here's the tricky part, Mike." Agent Norton said. "Someone looking at the collection wouldn't necessarily know whether items were stolen. Unless, of course, Arthur told them, and that doesn't seem likely. We aren't even sure who Arthur allows to see his collection.

"We need to find out," Norton continued, "first, if anyone has seen the collection, and we think Hudson might be a good bet for that. Second, we need to know if there are stolen artifacts in the collection. That would give us the information we need for a warrant."

"As you said, they're not likely to be labeled stolen," observed Mike. "How would anyone except an expert know what was stolen and what wasn't?"

"You're right, of course," Simpson said. "We have a list of stolen artifacts traced to this area. We just need to find out if any of them are in Arthur's possession. Then we can get the warrant. You can help us do that."

Chapter 22

The agents paused in their presentation, everyone looking at Mike, waiting for him to speak. A full fifteen seconds went by. Feeling stressed, Mike lost focus. He was on the verge of saying something, although he wasn't sure what, when Agent Norton lost patience and started in again.

"We know you've been having some problems since your wife died. We talked with your boss in D.C. He told us what he knew, which wasn't a whole lot. Except that a District psychiatrist said a few months ago you weren't ready to come back to work."

Mike began to breathe deeply. He tried to fight the anxiety welling up .

I am Mike Chance. I am here. I am real.

He felt safe talking to Dr. Rider about his problems, but who were these people to be checking on him. What had Justice told them? Why had he involved him in this without any warning?

"Mike," Justice said, "they asked me whether you were in shape to give a hand with this thing. It's been six months since you came down here. You've had time to get back on your feet. The agents wanted to know if you're able to help, if only in a small way. I told them the little I knew, but only you can judge."

"All we're asking, Mike," Agent Norton said, "is that you get to know this woman. You're a good looking guy. Take her for a drink. Whatever. Turn the conversation to artifacts and collections. See where it goes. Tell her the police know about George Arthur. That he's a big-time collector and there are questions about where he got some of the artifacts in his collection."

Mike began thinking this whole idea sounded crazy.

He's supposed to take her out on a date?

"Come on! You guys don't need me. Talk to her yourselves."

"We could," Agent Norton agreed. "And it may come to that. But quite frankly we think she might be more forthcoming with someone she knows."

"So I chat her up, then ask her if she's seen his collection. Why would she tell me if she had? We've never really formally met. How can you say I'm someone she knows?"

"But she knows who you are. You're the person helping these Jefferson folks stay out of trouble. You'll be a lot less threatening than we would be," Simpson answered.

"Look," Agent Norton said, "all you have to do is tell her you found out through the police grapevine that Arthur is being investigated by the FBI. That he has stolen artifacts. And to top it off, the FBI knows he's a Klan member."

"If I can get to talk with her, and that's a big if, and if we get to this kind of conversation, what's to stop her from warning this Arthur person about the FBI? I'm not sure this makes sense."

It was Agent Simpson's turn.

"Here's our thinking. If she's somehow connected with his racket then, yes, she may just string you along and then warn Arthur. But what's he going to do? He may try to stash the collection somewhere, but we'll be watching. If Arthur is in possession of just half the stuff we think he has, it won't be easy to move."

"But," said the other member of the FBI team, "let's say she's on the straight and narrow and she doesn't know Arthur's a crook. We've checked up on her. We don't think she would be hanging around with this guy if she knew he wasn't legit. And certainly not if she knew he's a Klan member. We're hoping the info you provide will make her nervous, make her worry she's involved with someone who can ruin her reputation. If she trusts you, she may tell you what she knows about George Arthur."

Mike thought of the ways he had seen undercover operations go bad, especially ones that started out badly. And this one, he thought, looked like another example. Where do these guys learn this stuff?

"Look, gentlemen, I'm not sure I'm the right person for this. As you said, I've got some problems I'm still dealing with." Glancing at his partner, he added, "Justice knows that. I'm not sure why he thought I could help."

Before Justice could defend himself, Agent Simpson started in again.

"Mike, if you don't feel you're up to this, we understand. But perhaps we should tell you something more."

All will be revealed, Justice had said. Up to this point, Mike realized it clearly hadn't. He wanted to leave and not listen to what the two agents had to say, but resigned himself to see what was yet to come.

Detective Springer spoke up first.

"Perhaps I can help here." He looked at the two agents, who both nodded for the C'ville detective to continue.

"Mike, there are a couple of things you may not be aware of. Some recent developments have brought the FBI into all of this. I assume you've been following the news about the Crawford and Maxwell murders."

"Who hasn't," Mike responded.

"A lot's gone down since you and I talked. As you know, Reverend Maxwell was murdered the same night Smith and his buddy Cooke got into the shootout in Richmond. Pathology results indicate the minister died early enough that the two of them could easily have killed him and then driven back to Richmond, where the local police caught up with them.

"We're confident Smith is involved in both killings. And we're pretty sure Cooke helped him out by driving his truck here from Richmond. We found out they visited Crawford's widow earlier in the day. Visited isn't the right word. Terrorized, I should say. They threatened her over this so-called Jefferson document. She told them she didn't know anything about a document, but she believed they were going to kill her just the same. Hoping to get them to go away, she told them her husband's minister knew about the document. This happened sometime in the morning on the day of the killing.

"We can place both of them at the scene of the murder later that night. A woman came forward who will testify she saw Cooke's truck parked on the same block as the minister's church. Our witness says she saw two men in the truck, but it was too dark to see them clearly. She told us they kept getting out and pissing on the sidewalk side of the truck. She forgave them the first time, but when she saw them pissing the second time, and the truck hadn't moved, she decided to call us. The dispatcher sent a patrol car, but the officer was diverted to a domestic dispute call. Later, when the officer drove down the street where she reported the truck, it had gone. He went off duty soon after.

"The next day the officer finds out the truck in question was parked on the same block where the minister was killed. I went to see the woman who called in, but the next door neighbors told me she went to visit her sister. They weren't sure where, but thought she would be gone only a few days, maybe a week. We left a message on her answering machine. She called yesterday and I went out to interview her. She had no trouble remembering that night. She was still mad we never showed up to chase those guys away. Lectured us about all her tax money going for nothing. I explained what happened, that the officer got pulled away, and that when he came back the truck had gone. That seemed to appease her.

"The truck apparently left about a half hour after she called in, but she wanted us to know that when no cops arrived, she did her citizen's duty. She wrote down the license plate as the men drove off. Still had it right beside her phone. Gave us a pretty good description of the truck as well."

"I assume it was Jimmy Cooke's," Mike said.

"It was Cooke's, all right," Springer declared. "It's possible Cooke is the one who killed the minister," the detective continued. "We understand he can run crazy at times. Blood work says he was on speed. The Richmond cops found a knife on him with traces of blood that match Maxwell's. We confronted Smith with what we had on them. It seemed like he wanted to say something, but he has a lawyer now who won't let him talk. Smith originally told the detectives who interviewed him that he and Cooke hadn't been doing anything special, that they parked somewhere in Charlottesville to drink a few beers before going back to Richmond."

The two FBI agents started to interrupt at once. Agent Norton got in the first word.

"Mike, we're also aware that Smith knows George Arthur. He's been seen by our informer more than once at the Richmond house."

"We're thinking Smith works for Arthur," Simpson said. "That maybe Arthur hired Smith to help find the Hemings letter, and that's why Smith went after Crawford, then the minister. If this is how it went down, then we can get George Arthur for a lot more than stealing historic goodies. And if the Klan is involved, we've got a possible hate crime with the killing of the black minister. We could bring down a bunch of these crazies! That is, if we can tie George Arthur to it all."

"Mike, we need your help to do that," summed up Agent Norton. "When the group meets again we'd like you to talk with this Hudson woman. Find out if she's seen Arthur's collection. We can provide some pictures of stolen artifacts. If she's seen his collection, all she has to do is confirm one of the stolen items is in his collection. Will you do it?"

Chapter 23

The meeting with the FBI agents and the C'ville police broke up before noon. In the end, Mike's desire to be more than an outsider and get on with his life helped make the decision for him. Yes, he'd do his best to meet this Hudson woman when the Bunch met on Friday.

On the way down in the elevator, Mike stared at the blinking lights signaling the floors on their descent and avoided saying anything to Justice. He trusted his behavior made it clear he wasn't happy about what transpired upstairs. Justice took the obvious hint and also said nothing. As they left the hotel, however, Mike couldn't remain quiet any longer.

"I don't think I deserved that kind of treatment," Mike said. "We used to share plans. At least we did when we worked together. You left me completely out of the loop on this one!"

"Mike, look, I didn't have a choice. You know how the feds can be. They asked me to keep you in the dark until they checked you out and did more background work on this Hudson woman. The captain also leaned on me to help them. You know how he deals with the agency. Do them favors and then they'll owe us."

"Okay, but why not bring me in on it before you spring these guys on me in some hotel room. You could have briefed me last night."

"You're probably right. But I have a stake in this, too."

"What do you mean?"

"For one thing, remember, I went back to the District hoping to leave the department on a good footing. Not jeopardize my pension, for example. And not let folks down. I've put in a lot of years there. So when the captain talked to me about cooperating with the FBI and the local police down here, I decided it was good for everyone."

"Except me."

"Wait a minute, Miguel. How do you know it isn't good for you? I know you're still wrestling with things, but you do need to move on. This little project might help. I don't want to sound like I understand exactly what you're dealing with, but I do know that over the past weeks you seem to be handling things pretty well. Kelly told me that, too."

"You talked with my sister?"

"It was part of the background they asked me to get on you. She and Steve think you've been doing much better recently. Especially since you've been talking to the local shrink."

"Justice, you don't understand. One of the things that hits me now and then is the feeling that I'm somehow outside my body. Outside my real self. When I get excluded from things, by the local cops, and now you, it makes me feel even more of an outsider. Maybe that doesn't make sense, but it's how I feel."

"I'm sorry, but perhaps you don't appreciate where I stand on this."

"Stand on what? An undercover operation?"

"No, not that. About this guy George Wallace Arthur and the Klan. And that a black minister, who from what I can tell was a pretty decent guy, gets himself knifed and killed. You've never asked me what I think about all of it. Or the Hemings document, Jefferson and Sally, his black slave. Oh, right, sorry, his servant, as they used to say."

Justice's comments set Mike back. He realized Justice had a point. They hadn't talked about any of this. Mike recognized he'd been self-centered in his thinking. Concerns about his mental health, memories of Kirsten and their interrupted life together occupied him most.

Even this Hemings document was just a case to be solved. He hadn't thought much about its significance, except why it might be worth stealing and who would kill to get it. A Hemings or Jefferson descendant? A collector? He certainly hadn't considered what it might mean to his black partner.

They had been walking east down the mall. People sat outside eating lunch, enjoying the warm autumn day. Justice pointed to a restaurant and suggested they get a bite to eat and continue their conversation. They found a table under some trees and looked over the menus the waiter produced.

Looking up from his menu, Justice said, "Did you know that Jefferson owned more than six-hundred slaves?"

Mike had heard something to that effect, but he knew a rhetorical question when he heard one, and also when it was best to play dumb. He looked at Justice, knowing his partner wanted to say more.

"They say Jefferson tried to keep families together, but that didn't always happen. Young children were torn from their parents. This means for many of my people the past is a blank slate. They don't know where they came from. Auntie Blossom says I might be related to the same slave family that produced Gabriel, but it's all guesswork and wishful thinking."

"Gabriel?"

"He led a revolt against white slaveholders in Richmond. Around the year 1800, I believe. Gabriel and his followers planned to attack people who oppressed blacks, then set up a city that welcomed people of both races."

"What happened?"

"What do you think happened! He failed. Just like the others. The whites caught him, hung him and his followers. Same thing happened to Nat Turner some years later. Except they skinned him alive. These revolts scared the hell out of the white people in Virginia.

"A possible slave revolt was always on the mind of white folks," he continued. "And when one actually happened it caused the whites to tighten up all kinds of slave laws. Virginia wasn't too kind to blacks in those days. Some say it still isn't."

Mike started to comment, but saw once again that Justice wasn't finished. A server arrived to take their orders.

"The funny thing is," Justice said when she left, "people in those days deceived themselves into thinking they were being kind to us blacks. Christian ministers preached that slaves should obey their masters like they would obey God. That it was their Christian duty. I guess they thought the blacks would grow closer to God that way. Save their souls, that kind of thing. And, of course, not cause trouble, like Gabriel and others.

"It's one reason I don't go to church anymore. That is, after I was out of Auntie Blossom's sight. Man, how she loved to sing in the church choir! When I learned my people's history, I realized religious people could spin any story they wanted if it suited their needs."

"Justice, I think I missed some lessons in school. I haven't given much thought to all of this. Obviously you have."

"Well, let's just say I have some definite views on the matter," Justice said with his smile again.

"You see, I'm not too sympathetic to your Thomas Jefferson. Granted, he was one among hundreds of the so-called respectable folks who held slaves. George Washington, too. Even the great Lincoln for the longest time was set on sending us back to Africa or maybe South America. It's hard to indict them all. But it doesn't make it right."

Mike didn't know how to reply and tried to redirect

the conversation in order to recapture some of the ground he had lost by neglecting his partner's feelings.

"What do you make of this Hemings letter?" he asked,

"What do I think about the letter? If it's real, and we learn more about Sally and Jefferson, that's fine. But to me, it's just more history. Nothing in that letter is going to change what happened in this country between blacks and whites. So what if we learn for certain she had his children, that Jefferson took advantage of a female slave? Everyone knows that white masters did that. Monticello wasn't the only plantation with mixed-race kids running around.

"We know what it was like two-hundred years ago. It wasn't very nice. Okay, today things are better in many ways, but there's a lot more to do. Worrying about how some folks got born way back then doesn't help people today a whole lot."

Mike's face reddened with embarrassment. He started to say something, but just then their lunch arrived.

"Don't get me wrong," Justice said, after taking a bite of his sandwich. "What I'm trying to say, is one more story about a white master taking advantage of a female slave isn't really news. Even if it was Thomas Jefferson. People looked up to JFK, the guy who got us the Peace Corps, stared down the Russians over Cuba, asked us what we can do for our country. All of that. But we know he was flopping on top of women in White House bedrooms. And Clinton. Both of them married. Even our own Martin had women problems. How many examples do we need of powerful men abusing women?"

Mike remained silent.

"I don't think you heard the story behind the guy we took in the night Kirsten had her accident."

"You mean the Redskins T-shirt? The one who shot

his young wife?"

"The same. You had left town by the time the case went to trial."

"I remember what we found in the stairwell. The memory still haunts me."

"Me, too. Because it's another example of what I've just been talking about. And I guess because the young woman was black and he was white."

"They were married, weren't they?"

"If you want to call it that. At the trial her relatives testified she had been down and out and that he sweet-talked her into a relationship. Got her to marry him with promises of a decent future. Turns out that soon as they got hitched he starts abusing her. Her brother said she tried to leave him several times but he forced her to stay. It's likely she was trying to run away the night he shot her."

"After she threatened him with a knife?"

"No one ever found a knife. She was shot in the back. The judge gave him sixty years. Men taking advantage of women they hold power over. I doubt if it will ever end."

Justice's passion startled Mike. Nothing like he had seen before, even after seeing young kids shot down in the District.

"I guess I'm on my soapbox. Sorry." Justice shrugged. "We better finish our lunch."

They both began to eat, but after a few bites Justice couldn't help unleashing more of his thoughts.

"What matters most is what we can do now. If we can get some of these hatemongers like George Arthur and his Klan buddies put away, then maybe, just maybe, things will be a little better for both black and white folks.

"So, Miguel, if I have to trick you a bit. Maybe push you in a direction you might not choose to go, then I'm going to do it. That's just the way it is."

Mike looked at his half-eaten sandwich. He had been put in his place and knew he deserved it. Justice turned the discussion back to what the feds had in mind.

"I don't think the FBI plan is a bad one. Even if you don't get very far with the Hudson woman, she may say something to Arthur that will stir the pot. All they need is for him to make one bad move and then they can come down on him."

"I said I'd do it, Mike said. "But I'm still skeptical it'll work. What about the Hemings letter? Who do you think has it?"

"Beats me. Maybe this Smith character got it from the minister before they killed him. If he didn't and it's still out there, we may never know. I have to think that when Smith sees the charges against him he'll make a deal however he can. Talking about the letter would be a start. Maybe he'll implicate Arthur. Then things will look better for us.

"And consider this," Justice continued, "let's suppose Smith did get hold of it and gave it to Arthur before he and Jimmy what's-his-name got into the gunfight with the Richmond cops. Then we're back to the plan the feds set up. Maybe this Hudson woman will know something about it."

"Like I said this morning, why would she tell me?" Mike asked.

"I don't know, but why don't we see? You've got a couple of days to work on your pickup lines."

"I'm not picking her up! The more I can convince her of the seriousness of what she's gotten herself into, the better. That doesn't call for pickup lines."

"Okay, buddy, you're in the lead here. But every woman I know likes a little flattery, and a little flirting. If I was better at it, then maybe I'd be married."

"You know why you aren't married," Mike said, laughing. "You're the stereotypical bachelor who likes things the way he likes them. Not how someone else likes them!"

"Okay, maybe. But that doesn't mean I don't know how to interest a woman when I want one."

"I'm not sure I can flatter any woman these days. It doesn't feel right."

"Then what do you plan to say on Friday?"

"If I can get Ms. Hudson alone, I guess I'll try the story the agents came up with. Tell her George Arthur is under suspicion for stolen goods. See if it unsettles her, then find out where it all goes from there. It may depend on what happens at the meeting with the Jefferson Bunch.

"They're going to want to talk about the minister's murder. They didn't meet last week and by now they'll have lots of questions. I understand from a couple e-mails that some are thinking about going to his funeral. Apparently it's been on hold until a brother comes down from New York. I'm sure they'll bug me about the police investigation."

"You're going to have a busy night."

"That's not all. I didn't tell you, but last week I talked with the curator and one of the archaeologists at Monticello. From what they told me, there doesn't seem to be any way this letter could have come from there. I can pass that bit of information on to the group."

"Maybe this is a fight between some collectors," Justice suggested.

The pair stopped talking while the server asked if they wanted dessert. When they declined, she left after placing their bill on the table.

"I guess it could be anybody at this point," Mike responded. "But as far as knowing how Crawford ended up with the letter, we seem to be at a dead end."

Justice groaned at his choice of words.

"Sorry, bad pun," Mike added, and then continued.

"The Monticello archaeologist I spoke with gave me the name of one more person to talk to. He's a graduate student at the university who's writing his dissertation on work he did at an archaeological site on the mountain. He did his digging when Crawford worked security there and seems to have known him. Maybe if I talk with him I can get some more background on Crawford."

"You don't think that this student and Crawford were in it together?" Justice asked.

"I never thought about that, but I'll keep it in mind when we meet. He works part-time at the university museum. I called there, but his supervisor told me he's out of town until next week."

"Sounds like a plan, but first you have your undercover assignment--sweet talk the lady on Friday night into divulging what she knows about the bad man's secret treasures."

"I can tell you it won't be sweet talk," Mike blurted.

"I don't have anything as exciting lined up. No pretty women and no secrets to find. I'm going back to the District today. Want to keep the captain informed about what's going on. He'll be happy we're helping the feds. I'm not sure anyone really gets these favors back, but the captain is the one in charge of inter-agency politics. And I've still got some loose ends up there to take care of."

"Unless I completely fail in all this, we probably should plan to meet on Saturday morning to take stock," Mike said as they paid their bill and got up to leave.

Justice put his hand on Mike's shoulder.

"See you then, partner, and don't do anything I wouldn't do." Justice winked.

Chapter 24

George Wallace Arthur followed the news stories of the past ten days with increasing anger. He had no trouble understanding the sequence of events. Smith obviously didn't listen when he told him to lay low and stay out of sight. Two more people had died with Bob Smith in the vicinity. One of them had to be a person Smith recruited to help him carry out his crazy schemes. The other, the C'ville minister, must have known something about the Hemings-Jefferson document and the two idiots went after him. Leave it to Smith, George thought, to screw up at the minister's place, just like he did at Crawford's house.

George couldn't be sure what Bob Smith would tell the police. No one would consider Bob capable of working on his own. When the police point out that the death penalty is a possibility, George figured Bob probably will say whatever he has to in order to save his skin. His greatest fear was the trail would lead to him. Even though he knew nothing about Smith's connection with the minister, he did know that Bob had been at Crawford's the night he was killed. George worried that fact in itself might implicate him in a cover up. He still hadn't decided whether Bob lied when he said he didn't kill Crawford. And the Klan? Would it be brought into this? To buy time, George arranged legal counsel for Smith. Just make sure he keeps his mouth shut, George instructed the attorney, and "keep me out of it!"

* * *

Andrea Hudson, along with other members of the Jefferson Bunch, also closely monitored the news stories following the "Richmond shootout," as the media labeled it. The *Washington Post*, with readers both in Richmond and Charlottesville, picked up the story immediately. Andrea saw a story in the *New York Times* a day later-- Charlottesville murder, police shooting, Richmond man killed after firing at officers, cop wounded, SWAT team, accomplice in custody, a secret letter, Sally and Jefferson again. What more could reporters and their readers want?

Since Monday, Andrea had been in Boston consulting with a client. She flew into Richmond late afternoon on Thursday, the day before the Jefferson Bunch was to meet. Before driving from the airport to Charlottesville, she wanted to see what George Arthur thought about the events detailed so sensationally in the media. Ever since telling him about the possible artifact, he had questioned her regularly about the Jefferson Bunch's plans to launch an investigation. She hadn't told George everything had been put on hold. Given all that happened, the police now would be conducting their own investigation. Although Andrea didn't doubt George would love to get his hands on the letter, she assumed he would take its apparent loss in stride. Collectors must have to deal with being out-bid, or out-raced, when looking for artifacts, she thought.

Andrea used her mobile to call George's office from the airport parking lot. Such calls in the past usually found George eager for a quick assignation at his house. He had provided her a key so she could let herself in if he was held up at the office. The secretary told her Mr. Arthur went home with a headache a couple of hours earlier. I'm sure he will be in tomorrow, she added. Andrea thanked her and pressed George's home number on her phone. At least she would inquire about his health.

George sounded distracted, not all that coherent, his words at times unclear, but she had no trouble understanding he wanted to see her. Insisted on it.

Andrea didn't like being ordered to come to his house. Becoming uneasy by George's tone of voice, listening to him slur his words, as well as being tired from the trip, she decided it would be better not to see him today. When George took to pleading with her, however, she relented to a short visit. She wondered whether something more serious than a simple headache had brought him home in the middle of a work day. Perhaps she could help in some way, she thought.

A little after 5 p.m., Andrea drove up to George's house in the fashionable Monument Avenue Historic District. Before she could press the bell, George opened the door, drink in hand. Andrea knew him to have a drink at lunch or maybe one in late afternoon when they had finished sightseeing and stopped at a bar. However, he usually didn't drink any more until evening. Today, he had clearly broken precedent.

She didn't forget that their first sexual encounter began in his museum room after George had one too many. That she didn't stop him still bothered her and she made an effort ever since to be on guard. They had sex after that, but Andrea made sure it was on her terms. When George was sober, or mostly so, he made a decent lover, but his drinking concerned her.

George greeted her loudly at the door. He teetered as he aimed his mouth toward hers for a brief kiss.

"I'm glad you came," he slurred. "We need to talk."

He turned and Andrea followed him down the long hallway.

"Well, you didn't sound right on the phone," she said to his back. "I thought I should check on you. I can see you started partying a bit early today."

"Just a couple. Been a hard few days at work. Come, I'll get you one."

He stopped and reached to put his arm around her. Andrea stepped away.

"I don't want a drink. I have to drive home yet today."

"Oh, come on. Have a drink. You can sleep over. And I can sleep over. Over you. Get it?"

George burst out in a drunken giggle, spilling his drink as he turned toward the living room. Andrea followed, uncertain of what was going on.

"No, George. I said I don't want a drink. I really just came because your secretary said you weren't feeling well. But it appears you aren't feeling much of anything."

"Funny. Funny. Sit down. Let's talk. Then we can, you know, talk about that sleep-over-over," he said, obviously pleased with his humor.

George staggered ahead of Andrea and fell onto the sofa in the living room, somehow managing to keep his drink upright. Andrea moved to sit in a chair across from him. Her work involved entertaining clients and their backers, so drinking couldn't be avoided. It sometimes got out of hand, however, and then usually turned out badly. After one evening of drinking, a client pulled her down onto a plush rug in his apartment and tried to tear off her clothes. He wasn't a client anymore. She left him with bruised testes from a none-too-gentle squeeze.

"George, I'm not staying. You need to get some coffee. Maybe go to bed for a while."

"Didn't I just mention bed," he laughed, before slurping his drink.

Watching him, Andrea saw his manner quickly change. He glared at her from his nearly prone position on the sofa.

"Don't go. Stay here. I said we need to talk."

Andrea was becoming more and more uncomfortable. She had never seen George like this. Even when he had a few drinks he always seemed to remain in control. She wondered if something went wrong at work. Andrea didn't move to get up, but also didn't sit back in her chair.

"I want you to stay away from that Jefferson group in Charlottesville," George spit out.

"Don't you want to find out what happened with the Hemings letter? Even with the investigation in the hands of the police, I may be able to get inside information about what they find. I told you there was a cop there last time. He seems to know what's going on with these murders. He might know something about the document. I thought you'd like to see where all this ends. Even if you can't own it."

"You didn't hear me. I don't want you going back there. No one knows who has the document. And I don't want anyone to know about my interest in it."

"George, we agreed I wouldn't identify you. And I haven't. No one knows you were planning to finance an investigation."

She looked at George, who didn't seem to register what she had said.

"Okay, if you aren't interested anymore, that's fine," she said angrily. "But whether I go to these meetings or not is my business. We can continue this conversation when you're sober. I'll give you a call."

Andrea stood and turned toward the hallway leading to the front door. Based on past experience handling drunks, she should have been prepared for what happened next.

George quickly moved from the couch, letting his glass bounce onto the white rug, spilling its contents. He grabbed her from behind. Andrea tried to push him away, but he dragged her back a few steps and pulled her down on top of him onto the sofa.

"Then before you leave let's do the over and under thing," George demanded into her face, pawing at the top buttons on her blouse with one hand while the other hand pressed down on the small of her back, keeping her from moving off him.

"George! Stop!" Andrea screamed, struggling to push herself up.

Looking into his angry face, spit hitting her as he raged, she relied on the tactic which worked so well in the past, this time employing her knee. George yelled. He dropped his hand from her blouse and loosened the force against her back.

"You bitch!" he cried out.

No longer pinned down, Andrea raised herself and delivered a crunching blow with her elbow to his nose-- in the exact manner her self-defense teacher had instructed. George threw her onto the floor, his hands reaching to catch the flow of blood from his nose, his eyes showing hate.

Andrea stood up and raced for the front door.

"You slut," shouted George through bloody hands. "You'll never work around here again."

Slamming the door behind her, she heard George continue to yell muffled obscenities.

Andrea managed to start her car and head on to Monument Avenue. She pulled over after driving a couple of blocks, flushed and breathing fast, unable to stop trembling. Sitting in the car with the engine running, she tried to calm herself. She felt violated. And disgusted. This drunk who tried to rape her was someone whom she had been sleeping with, supposedly a friend.

After a few minutes the shakes subsided, anger replacing the terror she had experienced. She straightened her clothes and started the drive to C'ville. Her phone rang several times on the way home. She ignored it before finally turning it off.

Chapter 25

The meeting of the Jefferson Bunch on Friday went pretty much as Mike expected. Discussion centered on the murder of the minister and on speculation about possible connections between the Crawford and Maxwell killings. Members put many questions to Mike about the investigation, which he mostly ducked by saying he didn't really know much other than what was reported in the media. The conversation then turned to the Hemings letter. Everyone had an opinion about who might have it. Whoever killed Crawford. Jeremiah's killer. Crawford's widow. Someone the killer handed it off to. Maybe Jeremiah hid it.

Mike passed on what he learned during his visit to Monticello. Although he had gained some insight into the workings of the Monticello operation, he said, nothing he learned shed any light on the document's origin. He had one more person to interview, a graduate student who had worked on the hill just before Crawford retired. Mike said he'd let the Bunch know if he discovered anything new.

The meeting ended with members talking about Preacher Maxwell's funeral, now set for the coming Friday, a week away. It wouldn't be in Charlottesville, however. Jeremiah's brother came to town to make the arrangements and insisted the body be taken back to New York so that other relatives and friends would be able to attend. No one in the Bunch considered traveling that far.

Throughout the meeting Mike looked toward Andrea Hudson, so often that she became aware of it. She smiled at him once or twice, causing Mike to blush, darkening his light brown features. He worried about what she might think of his furtive glances and whether he would be able to get her alone.

When the meeting ended, Andrea was among the first to get up to leave. Mike planned to go out the door immediately behind her, hoping to catch up to her on the walkway outside. He worked on what to say while he watched Andrea put on her coat. Trying not to appear in a hurry, he managed to exit the house a few steps behind her. Jonathan Turner's house had a small front stoop on which Andrea Hudson stopped suddenly. Mike bumped into her, nearly pushing her down the single step to the ground.

"I'm sorry," he said quickly.

"Oh, it's quite all right. My fault. I wasn't sure why I stopped, but I wanted to talk to you anyway."

Mike immediately worried his behavior during the evening's discussion had upset her. They moved off the front step and stood in the middle of Jon's walkway. Other group members said good-night as they walked around them. When the last person went by, Andrea began the conversation again.

"You seemed to look at me in there like you wanted something."

"I have to apologize again. Sorry if I was rude. As a matter of fact, I did. I wanted to pass on some information I received that concerns you. Maybe I could walk you to your car while I explain?"

"Why not," she said, somewhat stiffly, Mike thought. Or was it simply her uncertainty over what he had said.

"It's down the block on the right."

"I have to admit," Mike said, while they walked, "I wasn't exactly telling the truth in there. I do know more about the investigation, or at least part of it. And it involves you."

"What?" Andrea stopped to confront Mike.

"It seems you've been seen with a man named

George Arthur."

"Who told you that?" she asked defensively. "What business is that of yours?"

"Not mine exactly, but I heard through the police grapevine that this Arthur is mixed up in some bad business. I thought you would want to know."

Mike watched her face as she took in what he said, clearly not appreciating his words.

"Look," he said quickly, "maybe we could talk about this somewhere other than on the sidewalk."

Andrea glared at him and Mike started to think he blew it.

"Okay," she said defiantly. "Yes, I think we better talk. I haven't eaten since this morning. I'll meet you at the Taco Bell on Pantops. It's close to my house. Can you find it? Top of the hill and turn right at the light."

"I can find it."

Before he could say more, she turned and walked toward her car.

Watching Andrea Hudson drive off in a dark blue BMW, he remembered that exactly two weeks ago on this same street, and at about the same time, he had watched the preacher drive away. 'God bless you,' he had said to Mike before getting in his car. Another bloody mess, Mike thought, and shuddered as he got into his car.

Mike headed toward the by-pass. He congratulated himself on managing at least to get past the most critical hurdle--she had agreed to talk. He spotted her BMW in the parking lot and slipped his car into an adjacent spot. Breathing deeply several times, he walked toward the restaurant where he found her sitting at a booth sipping a fountain drink.

"I hope you don't mind meeting here," she said as he approached the table. "Would you like something to eat? I'm starved. It's been a long day."

Mike sensed her mood had improved, but he saw she

looked worn out.

Having spent time visiting his relatives in New Mexico, Mike knew how he wanted Mexican food to taste. It wasn't what they served at Taco Bell, nor did any so-called Mexican restaurants in the area serve what he ate in the southwest, and which he often yearned for.

"I'll just have a Coke," he answered, standing next to the table. "You go ahead and eat."

"I've already ordered. It's coming up now. Excuse me. I'll get you a coke. Regular or diet?"

"Regular is fine. Thanks."

As she left to get her order, Mike slid into the booth. He wondered whether he should offer to pay for the Coke. He hadn't eaten alone at a restaurant with a woman other than Kirsten for a long time. When Andrea came back with her order, Mike took his Coke from the tray and reached for his wallet.

"I think I can handle a Coke," Andrea said with a smile. "Besides, you're supposed to give me some sort of inside dope on George Arthur. Call it a trade."

Mike appreciated the entry into the central topic of the night. He thanked her for the drink, took another deep breath, and launched into the story he had prepared.

"I'm not sure how to approach this, but I'm worried about the Jefferson Bunch."

"Worried? Why? I thought you said this was about me and George Arthur?"

"Well, it is. But it's related. I'm worried about what might come down on them given their interest in a Hemings document and the murder of one of their members."

Andrea looked confused.

"I think you have to agree they're a decent bunch of folks," he began.

"Okay, and . . .?"

"It's just that I wouldn't want to see them get mixed up in something illegal."

"I can't see how they would do something illegal," Andrea said, still puzzled. "We voted not to get involved with a private investigation. No one tonight suggested otherwise."

"It has to do with what I heard on the police grapevine. They're aware you know someone who's interested in buying the Hemings document. That is, if it can be found. The police and the FBI are sure that person is George Arthur."

"FBI! Why the FBI? What is going on? Have they been tailing me? Why?"

Andrea put a taco down and reached for her drink to prevent choking on her food.

"Not you, but George Arthur. He's known to be a collector of historic artifacts. Since you've been seen with him, the feds figured he was the person looking for the Hemings letter."

"Whoa!" said Andrea. "First, who told the police or the FBI that I knew someone willing to finance an investigation? That was something I only told the group."

"I'm afraid I'm responsible. It came up in a conversation I had with the local cops when we were talking about the Crawford murder. I told them about the Hemings document and that it was important enough for someone you knew to offer to shoulder the expense to search for it."

"I'm getting lost here," Andrea said, now composed enough to begin eating her food again. "Do the police think George killed this Crawford person? That's crazy."

"No. They don't think Arthur killed Crawford or the minister. At least I don't think they do. But they're thinking that maybe someone working for him may have. This Bob Smith, for example. He's in the Richmond jail and charged with two murders. Smith's been seen with Arthur. "

"Why would George be involved with all of this?"

"Okay, here's where it gets a little murky. The FBI has been looking into stolen historic artifacts, chiefly from museums and private collections. The trail led them to Richmond."

"Richmond is a big place. Why would they single out George? He's respected around town. He's a carpet dealer, for crying out loud. Okay, he has a collection, but so must dozens of others."

"There are some reasons why Arthur is high on their list of suspects. I'm not sure I should be telling you anymore." Mike decided against playing the Klan card just yet. "The thing is," Mike continued, "if Arthur is crooked and maybe even mixed up with the killings, then it could bring the Jefferson Bunch into it."

"I'm not sure I buy all this. George is an avid collector. That's true. I've seen what he has. It marvels many museums. There's no doubt he would love to get his hands on a Jefferson-Hemings document. But traffic in stolen goods--that's how you guys say it, isn't it--I have trouble believing that."

"You've seen the collection?" Mike asked, somewhat excitedly.

"Yes. He showed it to me one day."

"Then maybe you can help out the authorities."

"How would I do that?"

"The FBI has a list of stolen artifacts they think might be in Arthur's collection. If you could testify you saw some of these artifacts, then they could get a search warrant."

"I can't be expected to remember what he has! He's got hundreds of things. They look pretty much like any museum pieces. Swords, uniforms, photographs, guns, flags, and so on. I don't think I could tell you if a particular artifact was there. I wasn't there very long.

"Besides, a sword is a sword," she added. "I'm not that interested in old military stuff anyway. I made a fuss over it to impress George. I would have liked it better if he had an art collection."

"What if I showed you some pictures of artifacts?" Mike said as he reached for a folder he brought with him. "If you could just look at these and tell me if any look familiar. The feds gave me a half dozen printouts of things missing from places around the country."

"Like I said, it all looks the same. But let me see."

Mike handed her the small stack of photos. While she studied them, he looked across the table and commented as best he could on what was in each photo.

"I'm not that good either at identifying artifacts. That one on top, for instance, is a revolver used by Jeb Stuart. I only know that because it says so on the back of the photo. It was stolen from a private collector in Virginia."

"It looks like several revolvers George has in his collection. I'm afraid this is hopeless." She scanned again the photos spread out on the table.

"And what's this? It looks like an old musket?"

"It's a Whitworth rifle. A favorite of snipers in the Civil War. I'm told something like this can fetch forty thousand dollars in a sale to military history buffs. The other rifle," Mike said as he reached across the table to point at a photo, "is a Tarpley carbine. Very rare. Stolen from an antiques store in North Carolina."

"Mike, I really can't help. When I look at these pictures up close, I can see differences. But, honestly, when I was looking around George's room one gun looked like any other."

"What about this?" Mike asked, pointing at a photo of a painting. "It's a portrait of Robert E. Lee painted around 1864. Someone stole it from a Smithsonian museum in Washington just a few months ago. The feds say there are middle men who look for museum employees who will take a payment to smuggle out an artifact. They pay a sizeable sum of money for them to do it, and then charge a collector an even larger sum."

"George did show me a painting of Lee. Or maybe some other general. I'm really not sure. I can't say this was the same painting I saw. They all had beards and wore grey uniforms! I'm sorry. Maybe he did tell me it was Lee. He was quite proud of that. But whether it was the painting in the photo, I don't know."

"I'll talk to the FBI about it. This may be enough to get a search warrant. In my experience it all depends on the judge. "Consider this for a minute," he continued. "What if you knew specifically what to look for? Now that you've seen these pictures, do you think you could recognize them if you went back? I'm sure we could get more pictures. All you would have to do is confirm that one or more of the items was there."

"That's not going to happen," Andrea said forcefully.

"Look, I know he's a friend, at least I assume he is. But you could also see this as a way to clear him." Mike knew he was definitely winging it.

"You don't understand. We're not speaking anymore."

"Did he fire you?" Mike asked, not knowing if she even worked for him.

"It's really not any of your business. Not anyone's, not even the FBI's. But I can tell you I'm not going back in that house."

Mike hadn't anticipated this response in the many dry runs he played out in his mind over the past few days. Trying to decide where to go next, he backtracked. "Did Arthur ever say anything? Do anything? Something that might suggest items in his collection were not altogether legal?"

"No. If they were stolen why would he tell anyone? I

assume if you've got stolen stuff you'd keep that fact close to your chest."

"Where is the collection?" Mike asked, thinking he could at least bring back some information about its location.

"It's in the lower level of his house. All locked up. Steel door, electronic keypad and everything."

"Sounds a bit over the top."

"George said his insurance company requires it. This isn't a mom-and-pop collection. Like I said, I don't really know one old gun from another, but the collection is impressive. Like a real museum. Overhead lighting, glass cases. He didn't say, but I assume the room also has automatic temperature and humidity controls. And obviously a security system."

Mike tried a different tack. "I have to say," he began, "that I haven't been entirely open with you."

"Oh?"

"I am worried about the Jefferson group being associated with Arthur and these murders. But that wasn't the main reason why I wanted to talk. The FBI wanted me to see if I could enlist you to help them catch Arthur at whatever he's up to. They realized you might refuse to help, maybe because you're too close to him. However, even if that were the case, they reasoned you might tell Arthur the authorities were on to him. If you did, it might stir things up enough for them to get a line on him."

This definitely had not been part of what he rehearsed. Why did he suddenly tell her all this?

"Well, I'm sorry to disappoint you boys, but I don't see how I can help. And I sure as hell don't intend to tell George anything. You can tell everyone that."

"What if you had something he wanted?"

"What are you talking about? Like what? You mean the Hemings letter? No one knows where it is. You know that."

"Okay, maybe not the actual letter, but what if Arthur thought you had it."

Mike was really winging it now. He wasn't sure what he meant, but it felt good to be in the game again.

"I can't imagine George falling for that."

"Maybe you're right, but if we could figure something out, would you be willing to contact Arthur?"

"What would I say to him? George, despite the fact I hate your guts and we aren't talking to each other and I don't want to see you again, I found the Hemings letter if you still want it."

Andrea chuckled at the absurdity and Mike, too, had to smile.

"I'm sure we can work on a story. What if George Arthur thought you were out for his money, for example. Perhaps looking for some sort of commission. Then maybe what was going on between you two wouldn't matter. From what you say he wants the letter badly. A possible deal might be especially attractive if you made it clear the letter is in the hands of someone who wants to make a sale on the quiet. If the FBI is right, Arthur should be used to dealing with people like that. "

"I don't know. How does that get him jailed for stealing artifacts? You can't arrest him for buying something that doesn't exist. He's always in a position to say he thought the purchase was legit."

"I don't have all the answers," Mike admitted. "But if the warrant doesn't come through, would you help to set up something that will make him bite? And maybe get us access to his artifact room?"

"I guess the way I feel about him now, yes. I might be able to help. But I'll need to know more."

And I'll need to know more, Mike thought. He wasn't sure where he had landed and wondered whether he told her too much. But he also had a feeling he could trust her.

"I better be going," Andrea announced. She scooped up an empty taco basket and made ready to leave the table.

"Thanks for talking to me," Mike said as he moved to get up.

"I guess I have to thank you as well," Andrea said, standing next to the table. "I can't see myself ever getting involved with George Arthur again. But if the thought ever crossed my mind, I now have more reasons to keep my distance."

They walked together toward their cars. Andrea said good-night, walked around Mike's car and pressed the remote key to open her door. Mike looked across the roof of his car, thinking for the first time tonight, how attractive she was. She turned to look at him.

"Maybe we can do this again. Some place a little nicer than fast food."

"I think I'd like that." Did he?

They exchanged contact information. Andrea looked up as she finished entering Mike's number in her phone.

"Besides," Andrea added with a slight smile, "you never asked me if I know the combination to George's room."

Mike didn't know what to say in response. Was she kidding? He finally sputtered, "Do you really? How did you get it?"

But Andrea had gotten into her car, put it in gear and pulled out of the parking space.

Chapter 26

Once again Mike found himself seated at his sister's kitchen table on a Saturday morning while he waited for a call from the C'ville police. After meeting with Andrea he had left messages both for Dixie and Miles Springer. He suggested they re-group to decide what direction to take given his conversation with Andrea Hudson. He assumed they'd alert the FBI agents.

Tammy never got up early on Saturday unless she had to be somewhere and today nobody needed her to go anywhere. Her father had already been in the kitchen to drink a cup of coffee with his wife and brother-in-law before heading to his university office. "Sorry to go, but I have a grant deadline. And people think college professors teach one class and then play golf," he joked on his way out.

Mike appreciated the quiet time with his sister. They talked about their mother and how they both needed to make a trip out west to see her. Since Mike rarely called, his mother took to phoning Kelly to check up on him. Kelly passed on news about their mother, which helped Mike believe he wasn't avoiding her. Mother and daughter had talked on the phone last night and the conversation apparently resurrected memories in Kelly of the food their mother used to make. This morning his sister made *huevos rancheros*. Tammy wouldn't go near them and the red chili ladled on top of the eggs and tortillas bothered Steve's sensitive stomach. It was a perfect breakfast for the two siblings to share.

"Too bad Justice isn't here," Kelly said as she served them both. "He loves this food."

"He's coming down today, but I don't know when."

"He's been a big help, hasn't he."

"Yeah, he has. He's been working as a liaison between the feds and the locals on a case."

"That's not what I meant," Kelly said.

"What do you mean?"

"It's just that you seem more relaxed when he's around. And it's Justice, isn't it, who's helping get you back into police work?"

"He does create a comfort zone around me. I'm not sure why that is. But as to getting me involved again? I don't know. It's been something of an eye opener."

"You mean about the case, or whatever you two are working on?"

"Yes and no. I guess I haven't said much about what we're doing. Kirsten and I made it a rule not to talk shop at home. She had to deal with some pretty awful things at the hospital, so the rule worked for both of us."

Kelly couldn't help noticing that Mike seemed more at ease when talking about Kirsten.

"But what's the eye-opener?" she asked.

"It all goes back to the possible Hemings document that Professor McCabe talked about when he was here. Everyone has been trying to track it down and now it seems it's linked to a couple of murders."

"That poor Crawford man and the minister? This is about the document Paul wanted you to look for?"

"Seems so. The document could be worth a lot to a collector, maybe even enough to kill for it. But that's not what's opening my eyes. It's about Justice."

"Would it help to talk about it? You know I like Justice a lot. You may not have been able to pick up the pieces after Kirsten's death if it hadn't been for him. Checking on you, making meals, calling me every time he thought you were too depressed to take care of yourself."

"I know, I know. And that's part of the problem."

"I think I'm missing something here. Are you worried you haven't thanked Justice enough? I really don't think

. . ."

"No, not that. How can I explain? He's black!"

"Well, yes, I think I noticed that!" Kelly said with a tinge of sarcasm. "You've always treated him like color doesn't matter. Are you saying it does? If so, I don't believe you. Not you."

"But it *does* matter. In a way I really never considered. Here we are chasing after some letter that links a white man, an important one at that, to a black slave. To me the letter's simply something the bad guys want and are willing to do bad things to get. No different than a bag of drug money.

"But for Justice it's altogether something else. It's about him. About being black in a society that more often than not takes advantage of blacks. It did two-hundred years ago and still does today. At least in some places and by some folks. I've seen the way people sometimes look at Justice when we're on duty. Even when we weren't. Everyone knows there's racial prejudice and I guess I just accepted it. An unfortunate fact of life in the land of the free. I figure someday people will get over it."

Kelly looked up from her breakfast, her attention focused on her brother.

"I've missed seeing how Justice sees this case," Mike said. "I've been wrapped up in thinking about myself. Who I am. Where is my life going. All of that. It's all mixed up in these feelings of being outside myself. But the bottom line is that it's been all about me."

"You're being unfair to yourself. I think . . ."

"No, listen. Let me finish. This Hemings letter. It just doesn't have the same meaning for me as it does for Justice. Thomas Jefferson doesn't look the same when he's the one who kept your people in chains, bought and sold them. And possibly took advantage of a young girl who had no real choice but to obey him.

"I've never told you this, but earlier the same night Kirsten died, Justice and I had been at a crime scene. A young black woman had been shot by the man she'd been living with. A white guy, maybe almost fifty years old. I wasn't there later to learn what really happened. The other day Justice brought me up to date. This guy had been abusing her. She was trying to get away from him when he shot her.

"The past couple days I've been thinking about her. And about Kirsten. About who they were and how different their lives were. I began to wonder whether this black woman had a choice. You know, what was her life like that she had to take up with this guy. Did she have a choice?"

"Mike, these things are complex."

"What's complex?" a cheerful Tammy asked as she waltzed into the room, her eyes on the breakfast plates.

"I'm starved. Don't tell me you both ate that egg and chili stuff?"

"Good morning, Sunshine," Mike quipped, working hard to match the merry mood of his niece. "If you ate *huevos rancheros* you'd be showing your appreciation for your Hispanic heritage."

"I appreciate you and mom already."

"But how about your *abuela* in New Mexico?"

"I appreciate grandma, too. That doesn't mean I have to appreciate her food."

Tammy," her mother said, laughing, "Uncle Mike's only joking."

Kelly picked up both their plates, their food uneaten throughout their conversation, and moved toward the microwave.

"One of these days," her uncle said, "we need to get you out to Santa Fe and let you meet all your relations. Show you what good food they have. Like *tres leches*!" Mike patted his stomach.

"Oh mom, can we go?"

"Mike, see what you started," Kelly groaned with a smile. She put their plates in the oven for reheating.

The interruption by his niece would have been sufficient excuse to postpone their conversation, but the phone ringing provided even more reason.

"That's probably the call you've been waiting for," Kelly said to her brother. "We can talk more later. I'll wait on heating up your plate until you're done on the phone. And Sunshine here wants her breakfast."

Mike picked up the remote receiver from the kitchen table and proceeded down the hallway so he could speak privately. It wasn't Detective Springer or Dixie calling, as he expected, but Justice.

"Hey partner!" Justice began. "I'm told the feds want to meet again in about an hour, at ten thirty. Detective Springer got your message and asked me to get in touch with you. I'm coming south on 29, just past Culpeper. I shouldn't have any trouble getting there by then."

"Where are we meeting? Is the FBI still shy about being seen around town?"

"Seems that way. Springer told me we're to meet at the same hotel. If the room is different someone will be in the lobby waiting for us. We're all anxious to know how your date went last night."

"It wasn't a date!"

"Whatever you say, Miguel," Justice chuckled. "I'll see you in a hour."

Mike decided he had time to finish his breakfast and maybe another cup of coffee. Returning to the kitchen, he asked his sister if she needed any errands run while he was out. One immediate request was to drop Tammy off at a friend's house on his way downtown.

"It's Brandon Sorenson's house," Tammy said. "Mr. Sorenson keeps asking me about you. He knows the guy who hit Brandon and me is in jail. I forgot, but he wanted me to tell you thanks for helping nab him."

"I'm not sure the local police would appreciate me getting any credit for arresting the guy."

"But it's okay if Mr. Sorenson thinks so, isn't it?" Tammy smiled coyly.

"I guess so. Maybe it will help your chances with Brandon!" Mike replied with a wink at his niece.

"I'm not interested in Brandon! Not that way! Besides, if I was, I could get him by myself."

"Stop it you two," Kelly said, all smiles. "Tammy, eat some breakfast and then go get ready. Uncle Mike has to leave soon."

The two siblings made eye contact, signaling that their interrupted conversation would continue later.

Chapter 27

Mike and Justice arrived at the entrance to the hotel on the mall at the same time. Seeing no one to greet them in the lobby, they headed for the elevator and the room where they had met on Tuesday.

"Just remember," Mike said as they went up, "my meeting with Andrea Hudson was not a date."

"Whatever you say. But when a man and a woman go out to eat together . . ."

"Justice!" Mike exclaimed. He knew he was being ribbed and tried hard not to smile.

"Well, okay, but let's hope you made some progress. You know, past the small talk and on to 'whose place shall we go to?'"

"Justice, I said enough!" Mike jabbed his partner not too gently in the ribs with an elbow.

"Okay, okay, if that's the way you want it. No need to get violent."

The two smiled at one another, reminding Mike of the many good times he and Justice had when working in the District. They exited the elevator and walked toward the meeting room. Detective Springer opened the door.

"Everyone's here," Springer said, backing away to let them into the room. "And we have a new addition. This is Sergeant Miller from the Richmond Police Department."

A large man, almost the size of Justice, with reddish hair and cheeks revealing freckles of the same color, stood up from the table and shook each of the newcomers' hands.

"Eric Miller," he said. "I've been asked to help co-ordinate what's going on between C'ville and Richmond.

We've got your man Smith, but from what I've been told, there may be more fish out there."

"We were in Richmond the last couple of days," Agent Norton interrupted. "Briefing the local police on what we think is going on and talking about how to proceed. They've known about George Arthur's possible connection to illegal artifacts. We brought that news to them some months ago. They didn't know about possible Klan involvement or George Arthur's relationship with Andrea Hudson. Sergeant Miller was asked by his department to sit in on our discussions in order to facilitate communication."

"More than being asked," Miller said, clearly irritated. Looking at Mike and Justice, he added, "The FBI's been operating in town without telling us what's going on. Our police chief is upset, to say the least. He briefed the mayor, who is not happy either. I'm here on orders to make sure everyone knows what everyone else is doing."

Agent Norton started to say something, then hesitated. His partner took the opportunity to move the conversation away from turf disputes between federal and local law enforcement.

"Mike, I guess we should start with you," Agent Simpson said. "We understand you met with Andrea Hudson last night."

Mike gave Justice a cold look so he wouldn't make any date jokes.

"Yes, I did. I tried out what we discussed. Told her I learned from the police grapevine about George Arthur's involvement with stolen artifacts. She said she didn't know anything about that and I believe her. It turns out that something happened between her and Arthur. She didn't say what, but she isn't talking to him anymore. Clearly doesn't want anything more to do with him."

"Are you sure she wasn't just leading you on?"

Norton asked. "You know, faking a breakup so you wouldn't go any farther with this."

"I agree. She could be putting one over on you, trying to get you off their trail," Simpson said.

"I don't think so. I don't think she was faking it," Mike responded. "She seemed extremely upset with him. Denied, as I said, knowing anything about illegal activities on his part. However," Mike paused for effect, "she did tell me she saw his collection."

As if something they rehearsed, both FBI agents leaned forward in their chairs simultaneously.

"She called it 'museum like.' The whole thing was that impressive. It's on the lower level of his house. She doesn't know much about historic artifacts, especially military ones, so she really couldn't say for certain whether she had seen any of the items in those photos. With one exception. He apparently has a number of guns, but she said one gun looked like another."

"You said there was an exception," Norton interrupted.

"The painting. The one of Robert E. Lee from the Washington gallery. She told me Arthur has a painting like that and she was pretty sure it was of Lee. Said he was quite proud of it. But whether this is the same painting, she couldn't say for sure. But how many can there be?"

"I don't know," Norton said. "Probably more than one. We'll have to see if this is enough to get a warrant."

"Things are moving along," Simpson said, obviously happy with the news Mike delivered. "Thanks to you, Mike, we confirmed Arthur's got a large artifact collection. And it's in the house, as we thought."

"It's in a secure room. Heavy-duty door and all. Ms. Hudson said Arthur's insurance company requires him to keep it under serious lockup."

Mike nearly said something about Andrea claiming

to know the combination on the door, but then decided he didn't know for sure that she did. Had she been teasing him? Even if she did know it, he didn't see how it could be relevant.

"We'll have to wait on the judge," Simpson said. "See if we can get a warrant."

"One other thing," Mike said. "Ms. Hudson said she may might be willing to help us, depending on what we wanted from her. That's one reason why I think she isn't trying to trick us."

"Or she just wants to find out what we plan to do about Arthur," Norton responded.

"But why would she tell me about the painting?" Mike asked, frustrated at the agents' tone and their distrust of his cop instincts. "She wouldn't want us to get a warrant if she was on his side."

"I don't know, "Norton replied, "but it doesn't feel right to me."

"If she isn't talking to this guy, then I'm not sure what else she can do," Simpson said. "It's good to know about the size of the collection and its whereabouts, but I'm not sure it helps all that much. We can't break into the place. Our case would never get very far if we did. Without the warrant we're back to square one.

"I think what we need to do, warrant or no warrant," the agent said, "is turn our attention to Bob Smith. We've got to squeeze him for what he knows about Arthur, the stolen goods, and the Klan. We're due back in the District later today, but first thing Monday morning we'll talk to Smith. Until then he can stew a little longer."

Agent Simpson's statement brought an end to the meeting. The FBI agents and the C'ville police officers began talking about who else should be in Richmond during Smith's interrogation. Mike and Justice followed Sergeant Miller to the elevator.

"What do you think, Eric?" Justice asked, pushing

the down elevator button. "Do you think Mike gave the feds enough to get a warrant?"

"I'm not sure. Seems like awfully weak testimony on this woman's part. As you guys know, it depends on how the judge sees it."

The elevator took them to the lobby, where they exited and walked through the hotel doors into the sun. Miller said he needed to get back to Richmond and proceeded a few steps ahead of Mike and Justice, before stopping and turning to face the two detectives.

"I'll let everyone know what happens about the warrant as soon as the feds get us the word. I'm hoping because I was present they'll feel obligated to keep us in the loop. I think the agents are right to put pressure on this Smith guy, but I'm told his lawyer has stopped him from talking. Although that may change when he finds out what all we know. I've got to let the chief know the agents will be visiting Smith on Monday. He'll want some presence there. And it looks like the C'ville cops want in, too. Could get crowded in the interview room. Nice meeting you guys."

They watched Sergeant Miller walk down the mall. Mike realized that he and Justice might not be needed anymore. He had contacted Andrea Hudson as he was asked. Justice had played his liaison role. The FBI and the local police in the two cities appeared to have everything in hand.

"I guess we're done with this business, partner," Justice said, putting Mike's thoughts into words. "They don't seem to require our services in order to wrap this up."

"Looks that way. But the Hemings document still hasn't shown up. Wouldn't you like to find it?"

"You know my feelings about it."

"There's one more thing," Mike said. "I didn't tell the feds everything Ms. Hudson said."

"Ms. Hudson? Sort of formal isn't it?"

"Come on! No more. Okay, Andrea. But it doesn't mean anything."

"Whatever. So what else did she say?"

Mike related Andrea's parting words about the combination to Arthur's artifacts room.

"But you know the feds are right," Justice said. "We can't just walk into the place without permission. Before you start thinking things you shouldn't think, wait until we hear from Richmond about the warrant."

"Okay, let's see what happens. In the meantime, can you come for dinner tonight? Kelly wanted me to make sure to invite you. Steve is cooking steaks on the grill."

"That sounds like something I'd be foolish to pass up. I've got to check on Auntie Blossom's house. I guess I mean my house. I have an appointment with a contractor at four. Auntie didn't exactly put a lot of money into the upkeep on the house, so there's a lot that needs to be done. Sooner than later, I'm afraid. I think I can get there by six, if that's okay."

"I'm sure it is. I'll make sure the beer is cold."

Chapter 28

Mike didn't need to put beer on ice. Steve Cummings made margaritas for the adults, joking as he usually did when serving these tequila drinks, that among his wife's New Mexican recipes, he liked this one the best. The mild fall weather allowed them to sit in the sunroom and open the large sliding doors. The room sat above the apartment Mike occupied, mostly hidden from neighbors, overlooking woods to the rear of their house. Charlottesville's rolling hills and ravines meant many houses abutted forested tracts and streams. It created a park-like setting, but also left the local deer population seemingly free to roam at will. Drivers frequently met them crossing city streets when the meandering deer went searching for residents' edible landscapes. Living in a city, with the impression of being in the country, made the wandering deer a manageable inconvenience.

"Let me know when I should put the steaks on," Steve said to no one in particular, speaking from a chair he appeared unlikely to move from for a while.

"I can't believe you guys will eat meat from helpless animals locked in pens, then shot in the head before they're slaughtered," Tammy said from her corner on the sofa.

Her parents were accustomed to such commentary, and Mike had heard his share since he came to live with them. However, she caught Justice off guard with her remark.

"Tammy, we've had this conversation before," her mother said. "Everyone must make their own choices about food. We're happy you're a vegetarian. It's your choice, but we choose to eat meat once in a while."

Justice, looking uncomfortable having to defend his

food habits, said, "People have been eating meat since they started walking upright. Probably before that."

Tammy started to answer, but her mother shook her head. "Tammy, now is not the time for this discussion. We apologize, Justice. Tammy can get carried away."

Kelly gave a stern look at her daughter, meant to bring the discussion to an end.

Maintaining the pained look adolescents probably practice in the mirror, Tammy mumbled the last word. "Okay, but if all of you have heart attacks from eating red meat, don't blame me."

"We promise not to blame you," her father said, sipping his margarita. Turning to Justice, Steve asked about his plans now that he was a property owner in C'ville. "Mike told us you're considering living here."

"I am," Justice replied. "I've given a lot of thought to what I want to do. Auntie Blossom's gift allows me some options I didn't have before. Like I told Mike, I won't miss all the stuff that goes with the job in the District."

At this moment Justice's phone chirped. He excused himself in order to answer it in the living room. Steve took the opportunity to say he'd put the steaks on, playfully sticking out his tongue at his daughter on the way to light the grill. Kelly headed for the kitchen to prepare a salad and side dishes, as well as a cheese and mushroom quiche for Tammy.

Mike and his niece were discussing her plans for the evening when Justice returned to the sunroom.

"The FBI didn't get the warrant," Justice said. "That was Springer on the phone. He just heard and wanted to pass along the news. The judge didn't think we had enough to go on. Especially since we're relying on the word of someone who can't say for sure what she saw and may have a grudge against our man. I guess everything Ms. Hudson told you got passed on."

"That doesn't seem quite right," Mike said.

"If it's any consolation, Springer told me the Richmond police have a slightly different take on things. The judge who refused the request just so happens to play golf with Arthur. They may not be buddy-buddies, but they know each other. The Richmond cops think Arthur's reputation as a business leader in the city probably influenced the decision as well. Anyway, the judge isn't going to sic the police on him without a stronger petition."

Tammy had been listening intently.

"Is this about the missing secret letter?" she asked excitedly.

"Maybe and maybe not," her uncle replied. "Don't you think your mother might need help in the kitchen?"

Tammy recognized the not-too-subtle hint and proceeded out of the room, although whether it was toward the kitchen wasn't clear.

"The feds are right, then," Mike said. "Seems the next step is to turn the screws on Bob Smith. See if he can be scared into implicating Arthur. But, like we discussed earlier today, we're no longer part of it."

Steve yelled a "five-minute warning" from the lawn below the sunroom. Kelly poked her head into the sunroom and asked Mike to see what people wanted to drink with dinner.

Justice's future plans continued to be the topic of conversation at the dinner table. His immediate plan included moving to Charlottesville and fixing up his aunt's house. Landing a job would come next. Justice said he had enough money to hold him for a while. Eventually he'd have to find an income stream, since he wanted to save some of his aunt's money for retirement.

Justice reported he intended to deliver a letter of resignation to his department chief this coming week. Mike then surprised everyone by announcing that he, too, was ready to submit his resignation.

"I guess I should have said something earlier. I think you all know I've been thinking about quitting. Justice can deliver two letters. Okay partner?"

"I'm sure the chief will be real happy," Justice quipped, rolling his eyes. "Already shorthanded and now two fewer officers to answer the call of duty. Yeah, that will make him real happy."

Kelly smiled broadly. "That's so great. I'm sure both of you can find something to do here in Charlottesville."

She then looked at her brother somewhat apprehensively. "Mike, you are planning on staying here?"

"For now? Sure. I don't have a lot of choices. Thanks to you and Steve I have some time to make a decision about what comes next. That is, if you'll put up with me a little longer."

"Don't be silly," Kelly said.

"Stay as long as you want," Steve added.

"And you can keep looking for the secret letter," Tammy said, which led Justice and her parents to look at Mike for his answer.

"Not my job," Mike responded. "Besides, I'm thinking of becoming a farmer, raising carrots and lettuce for rabbits and other vegetarians."

"Not funny," declared Tammy, but unable to keep a smile from forming. "Why can't you look for that letter?" she asked. "You've already been helping, but you aren't on duty, right? I mean you're deactivated or something like that. And if you quit you'll need something to do."

"Tammy," her mother said, "let your Uncle Mike alone. "What's most important is that he'll be close. Hopefully for a long time. Let's have dessert in the living room. It's cherry pie."

The announcement got everyone moving from the table. Kelly made a point to walk over to her brother to give him a hug.

"I'm so happy," she murmured. Letting go of him, she asked loudly over his shoulder, "Who wants ice cream with their pie? And who wants coffee?"

Tammy went upstairs to get ready for a night out with friends. The adults moved to the living room to eat dessert. Both Mike and Justice went through a list of things each might do in Charlottesville, with Kelly and Steve throwing out more ideas. Justice was giving serious thought to opening up a small restaurant in the Belmont area, a part of town becoming a popular location for trendy eateries. Mike joked that he might look for a security job at Monticello. The evening turned into one of the most pleasant Mike had experienced in some time. Maybe because he made it official he wasn't going back to his job, or maybe because he felt flushed with support from those who meant the most to him. Mike wondered if it was time to stop seeing Dr. Rider.

Tammy still hadn't come home when, around ten o'clock, Mike headed downstairs to his apartment. Kelly remained curled up on the sofa with a book, having lost the coin toss with Steve to see who would wait up for their daughter to arrive before her 11 p.m. curfew.

He'd already gotten into bed, prepared to turn off the light, when the phone rang from atop the desk across the room. Flipping back the covers, he jumped up to answer it.

"Hello?" he said hesitantly, not recognizing the caller's number, and unsure who would be calling him. He glanced at the clock by his bed. Ten thirty.

"Hi! I hope I'm not getting you out of bed," said a woman's voice. "It's Andrea. Andrea Hudson. You know, the girl who hangs around with bad guys in Richmond."

Mike laughed.

"No, no. I was just reading," he lied, the way everyone does when disturbed in bed at night by a phone call. "How are you?"

"Fine. Thanks. I'm sorry if I'm calling too late."

"No problem."

"It's just that I've wanted to tell you something I didn't mention last night. At the time I wasn't sure I should say more. I guess I held out and it's been bothering me."

"You mean about the combination on the lock to Arthur's collection?" Mike asked. He wondered whether she was confessing she had been joking.

"Not exactly. I apologize for being, well, you know, for being so coy about it. I guess I was still digesting everything you said and I didn't know for sure what you wanted from me."

"You mean you do know the combination?"

"I think so."

Mike wasn't sure what Andrea was trying to tell him.

"When he took me down there I saw him work the combination. Or at least part of it. The first four numbers were 0415. Then he blocked my view. I'm pretty sure there were eight numbers. I could tell by the way he punched the keypad. I'm willing to bet the last four were 1865."

"You've lost me."

"April 15, 1865, 04151865, is the date of Lincoln's death. George was obsessed with that date. He must have mentioned it to me a dozen times in some context or another. I guess it should have told me something."

"You're quite the detective." Mike said. Then added, "I'm not sure what the police can do with it, but I'll pass it on. I learned tonight that the FBI failed to get a warrant based on the information you gave us. The judge wouldn't bite. Said it wasn't enough. I guess I owe you an apology, taking you through all this stuff and no pay off."

"Not at all. Like I told you last night, you helped me gain a better perspective on George Arthur. I'm afraid I look pretty much the fool. I keep thinking about who that bastard really is and what he tried to do. I was hoping you'd get the warrant."

"You couldn't have known who he was. I'm sure he looks every bit the respectable business man. I've heard he has a good reputation around town. In fact, that's one of the reasons the judge wouldn't approve a search warrant. No one except the feds know he's mixed up with stolen artifacts and the Klan."

"Klan? You mean Ku Klux Klan?"

Damn, thought Mike. He hadn't meant to tell her that.

"The FBI think so."

"I didn't know those nuts were around anymore. Now I really look like an idiot."

"I'm sorry. I shouldn't have said anything. It slipped out. You didn't need to know. The FBI and the police are trying to see if there is a connection between the Klan and the killing of Crawford and the minister, and maybe even with the stolen artifacts in Arthur's basement."

"I'd like to see him rot in jail. I really wish I could do more. That was one reason I called. I know it's late, but it took me a while to work up the nerve. I said there was something I didn't tell you. Besides the combination, I mean."

"Oh?"

"I have a key to Arthur's place. He gave it to me so that . . . this is hard to say . . . so that if I was coming to see him and he wasn't there, I could let myself in. I never had a reason to use it," she added quickly.

"I'm not sure what can be done with it. Even with a key the feds or Richmond police can't let themselves in without permission."

"I guess you're right. I just thought you should know about it. Looks like I'm not being very helpful."

"No, you are. I mean everything helps. I'll tell the people working on the case about the combination and the key. Maybe they'll see some way to use it."

"I seem to have interrupted whatever you were doing for no good reason. Sorry. But maybe I can make it up. Could I buy you a drink? A real one, not a Coke this time?"

Mike paused. Was he being asked out on a date!

The phone. Look at the phone. It's in your hand.

"Hello. Are you still there? I didn't mean you have to," Andrea said with an uncomfortable chuckle.

"No. Sorry. I mean yes. I'm here."

I'm Mike Chance. I am real. I am here. Breathe deeply.

"Look, I should tell you something. My wife died about nine months ago . . ."

"I'm sorry. I didn't know. I'm out of line here. Not being very helpful continues."

"No, really. It's not that. What I'm trying to say is that it just caught me off guard. It's been a long time since a woman asked me out."

"We're talking just a drink here," Andrea said, laughing.

"I know. Of course. And, yes, I'd like a drink." Now! Mike thought. "I mean meeting for a drink would be great."

"How about Whistles? It's on the mall. They have a nice bar area. Do you know it?"

"I can find it."

"I have a conference call at six tomorrow evening, but I'm free later. How about eight o'clock? Unless you have a problem drinking on Sunday. Oh! I didn't even ask. Do you drink? I mean a Coke is fine, too."

It was Mike's turn to laugh. "I really haven't ruled out any days of the week for having a drink. And I've been known to drink something more than a Coke. Eight o'clock is fine."

"I'll see you tomorrow then," Andrea said, leaving

Mike staring at the phone in his hand.

Plastic. Keypad. Screen. I'm Mike Chance. I'm real. I'm here.

Chapter 29

Mike arrived early for his meeting with Andrea at the tavern on the pedestrian mall. He ordered a beer to calm himself, although he worried that maybe you weren't supposed to order before the other person arrived, especially the one who invited you.

To keep his mind occupied, he went through what happened earlier in the day. He had been rather distracted at breakfast and Kelly asked if he hadn't slept well. He ended up telling her that he had an "appointment" to meet Andrea Hudson later that evening, the woman who helped with the police case. To Kelly's credit she didn't tease him the way Justice had. No comments about a date. She simply said she was glad he was involved with something and meeting new people.

When Justice phoned later in the day the conversation went differently. He called Mike to tell him he planned to drive to the District tomorrow and wondered if Mike would have his resignation letter ready. Mike had forgotten about typing a letter, but promised he'd have it ready for Justice to pick up in the morning.

When Justice asked if he wanted to go out that night for a beer with him and Dixie, things went downhill, as least in Mike's view. He simply could have said 'no thanks,' or, 'I'm too tired,' or 'I have to do something for Kelly.' Anything other than telling Justice about Andrea's phone call and that she had a key to George Arthur's place. Mike explained he planned to meet her later that evening to talk things over.

"And what things might that be, Miguel?" Justice wisecracked immediately.

"Look, I'm sorry I mentioned it. When she called late last night she offered to buy me a drink. As a way of apologizing for holding out about the key. That's all. Maybe the feds can find a way to use the key. I thought it would be a good idea to talk some more with her, especially since the FBI doesn't seem to believe me that she's on our side."

"If you think you need chaperoning, Dixie and I could sit in. You're a bit out of practice. This Hudson woman could take advantage of you."

Mile could hear the teasing in his voice, but at the same time he became irritated with his partner's continued attempts at humor on his behalf. "Justice, just leave it alone."

"Okay, but I expect a complete report tomorrow. Every intimate detail."

Mike sipped his beer and smiled as he remembered Justice's last remark, unable to stay mad. Mike looked toward the entrance to the bar. He glanced at his watch. It was 8:15. He did remember that part of meeting women--they often were late. At least Kirsten was. Which fit them both, given Mike's tendency to adopt his mother's Hispanic attitude toward time. He thought of a bumper sticker he saw in Santa Fe--*Carpe mañana.*

By 8:30 Mike began thinking he'd been stood up. But why? Andrea joked it was just for a drink. There was no need to think anything else might happen between them, and she certainly sounded like she wanted to help. Her number would still be on his phone from last night and he thought about calling her. Maybe she had car trouble, or worse, had a traffic accident. But then why didn't she call him? He checked his phone, thinking maybe he missed her call, but found no missed calls. And no one answered when he attempted to contact her.

Mike wasn't sure what to do. Stay here and wait? Go to her house? That would only work if he knew where she lived, which he didn't, other than it wasn't very far from the Taco Bell where they met on Friday. He began to worry that maybe something serious had happened to her and decided to call Justice for advice.

When Justice answered, Mike quickly said, "No jokes. I've got a problem."

Mike could hear noise from the bar where Justice and Dixie were drinking. He explained that Andrea had not shown up and he worried something might have happened to her. Justice passed this on to Dixie who said it was kind of early for this kind of thinking. She took the phone from Justice.

"I'll have a patrol car go by Andrea's house. Just in case. She's a key witness in the Arthur case, so maybe some extra precaution is a good idea."

Mike reminded her of Andrea's last name and that she lived somewhere in the Pantops area. Dixie said the dispatcher would get her address. Dixie told Mike not to worry and that she'd call him when the patrol car got there and the officers determined what was up.

"She's probably sick in bed and overslept," Dixie reassured him, before putting Justice back on the line.

"Partner. Truth is, I thought perhaps you and Andrea were meeting for another reason."

"Damn it, Justice, no jokes. She could be in trouble."

"No, not that. It's just that with this key and all that, I began to wonder if maybe you two would try to get into Arthur's house."

Justice waited for his comment to sink in.

"It crossed my mind, but we're out of this, remember? The feds don't need our help and we could end up making a mess of their case."

"What about Andrea? Do you think she would go back to Arthur's for another look? By herself, maybe when he wasn't there?"

"I hadn't thought of that, but I guess it's possible. If

she isn't home maybe we could contact Eric Miller in Richmond. Do you think you could call Miller and see what he says?"

"It might be a good idea," Justice said. "Not the first time that the public tries to help the law. Let's just hope she hasn't gotten herself into trouble. But then again, maybe something important came up and she's just late. Where are you?" Justice asked.

When Mike told him the name of the restaurant, Justice said he and Dixie were at the other end of the mall, the same place they met before.

"Come on down here. We'll see what the officers turn up. If she isn't home then maybe a call to Miller is in order."

Mike downed what was left of the second beer he had ordered. He then left a generous amount of money on the table so he wouldn't have to wait for a credit card transaction.

Justice and Dixie weren't hard to find. As he approached their table, his partner asked if he wanted a beer. Slipping into a vacant chair, Mike declined, saying he already had two. He still needed to drive home.

The three of them discussed the possibility Justice had raised, that Andrea might try to do something on her own to get more evidence on Arthur. It may have looked simple, Justice said.

"All she would need to do is use her key, slip in the house, use the combination on the lock, and take some pictures of his collection using her phone. Then quickly get out again. Ten minutes tops. Assuming Arthur wasn't there."

"And assuming he hasn't changed the combination," Mike said. "I don't want to even think that she tried getting in."

A few seconds later a call came from the C'ville officers in the patrol car. Dixie listened for no more than ten seconds and said, "No. Nothing more now. Thanks."

"The officers said the place is dark," she reported. "They knocked on the door, but no one answered. They asked if they should do more. As you heard, I said not now. I think it's too early to start breaking down doors. I'll call the dispatcher to see if there have been any traffic accidents in the last hour. Mike, do you know what kind of car she drives?"

"A blue BMW."

Dixie called the station and found out that no traffic accidents involving a BMW had been reported in the last couple of hours. She said the dispatcher was sure nothing serious had happened in the last twenty-four.

"We only know about Charlottesville," Dixie said. "We could contact the Albemarle County Police, then maybe the state troopers. But if there had been something serious, word would have gotten passed on to us. Justice, maybe you better call Miller and see what's going on in Richmond before we start calling hospitals."

Justice made the call, but only reached Miller's voice recorder. He left a message explaining that Andrea Hudson had gone missing and asked if he knew anything about her whereabouts. The wait for Miller's call-back seemed to take a long time, but wasn't more than fifteen minutes.

The Richmond officer told Justice he's off duty at home, but wanted to so some checking before he called. By this time, the threesome had exited the bar and were walking slowly down the mall. Justice listened to what Sergeant Miller had to say.

"I finally tracked down the FBI agents. They're in Richmond getting ready for tomorrow's grilling of Smith. But there's more."

Justice motioned Mike and Dixie to stop.

"I talked to the agent named Norton. He was in an I-told-you-so mood. The feds really didn't believe Mike

Chance that the Hudson woman wouldn't tell Arthur that we're on to him. So they went with their original plan, which was to watch the house and see if Arthur tried to move any of his stuff. Two agents from the Richmond office had his place staked out all day. They're still there, I'm told. It seems you have to ask the feds to get any info. Doesn't pay to wait for them to tell you. My chief didn't know about the stakeout and was furious."

"What did you mean about the 'I-told-you-so attitude'? Justice asked. Mike and Dixie looked on curiously.

"I guess you want to know what happened earlier today," Miller said.

Justice rolled his eyes, which brought even more curious looks from Mike and Dixie.

"The Richmond agents watched Arthur leave his house this afternoon. Apparently on his way to play golf, since they saw him put a golf-club bag in his trunk. Within five minutes a woman drives up, parks in the driveway, runs up to the house and lets herself in. Then things got even more interesting."

"And that was?" Justice said, clearly impatient with the pace of Miller's report.

"Well, the agents reported that within another five minutes Arthur comes back. Parks his car behind the woman's car and goes into the house."

"Did they say what kind of car the woman was driving?" Justice asked. Both Mike and Dixie stood anxiously nearby.

"A blue BMW."

"Do the feds know that Andrea Hudson drives a blue BMW?" Justice asked.

Mike looked on painfully following Justice's question.

"They do," Miller replied, "and that's why they have the I-told-you-so attitude. They're convinced the Hudson woman warned Arthur about us and drove to Richmond today to help him. They're waiting to see what happens next. So far no one has come out of the house. They think, now that it's dark, the two of them will load up Arthur's stolen stuff."

Justice watched Mike and Dixie become more and more upset at being left out of the conversation.

"Look," he said to Miller, "can I call you back in a few minutes?"

Justice ended the call and relayed Miller's information to Mike and Dixie.

"This doesn't make any sense," Mike said, almost shouting. "Why would she make an appointment with me and then go help Arthur? She hates the guy for what he did to her. I'm sure of it."

"Whoa, partner," Justice said. "Let's look at the possibilities."

Before they could do that, Justice's phone rang again. Justice answered and mouthed "Miller" to Mike and Dixie.

"What's up?" Justice asked.

"Shit hit the fan over here. I just got a call from my chief. He wants me at Arthur's house right away. There's been a shooting. An FBI agent is down and someone coming out of Arthur's house is dead. I don't know anything more. Maybe one of you should get over here."

Justice put down his phone and passed on to Mike and Dixie what the sergeant said. He immediately put a hand on Mike's arm when it became obvious his partner was turning to go to his car.

"Just hold on everyone," Dixie said. "I need to call Detective Springer. See what he knows and let him know what we know. I doubt if Miller had time to include him, although maybe his chief did."

"We should drive over there," Mike said. "I feel responsible. I'm the one who suggested we couldn't use her key. She must have figured she was the only one who could get in there."

"Hang on, Mike," Dixie ordered. "I don't mean to be the law here, but you really don't have any business over there. Neither does Justice, and unless I get permission from Springer, I don't either."

Chapter 30

Detective Springer was on his way to Richmond when Dixie reached him. He'd known that the Hudson woman had been seen at George Arthur's. Agent Norton had called him that afternoon. Springer couldn't decide whether the agent called because the FBI wanted to gloat over the discovery that Hudson and Arthur met up, as the agents suspected they would, or whether he acted out of inter-agency good will.

Not long before Dixie called Springer, the Richmond police chief had phoned to tell him about the blowup at Arthur's place.

"I'm on my way there now," the police chief said.

The detective could hear the car's siren over the phone. The chief indicated Springer didn't need to come to Richmond, but he left it open for him to come if he wished. He promised the Charlottesville detective that he'd be briefed as soon as it could be determined what happened. Nevertheless, Springer decided to head out immediately, but told Dixie, in no uncertain terms, to stay in Charlottesville. Wanting to keep his sergeant and the D.C. cops in the loop, he suggested they go to the station and wait on his report. The detective said he'd call as soon as he knew the whole story.

Mike called his sister to say he'd be late, although he didn't know how late. He must have sounded upset because Kelly started to ask him what was wrong before she realized he'd broken the connection. Dixie led Mike and Justice to the police station and arranged for coffee to be brought to Springer's office, the same office in which Mike and the detective had chatted before Dixie discovered the preacher's body.

* * *

Close to midnight, Detective Springer called from Richmond. The three had been waiting for more than an hour. Dixie hit the button to activate speaker phone.

"Let me give you what I've found out so far. The place is crawling with news media. Chief Brown already gave two briefings to the press, but they've been short on details. Off the record, here is what I've been told.

"I found out earlier today that the FBI agents on stakeout saw first Hudson, and then Arthur, go into the house. The feds believed the two of them would move Arthur's collection from the house some time tonight. Earlier this evening, around nine o'clock, a couple of people emerged from the house carrying a large duffle bag. The agents moved in. It was dark and no one could see very well. The agents announced themselves, but then what happened gets a little fuzzy. One of the persons coming out of the house fired a shot and hit one of the agents. When he went down the other agent returned fire and killed the shooter."

"Who are we talking about?" Mike asked, unable to sit still any longer. "Where was Ms. Hudson?"

"That must be your voice, Mike. Hang on a minute. I'll get to that.

"The dead man is someone named Billy Lee Jackson, a friend of George Arthur's according to the FBI. Also a Klan member. But let me try to do this in order. Then I want to head home.

"The other person carrying the duffle bag, which wasn't a duffle bag, was George Arthur. He supposedly screamed 'don't shoot' and the agent who wasn't hurt told him to lie face down on the ground. Things slowed down as the agent called for help from his people and from the Richmond police. He then tried to help his wounded partner while keeping his gun on Arthur and Jackson. He didn't know Jackson's status at the time.

"That's where everything stood when the medics and

reinforcements arrived--one dead man, a wounded agent, and George Arthur on the ground. Now get this. What looked like a bag in the dark was actually a large, rolled-up rug. Everyone assumed it held some of Arthur's stolen artifacts. People were running around, checking on the two who had been shot, handcuffing and reading Arthur his rights. Then someone decided the house needed to be searched. They hadn't found the woman and it was possible others were inside as well. One of the FBI agents went in with some Richmond police.

"Only then, maybe five or ten minutes after help arrived, someone unrolled the carpet. Damn if it wasn't the Hudson woman. Tied up and gagged. She wasn't in great shape. Her face bruised and possibly in shock. But she's alive."

"Damn," Mike exclaimed.

"Hang on Mike," Justice said. "Let Detective Springer finish."

"Sorry, Mike," Springer continued. "I guess you knew her the best."

"What happened? Where is she?"

Thinking, but not saying, that this was a dumb question, Detective Springer said, "As you might imagine, she was taken to the hospital. Chief Brown told me just a few minutes ago that the initial report is that she is pretty well banged up, but nothing life threatening. She's under sedation for the night."

"Well, it's obvious she wasn't helping Arthur," Mike declared.

"We don't know that yet," Springer responded. "The feds are suggesting she and Arthur might have had some sort of argument which turned nasty. Look, I'm getting into my car now and going home. It's getting late. We can discuss this in the morning. The FBI and the Richmond police are in charge. They only invited me over here because of the Hudson connection."

Dixie turned the speaker phone off and the three sat in silence for a few moments.

"God, what a bloody mess," Mike said, almost to himself, then found that he was trembling.

"We never should have gotten her involved in this," he said more loudly.

Dixie and Justice took turns saying what anyone would in this situation. Andrea Hudson went there on her own. No one would have let her do it if they'd known. They had only asked her to identify some artifacts. Nothing more. It wasn't anyone's fault. Except maybe hers, for trying this on her own.

"Besides," Dixie said, "as Springer said, no one knows yet what went down inside the house. She might have gone there to help Arthur and they had a fight. From what you told us, it sounds like they had one before."

"You don't understand." Mike said, irritated that no one treated his views seriously.

He had been the one who talked with her. His cop instincts should be trusted. He could tell she hated Arthur. She arrived at Arthur's house after he had left, the agents said. Maybe he forgot something, returned to get it, and surprised her. Mike looked around the room, not seeing clearly. He found himself looking at the scene from somewhere above. Still an outsider.

Why does she have blood on her face? I should have been there. Where am I?

"I think we do understand," Justice replied. "Dixie is just saying that all the facts aren't on the table yet."

Justice saw that Mike wasn't listening.

"Mike!" Justice said loudly, causing Dixie to look curiously at the pair.

Mike slowly turned his attention to Justice. "She was just trying to help me. Us," Mike managed to get out. "I need to go see her."

"Tomorrow, Mike," Dixie said, studying him closely.

"Dixie is right," Justice said. "Let's get some sleep and talk to Springer in the morning. By then we'll have a better idea what happened over there. Ms. Hudson is being taken care of."

Justice wasn't about to let his partner drive home, given how spaced-out he appeared. Mike offered little resistance and Justice dropped his partner at home after midnight. He reminded Mike that all of this was not their problem and he could check on Andrea Hudson's condition the next day.

Justice had planned to return to the District in the morning, but decided he'd better stay around to see this business finished. And to check on his partner, which he did when he called the Cummings's house around 9 a.m.

Kelly answered the phone. Justice remembered to thank her for Saturday night's dinner, before asking if Mike was up yet, explaining they'd been out late the night before.

"I heard him come in late. I'll go see if he's awake. Wait a second."

Carrying the phone, she went to the lower level. She got no answer when she knocked on the apartment door. She opened it and looked in. Mike's bed had obviously been slept on.

"Justice, he's up and gone already."

"Oh darn." Justice never swore. "I think I know where he went."

"Is Mike okay?" a worried Kelly asked. "What's going on?"

"Don't worry. It'll be okay. Someone he knows got hurt in Richmond last night. I'm pretty sure he went to check on her. I just didn't think he'd go this early. I dropped him off last night so he didn't have his car at your house. His car was parked near the mall."

"Is this the woman he met last night?"

"Yes, but he never met with her. She got mixed up in some trouble before she could meet him."

"I bet he got a ride from Steve. He had an early morning meeting at the university. Mike probably asked for a lift to his car. Maybe I should call Mike, but I hate to be checking up on him."

"I'm sure he'll report in soon," Justice said. "If he contacts me, I'll tell him to call you."

Mike phoned both Kelly and Justice shortly after the two had talked, ignoring his rule against using a cellphone while driving. Yes, Steve drove him to his car early that morning. He was now on his way to Richmond to visit Andrea Hudson in the hospital. He'd be back later today.

Mike also called the Metropolitan Hospital in Richmond. Identifying himself as Mike Hudson, he confirmed that his "sister" had been admitted last night. That was all the information the hospital would release over the phone. He didn't like the subterfuge and knew it could bring him trouble, but he had to see if Andrea was going to be all right.

Chapter 31

FBI agents Simpson and Norton met for breakfast in Richmond about the same time Mike drove from C'ville toward Virginia's capital. They couldn't have been more pleased about how things turned out the previous night, except, of course that one of their agents had been wounded. This fact, however, didn't keep them from congratulating themselves over bacon, eggs, and grits at a downtown diner. Agent Simpson had called the hospital and found out that their wounded colleague would probably be released later in the day. The bullet passed through the upper arm, with no bones hit.

George Arthur was in custody. When searching his house, the agents found the door to Arthur's collection open. Many of the artifacts had been boxed, obviously intended for removal. The agents agreed that Billy Lee Jackson had been helping Arthur pack.

It didn't take long to identify several of the artifacts on the agents' list of stolen goods. One of them was the painting of Robert E. Lee from the Washington gallery. A thorough inventory would be made when an historic artifacts expert arrived from the District later that day.

The FBI agents continued in their belief that someone had warned Arthur he was under investigation. In their view that someone was Andrea Hudson. Her doctor wouldn't let anyone speak with her last night, but said she might be ready for a brief conversation later in the afternoon. When they did talk with her, both Norton and Simpson assumed she'd confirm the scenario they described for themselves--Andrea Hudson arrived at Arthur's house to help him hide his stolen artifacts, there had been a fight between Hudson and Arthur, it got violent and the Hudson woman ended up being carted out of the house in the rolled carpet.

The agents had accompanied George Arthur and the Richmond police to the city jail. No one had worked out all the charges, but likely would involve both federal and state statutes--interstate transport of stolen artifacts, kidnapping, assault on federal agents, and, possibly conspiracy to commit murder. Then there was the link to the Klan. They would start today looking into the background and friends of Billy Lee Jackson. It was possible that other Klan members were mixed up with the stolen artifacts and the C'ville killings.

The agents believed they now had considerable leverage against Bob Smith. To make sure Smith realized the seriousness of his situation, they insisted the Richmond police march Arthur past Smith's cell.

"Make enough noise to wake Smith if he's sleeping," Agent Simpson told the officers guarding Arthur.

One of the guards obliged by running a tin cup across the bars as they passed his cell. The agents laughed out loud when Smith looked out between the bars to witness Arthur in handcuffs, walking between two guards.

"Mr. Arthur! What are you doing here?" Smith blurted out. The prisoner looked the other way.

"You'll soon find out," Agent Simpson answered.

The FBI postponed their interrogation of Smith until more details of the previous night's events became clear. They could wait, and it might help if Smith had some time to consider reasons George Arthur also was jailed.

Mike Chance didn't know anything regarding Andrea's condition and it didn't occur to him that she may not be able to see visitors. He just had to make sure she was going to be okay. Justice had gently questioned him on the phone about his motives in going to Richmond. To see if she was all right? Or did he need to prove himself correct, that the Hudson woman was on their side and not still hooked up with Arthur?

Mike thought about Justice's questions during the drive to Richmond. He acknowledged Justice probably came close to the truth. He needed to find out what went on between Andrea and George Arthur in order to confirm that his cop instincts were still good. But Mike also felt guilty over the whole business, and knew he needed to see the damage done by bringing her into this mess. Also, for reasons not yet clearly articulated to himself, he recognized he cared about this woman.

Mike's anxiety level increased as he approached the hospital--a place of healing, and at the same time the scene of death and dying.

I'm Mike Chance. I am here. I am real.

His mantra was still inside his head when the receptionist at the information desk asked him which patient he came to see. After he spoke her name, the woman, reading from her computer screen, informed him that Ms. Hudson was not permitted visitors at the moment. She said he should come back tomorrow.

"I'm her brother," Mike announced. "I just got word this morning that she's here. I couldn't get any information over the phone so I drove as quickly as I could from Charlottesville."

"If you're a relative then maybe you should talk to someone at the nurse's station. Take the elevator to the 6th floor. Turn right when you get off. You'll see the nurse's station a few steps down the hall. Ms. Hudson is in room 615."

Mike thanked her, thinking she deserved his gratitude both for the information he received and that she hadn't asked for identification.

Stepping off the elevator, that peculiar hospital smell--antiseptic, sickness, bed linen, cleaning agents, death--wafted over him. Kirsten's nurse's uniform brought home traces of the same smell. He steadied himself, then walked toward the nurse's station without seeing room 615. Although tempted to keep going as if he had every legitimate reason to be there, Mike slowed down when the nurse on duty eyed him warily. He stopped and tried to look like a concerned relative, which he was. Concerned, that is.

"I'm Andrea Hudson's brother. I just learned today she was hurt badly in some kind of incident. I understand she's on this floor."

"She is. But I'm afraid the doctor said she shouldn't have visitors. She's sedated and last time I checked she was resting comfortably."

"I drove over from Charlottesville as soon as I heard. I only have today as I'm leaving the country on business tomorrow. I just need to see she's going to be okay."

What's the phrase, he thought, "in for a dime, in for a dollar?"

"Well, let me see what I can do. I'll page the doctor and see what he says. Hang on a sec."

Mike found a chair not too far from the nurse's station. Sitting down, he tried his best to keep his mind clear of the fog attempting to roll over him. One minute turned into ten. The doctor had not yet called, nor turned up. Mike had trouble focusing.

People get hurt and come to hospitals. Some never make it to the hospital. Some just die on the floor in a pool of blood.

The nurse stood in front of him.

"Mr. Hudson, are you all right? Mr. Hudson!"

"Oh. Yes, I'm good. Just worried about my sister."

"The doctor seems to be unavailable right now. I should get his permission, but if you promise not to stay for more than a minute or two, I'll let you in. As I said, your sister's sedated and probably not awake."

The nurse led him down the hall and opened the door into a darkened hospital room. Mike followed her in. When his eyes adjusted to the dim light he could see

Andrea lying in bed, her face covered in bandages. An IV drip hung nearby. Mike dug his fingernails into his palms and began to sweat.

"Ms. Hudson? Andrea. Your brother is here," the nurse whispered. Andrea didn't move.

"Mr. Hudson, I'll leave you alone for a few minutes. But as you can see, she's asleep. She needs rest. She experienced quite a trauma."

The nurse opened the door to the hallway and the bright hall light did what the nurse's whispered announcement did not. Andrea stirred and opened her eyes.

"Andrea, it's Mike."

She didn't answer right away, struggling to come back from wherever she had been. Mike watched anxiously.

A bloody mess. Why did it happen? I should have been there. Where am I?

"Mike? Why are you here?" her voice weak.

Mike fought through his own fog.

"I had to see how you're doing. I'm so sorry about what happened."

"Just a continuation of me not helping much," she replied so quietly that Mike had trouble hearing her.

"I messed up everything."

"Look, don't try to talk. You need to sleep. I'm just happy to see you're going to be okay." Did he see that? "And you didn't mess up. Thanks to you, George Arthur's in jail."

"I don't remember much," she said, and slipped back into a drugged sleep.

Chapter 32

When Mike drove west toward C'ville, he knew he'd be returning to Richmond to check on Andrea. Hopefully the nurse wouldn't remember that he was supposed to be out of the country. Trip canceled? State Department advisory for where he was going? Obviously, the FBI would be visiting her as well when she was up to talking to them. Mike didn't doubt, however, that what Andrea said today meant she had been trying to help get evidence on Arthur. He assumed the FBI would find that out, too.

Approaching the exit to Charlottesville, Mike's mind traveled back to what had started it all. No one had yet found the so-called Hemings document. The Monticello people had patiently answered his inquires, but didn't provide much useful information. How Stanley Crawford ended up with a two-hundred-year-old letter was a mystery to them. If the experts didn't have any good ideas, what was he supposed to do? Mike reminded himself it wasn't his business. Still, it remained a loose end hanging in front of him.

He spotted Justice's car in the driveway when he arrived at his sister's. Mike realized he should have called him on the drive back, but his mind had been filled with other thoughts. He was relieved that Andrea would recover, but he also couldn't shake thoughts and images of her being bloodied at Arthur's place. And then there was his reaction in the hospital. He grudgingly admitted to himself that he wasn't done seeing his therapist.

Kelly and Justice were seated in the kitchen when he arrived at his sister's house. Mike sat down across from his partner. Both Kelly and Justice immediately asked about "Ms. Hudson." He told them what he could. He added that his brief conversation with her confirmed what he always knew--she went to Arthur's house to obtain evidence and not to tell him the feds were on his trail.

"Have you eaten anything today?" his sister inquired of Mike.

"I guess I haven't gotten around to it."

"Justice, what about you? Can you stay for lunch?"

"If I keep eating at your house I won't fit in my pants anymore. I appreciate the offer, but I ate a big breakfast, and I need to get going. I've got these letters of resignation to turn in. I just stopped by to check on Miguel here. And his love interest."

"Justice! You said you were leaving," Mike said, more angrily than he intended.

"Love interest?" Kelly asked, looking at Mike. "Ms. Hudson?"

"I guess I'll get myself going now," Justice said as he got up and backed toward the kitchen door. "Kelly, thanks for the coffee." He headed down the hallway to the front door.

As Justice beat a retreat, Mike cautioned his sister about following up on his partner's remarks.

"This is something in Justice's head. I appreciate him trying to move me along. No, damn it, I guess I really don't appreciate it. It isn't something I want to talk about, okay? Sometimes Justice goes a little too far with his teasing. I feel responsible for getting Andrea, Ms. Hudson, into this. She got hurt because I roped her into something she didn't need to be involved with. I don't want any more bloody messes." Mike cringed at his choice of words.

"Listen, I can make my own lunch. I just need a sandwich."

After lunch, Mike realized how tired he was. A

restless night and the morning's trip to see Andrea had taken its toll. He surfaced more than three hours later. Returning to the kitchen, he found Kelly beginning preparations for dinner. She told him Tammy was upstairs doing homework not due until Wednesday.

"Tomorrow's a teachers' in-service day," Kelly explained. "It's easy to say it's really a teacher's holiday, but anyone who can live with a room of 7th-graders for nine months deserves a break now and then.

"I told Tammy if she got her homework done that she could go to the mall with friends tomorrow, and then to a play at the high school tomorrow night. It's a school night but one of her good friend's older sister is starring. Steve's working late today."

"What's for dinner? Can I help?" Mike asked, thinking it seemed like he had just finished lunch.

"Just getting the rice started. I'm making burritos. They're good for when Steve works late since he can heat them up easily. I hold down the chili on his. Chicken ones for us and veggie for Tammy. It's still early. Why don't you grab a beer? Today's paper is in the sunroom."

During dinner over burritos and salad, Tammy talked excitedly about having no school the next day and the play that she had wrangled permission from her mother to see. At the same time, she made it known that she completed nearly all her homework, fulfilling her part of the deal.

"Maybe you could get used to not doing things at the last minute," her mother said.

"I'll probably forget everything by Wednesday," Tammy replied. "I'm only doing it tonight because you blackmailed me into it. You should have her arrested Uncle Mike. Isn't blackmail illegal?"

"Let's see. Maybe the charge should be trying to make her daughter responsible and a success in life."

"I knew you'd side with Mom. May I be excused so I

can finish the homework that I'm illegally being forced to do two days in advance?"

Mike raised an eyebrow toward Kelly, who rolled her eyes, both smiling as Tammy exited the room.

"I can clean up," Mike offered.

"There's not much to do. Just sit there and keep me company. I want to ask a different favor. You want coffee?"

"No thanks. What's the favor?"

"I have to be at a meeting of nonprofits here in town for most of the day tomorrow. I wondered if you can keep an eye on Tammy. She wants to go to the mall with friends sometime in the afternoon. That's fine, but I'd feel better if you were on call. Steve's Tuesdays are really hectic and I may not be able to get to my phone."

Mike started to say that he needed to drive to Richmond, then thought back to something that occurred to him earlier. If Andrea was up to it, the FBI and Richmond police would want to talk with her. He would likely just be in the way. Perhaps best to give it another day.

"I can do that," he said. "Some uncle-niece quality time would be good. For me, at least. We'll see what she has planned. I also don't mind just sitting around while she goes in and out."

The next morning, a few minutes past eight o'clock, something unusual occurred in the Cummings household. Kelly's conference downtown began at nine. Steve had already left for work. The siblings were drinking a second cup of coffee at the kitchen table. Looking at the clock on the wall, Kelly quickly finished her coffee. She asked Mike if he wouldn't mind putting the dishes in the dishwasher while she got ready to leave.

Tammy strolled in before Kelly left the kitchen. Not exactly bright-eyed and bushy-tailed, but, nevertheless, mostly awake. Neither Mike nor Kelly could hide their surprise.

"I need to put this on the calendar," Kelly joked.

"What on the calendar?" Tammy asked.

"There's no school today, nor soccer practice, but my daughter is out of bed before nine o'clock. I don't think that's ever happened before. At least since 4th grade."

"Okay, enough with the jokes or I'll go back to bed."

Looking at her uncle, she said, "Mom told me last night that we were going on some kind of outing today. I thought I'd better get up before you left without me."

"Tammy! I said Uncle Mike might be willing to take you somewhere if you didn't have other plans. Not that he would for sure."

"Do you have plans?" Mike asked.

"I told Melissa and Ellie that I'd go with them to the mall later this afternoon. If that's okay?" Tammy looked to her mother for approval and Kelly nodded.

"But my morning is all yours, Uncle Mike. And lunch, too," she said with a hopeful smile.

"I can think of something if you're interested," he replied. "You wanted me to track down that secret document. Well, I'm down to my last possibility at coming up with any useful information."

"You mean I get to be in on the chase?"

"Not a chase exactly. You watch too much TV. When I talked with people at Monticello they gave me the name of someone to talk to. He used to work in the archaeology department around the time this man Crawford worked security. They said if anyone might know how Crawford got hold of a document, it would be him. His name is Kevin Nesbitt. Works part-time at the university museum. He's been out of town and wasn't expected to be back until yesterday."

"Do I have to look at all the paintings?" Tammy made a face to show how bored she would be.

"I've never been to the museum so I don't know

what's there. But no, you don't have to look at anything, but it will be up to Mr. Nesbitt if he wants you to sit in on our conversation. I'm assuming he'll talk with me, although I haven't contacted him directly. His boss told me yesterday when I called that he was back and that I should stop by anytime this morning. She assured me Nesbitt would want to meet with me. He apparently goes on and on about the excavations at Monticello."

"But you'll ask him if I can listen, won't you?"

"Of course."

"Looks like you two have a plan," Kelly said. "I've got to run. Thanks Mike. Tammy, you listen to what Uncle Mike says. Okay?"

"I will. I will. We're having lunch, too, right?" Tammy asked as her mother headed out the kitchen door.

"Sure. You can pick the place. There's a great burger place . . ."

"No!"

"Just kidding. Anywhere you want, even if they only serve lettuce and carrots."

"Melissa told me about a great place near the mall that's almost all vegetarian. Her parents, unlike some I know, like vegetarian food. It's Ethiopian, she said. Whatever that it."

"Okay, even Ethiopian. The museum opens at ten so you've got time for breakfast while I finish the newspaper. If it turns out that if Ethiopian is just grasshoppers and tree roots then we can do pizza. I heard it sometime comes without meat."

Kelly came down from upstairs, grabbed her briefcase, and managed to kiss both her brother and daughter on the top of their head before going out the front door. Mike continued to read the local paper while Tammy ate her cereal.

Mike and Tammy walked in the front door of the museum less than five minutes after it opened. They approached a woman sitting on a stool at an information desk to the right of the entrance.

"Welcome to the University Art Museum," she said brightly. "Have you been here before?"

"No, we haven't," Mike answered. "We'd like to look around." Just as the woman started to hand him a museum guide, Mike added, "But before we do, I'm wondering if I might be able to talk with Mr. Nesbitt. I spoke with a Ms. Singleton yesterday. She said he'd be in today."

"Let's see what I can do. Mary Singleton's our director. She's out right now, but before she left she mentioned you might be in. You're a private investigator, right? I don't know if Kevin knows you're coming. He does restorations and repairs for the museum. He's working in the Object Gallery upstairs. I'll give him a call."

The receptionist picked up a phone and punched in some numbers.

Tammy stood next to her uncle, beaming. She hadn't realized her Uncle Mike was an official PI. Then again, Mike didn't know he was either. Whatever he had said to Ms. Singleton, she obviously got the idea he was a private investigator. Looking down at Tammy's wide-eyed expression, Mike couldn't bring himself to say otherwise. His business was private and he was investigating. That would do, he decided.

"Kevin, there's a private detective to see you," the receptionist said when someone answered on the other end.

Turning back to Mike and Tammy, she announced that Kevin would be down in a few minutes, as soon as he puts some things away.

More than a few minutes passed and Kevin had yet to appear. Tammy, growing impatient, drifted into a side room to look at paintings she swore she wouldn't look at.

She then returned to ask the receptionist the location of the restroom. The woman pointed toward the rear of the first floor, near the bottom of marble stairs leading to the second floor.

After a few more minutes the receptionist addressed Mike, who was studying a nearby painting.

"I don't know what's keeping Kevin. He must be in the middle of something. Why don't you go upstairs to where he's working. I'm sure he won't mind. Take two rights when you get to the top. It's the Object Study Gallery. You'll see a room with a glass case and lots of different artifacts."

"Thanks. Please tell my niece where I went, will you?"

"Certainly."

Mike ascended the wide stairs and found the gallery. He saw cleaning supplies on the floor in front of a glass case, but no one was in sight. Mike began to retrace his steps. When he re-entered a main exhibit room, he saw a man in working clothes about to descend the stairs.

"Mr. Nesbitt? Kevin? Can I have a few words with you?"

"Not now," came his response.

The man ran down the stairs while keeping his eye on Mike.

"Just a minute! Please," Mike said, perhaps too loudly, as a museum security guard standing next to a statue glared at him from across the room.

Mike hurried toward the top of the stairs. He saw Kevin Nesbitt disappear around the bend in the stairs. The next thing he heard was a man yell, "Look out."

Then he heard Tammy scream, followed by a muffled crash.

Mike raced down the stairs. Making the turn, he saw his niece sitting on the floor at the bottom of the stairs. The man Mike had been chasing lay sprawled on the floor a few feet away, his hands over his mouth and nose, blood running through his fingers onto the floor. Mike slowed, steadying himself. He paused on the stairs, feeling somewhat dizzy.

I'm Mike Chance. I am real. I am here.

Tammy looked up at her uncle as he came down the last few steps.

"Uncle Mike, I'm sorry. He didn't see me. I tried to get out of the way but he wasn't looking."

She put her hand to her mouth, eyes fixated on the fallen man stretched out on the concrete floor a few yards away.

"It's okay, Tammy. Are you all right?"

"I think so. Just scared me, that's all," she announced as she stood up.

"She's right," the receptionist said as she came running toward the scene.

"I was walking over to tell her you went upstairs when Kevin came flying down the stairs. He tried to avoid her, but he tripped and hit the floor pretty hard."

A museum guard ran over to the group and the receptionist explained again what had occurred.

The guard used his phone while Mike approached Kevin Nesbitt, wondering what triggered all this. The young man bled profusely around the face. Mike judged he might have broken some front teeth and possibly his nose when he hit the floor. Tammy looked away from the bleeding, moaning man.

Mike felt himself slipping. The fog rolled in. He looked at a painting on the wall opposite the stairs. He repeated to himself the mantra Dr. Rider had given him. Taking a deep breath, he turned back toward the bloodied man.

The receptionist stood frozen in place, also clearly disturbed at the sight of Nesbitt's bloody face. Her voice louder than usual, she asked, "Kevin, are you hurt badly?"

"Can you find a wet towel, please?" Mike asked.

"Oh, yes, of course." She hurried off toward the restrooms.

"I'm sorry," Kevin mumbled through broken teeth. "I didn't mean for him to get hurt." He began to cry.

Mike knelt next to the injured man, who tried to continue talking. Kevin's words sputtered and he began choking, spraying particles of red on Mike's face and shirt. Mike focused on the injured man's shoes and said, "It's okay. I shouldn't have shouted."

The receptionist arrived with a handful of wet paper towels, which she handed to Mike. He wiped his own face with one and handed the remainder to Kevin. The security guard took a phone from his ear and announced that help was on the way.

"It wasn't what he thought," Kevin said, his words muted by the towels he held over his mouth. Sirens could be heard in the distance.

"Who thought? What wasn't? I don't understand," Mike said. He moved his eyes from Kevin's shoes, trying to avoid looking at the blood soaked towels, mentally moving away from the scene in front of him.

"I'm sorry. I really am. I didn't mean for people to get killed," Kevin murmured indistinctly through the bloody compress.

Chapter 33

Tammy spent the early part of the afternoon at the police station. Mike didn't know what else to do with her until it was time to meet her friends on the mall. She enjoyed every minute of it, sitting contentedly in the reception area, watching people go in and out. Mainly cops, who often said hello and asked if she needed anything. Sometimes citizens brought their complaints or asked for help at the reception window. Much to Tammy's disappointment she learned that the police brought any persons under arrest through another entry.

A C'ville patrol car and two university police cars had showed up at the museum soon after an ambulance arrived. The university police took over traffic control while the city officer approached the museum. Sergeant Alice Dixon came through the museum door a few minutes after the EMTs.

She stopped a few feet inside, trying to understand the sight before her. A number of people stood near the rear of the large first-floor exhibit room. She recognized the young Cummings girl, whom she had interviewed some weeks ago. The girl stood beside her uncle, Mike Chance. An obviously nervous woman hovered nearby, talking quietly with a museum guard. In front of them, a man lay on his back, holding towels over his lower face. EMTs were checking the injured man's pulse and beginning their questions. Blood was everywhere, including on Mike Chance's shirt.

Dixie couldn't be blamed if her initial impression was of an altercation between Mike Chance and the man on the floor. Mike appeared to be the winner, since he was still standing. She pulled out her notebook and walked toward the gathering.

"Dixie!" Mike exclaimed. "I'm glad it's you."

Dixie smiled slightly, but remained uncertain how she should treat the Washington detective. The EMTs bent over Kevin Nesbitt. Dixie moved closer to observe their patient.

"What happened here?" she asked, now looking at Mike. Until she learned more, Mike would be viewed as someone other than a friend and colleague.

"He tripped coming down the stairs. I came here to talk with him. When he saw me, he started running toward the stairs. He fell near the bottom when he almost collided with my niece."

"That's right. It was really strange. I couldn't tell what was happening," the museum receptionist said to Dixie.

"I saw Kevin come running down the stairs and almost run into the girl there. He tumbled and hit the floor pretty hard. You would almost think he was trying to escape from the detective here."

"And you are?" Dixie asked, a pen held ready to write in her notebook.

"My name is Gloria Pepper. Like salt and pepper, like my hair." She ran her fingers through her hair. "I'm the receptionist at the museum. I work three days a week. Usually I'm off today, but Albert was sick and . . ."

"Hold on," Dixie said. "I'll get back to you in a moment."

Dixie turned toward Mike again, who said, "I'm pretty sure I know why he ran. Ms. Pepper may be right. I think he thought I came to arrest him. Or at least confront him about what he knew."

"What he knew?"

"Yes," Mike said, unable to withhold a tone of satisfaction.

"I'm pretty sure this is about the Hemings document."

Mike and Dixie halted their conversation while they

watched the EMTs help Kevin Nesbitt to his feet, supporting him briefly to make sure he could stand safely. Seeing that their patient didn't appear to be hurt too badly, they judged he could walk on his own. One of the EMTs told Dixie they would take him to the emergency room to be checked out. His nose didn't seem to be broken, but he definitely would be needing a dentist. An EMT had provided a fresh towel for Kevin to hold against his mouth and nose.

"Can you give me your name?" Dixie asked Nesbitt, not sure whether his injuries would permit him to speak.

"Kevin Nethbit," he mumbled through broken teeth after lowering the towel.

"I work here. I'm sorry for the trouble."

"I'll need a statement from you. And you, too, Mike," she said, looking in his direction. "I'll have an officer meet the EMTs at the hospital and wait on Mr. . . . .?"

"Nesbitt," Mike offered.

"Mr. Nesbitt, you aren't under arrest, but I will need to talk with you. If you're feeling up to it, would you be willing to come to the police station after they see you at the hospital? I'll have someone drive you."

"I guess so. It hurts a bit, but I think I'll be okay. There are some things you need to know."

Kevin looked resigned to what was going on, but also somewhat relieved.

Dixie asked Mike to meet her later at the station. She wanted to get statements from the receptionist and the security people before leaving the museum.

Looking at the Cummings girl, she said, "It's Tammy, isn't it? I talked with you at your parents' house. Remember?"

"Of course."

"I hope you don't mind trailing along for now. Your parents can come get you. I can get everything I need from your uncle."

Mike quickly explained his role as parent for the day. He asked Dixie if the two of them could meet her after getting some lunch. That was fine with Dixie, who now understood that this had been an accident, although one with some contributing factors that weren't yet clear.

Tammy had to settle for pizza on the mall. Mike wasn't ready for a sit-down lunch of vegetarian food. Especially since he looked like he had just finished butchering some cows. Not a comparison, however, he used with his meat-sensitive niece.

Dixie hadn't returned from the museum when Mike and Tammy arrived at the police station. They sat down in the reception area to wait.

When Dixie arrived, she asked Tammy if she would mind waiting a few minutes while she talked with her uncle. Mike promised Tammy not to be long and Dixie led him to one of the interview rooms.

There wasn't anything he could add to what he already reported at the museum. Except to say once more that Kevin Nesbitt appeared to be frightened by his appearance at the museum and fell while trying to avoid him. Mike told her what Kevin said after hitting the floor, and that he clearly was upset about something.

Mike explained that he was planning to ask Nesbitt about his work on the archaeology dig at Monticello and also about what he knew of Stanley Crawford. Mike reiterated that he believes Nesbitt knows something about Crawford and the Hemings document, and that's why he ran.

When they returned to the reception area, Dixie asked Mike to wait while she briefed Detective Springer on the morning's events.

"He might want to question you as well," she said. She opened a door and went down the hall toward offices in the rear.

Tammy took the opportunity to ask her uncle for

permission to meet her friends at the frozen yogurt shop on the mall. She got his okay with a promise she wouldn't leave the mall. They agreed Mike would call her when he was done at the station. Tammy phoned her friends to say she was on her way. Mike overheard her tell one of her peers that she was at the police station and would "explain" when she saw them. He realized she had a great story to tell and was going to love telling it.

Dixie emerged from the rear of the station to say that Miles Springer would like to see him. At the same time, a police officer arrived with Kevin Nesbitt. The grad student's nose was supported by a stiff bandage. His mood was still of one resigned to whatever was going to happen next, although he looked less apprehensive than before. Dixie could see jagged teeth behind Kevin's split lips. She asked whether he would like some soup or soft drinks brought in, not wanting to suggest something harder to chew. Kevin shook his head. Dixie retreated once again to the offices in back while Mike waited quietly with the officer and Nesbitt.

She returned to the reception area to inform Kevin that two detectives would like to speak with him. Continuing to exhibit total indifference to what was transpiring, Kevin simply nodded, then looked down at the floor.

"Mike, do you mind waiting while I take Kevin to the interview room? I'll check with Springer to see if he wants you to stay."

"No problem. I'll be here."

Dixie led Kevin Nesbitt down the hallway and introduced him to Detective Springer, who in turn introduced his partner, both of them standing outside the interview room. Dixie asked Springer if he still wanted to see Mike Chance. The detective told her it could wait. Springer led Kevin into the interview room while Dixie started back to the reception area. However, the detective called to her before she had gone very far down the hallway. He stepped away from the interview room and approached Dixie.

"On second thought, it might be a good idea if you and Mike Chance listen in on the interview. Mr. Nesbitt said he doesn't want an attorney present. Looks like he simply wants to get something off his chest. The two of you are in the best position to determine the accuracy of his statement, particularly as it relates to the Hemings document, which I know next to nothing about."

Mike was pleased to be included. Dixie led him to a room adjacent to the interview room, where they could hear the conversation via audio feed. A monitor provided video from a camera located high above the room's occupants.

The interview lasted more than an hour. When it was over, Detective Springer informed Nesbitt that he would not be allowed to leave the police station, and placed him under arrest for his role in the death of Stanley Crawford. He would likely be charged with murder, but pending a review by the city attorney, the charge may be reduced. He told the now completely deflated graduate student that any change in the charges would depend on whether sufficient additional evidence could be found to support his story. Broken teeth became the least of Kevin's problems.

Mike phoned Tammy to tell her they would need to head home soon, and that he could give her friends a lift if they wished. He then called Justice in D.C. to give him a brief rundown of the day's events. Mike indicated he had learned the circumstances which had drawn them into the Hemings-Jefferson business, and would fill him in later that evening.

Despite Tammy's pestering during the car ride to her friends' homes, Mike refused to say what he learned after Tammy left the station. He said, truthfully, that it was confidential police business. He did win some favorite uncle points, however, by telling her friends that it was Tammy's entry from a side hallway that had thrown the running man off stride. Her timely appearance resulted in his fall and eventual arrest by the police.

Tammy was still in hyper-drive when Kelly came home. She told and retold her mother about what happened at the museum. How she caused "the crook" to trip. How the ambulance and then Officer Dixon came. How Uncle Mike took her to the police station where she had to sit for over an hour. But she didn't mind. That she didn't get to eat Ethiopian food as Uncle Mike promised, because he had blood all over him. And that he ate sausage pizza while sitting next to her, and how gross that was.

Kelly had been genuinely concerned when Tammy started her story, especially when she saw her brother's blood-spattered shirt. Mike could see Kelly's face as she imagined all kinds of possibilities about what it had been like for her daughter. He quickly told his sister it wasn't his blood and things weren't as bad as they might look. She began to relax when Mike rolled his eyes during Tammy's lengthy recitation of the day's events. Of course, when her father got home, Tammy began telling her story all over again. Both parents agreed that a day out with Uncle Mike wasn't something they could ever match.

Tammy left soon after dinner to go to the play her mother had promised she could attend. Mike gave Kelly and Steve a brief summary of exactly what happened to him and their daughter.

He reported that Kevin Nesbitt, the graduate student they went to see, was in jail and various charges were being prepared. What the police learned from Kevin Nesbitt would no doubt be in tomorrow's newspapers, he said, but felt it should come from the C'ville authorities, and not from him. When the police released their statement, Mike told them, they would learn how Stanley Crawford got hold of a Hemings document and how, apparently, he was killed.

Mike said he didn't learn anything new about the minister's death, only that he was quite sure that he was killed by people looking for the document. The document did exist, he said, but it wasn't what the Jefferson Bunch and others thought it was. Kelly and Steve appreciated the review of the day's events. Steve, chuckling, thanked Mike for introducing Tammy to law enforcement first hand.

When the evening drew to a close, Mike knew to whom he wanted to tell everything he learned today. Saying good-night to his sister and brother-in-law, he descended to his apartment, sat down on his bed and punched a number on his phone.

"Justice," he said, when his partner answered, "are you sitting down? I've got a long story to tell you."

Chapter 34

Lying on his bed, Mike relayed to Justice what he had learned about the mysterious Hemings document.

"Kevin Nesbitt worked at Monticello for nearly two years, earning a promotion to crew chief during his second year. He reported to one of the senior archaeologists overseeing excavations on the mountain. Kevin received permission from the Monticello Archaeology Department to use data collected during the excavations for his dissertation at the university. After completing his field work last spring, he left Monticello so that he could concentrate on writing his dissertation. That was about four months ago. Since then he worked at the museum part-time."

"This guy knew Crawford?"

"Yes. That's why the Monticello archaeologist suggested I talk with Kevin. But he clearly didn't want to talk with me. He took off when I approached and fell running down some stairs. Smashed his face on the floor. An ambulance came and then Dixie showed up. She had him go to the station for questioning after he got patched up. Which is what he wanted. He was ready to get the whole thing off his chest."

"You mean he's the one who stole the Hemings document?"

"Not exactly. Let me explain."

To provide some background, Mike told Justice what he learned from Dr. Abigail Parker at Monticello. That the Foundation regularly offers a field school for archaeology students at the university. In their summer months on the hill they learn the painstaking, but exacting, work of excavation, site recording, artifact cleaning and identification. Everyone benefits, the archaeologist explained. The students receive an introduction to archaeology while learning something of Monticello's history. Part of that history lesson, she said with obvious pride, includes the fact that Thomas Jefferson has been called the "Father of American Archaeology." The Founding Father had anticipated modern techniques when excavating an Indian mound near Charlottesville. For their part, the Monticello archaeologists got much needed help from the students and the opportunity to pass on their expertise to a new generation of scientists.

Mike told Justice that Kevin described a common form of initiation for novice archaeology students. Experienced members of the team would sometimes "salt" a dig with an anomalous artifact, one that had no good explanation for being there. A simple prank, for example, might be to put a shard from a Coke bottle in a layer of dirt containing artifacts from the 18th century. The goal, of course, was to confound the novices and then see where it went from there. Such tricks typically were frowned on by the senior staff, but they usually cut the playful veterans some slack.

"That's where it all began," Mike said.

"Uh-oh. I think I see where this is going," Justice responded.

"Kevin and another graduate student decided to take this game to a higher level. Although the residences of both Sally Hemings and her mother had been excavated some years ago, the new students learned about the investigation of these sites during their classroom time. Once that happened, Kevin said the novices couldn't help discussing the Jefferson-Hemings story. Did he or didn't he? How would we ever know for sure? He reported one student jokingly remarked that a time-traveling eyewitness was needed--someone going back to the past and then returning to the present with news of what was going on."

"That would help with a lot of cases," Justice interjected.

"Kevin claims he couldn't remember whether he or the other student came up with the idea of planting a letter from James Hemings in the root cellar of a newly uncovered building near Mulberry Row. That's an area where there were slave quarters."

Justice interrupted. "They were playing games!"

Mike smiled through the phone at his partner, who was experiencing the same awakening he had that afternoon.

"Yes, it all began as a joke. Kevin explained how it wasn't hard to prepare a reasonable facsimile of a letter. A sample of James Hemings's handwriting exists and was easy to copy. They used a quill pen and black ink, which, Kevin said, any tourist can buy at the Visitors Center. The paper came from a local stationary shop. Apparently, it looked much like what was available in Jefferson's time, or close enough. Heating it slightly with a candle and dirtying it produced an old appearance. Kevin admitted having fun composing a message that would get everyone excited. He directed the words to James's mother, Elizabeth Hemings.

"The message said that he, James, knew that Mr. Jefferson promised Sally, if she slept with him, to free any children she had by him. He was writing, so the letter continued, because he was leaving the mountain. He wanted his mother to know of the master's promise. She should make James's testimony public if Mr. Jefferson ever broke his promise."

"But where could he put a piece of paper in an archaeology dig? Justice asked. "I think I'm missing something here."

"They had a plan, quite a simple one. The two graduate students put the letter in a corked bottle. Many wine bottles have been dug up over the years. Kevin said it was almost impossible to see inside the dark-colored bottle, but he smeared the bottle with wet dirt to make sure its contents weren't visible.

"He and his friend knew better than to mess with the site by burying the bottle in an area not yet excavated. Instead, they placed the bottle with the letter where digging had commenced. They chose an evening when other members of the team had left for the day and the site was protected by tarps. What happens, Kevin explained, is that when an artifact is discovered, it's placed in a bag with a record of its exact location on the site. The bag goes to the lab, where the artifact is cleaned, typically by other students, and then placed on a shelf to dry. After that, the artifact is identified, a computer record made, and the artifact stored."

"But how did Crawford get it?" Justice interrupted once more.

"I'm coming to that. Kevin said that anyone could easily untie the clasps on the plastic tarp. After placing the dirty bottle with the Hemings letter under the tarp, Kevin said they expected the field students to find it the next morning when they resumed digging. It was possible, Kevin admitted, that a student might immediately take the bottle to one of their supervisors for inspection. Otherwise, Kevin and his accomplice expected the letter to be found by students when the bottle was cleaned. He said it really didn't matter what happened at this point. The students and the senior archaeologists would know that a letter inside a bottle could survive intact for two-hundred years. Sealed bottles had previously been found on the hill, some with their liquid contents still inside.

"It wouldn't take long for the bottle to be opened, exposing its contents, and the letter examined. Kevin and his friend figured the staff archaeologists would quickly recognize it was fake. In the meantime, the letter and message would produce a buzz among everyone at the dig. And hopefully a good laugh when the letter was discovered to be what it was, a prank."

"I still don't see how Crawford got it," Justice said.

"Just wait. Kevin said they planted the letter when he had the next two days off. His friend was leaving Monticello for good the following day, going back to graduate school in Kansas. He was sure that when he returned from his days off that everyone would still be laughing over the document. It would have been identified by the senior staff for the forgery it was. But when he returned, no one said a thing. He discreetly asked whether anything of significance had been discovered the last couple of days, but no one mentioned anything new. He even checked the site to see if the bottle was somehow still there. Which of course, it wasn't."

"So Crawford got there first!" Justice said.

"Hang on partner. At first Kevin thought he was now the butt of the joke, that the bottle had been found and easily determined to be a fake. He decided everyone was waiting for him to admit planting it. Then he became concerned that one of their supervisors hadn't been thrilled with the prank. Maybe one of the senior professionals initially claimed it was real. Not good to embarrass your boss. He worried that he and his friend had gone a little too far with this joke.

"Kevin kept quiet, and waited. He called the other student after a day or so and explained what had happened, or, rather, what had not happened. They both judged it best for their careers to just forget the whole thing. Wherever the bottle went, they hoped no one would find out who had planted it. Kevin left Monticello a week later to write his dissertation. He claimed his friend knows nothing about what happened next.

"Kevin admitted he knew Stanley Crawford. Said he

seemed like a nice guy. Crawford regularly came by the digs, often asking what the archaeologists had found. Kevin occasionally took time to talk with the guard about their progress.

"It appears Crawford retired a few weeks after Kevin quit the hill. Kevin told the detectives he had no idea the security guard had been taking artifacts from the excavation sites. One or two items wouldn't be missed since they had yet to be completely uncovered and removed."

"Okay, I'm with you," Justice said. "The bottle with the message becomes part of Crawford's collection. But how did Kevin know it was Crawford who had it if he didn't know Crawford was stealing stuff from up there?"

"It went like this. A few months later, Kevin's at a downtown bar and overhears Bob Smith talking about a man who claimed to own a letter written by James Hemings, and was looking to sell it. Of course, Kevin immediately became interested. He joined Smith for a beer in order to hear the story first hand. From Smith's description, he recognized the person with the letter was Stanley Crawford, but he didn't say anything to Smith. Kevin assumed Crawford must have been poking around under the tarp and discovered the bottle with the letter, and believed it to be a real letter written by James Hemings. He decided Crawford must have gotten the letter the same night they had planted it, which would explain why no one on the hill had said anything."

"Why didn't this Nesbitt guy report what he learned to the people at Monticello?" Justice asked.

"Kevin said he knew he should have revealed the prank and where the letter had ended up to the Monticello archaeologists, but he worried once again that his career would be jeopardized. He had almost finished writing his dissertation and didn't want to spoil what he had worked so long to achieve.

"At this point in the interview, Kevin started to cry. He told the detectives all he wanted to do was contact Crawford, explain that the document was a fake, and get it back. When Crawford learned it wasn't real, Kevin assumed he would give up trying to sell it and turn it over to him.

"I have to say," Mike said, pausing in his story, "I started to feel a bit sorry for Kevin."

"I'm not sure I do," Justice said. "But then I wasn't there. What happened next?"

"He telephoned Crawford, told him who he was and that he remembered Crawford from when he worked at Monticello. Crawford remembered him as well and the conversation initially went well. Kevin said he had heard Crawford possessed a James Hemings letter and asked if he could see it. He suggested there were some things Crawford should know about the document. At this point, Crawford got spooked. After all, he had stolen an artifact from the dig and one of the site supervisors was calling him about it. Recognizing Crawford's panic, Kevin quickly told him not to worry, that the letter was a fake.

"Crawford got angry. He accused Kevin of wanting the letter for himself, that Kevin was only saying it was fake so he could get the letter for nothing. They argued about this, but Kevin still didn't say why he knew the letter was fake. He apparently held on to the idea that he could get the letter back without identifying himself as the one who manufactured it. Crawford refused to meet with Kevin and hung up."

"I bet Kevin didn't take no for an answer," Justice said.

"You're right. Kevin thought if he met with Crawford in person, he could easily show him the letter was forged. All he had to do was tell Crawford what was in the letter without even seeing it. He went one night to Crawford's place, a corner house in the Woolen Mills area, around nine o'clock, possibly a little before nine. He wasn't sure of the exact time, nor could he remember the exact date, only that it was a Monday.

"He drove around the block a couple of times. The second time round he saw a light from a window in a room at the back of the house. Kevin parked his car on the side street so he could approach the house from the rear. He walked to the house through the backyard.

"Peeking in a window, he saw Crawford sitting at a desk in what appeared to be an office or den. Kevin said he decided not to knock, hoping to avoid a confrontation at the door and possibly allow Crawford to shut it on him. Trying the door handle, he found the door wasn't locked. Kevin said he simply walked into the room.

"He surprised Crawford, of course, who recognized him and said something like, 'What are you doing here? I thought it was clear I didn't want to talk to you. You aren't supposed to be here. I told you I don't believe what you said about the letter. You're going to ruin everything.' Or some such words. Kevin tried to reason with him, but Crawford demanded he leave.

"Crawford apparently kept looking past Kevin to the back door, as if expecting someone. He was really upset, Kevin said. Continued to say he wouldn't show him the letter, fearing Kevin would take it. Crawford then goes to his desk, opens a drawer, pulls out a gun, and again orders Kevin out of his office. Now Kevin gets spooked. He said he kept pleading with Crawford. Kevin even recited the contents of the letter word for word. Either Crawford didn't hear him or didn't want to hear him. Maybe Crawford didn't want to accept the idea that his grand plans for the letter were coming apart.

"Kevin claimed Crawford came toward him, pointing the gun at him, yelling at him to get out. Crawford got so close and was acting so crazy that Kevin said he got scared and tried to push the gun away. They wrestled and the gun went off, hitting Crawford, who then dropped the gun. He clutched his groin area with both hands and fell to the floor beside the desk. Kevin claimed he was sure Crawford wasn't dead, that someone would hear the shot and come to Crawford's aid. Kevin started crying again as he described what happened next. He reported that he ran out the door across the backyard to his car. 'I know I should have stayed to help,' he told the detectives."

"Well, he didn't, did he," Justice commented. "I'm definitely not feeling sorry for him."

"Perhaps you're right. Ever since then, Kevin has been living in fear the police would track him down. He followed the story in the news and saw that Crawford had died. He repeatedly expressed his guilt to the detectives about running away, and then not coming forward. He said he was afraid he would be tried for murder, when it had been an accident. Kevin then watched everything go from bad to worse. Someone else had been killed, apparently because of the letter he and his friend had planted. At the museum, when the receptionist called to say there was a detective waiting to see him, he panicked. He had no idea why he ran. He didn't know what else to do. His career was ruined. During the interview, he kept repeating over and over that it was a joke. Just a silly joke."

"So it appears that Bob Smith wasn't the one who killed Crawford," Justice said.

"No, he didn't," Mike agreed.

Mike told Justice how he believed the whole business had played out. Kevin must have arrived at the house a short time before Bob Smith showed up for his appointment with Crawford. Kevin couldn't have been there for more than a few minutes. Remember, he said to Justice, Beatrice Crawford came into the room twice.

First, immediately, or almost immediately, after she heard the car noise in the front of the house, and then again after she opened the strongbox and threw its contents in the waste can. Then she called 911. She must have gone in the first time when she heard Bob Smith leave from the front of the house.

"Despite what Kevin thought," Mike said, "it's unlikely the gunshot would have been heard by Crawford's wife. It came from a room at the rear of the house, and close to Crawford's body. His wife was, by her own account, watching television.

"As I said," Mike continued, "Kevin wasn't sure what time he got there, except that we know now it had to be before nine o'clock. Bob Smith never saw Kevin and Smith left in his car just as Beatrice Crawford's show ended."

"This may get his widow off the hook," Mike explained. "It's clear she ditched the porn before calling 911. Even if she did delay calling, it may not have made a difference. Stanley Crawford possibly died before his wife came in the first time. Taking time to throw away the porn from the strongbox might not have mattered."

"Then you think Crawford was already dead when Smith and then his wife showed up?"

"It's possible Bob Smith got there when Crawford was already dead, or at least looked dead, which is what Smith has repeatedly claimed."

"I don't feel sorry for him, either" Justice declared.

Chapter 35

On Wednesday morning Mike drove again from C'ville to Richmond. Guilt feelings overwhelmed him. He needed to check on Andrea. He regretted more than ever letting the FBI pull her into their scheme.

The trip wasn't an easy one. He fought off thoughts of being outside himself, of death and dying. He tried to reason with himself that everyone had morbid thoughts when visiting people in the hospital. It was one more thing to talk over with Dr. Rider. He hadn't seen her in two weeks. Before the events of the past few days, he thought maybe he could wean himself from therapy. All that happened recently suggested otherwise. He acknowledged he wasn't quite ready to stand alone on his own two feet. Nevertheless, he had cancelled today's therapy session. Seeing Andrea was a priority.

As Mike walked off the hospital elevator, he continued to battle thoughts of being outside himself. Lost in his fog, he almost collided with the nurse who had helped him on Monday.

"Mr. Hudson. I hope your trip went well."

"Uh, yes, it did. Very quick, it turned out. How is my sister?"

"Much better. Some law enforcement officers just left. They've been going in and out, yesterday and this morning. I've been reading in the newspapers about what happened to your sister. The shooting and all. It's so awful.

"If she isn't too tired from all the visits," the nurse continued, "I'm sure she'll want to see you. You know where her room is."

"Yes, thank you."

Mike started down the hall, trying not to look into

the rooms along the hallway. Why were so many doors open? Who wants to see people sick and dying!

Why did she have to die! Where are we when we die? Why am I the one still alive?

Opening the door slowly, Mike poked his head inside. He saw Andrea sitting up on the bed. "Can you stand another visitor?"

"Mike! Of course. Why are you back here? You don't need to come every day."

"Well," he said laughing, "I haven't been here since Monday, so it hasn't been every day. You were pretty groggy last time I came. I just want to see how you're doing."

"I'd be a lot better if the FBI and the Richmond cops would just let me alone."

"We don't have to talk about it if you don't want to." Mike pulled up a chair and sat down next to Andrea's bed. "You're looking much better."

"Thanks, liar. My jaw still aches, but I'm not so sore anymore. My face is a mess. I have some bad cuts. They took off some of the bandages this morning. I still don't remember everything that happened. And these FBI guys make me so mad. From the questions they ask, they seem to think I was in on this, that I warned George that the police were on to him."

"I know you didn't, and I told them that."

"It was a stupid thing to do, but it seemed like it would be so easy."

Andrea paused, tears forming. She looked away before turning her face back to him.

"George always plays golf on Sunday afternoons. I figured I'd just wait until he leaves, get in with my key, take a few pictures and get out. Then you guys would be able to see what's in his collection.

"My plan started off okay. I waited down the street until I saw him drive off, then drove up and let myself in.

And I was right about the combination! When I opened the door to the room, I saw this man packing boxes of stuff. He was as surprised as I was. Scared the hell out of me. I think I screamed. I started to back up and get out of the house as fast as I could. But he chased me and grabbed me from behind when I went up the stairs. Turned me around and hit me across the face. After that it's a bit of a blur.

"I think I fell back down the stairs. He broke my nose, or maybe I broke it when I fell. Anyway, I remember being on the floor with him standing over me talking to George on his phone. At least I'm pretty sure it was George. They had this heated conversation, lots of loud words. That's all I remember. I may have blacked out after falling down the stairs. The doctor said I had a concussion."

"Maybe you shouldn't talk about this," Mike said, imagining her at the foot of the stairs.

"I think I need to. I want you to know what happened. I didn't help George. I swear."

"I know you didn't. Please don't worry about that."

"Let me finish. George must have come back to the house. I'm not sure how long that took. I don't remember him being there, but one of the FBI agents says he showed up soon after I went in. He must have come back when his buddy called him. Everyone thinks I was there to help him get away! The agent said that we must have had a fight and that's why I look this way. They say the only way George would have known about them closing in was if I had warned him. That I contacted him after you and I talked on Friday night."

Mike didn't know how to respond. She wanted to reassure him that she didn't help Arthur. He knew she didn't, but he also knew he wanted to find out what happened inside the house, what she had gone through on his account. He knew the FBI wouldn't tell him anything. Andrea was clearly worked up, but at least he was a sympathetic audience. Unlike what she must have endured the last couple of days.

Andrea's hand clenched the sheets of her bed. "The one who pulled me down the stairs. They tell me he's dead. That's one good thing, I guess. I don't remember much of it, thank God. They told me I was rolled up in a rug. That George and his friend were taking me to a car when the shooting started. The bastards."

"George is in jail, you know. They'll nail him for a lot of things. I can guarantee you he won't be around for a long time."

Andrea started to break down at this point. Mike reached for her hand.

Where was he? Look at your hand. It's holding hers. She must have suffered falling down the stairs. I should have been there.

"Mike? Are you all right?"

"I should have been there," he murmured.

"Don't be silly. You couldn't have known what I was going to do. It's my fault entirely."

"But if I had been there, I . . ."

"If you had, it may have been worse. The guy could have shot you. Don't think that way. It wasn't your fault."

Mike was moving outside himself. He looked away from Andrea and stared at a water pitcher on the table next to the bed.

"But there would have been no need to come down the stairs," he murmured.

"I had no choice. He pulled me down. I told you."

Mike didn't respond. He didn't move, his eyes locked on the pitcher of water.

Andrea watched Mike, saw he wasn't listening.

"Mike? Are you okay?"

"What?" he said, slowly turning toward her, tears in his eyes.

Andrea studied him, saw the tears, and realized what was happening.

"Mike, you aren't talking about me, are you? This is about something else. Is this about your wife? You never told me how your wife died."

Mike wasn't sure where he was or who he was talking to. Images of that January evening floated through his mind--sitting beside Kirsten at the foot of the stairs, blood on her face, not moving, eyes vacant, holding her hand.

"Mike, I'm not sure this is the time to talk about what happened."

Mike looked directly at her and tried to collect himself.

I am Mike Chance. I am here. I am real.

"It's okay," he said, not confident it was.

"Sometimes I have flashbacks. My therapist says it's to be expected. It's just that I haven't had them for weeks. Thinking about you at the bottom of the stairs must have triggered them. My wife died falling down our townhouse stairs. I was at work and she was on her way to unlock the door for when I got home. The dog tripped her."

Outside of his family and Justice, Mike hadn't described what happened to Kirsten in this detail to anyone. Therapists don't count.

"I'm so sorry. Maybe sometime we can talk more about it if you like."

"I might like that. Maybe not right now, though."

It crossed Mike's mind that he was the one being comforted. "Maybe when we're both a little more ready," he added.

"You know, Mike. Maybe it isn't such a good idea to visit me."

"No. No. I can handle it. I feel responsible."

"Is that why you're here? Because you feel guilty?"

"Well, maybe, partly. I just want to make sure you're okay."

"I'm going to be okay. Wasn't too sure of that a couple of days ago, but now I think I'll be fine. Eventually. It's not the beating I took. Bruises heal quickly. It's, well, knowing I was such a fool being with George."

Mike didn't know what more to say.

"Look, Mike. When I say that maybe you shouldn't visit anymore, it isn't just about you."

What had Justice said to him? It's not always about you. But is it?

"I need some time to get over this," Andrea continued. "I need to think about how I got involved with George Arthur. He's a thief. Worse than that, he's a racist. He tried to rape me once, the day before we met at Taco Bell. He's evil. Why didn't I see that? What's wrong with me?"

"Whoa!" Mike said, smiling slightly. "That's a lot to take on by oneself."

"Maybe I'll need the name of your therapist!" Andrea said with a laugh. Then realized exerting those muscles in her face brought on pain. "Ouch! That hurts."

"You okay?" Mike looked for the buzzer to signal the nurse.

"I'm okay. Just no more laughing. Mike, I just want you to see that I'll need some time. It's not about you, it's about me. I'll let you know when I'm ready. I want to see you again."

"I would like that. Yes, when we're both ready."

Mike looked more closely at her and saw apprehension in her eyes, but also concern for him. He knew he wanted to see her again, but he also knew he wasn't ready either. Both of them had some healing to do.

"I'm glad," Andrea said. "I promise I'll be in touch.

That is, if they don't lock me up for conspiracy to commit theft."

Mike laughed. He carefully let go of her hand, not conscious until that moment that he had been gently holding it.

"If they do, I promise to bring you cookies."

"Thanks, that's a real comfort," she said jokingly. "Ouch. You better leave before my stitches split!"

A smile lit her battered face while she patted his hand.

Mike stood up, turned to go, and gave a small wave of his hand when he reached the door. On his way down the hall, his mind swirled around Andrea and the things she had said. Things they both said. The emotion that wanted out. He nearly collided with someone walking the opposite direction.

"Hey! Watch it!" said a voice. "Have you been drinking?" Sergeant Miller asked teasingly. "I'm sure someone around here can test your blood-alcohol level."

Mike glanced up at the smiling police officer.

"Sorry, had my mind on something else. Been talking to Ms. Hudson."

"Yes, I know. The nurse said her brother was with her. Unless you left him behind, I think I smell a little lie."

"In my defense, I was here on Monday to see how she was doing. Tried the old relative-needs-to-see-her story. Today, I didn't think it appropriate to change my story. We were just talking."

"Since it's your first offense, I won't take you in. Or worse, tell the nurse. I'm here to talk with Ms. Hudson as well. I've got orders to drop in everyday to see if she can remember more about what went on in the house."

"It doesn't seem like she can, but I guess you have to take a stab at it. Go slowly. It's painful for her to think about what happened."

"I will, but I'm afraid I have no choice. Orders."

"I do know she's upset you guys don't believe her, that she was only trying to get evidence for us. I'm certain she was only trying to help."

"It's really the FBI guys who won't give up on that. They think she was the only one who could have alerted Arthur and got him packing. The feds claim she called him after she talked with you. They're looking into her phone records. However, some of our people have another idea."

"About who told Arthur?"

"Remember the judge who wouldn't issue a search warrant?"

"How can I forget. That's why Ms. Hudson got into this mess. When we couldn't get the warrant, she thought she'd help us out."

"His name's Morrison. Maybe you heard he plays golf with George Arthur. Or did. Turns out the judge has been under investigation for some time. Seems he's been taking bribes. The U.S. Attorney's office has him under surveillance. According to what they told one of our guys, Morrison plays golf for money. Big money. He owes several people, including our one-and-only George Arthur. We're talking a lot of money. It wouldn't be a big jump to think that Judge Morrison warned Arthur after we tried to get the warrant. Maybe to cancel some of what he owes Arthur."

"Makes sense."

"Yes, it does. We can't prove anything yet. The investigation's still ongoing, but we know the judge's phone was tapped. I'm not even supposed to be talking about it. Anyway, I don't think the feds will stick to their version very long. Too many things just don't add up. I hear Arthur claims he never touched her. Says Billy Jackson knocked her around. The feds just don't want to admit they're wrong. Seems to be a trait in people housed in Washington."

"Thanks for telling me this."

Mike shook Miller's hand and walked toward the elevator.

"Don't worry, Mr. Hudson, we'll take good care of your sister," the nurse said as the elevator door closed.

Chapter 36

Justice arrived back in town late Friday morning. He stopped at the Cummings house to ask Mike's help the following Monday when he drove a rental truck back to the District to get his furniture and belongings.

"It's time I moved into auntie's house," he told Mike.

Until his furniture arrived, he had been sleeping on the floor, much to Kelly's consternation. She had wanted him to use their guest room. His excuse had been that he needed to be in the house to keep an eye on the contractors. "You know how it is when people are in your house doing work," he explained.

Tammy was at school. Steve stayed home to work in his upstairs study, but came down when he heard Justice arrive. Kelly and Mike were sitting with Justice at the kitchen table when Steve entered the kitchen.

By now everyone was pretty much up to date on the myriad happenings of the past week. The news media enjoyed a field day with stories of the Hemings letter faked by a graduate student at the university and its connection with the killing of two Charlottesville men. Then there was the wounding of an FBI agent, the killing of a man known to be associated with the Ku Klux Klan, and the assault and kidnapping of a Charlottesville woman in Richmond. The news reports noted that these latter events occurred at the home of a prominent Richmond business man, who the FBI arrested on charges of buying stolen historic artifacts. This person also might be involved with the killings of the two Charlottesville men. All of this guaranteed prolonged news coverage over the entire Mid-Atlantic region.

After Mike assured Justice he would be free on Monday to help him move, the conversation centered around Justice's plans to start a restaurant. What began as a somewhat whimsical idea had now coalesced in his mind as a real possibility. Justice put up with a barrage of questions about the kind of restaurant he had in mind, the menu, the seating, and so on.

Talk inevitably shifted back to recent news stories. It would be weeks before everything got sorted out with regard to the roles played by Kevin Nesbitt, Bob Smith, and George Arthur. And those of the lesser actors, now dead, Jimmy Cooke and Billy Lee Jackson.

Mike believed Kevin's account of what happened and expressed the hope that he wouldn't get punished too severely. A prank had gone very wrong and three people died, but it seemed to Mike that Kevin wasn't out to hurt anyone. His archaeological career, as Kevin feared, was no doubt over. That surely was one form of punishment. It would be up to his defense attorney to convince a jury of the truth in Kevin's account of events at the Crawford house. He would no doubt go to jail, but, Mike guessed, not for murder.

Both Mike and Justice agreed that the authorities might not get George Wallace Arthur for conspiracy to commit murder. However, he'd certainly go to prison for stealing artifacts and kidnapping. Justice said Dixie had passed on a rumor that Bob Smith was ready to tell all, especially since it seemed he was off the hook for Crawford's killing. The blood on Cooke's knife had matched the minister's and Smith hoped to escape that murder charge as well. He wouldn't be free anytime soon, but should avoid the death penalty.

Mike said that he found only one unconnected dot-- the Hemings letter.

"Okay, it's a fake," he said. "But where is it? I don't believe Bob Smith knows where it is. If he did, he would have offered it up by now to support his story.

"We know Crawford had it because the preacher saw

it. But we can be pretty sure Jeremiah didn't get hold of it. He got killed for nothing."

"It really doesn't matter much anymore, does it?" Justice shrugged. "Maybe something to let be."

"No, you're right, it probably doesn't matter," Mike replied. "The police have Kevin's confession, but it's bugging me. I was lying awake last night thinking about it. You always told me we should tie everything up before leaving a case. No loose ends."

"I guess so," Justice said. "But this isn't our case. We don't have cases anymore. Remember, we resigned. Besides, I'm really not interested in chasing all over trying to find this thing. You know what I think about all the interest in the Jefferson and Hemings affair, or non-affair. Let's move on, folks! We have more serious problems in this country to deal with. Let's concentrate on the present."

"I'm sorry, you're right," Mike agreed. "But do you want me to tell me you what I think?"

"Do we have a choice?" Justice asked with a smile.

"I have an idea where the letter is," Mike asserted.

"What? Where?" Kelly and Steve asked in unison, who to this point had been listening quietly while Mike and Justice summed things up.

"First, listen to my thinking. We know that Kevin Nesbitt never saw the letter when he went to Crawford's. At least he said as much and he certainly has no reason to lie. In fact, it would be better for his story if the letter were found. It would confirm that the whole thing was a joke gone wrong."

"But we're pretty sure that Bob Smith never saw it either," Justice said. "So where does that leave us?"

"Dixie told me that Kevin identified one of the bottles Crawford had in his box as the bottle they used to protect the letter. At one time Crawford must have had the document in his strongbox."

"Okay, had it. But tell me wise man, who has it now?" Justice asked.

"No one," Mike said, exhibiting a playful smile.

"Look, you just said there had to be a letter. Someone has to have it," Justice said, obviously put out with Mike's delaying twist.

"Yes and no," Mike said, but hurried on as Justice looked ready to strangle him from across the table.

"Consider this. Crawford is waiting for Bob Smith to show up. He knows the buyer will want to see the letter. Now, if you were Crawford, would you just put it out on the desk for the buyer to see? I wouldn't. From what the minister said, Crawford was paranoid about someone taking it from him. I think Crawford would have put it somewhere close by. Out of sight until he saw whether Smith was for real and had something to offer."

"But we know it wasn't in the strongbox with the other artifacts," Justice said, now becoming more interested in the missing letter. "Unless the widow is lying and she has it. Is that what you're thinking? That she took it out when she removed the sex stuff?"

"I thought about that, "Mike answered. "And it's a possibility. We know she did go to the box before calling 911. But there's another possibility."

"And it is . . ." Justice said impatiently. Kelly and Steve looked at Mike, eagerly waiting for him to explain.

"I think it might still be in Crawford's office," Mike announced.

"We know the letter was out of the box earlier in the evening because Crawford showed it to the preacher. Jeremiah also said that after he saw the letter, Crawford shooed him out of the room fairly quickly because he expected a buyer soon. It makes sense, I think, to consider that once the letter was out of the box Crawford wouldn't put it back in. That is, I don't think he'd want to be opening the box in front of this buyer who he didn't know.

"I'm thinking he might have hid the letter somewhere in the office until he checked out Smith. It wasn't in the desk. We know the C'ville police went through that. But what if Crawford simply put it in a book, or behind a picture? He'd want it handy if he decided his buyer was serious and had the money. Kevin apparently got there only a short time before Smith. So if I'm right, the letter was already out of sight when Kevin showed up."

"Man, you weren't sleeping last night, were you," Justice commented. "Perhaps we should visit the widow Crawford. You hang a beautiful little smile on her and I'll bet she lets us look around."

"So you think it's worth a look?" Mike asked, feeling less sure of himself now that he had spoken his ideas aloud.

"Yes," Kelly and Steve said at the same time. "Why not find that loose end?" added Steve.

"I guess we better find out just to make you happy," Justice sighed. "Then maybe we can stop talking about this thing. Time's a wasting. It's been quite a while since Crawford died. His wife probably cleaned the place out by now."

Justice pointed his finger at Mike. "You have to promise that if it isn't in Crawford's office that you'll let the whole thing alone and help me build some tables for my restaurant."

"I promise."

The trip to Beatrice Crawford's house took only fifteen minutes. Justice drove. When he pulled up in front of the house, he suggested Mike be the one to talk to her, that he'd stay in the car.

"After what's happened, I doubt if she's all that comfortable with strange black guys."

Walking up the front sidewalk, Mike had trouble keeping out mental images of Crawford on the floor

covered with blood, while his wife ran around destroying
the porn he stashed in his strongbox. It wasn't clear, and
never would be, whether her obsession with Stanley's sex
material let him bleed to death.

A woman Mike assumed was Beatrice Crawford
opened the door before he could ring the doorbell.

"Are you a cop?" she asked, peering through the
screen door.

"No ma'am," Mike said truthfully, his resignation
letter having been delivered.

"You look like a cop! The police were here a couple of
days ago. I thought maybe one of them was coming back.
Who are you?"

"My name is Mike Chance. I was helping the police
with their inquiries into your husband's death. But I'm
not a cop. At least not anymore."

"Why are you here then? The police told me they
think a university student shot Stanley. As if that makes
a difference. He'd dead, and all because of some silly
letter that wasn't even real. What do you want?"

"It's about that letter, Mrs. Crawford. I was
wondering if you've cleaned out Stanley's office."

Mrs. Crawford wasn't looking at Mike anymore. She
gazed over his shoulder at the car with Justice in it.

"Who is that? I thought the minister was dead. I
didn't like him one bit. Wanted Stanley's money."

"He's a friend. He doesn't want to intrude. Mrs.
Crawford, it's possible the letter everyone was looking
for, and that your husband believed was real, may be
with his things in his office. Is everything still there?"

"Yes, everything is the same. I'm not going into that
room again. There's blood on the floor. I don't know
what else I might find there. No, I don't have any interest
in going in there. Maybe someday I'll ask somebody to
clean it out. Father Thomas would know who could do
that. Maybe the church can sell some of the books and

furniture at their annual yard sale. But then I will have to ask Father Thomas about . . ."

"Mrs. Crawford, could I just look around for a few minutes? I promise I won't take anything."

"I don't know if I want you to see what Stanley had in there. It's really none of your business."

"Do you mean the naughty pictures?" Mike couldn't believe he said 'naughty.'

"How do you know about that?"

"Like I said, I've been helping the police. Look, if that stuff is what's bothering you, holding you back from cleaning out the place, then tell you what. If I find any of those dirty pictures I'll take them away. Make sure they get destroyed. If there's anything like that in there, you won't have to worry about anyone finding it."

"Maybe that would be good. But you won't take anything else?"

"No I won't. If the letter is there, I'll show it to you."

Beatrice unlocked the screen door through which they had been conversing. Mike followed as she led the way to Stanley's den, office, man cave, whatever. The widow opened the door and stepped back.

"I'll wait in the living room. I told you I don't want to go in there."

Mike entered the room. He worried he had been wrong, that the police had come back to search further. Maybe he should have called Dixie to find out.

Looking around, Mike could tell Beatrice told the truth. The room apparently hadn't been touched since the crime scene people did their thing. Blood stained the floor around the desk. Yellow crime-scene tape still hung across the back door. A couple of desk drawers were slightly open. Some floorboards were lying next to a recess in the floor. This no doubt was where Crawford kept the strongbox, he thought. The box and its contents would now be in possession of the C'ville police. Books and objects on the shelves appeared to be undisturbed.

Beginning with the books on the shelves behind Crawford's desk, he began a systematic search of the room. It didn't take him long to find what he had guessed might be there. A large book in easy reach of Stanley's desk chair had the so-called Hemings letter inside its front cover. He carefully held it up for inspection. Although enclosed in a scratched plastic sleeve, he could read the letter without removing the protective cover.

The students had done an excellent job. He had the immediate impression he held something very old. Faded, no doubt because they had watered the ink, the script still jumped out from the page.

Sep 1801
Mama,
I am leaving the mountain & want to leave this with you in order that Sal will be treated right. When we was in Paris Sal told me the master promised to take care of her if she sleep in his bed & he told her he would free any child born by him. You know she have 5 childrin tho 3 died. Be sure Mr. Jefferson keep his word. I will not be here when you need what I am writing.
James Hemings

Mike could easily see how Crawford believed the letter to be real. But it wasn't. After all that happened, he found that he had to keep reminding himself of that fact. Professor McCabe had indicated James Hemings was literate and the students would know that, too. Kevin Nesbitt said they copied James Heming's handwriting from something he wrote that still survives.

At first, the number of children mentioned in the letter didn't make sense. Mike remembered the professor said there were records of six children. McCabe also told him that Madison Hemings mentioned a seventh, which he claimed died soon after his mother and Jefferson returned from France. Mike admitted to himself that his time with the professor and the Jefferson Bunch hadn't been wasted. A few months ago he wouldn't have been able to say how many children people said Jefferson had with his slave mistress.

Mike looked again at the date. When Paul McCabe and his wife had dinner at the Cummingses, Mike recalled the professor saying that James Hemings committed suicide. That was in 1801, if he remembered right. The number had stuck with him since 1801 had been his family's street address in Alexandria. James Hemings had been freed by Jefferson before that. He didn't recall when or where he learned that fact. The students must have meant it to look like the letter had been written just before James died. Mike also didn't remember the month James died, if he ever knew. It's possible, he thought, that James Hemings wasn't alive for all of Sally's births.

The letter suggested James Hemings knew of five children born before September of 1801. The grad students would know the correct number of children to mention in the letter. Unless a wrong number was part of the ruse? Mike knew he'd have to check with Professor McCabe about the exact number of Sally's children, when they were born, and when they died.

Holding the document in his hands, he couldn't help wondering if the letter might describe what actually happened between Sally and Jefferson more than two-hundred years ago. If that were the case, why might James Hemings leave such a letter? Did he not trust his former master? Had he heard people say vulgar things about his sister and the president? Was knowledge of an affair between the famous Thomas Jefferson and his sister too much to bear? Did James know he wouldn't return to Monticello? Is that why he would leave a message like this with his mother, Elizabeth Hemings?

Mike shook his head. Stop thinking like this, he thought. While he might enjoy this bit of fancy, he knew a letter from James Hemings didn't exist. He was looking at words written by two graduate students in the 21st century. What they wrote wasn't true.

Or was it?

Selected Sources

Jefferson, Hemingses, and Slavery:
Brodie, F. M. (1974). *Thomas Jefferson: An Intimate History.*
Egerton, D. R. (1993). *The Virginia Slave Conspiracies of 1800 and 1802.*
Ellis, J.J. (1996). *American Sphinx: The Character of Thomas Jefferson.*
Gordon-Reed, A. (2008). *The Hemingses of Monticello.*
Stanton, L. (2000). *Free Some Day: The African-American Families of Monticello.*
Stanton, L. (2012). *Those Who Labor for My Happiness: Slavery at Thomas Jefferson's Monticello.*
Wilkins, R. (2001). *Jefferson's Pillow: The Founding Fathers and the Dilemma of Black Patriotism.*
http://www.monticello.org/site/jefferson

Depersonalization Disorder:
Abugel, J. (2010). *Stranger to Myself: Inside Depersonalization: The Hidden Epidemic.*
American Psychiatric Association (2013). *Diagnostic and Statistical Manual of Mental Disorders* (5th ed.).
Simeon, D., & Abugel, J. (2006). *Feeling Unreal: Depersonalization Disorder and the Loss of Self.*

Charlottesville:
Moore, J. H. (1976). *Albemarle: Jefferson's County, 1727-1976.*

Richmond and the Civil War:
Campbell, B.(2012). *Richmond's Unhealed History.*
Davis, W. C. (1996). *The Lost Cause: Myths and Realities of the Confederacy.*
Lankford, N. (2002). *Richmond Burning: The Last Days of the Confederate Capital.*

Richmond and the Civil War (cont.):
Mitchell, M. H. (1999). *Hollywood Cemetery: The History of a Southern Shrine.*
Swanson, J. L. (2006). *Manhunt: The 12-Day Chase for Lincoln's Killer.*
Winek, J.(2001). *April 1865: The Month That Saved America.*

Monticello Archaeology:
Kelso, W. M. (1997). *Archaeology at Monticello.*
http://www.Monticello.org/archaeology

Jefferson's Promise

Acknowledgments

Most of us occasionally find ourselves in unfamiliar terrain, as when we walk a new mountain trail or visit a city for the first time. Often the signs don't seem adequate, and while we know where we want to go, we aren't sure of the right direction. It may be difficult not to get lost. Sometimes we *are* lost. This has been my experience writing *Jefferson's Promise*. Unlike other experiences of losing my way, however, there have been people along the path to point me in the proper direction. Gretel Braidwood, Sandra Brooks, Mark Davison, Jim Hall, Sue O'Keane, and Liz Zechmeister, are some of these folks. So, too, are Jennifer Briggs and Elizabeth Sawyer, both on the staff of the Monticello Archaeology Department. Beth took me on a tour of Monticello digs and helped put the right words in Abigail's mouth. Jerry Ortiz y Pino and Donna Bruzzese spent way more time reading and commenting on a draft than they had time. Sergeant Mike Farruggio of the Charlottesville Police Department provided much needed information about police procedures. All for the meager price of a lunch. Victor Ashear shared insights from his clinical practice into depersonalization-derealization disorder.

The idea for this book came from research I was doing at the Jefferson Library. Thank you, Jack Robertson, for providing a "job" that opened to me the resources of this great depository of the Jefferson story. I am especially indebted to Anna Berkes, reference librarian at the Jefferson Library at Monticello. She kindly read a draft, answered my questions, and corrected me where needed. The story line was aided by a class I took at UVA on Charlottesville's history when we first moved into the neighborhood of Monticello. Taught by Coy Barefoot, a local historian and radio/TV talk-show host, the course helped set the backdrop for *Jefferson's Promise*. Getting to the end was aided by the sage advice of publisher Robert Pruett and excellent directions provided by editor Erin Harpst, as well as the professional advice given by MaryJoy Johnson (see her novel on Amazon.com: *Road to Death's Door*). Thank you, Jim Gibson, for the cover design.

Finally, my wife Jeanne has been my muse and guide in this and in all my activities. She's the real writer in the house and without her, I would be seriously lost.

--The Author

NOV -- 2014

CPSIA information can be obtained at www.ICGtesting.com
Printed in the USA
LVOW06s1459210714

395322LV00001B/119/P